In the
Porches
of My
Ears

In the Porches of My Ears

Norman Prentiss

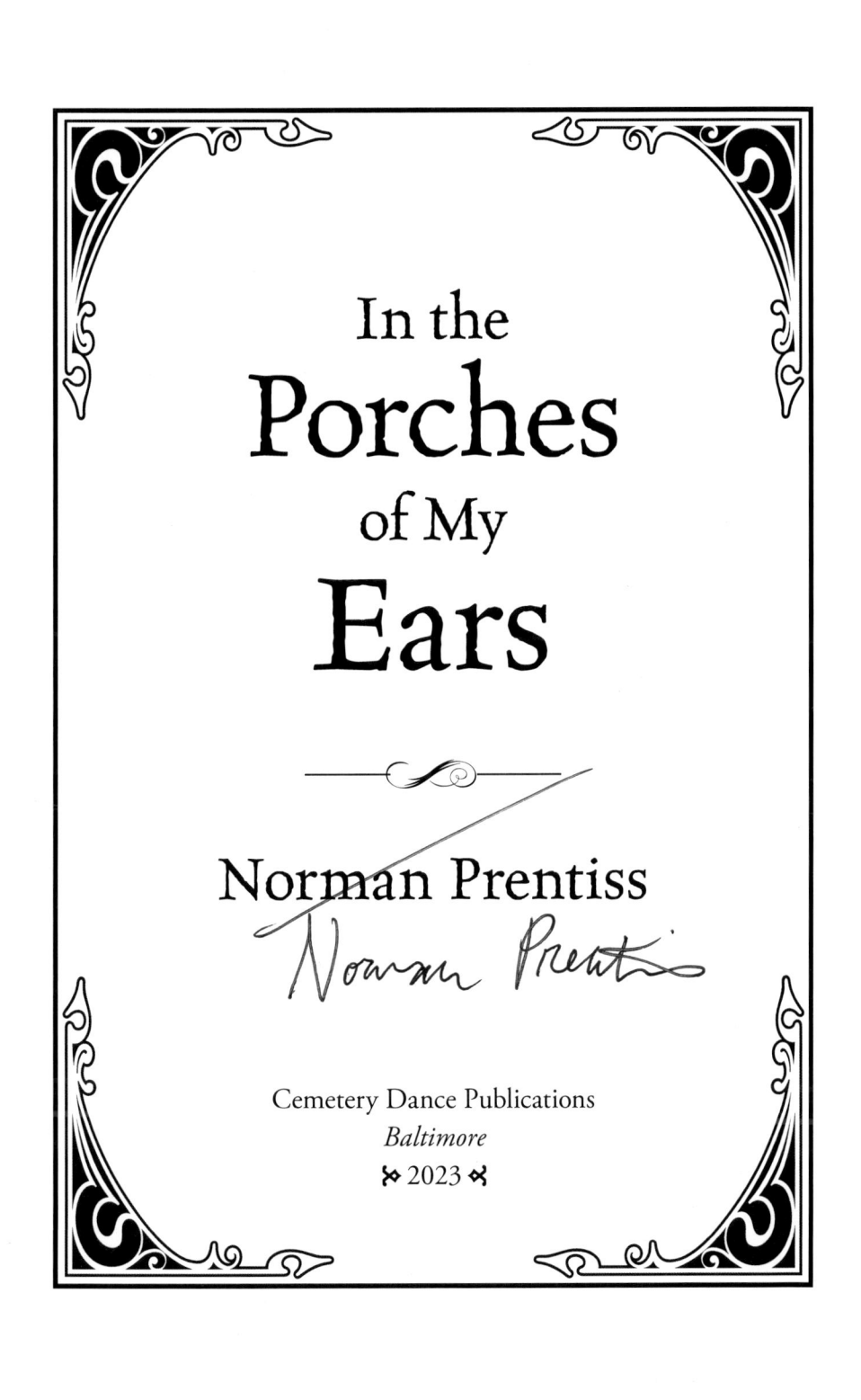

Norman Prentiss

Cemetery Dance Publications
Baltimore
2023

Copyright © 2023 by Norman Prentiss
All rights reserved.

No part of this book may be reproduced in any form or by any electronic or mechanical means, including information storage and retrieval systems, without permission in writing from the publisher, except by a reviewer who may quote brief passages in a review.

Cemetery Dance Publications
132-B Industry Lane, Unit #7
Forest Hill, MD 21050
http://www.cemeterydance.com

The characters and events in this book are fictitious. Any similarity to real persons, living or dead, is coincidental and not intended by the author.

Trade Paperback Edition

ISBN:
978-1-58767-872-1

Cover Artwork copyright © 2023 by Caniglia.
Interior Design copyright © 2023 by Desert Isle Design, LLC

Table of Contents

7	In the Porches of My Ears
21	The Storybook Forest
33	Interval
55	The Old Ways
71	Glue Traps
79	The Quiet House
99	Distance
109	The Shell
127	Burls
145	Beneath Their Shoulders
171	The Man Who Could Not Be Bothered To Die
183	The Everywhere Man
199	Control
205	The Transfer Student
221	The Thing With Feathers
243	Four Legs in the Morning
263	Invisible Fences

In the Porches of My Ears

HELEN and I should have paid more attention to the couple we followed into the movie theater: his stiff, halting walk, and the way the woman clung to him, arm around his waist and her body pressed tight to his side. I read love into their close posture, an older couple exchanging long-held decorum for the sort of public display more common among today's younger people. I felt embarrassed for them and looked away. I regret that neither my wife nor I noticed a crucial detail in time, but real life doesn't always inspire the interpretative urgency of images projected on a screen, and it's not as if a prop department provided the obvious clues: sunglasses worn indoors, or a thin white cane tapping the ground, sweeping the air.

Helen went ahead to get us seats, while I stood in line at concessions to buy bottled waters. We disliked popcorn for its metallic, fake butter smell and, more importantly, because we chose not to contribute to the surrounding crunch—a sound like feet stomping through dead leaves, intruding over a film's quieter moments. For similar reasons, we avoided candy, with its noisome wrappers, and the worst abomination of recent years, the plastic tray of corn chips and hot cheese dip. Fortunately, the Midtowne Cinema didn't serve the latter, making it one of our preferred neighborhood theaters. That, and the slightly older clientele who behaved according to that lost era, back before people trained themselves to shout over rented movies in their living rooms.

The Midtowne wasn't quite an art house, rarely showing films with subtitles or excessive nudity. Instead, it tended towards Shakespeare or Dickens or E. M. Forster adaptations, the big-screen, bigger-budget equivalents to television's *Masterpiece Theatre,* which I tended to prefer; or, closer to Helen's taste, romantic comedies more palatably delivered through British accents.

Helen had chosen the afternoon's entertainment, so we'd once again see that short, slightly goofy actor who survived an embarrassing sex scandal a few years back and still, *still* managed onscreen to charm the sandy-haired, long-legged actress (who was actually American-born, but approximated the preferred accent well enough for most, and smiled brightly enough to provoke the rest to forgive her). I brought the water bottles into the auditorium—two dollars each, unfortunately, but we broke even by saving as much on matinee admission—and searched for Helen in the flickering dark.

We were later than I expected. Previews had already started, and the semi-dark auditorium was mostly full. I knew Helen's preference for an aisle seat, on the right side of the main section, but the crowd had forced her to sit farther back than usual. I walked past her before a whispered "Psst, Steve," called me to the correct row.

She turned sideways, legs in the aisle so I could scoot past easily. I handed her a water bottle before I sat down.

"Is this okay?" she asked.

"Fine." I responded without really thinking. It was her movie choice, so it wouldn't bother *me* to sit too far back from the picture.

Helen gestured toward the man in front of me, then forked her middle- and forefinger to point at her eyes. I recognized the man from the couple I'd half-noticed on the way inside. He sat tall in his seat: his shoulders and gangly gray-fuzzed head, from my vantage, cut a

In the Porches of My Ears

dark notch into the bottom of the screen like the interlocking edge of a missing jigsaw piece. His companion was a good bit shorter, granting my wife a clear view of the film.

I knew Helen felt guilty because she liked the aisle, actually thought she *needed* it because she typically left to use the restroom at least twice during a ninety-minute film. The water bottle didn't help, obviously.

Music swelled from the preview's soundtrack, and a glossy country manor montage shimmered onscreen. Like a sequel to *Age of Innocence*, or maybe *A Room with a* Different *View*. "I can see fine," I assured her. Besides, the slight obstruction was better than having Helen climb over my legs several times once the film was in progress. "As long as there's no subtitles," I joked.

Helen pointed to her eyes again, and her fingertips nearly touched the lenses of her glasses. I could tell she wanted to say more, but she stopped herself.

"What *is* it?"

I spoke normally, just loud enough so she'd hear over the trailer's quoted blurb from *The New Yorker*, but from Helen's expression you would think I'd shouted "Fire!"

"Never mind," she said, especially quiet, but her message clear.

Then the man in front of me turned his head. It was a quick motion, almost like a muscle spasm, and he held the angle for a long, awkward profile. His shoulder pressed into the chair cushion, and he twisted his head further around toward me. From a trick of the projection light, I assumed, his eyes appeared fogged, the irises lined like veined gray marble.

His companion tapped him. "The movie's about to start." As if she'd activated a button on the man's shoulder, his head snapped quickly around, face front.

"Strange," I said, barely audible, but still Helen winced. I couldn't understand her agitation. In our shared interpretation of moviegoer etiquette, it was perfectly acceptable to speak quietly during the "coming attractions" portion of the show.

The exit lights dimmed completely, and the studio logo appeared on the screen. Then before the credits, a pan over Trafalgar Square, then Big Ben, then a red double-decker bus. Quick establishing shots so any idiot would know—

"We're in England."

The woman in front of us spoke with a conspirator's whisper, a quiet, urgent tone far less musical than the lover's lilt she'd expressed earlier when she tapped his shoulder.

Jeez. Thanks for stating the obvious, lady.

The credits began, yellow lettering over a long shot of the Thames river and the London skyline. The two main actors' names appeared first, then the film title.

In that same strident whisper, the woman read aloud to her companion. The stars, the costars, the "Special Appearance by Sir James So-and-so." The screenwriter, editor, for-God's-sake the music composer, and finally the director.

He can see for himself, I thought. He's not…

But of course, he *was*, and I'd been a fool for not realizing sooner. For a moment I held out a glimmer of hope that the man was simply illiterate. Once the credits ended, she'd grow silent and they'd watch the movie in peace. Wishful thinking, however, because I recalled how she'd held him close coming inside the building. Guiding him.

And I knew she'd be talking over the entire movie.

If we'd figured it out sooner, we could have moved. Dark as it was, I barely distinguished a few unoccupied seats scattered around the theater—including an empty to my left—but no pairs together. Helen and I always had to sit together. If the movie ended up being ruined for us, at least it would be a shared experience.

The commentary began in earnest. "She's trying to lock the door, but she's got too much in her arms. A purse, an accordion briefcase, a grocery sack, and a Styrofoam coffee cup. The lid's loose on the coffee."

Onscreen, the Emma- or Judi- or Gwyneth-person—possibly I've conflated the actor's name with the character's—juggled the coffee

In the Porches of My Ears

cup, the lid flew up and the liquid slipped out and over her work clothes. "Damn, damn, damn," she said in a delightful accent, and the audience roared with laughter.

"She spilled it," the man's companion told him. "A huge coffee stain on her blouse."

I hadn't laughed. The woman's commentary—I assumed she was the blind man's wife—had telegraphed the spill. Had the lid really been loose? Enough for any of us to see the clue?

"I can't believe this," I whispered to Helen, and she half-winced again. Finally, I realized the source of her tension: the commonplace wisdom that a person lacking in one physical sense gained extra ability in another—in this case, hearing.

Sure. His loud-mouth wife can ruin the whole film for us, but God forbid we whisper anything that might hurt the guy's feelings.

Helen risked a quick whisper of her own: "I'm sorry."

It wasn't her fault, of course—not really. But we'd been married almost fifteen years, and familiar intimacy brought its own yardstick for blame. The woman, her husband, the *situation itself* created the problem, and we could share disapproval of the couple's imposition, or shake fists skyward in synchronized dismay at Fates who brought us together at the same showing. And yet, Helen had eaten her lunch slowly this afternoon, had misremembered the show's start time, which in turn limited her seating options (and she *must* have the aisle seat, and *must* see these British comedies the first weekend of their release). So I blamed her a bit, then—the type of blame saved for those you love deeply, blame you savored as you indulged a spouse's habits and peculiar tastes.

Helen did the same for me. When she disliked one of my film choices—the somber violence of the latest *King Lear* adaptation, or any Thomas Hardy depression-fest other than *Under the Greenwood Tree*—I could sense her unspoken discomfort beside me, all while the film flickered toward an inevitable, tragic end. In an odd way, her discomfort often improved the experience for me, magnifying the tension of the film. Making it more authentic.

The tension was all wrong here, though, since nothing spoiled a comedy like an explanation. As the Rupert- or Ian- or Trevor-character blustered through confident proclamations, and Emma/Judi/Gwyneth mugged a sour expression, the blind man's wife stated the obvious: "His arrogance offends her. He's so self-centered, he doesn't yet realize he's in love with her."

Oh, really? Do tell.

It was easy enough to infer the same conclusions from the dialogue. I could have closed my eyes and done fine without the woman's incessant whispers. Score myself a hundred on the quiz. Besides, these romantic comedies all followed the same formula: the guy would Darcy her for a bit, she'd come around just when it seemed too late, there'd be a misunderstanding on one or both sides, until a ridiculous coincidence threw them awkwardly and then blissfully together, the end.

"Now she puts her Chinese take-out cartons in the trash, aware she's eaten too much, but also aware it doesn't matter, because she's alone."

A slight bit of interpretation there, against the whimsical Supremes song hurrying love on the soundtrack, but probably accurate. At that moment, I wondered exactly how many others in the theater could hear the woman's commentary. The people in front of them, surely, were in the same position as Helen and I: close enough to overhear, but too close to make a show of offense. Nobody else seemed to react to the voice: no grunts of disapproval, no agitated shiftings in the seats. There wasn't that ripple of cold scorn that chills the orchestra seats when a cell phone goes off during the first aria. Perhaps her whisper was one of those trained, *directed* voices, sharp in proximity but dropping off quickly with distance—as if an invisible bubble cushioned the sound into a tight circumference.

Lucky us.

I actually tried to control my indignation, for Helen's sake. We were both hyper-sensitive to extraneous chatter during a film, but this was her type of movie (though not, as was already evident, the pinnacle of the art form), and I was determined not to spoil her experience further by huffing my disapproval throughout. Instead, I touched the top

In the Porches of My Ears

of Helen's hand on our shared armrest. Our secret signal in the dark: three quick taps, for *I-love-you.*

It was a slight film, stupidly titled *Casting a Romance:* a reference to the Darcy character's job as a casting director for movies, then a pun on casting a *fishing* line, since he joins the girl and her father at a summer cottage, only to lose his stuffy demeanor amid hooks and slipping into lakes, and her getting a massive rainbow trout next to his emasculating tadpole. Somewhere along the way—about half-way between Helen's first and second trips to the Ladies' Room—I'd settled into the film, and into the commentary. I grudgingly appreciated it after a while—the woman's skill at selecting the right details, firing the narration rapidly into her husband's hungry ear. To keep myself amused, I played around a bit, closing my eyes for short stretches and letting the woman's words weave images around the dialogue. When Helen returned from the restroom, I didn't have the burden of summarizing what she missed: the woman's commentary easily filled the gaps.

After a while, I didn't mind being in the bubble with them. The shape of the blind man's head became familiar to me, atop his thin neck and leaning perpetually to one side to catch his wife's every word. That sharp underlying whisper became part of the film, like the experts' comments during a televised sporting event. I half-toyed with the idea she was an expert herself. For example, she whispered how the character left his jacket draped over the chair, and she warned, correctly, that the plane tickets would spill out. She also predicted the moment when he realized his embarrassing connection to the heroine's brother—the cad who'd tried to blackmail him into an acting job during the first reel. Her delivery was so good, that I suspected she'd seen the film before—perhaps even practiced with a notepad and a stopwatch, to pinpoint the precise moments to whisper crucial details or hiss clues that inattentive viewers might miss.

So, I'd grudgingly grown to admire her skill, almost to rely on it for my full appreciation of the movie. And then she did that malicious thing during the final scene.

She changed the ending. It was almost elegant how she did it, an interplay between the silences and the openness of the characters' final words. Onscreen, the man said "I still love you," and there was a faint rise in his voice, maybe the actor's insecurity rather than the character's, but the woman twisted a question mark over his declaration.

"They say they are in love," she whispered, "but they don't mean it. He reaches out to hug her—" and on the screen they *are* hugging, "but she pulls away. It is too little, too late."

I realized, then, how precarious this type of movie was: a teasing, near-romance, suspended over ninety brittle minutes. The main characters' relationship is simultaneously inevitable and fragile—a happy ending endlessly deferred, the threat of ruin always beneath the comic surface.

The actress laughed onscreen, a clear display of relief and joy, and the woman said: "She's bitter. It is a dry, empty laugh. Her face is full of scorn."

I reached again for Helen's hand beside me. We didn't speak aloud; our touch expressed the outrage well enough. This horrible woman at once betrayed the movie, *and* her blind husband.

I felt certain now that she'd rehearsed the commentary. How else could she best deliver her poison into his ear—at what time, and at how strong a dose—certain no additional dialogue would provide an antidote?

Thinking back, I realized something more sinister. The woman's descriptions of the lead actor had made him taller than the visual reality, gave him a thin neck and wobbled head that tilted awkwardly to the side, very much like…the head in front of me, a shadow rising above the seat to darken the bottom edge of the movie frame. She'd transformed the hero into a younger version of her husband, making the character fit how the blind man—for lack of a better word—*saw* himself. For him, the disappointed ending would be particularly cruel.

The camera pulled back from the onscreen couple's happy, final embrace, and a song blared from the soundtrack. The song was allegedly

In the Porches of My Ears

a cheerful choice, with an upbeat tempo and optimistic lyrics. Most people in the audience probably tried not to dwell on how the lead singer died of a drug overdose, just as the group verged on the brink of stardom.

The blind man's shoulders shook in uneven rhythm. His head, formerly tilted toward his wife, now drooped forward. I couldn't hear over the joyful soundtrack, but clearly, the man was crying.

Still, neither Helen nor I said anything—to them, or to each other. The woman had done an awful, unforgivable thing to her husband, but we decided it wasn't our place to comment. An overheard whisper is sacred, like the bond of a confessional. We needn't involve ourselves in another couples' private drama—even if its language had been forced upon us, even if (and I knew Helen felt this more than I did) the whispered words had spoiled our afternoon's entertainment.

My wife and I didn't need to voice this decision. It was communicated though a strange telepathy, refined over many years in darkened movie houses: a released breath after an exciting chase scene; an imperceptible shift in posture to convey boredom; a barely audible sigh at a beautifully framed landscape. We felt from each other what we couldn't hear or see. Helen's soft gasp had told me, "It's not worth it." I tapped my foot on the floor, as if to say, "You're right. I'll let it go."

Like many patrons of the Midtowne Theatre, we were "credit sitters." We wouldn't stay to the very end, necessarily—even the greatest film buff has little interest in what stylist coiffed the extras' hair, or who catered lunches for the crew—but it was always worth sitting through the list of characters, to recognize an actor's name and think, "Ah, I thought I'd seen him before. Wasn't he the one in...?"

But the blind man and his companion began to leave right away. The woman seemed to lift him from his seat. Together, they moved slowly into the aisle. Instead of guiding him, as she had upon entering the theater, it now seemed more like she was *carrying* him out, her arm around his back and supporting slumped, defeated shoulders. The house lights were raised slightly to help people exit, and I'd caught a brief glimpse of his sad expression. I wished his wife had given him more time to collect himself, before exposing his raw emotions to the bright, sighted world of the lobby.

In a bizarre, random thought, I wondered if she'd purposely ushered him out before the rapid scroll of names and obscure job titles made a mockery of her remarkable skill. She would have short-circuited trying to keep up, like an early computer instructed to divide by zero.

Helen and I waited through the rest of the cast list, maintaining our silence even as the real-life names of "Florist" and "Waiter #4" floated toward the ceiling. About a third of the seats were still occupied when we stood to leave. After we pushed through the double doors into the lobby, my wife took a detour to the side: another trip to the ladies' room.

I dropped our empty water bottles into the recycle bin, then stood aside near the front doors. A line stretched outside, people buying tickets for the next show, and a steady trickle emerged from the auditorium doors on either side of the concessions counter. They blinked their eyes against fresh light, and all of them had pleasant expressions on their faces. Some people, at least, had been allowed to enjoy the film.

I spotted the blind man beside an arch to the side hallway. He stood by himself, slouched slightly against the wall. His head bobbled indecisively on the thin neck, as if longing to lean toward his wife's voice.

The opportunity presented itself. Despite what Helen and I tacitly agreed to, I moved toward him, my tennis shoes soundless—to me, at least—over the lobby's worn beige carpet.

"Excuse me," I said, but before I got the words out, his face turned toward me. He looked older than I'd imagined, overhead lamps etching shadows under the wrinkles in his skin. Although he was dressed in casual clothes—a light blue short-sleeve shirt and twill pants—he stiffened into a formal posture which, sadly, made him seem more foolish than dignified. His eyes were expectant and vacant and puffy red.

"Excuse me," I repeated, stalling for time even as I feared one of our wives would return from the ladies' room. My voice was loud, but I couldn't control it—as if I needed to pierce the fog of his blank stare. "I just, um, I just wanted to say…"

In the Porches of My Ears

"Yes." It was the first time I'd heard him speak. His voice sounded weakened by his bout of tears, with barely strength to encourage me to continue.

People walked past us, oblivious. I squinted down the hallway toward the rest rooms. No sign yet of Helen, or the awful, whispering woman.

"The movie didn't end the way she described it to you." I blurted out the rest, before I lost my nerve. "The couple was happy at the end. Still in love. I thought you should know."

The blind man didn't react at first. Then I saw something like relief: his body relaxing, the tight line of his mouth loosening as if he sought permission to smile.

He swung his left arm to the side with a flourish, cupped his right arm over his stomach and bent his torso forward in a deep, exaggerated bow. He straightened, then spoke with a firmness I hadn't expected: "Oh, thank you. Thank you *so* much. I don't know what I would have done without your help."

It was a parody of gratefulness. The sarcasm settled into his face, an expression of scorn that immediately dismissed me from his presence.

Luckily, I spotted Helen approaching. I crossed to meet her in the archway, and I steered her across the lobby, keeping her distant from the blind man. As we reached the sidewalk outside, before the theater door swung shut with a rusty squeak, I thought I heard the blind man thank me again.

At dinner, we didn't discuss the film as we normally would. No revisiting favorite lines of dialogue, seeking subtleties in the script; no ranking of the performances or nuanced comparisons to films of similar type. Instead, we tore small pieces off store-bought rolls or rearranged silk flowers, their petals dusty in a white ceramic vase. We took turns saying we were hungry, wondering aloud when the minestrone soup would arrive.

Finally, Helen broached the subject. "I don't know what I was thinking. I wish I hadn't sat there."

"No need to blame yourself," I said. "I hadn't even noticed the guy was blind. And who'd ever expect his wife to describe the whole film for him?"

"I wish I hadn't sat there," Helen repeated.

That was pretty much all we needed to say about the matter. After the main course, though, when we decided not to stay for dessert or coffee, the waitress took too long to bring our check. In the awkward silence, I weakened and decided to confess. I told Helen about my curious encounter with the blind man in the lobby.

Helen shivered, like it was the most frightening story she'd ever heard.

LET ME TELL you about a different movie. It's another romantic comedy, this time about a long-married couple who stop everything so they can take a month to travel the world together. The man is reluctant at first, afraid to fall behind on his work accounts, and it's not their anniversary or either of their birthdays, and he's never been that spontaneous anyway. But she convinces him, and she's already booked the flights, the hotels, the cruise ship, and she's bought books and brochures and printed off pages and pages of advice from travel websites: little restaurants tourists didn't visit; special tours given only Sunday afternoons, *if* you know who to ask; "must see" lists for each city, itineraries to fill each day.

Before they leave, she surprises him with a wrapped package, and it's a digital camera with lots of storage space, so they can take as many pictures as they want. He'd never believed in photographs, thought taking them distracted from the experience of travel. On previous trips, other tourists were a nuisance with cameras, blocking his view or popping a flash to interrupt the soft calm of natural light. But it's a thoughtful gift, and he finds out he enjoys it: framing a waterfall or mountain or monument, with her in the foreground, and the fun of checking through the pictures that night in the hotel.

He had agreed to the trip just to please her, but soon her enthusiasm wins him over, and he ends up loving it. To be a better comedy,

In the Porches of My Ears

though, things need to go wrong: missed connections, bungled hotel reservations; a random "I'll have that" finger pointed at a menu, and lamb brains arrive at the table, or a five-pound exotic fish with bubble eyes staring up from the plate; or ill-pronounced words to a French street juggler—*fou* instead of *feu*, for instance, ("You called him crazy, m'sieu!")—and hilarious misunderstandings ensue.

But there's none of that. Similar things occur, but not often, nothing major. A forgotten toothbrush, rather than a lost passport. She's a fantastic tour guide, and he loves her more than ever. The trip is unforgettable, revitalizing. Okay, it's not that great a film: no conflict, no complications. But it's sweet.

After the trip, he has the memories, and the pictures. The woman smiles in all of them—leaning against the ship rail during their Hawaii cruise, the Nepali coast in the background; tiny in one corner, hair windswept, with the Grand Canyon vast behind her; at a table outside a Venice cafe, a glass of local vintage raised for the camera, and for him.

He's printed all the photos, hundreds of them. He fans a stack, like a cartoon flip-book, and the world rushes behind his wife's constant, smiling image. The heavy paper stock creates a gust of air, almost like a whisper.

Bladder cancer, it says. *Inoperable.*

Everything had seemed like one of Helen's fluffy, happy-ending movies. She kept it that way as long as she could.

The specialists call it bladder cancer, if that's where the tumor originates, even if the disease spreads to other parts of the body. Helen's frequent visits to the bathroom were a symptom, but the change happened gradually, and neither of us had noticed. By the time she got the diagnosis, things had progressed too far. Even with radical treatment, the prognosis wasn't good. When she found out, she decided not to tell me. Instead, she announced, "Let's take a trip!"

If this were really a movie, that omission makes for a more significant story. We were always a happy couple, but I was especially happy during that month-long vacation. *I* was happy. I can only imagine what really went on in Helen's mind, despite those ever-present smiles. Thoughts of aggressive therapy when she returned home; dread of long hospital days, pain still sharp through medicated fog. If she was lucky, maybe, a swift decline.

The trip wasn't for her benefit, but for mine. A beautiful, poignant farewell gift. And always, beneath the sweet surface of her romantic comedy, an awful, unnarrated tragedy.

I hate myself for not noticing it. Helen spared me the knowledge, as long as she could.

One day near the end, from the intensive care bed that she'd dreaded in silence, she revealed something very strange. I almost wish she hadn't told me—though I can understand why she needed to. Something else happened that day at the theater, after we sat behind the blind man and his talkative companion. In the ladies' room, when the film was over, Helen heard that whispered voice again, from the adjoining stall. The voice was clear and *directed;* Helen knew she was the only one who could hear it. The whisper began at the precise moment when my wife strained and began to empty her bladder. Helen remembered exactly what the voice had said: "It doesn't hurt. It's just a minor inconvenience, so you put it off. By the time you get to a doctor, it will be too late." As she repeated the words, Helen's voice, weakened by the cancer and the treatments, achieved a perfect, uncanny duplication of the woman's urgent whisper.

The hospital seemed instantly more sterile and hopeless and cold. Helen passed away that night, while I was home asleep.

And now, all my movies are sad. I go to them alone. I want to feel Helen's presence in the empty seat next to me, embrace those half-conscious signals we always shared in the dark. I want to tap the top of her hand gently, three times.

Instead, I lean my head slightly to the side. A whispered voice distorts the context of the film, makes the story all about me and my loss. It changes the ending, twists it into something horrible.

The Storybook Forest

IT wasn't a girls' ride any longer.

The giant teacups had lost their glossy white sheen, and the flowery trim had faded beneath new designs of chipped paint and cracked fiberglass. Craig aimed his flashlight over the nearest rim: dead leaves and broken branches settled into a wet muck at the bottom of the cup. The circular bench was broken in three places.

"Reading the tea leaves?" Eddie said, peering over his shoulder.

"Yeah. They tell me it's time to trash this place." Craig smacked the side of the cup with his palm. He expected a hollow thump, but it was firm and flat, like hitting a piece of drywall. They must have reinforced the frame with bent iron, poured concrete into the hollow fiberglass. Safer that way.

"This one's better," Skates yelled from the edge closest to the moonlit castle. He was climbing into one of the cups, his long legs straddling over the rim instead of using the rounded doorway opposite the teacup handle. His foot caught on the rim and he almost fell inside headfirst—not because he was drunk, yet, but because Skates was basically lanky and uncoordinated. His nickname altered his last name of Slate, and reflected his ambitions more than any success with the skateboard. He was mostly a wipe-out kind of guy.

Craig headed over, Eddie following like he usually did. Craig kicked a broken bottle out of their path, and it clanked against a pile of rusted beer cans. They obviously weren't the first who'd trespassed into Storybook Forest for a bit of underage drinking.

Skates set his carton of Buds on the flat round steering wheel at the center of the cup, then put his wide-bottom flashlight next to it, letting the beam shine up like a weak spotlight. "C'mon in. Got our own coffee table." He wrapped his T-shirt around a bottlecap, twisted it off, then took a loud swig.

The metal chain was still fastened across the doorway. Back when the park was open, vinyl padding covered the chain—white, if Craig remembered properly, sewn with pink thread to match pink roses painted on the cup. He brushed along the chain, brittle like sand beneath his fingertips, then found the hook-latch. He squeezed the release to open it, and the latch broke in his hand.

He must have cried out—startled, or maybe a sliver of rust lanced into his thumb or beneath his fingernail—because Eddie said, "Careful you don't get tetanus." That was Eddie, always giving advice after it was too late.

The chain clanked to the side of the cut-out doorway. Craig rubbed his thumb and forefinger together. "What is tetanus, anyway? Do you even know?"

That would quiet him for a few minutes.

The bottom wasn't as mucked up as in the other cups, and the bench around the inside perimeter was still intact. Craig stepped over Skates's legs and sat across from him, leaving space for Eddie. Each cup was designed to hold two parents and a couple of kids. They had plenty of room.

"Some ride," Eddie said. He clinked his quart bottle of Colt 45 on the center wheel. Eddie never shared, never pitched in with Skates's six-pack. His glass bottle always looked the same, with a heavily rubbed label. He probably filled the bottle with diet soda.

"This was the *only* ride," Craig said. "Guy who built the place wanted a different kind of amusement park. The idea was for kids to walk through these fake little houses, as if they were Goldilocks or Hansel and Gretel or something." Craig remembered how it pissed him off as a kid: they got to go to King's Dominion *once* when he was growing up—with its dizzying Tilt-a-Whirl, water slides, and the Rebel Yell coaster that his parents wouldn't let him ride. *Maybe when you're older,* but they never went back.

Instead, his family went to Storybook Forest for a half-day every summer.

"My sister loved it here," he said. "Hallie thought the place taught her how to read. How to love books, I guess."

"Yuck," Skates said, and Eddie punched him in the shoulder. "What's that for?"

"'Cause you're a douche." Eddie took a sip from his Colt 45. A faint hiss like carbonation came from the bottle. He screwed the cap back on, like he always did after each sip.

Skates started laughing. Nothing was *that* funny, and for a moment Craig wondered if maybe he should punch the guy too. Then Skates grabbed at the steering wheel. "Oh man, how fast did this thing go? I bet you had to hold on for dear life!"

All three of them were laughing now, a kind of pre-drunk high where stupid stuff managed to hit you the right way. "God, Craig, your mom must have been terrified."

"Stop it. You're killing me." Craig lifted a bottle from his half of the carton, popped it open.

"I mean, with this thing spinning and shit. It spins, right?" He held the wheel again, this time grunting.

"Put your weight into it," Eddie said.

"Yeah, it spins. It's gotta." He had that same determined look on his face like when he attempted a triple Ollie or tried to jump his board over the curb. He usually failed.

"Let me." Eddie grabbed the wheel too, and there was some confusion over clockwise or *counter-clockwise, you idiot,* and still nothing happened, then Skates grunted like grinding metal, or that movie sound a pirate ship makes when the deck lurches.

The teacup didn't spin, though. It tilted up off its saucer at a steep angle, as if some invisible giant lifted it to take a drink.

The big flashlight rattled off the wheel and onto the ground. Craig saved the carton, though he spilled his half-empty bottle in the process. He remained inside the cup, one leg balanced against the steering post. Skates had been in the end that arced into the air, and he'd kind of leaped out, arms and legs wide, and actually cleared the guardrail surrounding the entire ride—probably his most impressive aerial stunt ever, if he'd actually planned it, and if he hadn't tripped on his ass after he landed. Wipe-out.

Eddie was outside the dip, like he'd been poured out of the cup onto the metal platform. His foot was caught under the cup's rim.

"Careful," he said. Craig stepped down to help him, and the shift in weight curled the rim tighter against Eddie's ankle. Where the flashlight had fallen, its beam illuminated Eddie's expression: he smiled and winced at the same time, his face round and white in the glow, like a Tweedle-dum.

"Don't think that was supposed to happen." Skates dusted off the seat of his trousers and straddled back over the guardrail. "Somebody musta hit the reject button."

"Quit joking around and get this offa me." It was Eddie's teacher voice, since he liked to imagine himself as the guy who kept everybody else in line. But how often is a teacher flat on the ground, stuck under a giant cup? In that position, it would be wise not to get bossy with the students.

Craig was used to this tone, so it didn't bother him. The most important thing was to help his friend. Besides, they could tease him mercilessly later.

"Roll it *counter*-clockwise," Tweedle-Eddie said. "To the left. *My* left, not yours. Toward the castle."

Maybe it was too much clarification, like they were both stupid. Skates got called stupid often enough, and had the grades to back it up. He wasn't that strong either, but he was tall—which sometimes gave him leverage.

Craig knelt down, pushing against the cup to roll it to the left—per teacher's instructions—and it felt smooth, like Skates was working with him, but also like the cup was moving on its own. It may have been like guiding a planchette around a Ouija board, where the slider seems to move by magic, but maybe somebody's fingers are pushing that thing on purpose. To make the board tell the guy something he needs to hear.

He pushed, Skates pushed near the top—*leverage*—and the cup didn't so much roll to the left as it just kept tipping. Off the saucer, and over Eddie.

It sounded like a car crash. A heavy dent into the hollow metal platform, an echoing scrape against the matching saucer.

Eddie was silent.

Then, not so silent. High pitched complaints about how he landed, the rim barely missing his head, and his body cramped and curled around the steering post. Threats also, explaining what he might do to his friends once they got him out of there.

If he was really going to do those things, they'd be foolish to let him out.

Easier decided than done, anyway. When the ride had been operational, the main platform circled slowly, like a merry-go-round. There were a dozen or so cup-and-saucer compartments on the dilapidated ride, all attached to this metal platform. Their cup—the one they'd upended over their friend—had landed snug into the platform space between its vacated saucer and two other saucers. It was pinned in place at three separate points. The notched doorway had landed at an inconvenient angle, the opening mostly blocked by a saucer lip. Only a half-moon slot was visible, not big enough even for skinny Skates to limbo through. For Eddie, it was out of the question.

Skates retrieved his flashlight and shined it into the blocked opening. Eddie's face slid into the light, a prisoner looking out from his dungeon. A cloud of breath came from his mouth like angry smoke. He blinked, then shifted back into darkness. "Done looking?"

Skates shrugged and set the flashlight on the ground. He gripped the lid of the opening and tested it. "Heavier than I thought. Help me, Craig."

They couldn't lift it, and couldn't shift the cup to clear the opening. Eddie's fingers suddenly appeared in the opening, an extra pair of hands that for some reason Craig hadn't been expecting. They didn't help.

"We need something," Skates finally said, out of breath. "A crowbar or a log or something."

Craig shouted into the dark opening. "You'll be all right here?" As if Eddie had a choice.

"Leave me a flashlight."

"Mine's broken," Craig said. "We need the other one for searching and stuff."

Eddie sighed. He mentioned calling an ambulance or the police, then at once realized how stupid the idea was. What a humiliation it would be, caught trespassing in a kiddie park, and trapped under an upended, paint-flecked, fiberglass teacup.

Skates patted the side of the cup. "We won't be long."

"You better not be."

TROUBLE WAS, THE place really was a forest. Suburban property was plentiful when park designers conceived the idea for Storybook Forest, so they spread their attractions over a large area. Little kids would walk along park paths, discovering one presumably magical attraction after another. Hallie used to run from Jack Spratt's pumpkin house to find the giant shoe around the next corner. Dad would read the placard for her, until she learned how to read it herself: "There was an old woman who lived in a shoe. She had so many children, she didn't know what to do."

So Craig and Skates had a lot of ground to cover—especially since they didn't exactly know what they were looking for.

They found the house for the three little pigs. Not a brick one, which would be too much like an ordinary house, but the one made of straw. A fiberglass wolf used to huff and puff outside the door; his feet remained, legs snapped off at the ankles, and a few other broken pieces stomped into the ground. Once upon a time, the straw was simulated with bright yellow paint, brown now and making it more like a house of wet, dirty rope. The place seemed menacing in a way unintended in the park's heyday. It was smaller than a real house. Instead of sharp corners, the angles were rounded and out of alignment—a whimsical effect on sunny days when the house was fresh, but now it looked as if the place was melting. The windows were smashed. Craig imagined innocent children reaching across the empty frames, their soft wrists tearing over jagged glass.

The windows were too small to climb through. Craig shined a light inside, revealing plump, upright pigs that had been target practice for beer bottles. Ears and snouts were broken off, little pig hooves shattered into sharp claws. Judging from the smell, they'd also been pissed on.

If vandals could have stepped inside, the pigs would likely have been torn to pieces, like the wolf.

"Chinny chin chin," Skates said. He pushed his finger against the tip of his nose, turning it into a snout.

"Let's try another house." They followed the curve of the cracked blacktop path. Signposts had long-since disappeared, but a few joined shadows in the clearing identified the route: these were silhouettes of the remaining gingerbread children, baked to death in the witch's oven. The doomed children always seemed blissfully happy, hands linked and dancing in a circle. Mom and Dad bought cookies from the snack booth, and Craig and his sister sat at a bench beside the victim circle, biting off cookie arms and legs, and not at all feeling like cannibals.

"Long past its expiration date," Skates said. The house itself had grown horribly unappetizing. Giant gumdrop trim looked moldy, and gingerbread shingles were stale and drizzled with grime. The ice cream chimney was cracked down the side of the cone; a vanilla dip at the top was brown and lumpy, like a huge scoop of vomited oatmeal.

Inside was a single room, a large metal cauldron at the center and overflowing with garbage.

"Look at her feet!" Skates pointed and laughed at the brick oven. The witch's legs were painted dangling at the back of the open oven, presumably because Hansel and Gretel had just pushed her inside. "And check out the cage." A sign beside a grid of iron bars said, *Next Victims*. Skates laughed some more.

And that was what was wrong with Storybook Forest. It made you laugh. Happy little stories for happy little kids. There was no lock on the cage. You could climb inside, wrap your tiny hands around the metal bars, and know all along you'd never get cooked by the witch.

Craig hated the treachery of it all. The smiling storybook world where nothing bad ever happened. "They sanitized all the stories. I wanted stuff to be scary, like the thrill-rides at Kings Dominion, and it always disappointed me."

Skates pulled at one of the metal bars. It didn't budge from its concrete moorings.

"You know," Craig said, "the real versions of the nursery stories are pretty gruesome. The wolf eats Little Red Riding Hood's grandma—the woodsman has to carve her out of his stomach. And Cinderella wasn't like the Disney cartoon. The stepsisters cut off parts of their feet so the glass slipper would fit."

"That's kinda cool."

"I dragged us here tonight—pushed for it, even, when Eddie tried to talk us out of it—because I thought for once the forest actually might be scary. We'd break in late at night, and the place would be falling apart and maybe dangerous. Haunted. But it's not. It's just sad."

"I bet Eddie's pretty scared right now. He probably crapped himself when that cup fell on him."

Craig wouldn't laugh with him. "You didn't do that on purpose, did you?"

"No. Did *you?*"

"I mean, you said you didn't realize how heavy it was."

The Storybook Forest

"I said no." Skates attempted a serious expression, but it still came across like a smirk. He got in trouble for that a lot at school.

"All right," Craig said. "Let's keep looking around."

༄

OUTSIDE, CRAIG CUPPED his hands over his mouth and yelled into the air. "We're still here. We'll get you out soon."

No answer. Might have been too far away, and the sound didn't carry well. Just as likely, Eddie was giving them the silent treatment.

Skates did a two-fingered whistle, then made a few hoot-owl noises.

"Cut it out," Craig said. "He's probably sulking."

Still no signposts, but he registered where they were headed. In the midst of the overgrown forest a giant shoe loomed, a front door carved out of its heel. He remembered the windows in the sides and up the tall back of the shoe—like a tower, the old woman leaning out the top window to wave at her many children, some of them scrambling over bright blue laces, and she'd waved at him and Hallie, too.

She still waved, but she was headless. The filthy shoe looked like something a homeless giant had worn through, then discarded.

The door was open, but when Skates ducked inside he couldn't get far. Craig pushed in after him. A spiral staircase had fallen over, along with all the upstairs exhibits. A few small body parts were visible: several of the old woman's children had been crushed in the collapsing rubble.

Skates pulled at a plank that looked intact. It broke at his touch. The wood was rotten.

Craig recalled Hallie's sing-song recitation of the rhyme—*so many children she didn't know what to do.* How many children were there, really?

"This is a terrible rhyme," he told Skates.

"Dude, it's a lame-ass park all around."

"That not what I mean. The rhyme—I think it's about being poor. This woman's got all these kids, and she's freaking *old,* and doesn't have a husband or a job. They're living in a shoe, for Christ's sake. Real life, they'd be starving to death."

Skates kicked at another board. A tiny fiberglass hand holding a lollipop rolled off the pile. "What a shithole."

"Hallie actually cried when they closed this place down. But I guess she cried about a lot of things."

"Can't compete with that, can you?"

"Nope. Hallie always got her way."

"I'm sorry man."

"That's okay." Craig closed his eyes for a second, blacking out the flashlight beam and the trash and the pile of collapsed rubble. Everything but the memories. "I wish I'd never come here."

"We'll be out soon enough," Skates said. He set the flashlight on the floor, planted one foot at the bottom of the heap, and grunted and pulled at a curled metal bar. It was part of the broken banister, about five feet long once he'd extracted it. "This'll work like a big crowbar, don't you think?"

~

OUTSIDE, SKATES WHISTLED and did the hoot-owl a few more times. As they retraced their steps back to the teacup ride, he dragged the metal bar on the path behind him, a dragon's claw scraping at the blacktop. Craig held the flashlight, which began to dim; he flicked the power off now and then, to conserve the battery. Slivers of moonlight through the trees made it easy enough to see, as long as they stayed on the path.

"How about this," Skates said. "We get back there, pry the cup off him, and it's like one of those ghost stories where at the end the guy's hair has turned white from fear. Imagine Eddie with white hair. And he's lost his voice from being so scared, that's why he doesn't answer. He'll never talk again."

"We should be so lucky."

"Could be, you know, some serial killer followed us into the park. Waited for us to split up, like dumb kids do in horror movies. He'd go after the weaker kid first, the one who's alone and can't get away."

"And we'd be next."

"Sure. We're probably walking into a trap." Skates practically had to shout to be heard over the scrape of the metal bar. Now he lifted the bar and switched to a whisper: "We get there, and it's totally silent. The cup's been lifted and you point the light inside and nobody's there. But there's all these splashes of fresh blood."

"You're enjoying this a little too much."

"Or try this: We get there, and that dumb cup's still upside down, and Eddie's still sulking and saying nothing, and we creep closer and we hear...*chewing.* Teeth tearing at flesh, chomping on bone."

"Okay, you're really starting to spook me a bit." He wasn't really, but Craig figured that was the only way to get him to stop.

"One more. We get there, and Eddie *does* talk, says something like, 'Give me a hand.' The voice is a little hoarse, though, and I think maybe he's been crying like a baby, so I reach in through the opening. A hand closes over mine, and...it's *not* Eddie. It's not even human."

The punchline to his story echoed in the forest; the flashlight was off, the moon had gone behind a cloud, the trees were thicker overhead. "Good one," Craig said, not intending a compliment. His friend laughed, like someone who had lost his mind.

Ridiculous. Skates was joking around. Eddie was angry, but he was fine. After all, this was the Storybook Forest. Nothing terrible ever happened here.

Clouds drifted away from the moon. In the distance, the facade of a castle appeared through the trees, a sign they'd nearly reached the site of the teacup ride. One of the turrets was split down the side—painted Plexiglas instead of stone. Branches hatched thick shadows across the castle's decayed surface. From this angle, it really did look haunted.

They hurried up the path, hoping to rescue whatever was left of their friend.

2 Interval

IT hadn't seemed possible that Michelle could hate her job more than she did yesterday. The airline's Chapter 11 announcement brought a freeze in her salary, reduced benefits, and the threat of scaled-back hours, along with new layers of unpleasantness from travelers already inclined to complain to the wrong people about government-imposed carry-on limits and increased security delays. Too many customers asked her if they'd lose their frequent flier miles, as if that's the worst possible crisis—and Michelle, worried about the future of her job, smiled through the pretense of friendly skies and *Thanks for flying with us!*

But today. Today was worse. Apparently the skies hadn't been so friendly.

At issue was Flight 1137, from St. Louis by way of Nashville. The Delayed indicator flashed next to 7:55 pm on the Arrivals screen, and lingered long enough to nudge several waiting family members to the ticket counter at scattered intervals to request an explanation. A single monitor reported status updates for the small airport's half dozen active flights, and Michelle assured them this public screen was usually current. Still, she dutifully checked her computer for non-existent updates then shook her head a few key clicks later. Close to 8:50, *Arriving* flashed into the status column on the public screen, followed a few minutes later by *At Gate 16*. Then not.

"How could it be blank?" The tentative worry of the young woman's previous visits had steered into anger. She was out of breath after her third trip from Baggage Claim, and her stomach—probably seventh month or so—heaved with each agitated wheeze. "The plane has to be somewhere, doesn't it?"

"Let me check again for you."

As she waited for her computer to respond, Michelle smiled at the young boy standing beside his pregnant mother. The boy seemed distant, more puzzled about his mother's anger than about the whereabouts of his father's airplane. Poor kid. Probably just tired.

The info page for Flight 1137 flashed a new message in the status box.

"What? What's it say?" The woman leaned closer, her stomach pressing against the front of the ticket counter.

Michelle realized her face must have registered some slight surprise, and she corrected with a more neutral expression. "Nothing," she said. "Nothing. Just that they'll be making an announcement soon."

"What's that mean?"

Michelle shrugged. "It says 'Announcement forthcoming.' I don't know anything more than that."

The woman stared back at her, mouth slightly open. Michelle found it hard to return her stare and glanced instead at the child. His eyes blinked a few times, exactly in sync with the flashing message in the status box.

Michelle had quoted the information precisely as it appeared on the screen, and it was true she didn't have further explanation. Except the simple fact that she'd never seen this kind of vague entry in a flight's status column. That, and the chilling awareness that an airline would never flash a status code like Crashed, or Missing, or All Passengers Presumed Dead.

The woman turned, and she put her hand on her son's right shoulder then let him guide her away from the counter. Michelle

Interval

noticed the woman's long, straight hair, which hung almost to the middle of her back. She remembered the time she'd been pregnant herself, briefly, and her scalp had been strangely sensitive, her hair so unbearably heavy that she'd cut most of it off with a pair of scissors. But she'd lost the baby in the first trimester, and was sad about her hair too, for a while. So far along in the pregnancy: how could this woman stand it?

Her supervisor approached from the opposite end of the ticketing stations. Wade had heavy brown sideburns and glasses so tiny that he practically had to squint through them. He looked, simultaneously, like a twenty-year-old trying to be stylish, and a fifty-year-old trying even harder. Either direction, he was an awkward boss, uneasy with his authority. Yesterday, when he stumbled and stammered through the bad news about the airline's bankruptcy filing, people understood him only because the story had already been reported in the morning's newspaper. Michelle guessed Wade had known sooner, by at least a few days, and hadn't summoned the nerve to tell them.

He was even more flustered now than yesterday. "There's going to be an announcement. Flight 1137, uh, over the loudspeaker in a few minutes. We're gathering—you know, all the people here to meet the flight—gathering them in the Courtesy Office downstairs. Outside the Baggage Claim area, where most of them are already waiting."

"What happened?"

"I need you to come with me. We can close out your terminal."

True enough. Joanie and Erika could handle the few remaining departures that night, and her own shift was due to end within the half hour. Was he asking her to stay late?

"A lot of back and forth on the phone," Wade continued. "I've been told we need to keep people calm."

He still hadn't answered her question. "What happened?"

"Probably, uh." He pressed his thumb on the bridge of his glasses, pushing them tight against his face. "Probably what you think."

COURTESY OFFICE 2-C was a former smoking lounge, from the days when the airport allowed smoking in designated areas. Now it was a meeting area available for training sessions, policy announcements, sometimes even for staff birthday or holiday parties. They'd met in the same room yesterday, at 1:00 when the morning and evening shifts overlapped, so Wade could privately announce the pending bankruptcy. Perhaps the main office gave him the same advice at that time: *keep everybody calm.*

2-C needed a key card for entry, a benefit Wade impressed upon her as they headed downstairs. They needed to control who entered the room—only immediate family members (he didn't quite say "next of kin"). The airline's name was already tarnished by the bankruptcy announcement, and they needed to minimize further negative publicity. He'd already deflected calls from two different reporters. "Wouldn't be surprised if someone showed up here, tried to get some awful story to turn things against us."

All Michelle could think of was the intrusion on people's privacy. For the sake of an exclusive story, would a reporter dare sneak into the group, try to catch people's grief when it was fresh and agonizing and newsworthy? Not if she could help it.

Wade gathered his laptop computer and clipboard under one arm, then slid his magnetic card through the reader slot. The door opened with a click. A large refreshment cart was already inside the doorway, parked at a haphazard angle: two metal canisters of coffee, a tray of donuts, and a bowl of oranges. Next to it, dozens of in-flight snack boxes filled a bin, along with plastic bags of napkins and cups bearing the airline's logo.

"Let's line the tables along the outer wall," Wade said. "We can spread food out more easily."

The six long tables were usually pushed together in the middle of the room, forming a large conference table. The food items weren't

Interval

enough to cover all the tables; Michelle suspected her boss didn't want their guests to stare at each other while they waited for news.

Wade's arrangement of the chairs confirmed her suspicion. He set them up press-conference style, in rows that faced the lectern and projection screen at the front of the room. Then he opened his laptop and plugged it into the network and presentation system. Eventually, computer icons flickered onto the screen, then after a few clicks a large representation of the public "Arrivals" monitor appeared. The image was grainy, but easy to read even with the overhead light on. The status column next to Flight 1137 was still blank.

She looked over Wade's shoulder at the podium. The laptop's smaller screen was divided into four quadrants, like a security monitor. The upper left panel, surrounded by a yellow selection frame, indicated the projected image. Next to it was the evening's view from the front of the airport, taxis and shuttle buses and passenger cars rolling past in a jerking motion caused by the camera's slow refresh rate. On the bottom row, an innocuous view of a random runway, a plane safely landed and baggage being unloaded from beneath. The final quadrant contained another low-resolution image, but the refresh rate was better than the airport's typical security feed. Emergency lights strobed red over a darkening field: ambulances and fire trucks at the perimeter, a scorched stretch of ground, a few trees uprooted, patches of brush fire and the waving flashlights of police searchers.

Even though she expected it, the final panel sickened her. Michelle thought of that young boy waiting for his father—of however many other children, spouses, parents and friends might soon be seated in those rows facing the front, facing her to plead for news they didn't really want to hear.

Wade pressed a function key and the Arrivals board expanded over the divided quadrants on his computer. "Remember we have to stay calm, to keep the others calm."

Why had he chosen her, instead of Joanie or Erika with years' more experience? The answer was too obvious. They were pleasant enough, those women, but Wade had chosen a younger companion for this trial. A kinder emissary of grief. Joanie and Erika at least had attractive phone voices, and could field calls to the airline.

He placed a cell phone headset over his right ear and assumed a soldierly expression. "I'm calling them in." He gave a quick Go-ahead to someone on the other end, obviously already prepared for his call. Almost immediately, a message droned through the airport loudspeaker: "Families awaiting the arrival of Flight 1137 from St. Louis or Nashville, please report to Baggage Claim Level, Room 2-C Courtesy Office." Then, repeated twice more.

Michelle started to panic. She half-wondered if Wade followed a set protocol, or if he was being allowed to improvise. Shouldn't there be some police officers here? Airport representatives? Some kind of professional grief counselor? On-call specialists should be available to handle this kind of thing—even for a small out-of-the-way airport, and their small, money-losing airline. She wasn't trained.

"Here's an extra copy." Wade handed her a passenger list and a yellow highlighter. "Get ready."

NINETY-SEVEN PASSENGERS, ACCORDING to the total at the bottom of the third page. Just a number, just a list of names. As Michelle read over the list, she wondered if she'd checked any of these people in for the westbound portion of their journey. A few names seemed familiar, but she had no faces to connect to them.

No. Only the recent faces of the pregnant woman and her son; the tall, gray-haired man in a plaid suit; the heavyset woman with a two-liter plastic tumbler of soda from Seven-Eleven. And more faces soon to arrive.

The first wave was the roughest, a large group of about thirty who formed two separate lines outside the open doorway. Michelle asked the first woman in her line for identification, then compared the driver's license name against the relatives on her list.

∽ Interval ∽

"My daughter, visiting home from college." The woman was in her forties, thin and barely over five feet tall. With her small legs she must have walked quickly to get to the front of the line. Anxious as she was, her voice remained quiet and restrained. "I wish Lizzie hadn't gone to school so far away. But we still get to see her a couple times a year."

Michelle highlighted the daughter's name and waved the woman into the conference room.

The woman paused before entering and turned her head to ask, almost as an afterthought: "Do you know what's going on?" Again, the quiet voice, and Michelle responded in kind.

"Not really." Michelle felt the stares of people in both lines, their ears straining to listen. No such thing as a private conversation here: speaking to one meant speaking to all. "We're still waiting for information."

A murmur of frustration thrummed through the crowd. Most of them were strangers to each other, spoke only to themselves or the air. Michelle turned to the next person in her line, a man in a salmon-colored polo shirt. He held his license by one corner, extended as if he were making a credit card purchase.

"No, no." Wade's voice rose sharply above the random airport noise. He looked at a teenage girl and made dismissive motions with his fingertips. "Relatives only. Family members, like the announcement says. The rest of you will have to wait outside."

For a moment, Michelle feared there would be a small riot. "I've waited over an hour," the teenager said. She looked barely old enough to drive—probably on her first ever pick-up trip to the airport. "My best friend is on that flight." Several people raised exasperated arms, either in sympathy to the girl's plight, or angry about their own pending dismissal. They looked to people on either side for allies. Michelle had earlier conceded Wade's point about privacy, didn't want intruders to witness the coming grief. But she blushed now, aware of how this situation would look, how they'd assume her tacit approval of Wade's ruling as she stood there with her clipboard and highlighter, a pitiless gatekeeper who measured each supplicant, denied entrance to those deemed unworthy. As if their budget airline, already stingy with on-flight drinks and snacks, couldn't spare the extra coffee or donuts.

Then the crowd settled down, the collective mood flattened by the more important subtext to Wade's statement. She could see the realization slowly dawn on their faces, their eyes glazing over, jaws dropping slowly, hands lifting in almost-choreographed unison to cover mouths that needn't say what they're all thinking, have been trying for a long while not to think: *If they're only allowing family members, it must be something terrible.*

Michelle's eyes blurred, shifting the two lines of people out of focus so she didn't have to distinguish their expressions. The announcement repeated from the airport speaker, "Families awaiting the arrival of Flight 1137..." The tin voice, sterile and mechanical before, now sounded smug. It knew. It knew, and it withheld the truth deliberately.

A faint tug pulled the clipboard away from her chest. A tall man stood next to her, too close, really, but gentle as he looked over her shoulder and drew a slender finger down the list. "Robert is my...my partner," he said. "The last names won't match, I'm afraid." He reached the bottom of the page without success, and Michelle absently lifted it to reveal the second sheet.

"This one?" she asked, pointing to a Robert Braynard, listed with a local address.

"Yes." The man's eyes pleaded with her—as if she could not only admit him into the conference room, but also had some power over his partner's fate.

Was her boss listening? Wade seemed busy with his own crowd, the pregnant mother trying to coerce answers from his vague, avoiding mouth. Wade was a stickler for rules, especially when he made them himself. Family members only, as legally defined—and their conservative legislature wasn't anywhere close to approving same-sex marriage. Wade wouldn't let this guy in.

Michelle thought about her friend's brother who'd gotten sick a few years back—pneumonia as a complication from AIDS—and

⁓ Interval ⁓

remembered how Alice's parents wouldn't allow her brother's lover to visit the hospital room. Alice still hated her Mom and Dad for that. Her brother was dying, and it wasn't their place to judge. Grief is what it is; love is what it is.

And Michelle knew the others in her line were watching, waiting to see if she followed her boss' example. Their airport served a small city, mostly white, mostly Southern Baptist, and many of them would agree with the strict legal definition of family. At the same time, people who traveled by plane tended to be more worldly than the town itself—recruits connected with the down-sized military base, for example; international students attending Graysonville University and professors who moved here from out of state. She'd like to think—even here in the middle of the Bible Belt—she'd like to think people would be more compassionate in a time of shared crisis.

She barely looked at the driver's license the man held up. "Go ahead in," she told him.

⁓

AFTER THEY'D ADMITTED that initial group, Michelle and Wade moved inside. Other people showed up individually or in small clusters, lured by the loudspeaker's monotonous chant, or directed there by Joanie or Erika or an indifferent recorded message on the airline's answering machine. These new people peered through the thin rectangular window in the door frame, then tapped at the wire-meshed glass. When Michelle opened the door partway to check their identification against her printout, she tried not to meet the gaze of those who lingered outside the room, banished to the hallway as if their friendship had no value.

Did the people inside count as the lucky ones? There were fifty of them in the conference room now, all suspended over the cliff of a horrible grief. Occasionally, a ripple would start in one row or another, the beginnings of a protest eventually stifled by decorum. And false hope.

Wade held them off with a partial announcement at ten o'clock, told them simply that radio contact with the plane had been lost. *It may have been diverted to a different airport. We're working on locating it now.*

But Michelle had seen enough on Wade's laptop to prepare herself. The projected image remained constant, but her boss periodically cycled through the other camera views on his private screen. He tried to do this subtly—when none of the family members were close to his podium, and therefore couldn't catch a stray close-up of metal scraps, torn and burnt and bloody fabric, or a crisp white sheet on a stretcher pulled over shapes that didn't quite add up to a complete body.

Each glimpse was enough to force Michelle back into a noncommittal smile, to send her among the rows to collect napkins folded over half-eaten donuts, or see if anyone needed a different magazine or a coffee refill, decaf or regular, and no, we haven't heard anything new, not since the last time you asked, I'm sorry.

She grasped for a general way to refer to them in her mind, these almost-widows and nearly-orphans, these older men and women who'd soon cast the name of parent painfully into the past tense. Without intending to, she'd attached nicknames to some of them. "Big Gulp" for the woman with the soda tumbler; "Surfer Dude" for the 20-year-old with a slurred California accent. Then there was the stocky middle-aged man who looked like he'd slept in his clothes. His short brown hair had an uneven part on the left side, his face scratchy with a pepper stubble of beard. Maybe she'd been influenced by Wade's predictions, but this man's eyes, dark and darting around the room, seemed to *take notes*. So she'd dubbed him, "The Reporter." The nicknames weren't meant to be unkind—just a way to identify people, yet keep them at a distance. If Michelle registered the real name of the elderly black woman—if it was Gladys, for example, and if she held an infant granddaughter named Tammy—the knowledge would only make their suffering more tangible.

Occasionally she'd hear the ring of a cell phone, or overhear the tentative, nervous half of a phone conversation. She gathered nobody

Interval

at home had information either: whatever happened or hadn't happened wasn't yet enough to attract the national media, and local news sources remained silent or unaware. Unlike typical cell conversations, loud to the point of rudeness, people here whispered into their phones, unwilling to amplify their anxiety to the room. They hugged phones to their ears, turned their heads to hide the electronic devices as Michelle passed.

An unconscious symbolism seemed to control them. Michelle was playing at stewardess, and Wade had seated them as if they were on a spacious flight. People stayed mostly in their seats, for fear of missing an announcement the instant it was conveyed—but just as strong was the sense that leaving was impossible, would break the air-seal of the cabin, send them from safety into rooms governed by cruel gravity, with no solid footing beneath them.

A few of them, however, felt free to roam about the "cabin," in particular the boy who strayed frequently from his pregnant mother (slumped in the first row, her legs stretched wearily in front); and Robert's friend, who seemed more alone than any of them, an outsider in this group of legally-sanctioned relatives. Each time he got up for more coffee or to select from the snack offerings or choose a new section of *USA Today*, he returned to a different spot.

He settled near the African-American family now, leaving a respectful empty seat between them. The husband had turned away slightly to stare at the wall. The thin, neatly dressed woman held a baby, most likely a grandchild. Michelle wondered how the baby could be comfortable seated in the woman's sharp-boned lap, but the infant smiled, adorable and oblivious in a sun-yellow dress, with a white lace bonnet bow-tied beneath her chin. She seemed to enjoy the rhythm as her grandmother tapped one leg nervously.

"It will be all right," Robert's friend said to the old woman. "Don't you think?"

"Yes, I do," she said. "What I told my husband, the Lord wouldn't send us more than we could handle."

"No," Robert's friend said. "No, He wouldn't."

"This here's our granddaughter. We took care of her this week while our daughter was in Nashville." She spoke inclusively, but her husband didn't acknowledge the conversation. "Vanessa's been no trouble at all, have you dear?" She adjusted the bonnet, actually tilting it slightly off center. "'Course, the nice thing about grandkids is, you can hand them back to their Mommy before they get to be a bother." Her voice shook on the last words, her lower lip trembling.

"She'll be happy to see her mother again." Robert's friend reached a long arm across the empty seat and patted the woman on the knee. For a moment, her leg ceased the nervous tapping; the infant looked startled, but remained peaceful. The old woman smiled back at him.

It was good of him to offer comfort, Michelle thought. It was good of the grandmother to accept it.

TIME PASSED WITH agonizing slowness. The tension was nearly unendurable to Michelle, and she imagined it was exponentially worse for those with loved ones on Flight 1137.

Yet people remained remarkably calm. When the granddaughter cried, as babies will, everyone waited without comment for the sound to end. But at some point their civility and polite denial would break under the strain. And Michelle knew the shift would be dramatic, with one screaming outburst triggering a domino effect of fear and rage. And who could they take their anger out on? God wasn't here. Just her and Wade, two representatives from the airline.

Five minutes before ten-thirty. She wondered if people expected the announcement to be timed to the half-hour, like the start of television shows.

Wade needed to tell them. The longer he waited, the worse it would be.

Michelle backed away from the podium and stood to the side. Most of the people sat up straight in their chairs and faced the front of the room. They stared at the projected Status Board as if it were a curtain

Interval

ready to open. Each instant the imaged refreshed, a horrible ripple of anticipation trembled through the crowd.

Tell them, Wade. Tell them gently, but tell them.

In the middle row, Robert's friend looked directly at her boss instead of at the screen. He studied Wade, as if he could read something in his face.

All the while, her boss clicked at his keyboard. Was he composing some message? Michelle noticed a shifting cascade of colors reflected in the lenses of Wade's glasses. The images were too small, she was certain. It was impossible that someone could decipher a reflected picture in those tiny ovals of glass.

In the waiting audience, Robert's friend continued to focus on Wade.

Then the calm finally broke, in a shrill chaos more spectacular than anything Michelle had predicted.

"WHAT WAS THAT?"

Several voices at once. The scuff of rubber-tipped chair legs on thin carpet.

"My baby. My baby."

People clutching at their chests or squeezing their faces in their hands.

"Alan's briefcase?"

Standing abruptly, a half-empty coffee cup spilling to the floor.

"Sandra's jacket. That looked like Sandra's jacket!"

A rustle of newsprint. Quiet sobs in an awkward silence.

"It couldn't be..."

"Isn't that—?"

And the pregnant woman, closest to the front, crossing the gap with a sprinter's speed, tip-toed and stretching one arm over the podium to grasp Wade's lapel and pull his face closer to hers, her voice an awful, resonating snarl: "What kind of sadistic fucking game are you playing?"

Because, on the public screen—only for a split second, an almost subliminal flash—an image so horrific...Michelle couldn't be sure, it had happened so fast. But she thought she'd seen a nightmare collage, some awful collection of the worst fears in this room, carefully joined into a single terrible picture then projected onto the screen. All this time, had Wade simply been working on this perverse Photoshopped image?

"What?" Wade, flustered, looked behind him at the familiar Status Board that had been projected for so long. "What? I didn't—" But he also snapped shut the lid to his laptop, turning off the computer in a quick, guilty motion.

"Oh Lord, Oh Lord." The grandmother hugged the baby against her frail chest.

Wade stepped beside the podium, and the pregnant woman's hand hovered in the air where she'd previously held the lapel of his suit coat. Clearly, the group was ready to shout him down, attack him, but something about his defenseless manner made them pause. Michelle stayed back, not wanting the blame that came with Wade's authority. She felt the crowd lean forward, tensing as if to decipher the words of a man who stuttered or spoke in a foreign tongue.

And that's what it sounded like: an odd rasping whisper of syllables that started and stopped, less decipherable with each attempt. But he was *trying* to speak, Wade was trying, which was more than he'd done before, so they gave him space, they listened and waited for some meaning to break through.

As a result, the other voice broke through clearly, even at a whisper. "You did this." An accusation, from the man she'd come to think of as the Reporter. His glowering eyes focused on Robert's friend.

Where she stood, Michelle could see them both. Most people faced forward as her boss' voice cracked further and further from coherence, but the Reporter had turned ninety degrees in his chair, his legs in the aisle and chin near his shoulder to stare at the man across the room and two rows back.

"What?" One arm flew up, wrist flapping limp as if he'd been startled into a stereotypical, flamboyant gesture. Robert's friend didn't check to see if the Reporter intended someone else nearby, and Michelle

Interval

thought she understood. A gay man in this southern town no doubt lived through years of harassment: misunderstood by his parents; teased at school; jeered at outside bars by predatory frat brothers; finally finding love, but denied legal status by a government that should protect him. And all the while, a target for blame, as if just by existing he corrupted children, undermined the nation's morality, weakened the economy and the employment rate. *You did this,* the Reporter had said, and of course the word *this* meant everything, from the tension in the room to the strange projected flash of horror to the plane crash itself. Robert's friend was startled by the accusation, but not surprised.

"I know what you are," the Reporter said. "You shouldn't be here." He had obviously listened carefully when she'd bent the rules to admit Robert's friend into the room.

The gay man summoned a nervous laugh, then a wry, resigned, half-smile.

"It's not funny," the Reporter said. One leg was anchored beneath the chair, the stocky torso and a clenched fist rising from the seat to lunge across the aisle.

In the instant it took Michelle to cross to the space between them, she had the uneasy realization that, moments before, if the crowd had chosen to attack her boss, she would have allowed it. She would have stood back, let them knock Wade to the ground and punch and kick him, maybe would have raced for the door and left him behind without a second thought.

But this man had been her ally, comforting others even as he suffered the same terrible uncertainty. She would protect him. She didn't have a choice.

Her frame was slight, but she counted on southern gallantry. The Reporter wouldn't dare hit her.

"Miss, out of my way—"

"Return to your seat," she said, as confident as a stewardess repeating federal regulations. *Smoking is forbidden in the airplane lavatory. Please wait until the captain has turned off the Fasten Seat Belt sign.*

"You don't understand. You have no idea." He wouldn't hit her, no, but he put one palm flat against her shoulder and shoved her out of the aisle. Michelle caught herself on the back of a chair, practically falling into the Surfer Dude's lap. As she regained her balance, she was pleased to notice Robert's partner had escaped. And people from outside, the non-family members Wade hadn't permitted to enter, caught the door before it crunched shut. They surged into the conference room, agitated by the commotion of agony and confusion they'd heard through the walls.

The Reporter ran toward the doorway, and he wedged his thick body through the entering crowd. Michelle hadn't been able to stop him, but at least she'd given Robert's friend a head start.

The entire situation was too big for her to grasp, so she'd fixated on this tiny battle of wills. Michelle couldn't revive dead bodies from the wreckage, but she could damn well fight against prejudice and exploitation.

She followed the Reporter.

SHE FOUND HIM outside the room, the only person in the Baggage Claim area at this late hour. He aimed a digital camera at empty conveyor belts. So, she'd been right about him all along. Michelle thought of movie crime scenes where a police chief grabs a reporter's unauthorized camera and pulls a loop of film from the compartment, recorded images flashed away in an overexposed instant; or where a sheriff's boot heel cracks through a lens and view screen, scrapes metal and plastic into the asphalt next to a bloodstain and chalk outline. She didn't have that kind of bullying authority—only the force of her indignation. "Which newspaper?" she asked.

The Reporter held the camera at arm's length, between thumb and fingertips, with a continual pan and pivot of his wrist. "I'm sorry?"

She called his bluff. "You don't know anyone on that plane," Michelle said.

Interval

"No. I don't." But his confession wasn't the triumph she expected. There was a glimmer of weakness in his flat statement, something with the flavor of authentic grief. "*This* tragedy isn't mine," he said, and for a moment, despite herself, she pitied him.

But her emotions, held in check for most of the evening, now responded in quick reflexive jolts. When the Reporter next said, "He can't have gone far," a sneer in the pronoun set her off again. Michelle was certain she'd heard it: *He* used ironically, as if a homosexual doesn't deserve the masculine reference.

"Why are you looking for him? Maybe you need someone to blame for the sake of a story. Or maybe it's something personal?" Her voice got louder as she climbed inside rediscovered anger. "But it's chance. Random wind currents or pilot error or engine flaws or some other combination of bad luck. You can't scapegoat an innocent man simply because—"

"He's not innocent," the Reporter said. "And he's not a man."

"That's enough!" And she was pointing at him, jabbing his shoulder with her forefinger for emphasis. "You can't blame someone because you don't like the way he looks. Because you don't like the way he loves." How did she summon the nerve to touch him like that?—a small framed girl against this stocky bigot who no doubt played football or wrestled in high school, lifted weights twenty years later to fight back the gut from weekend drinking. And even more surprising, her outburst seemed to work. He dropped the arm with the camera and stepped back, a sadness and realization on his face, and she felt as if, in a one-minute confrontation, she'd startled him out of a lifetime of prejudice. No miracles for people on Flight 1137, sadly, but maybe a small miracle here.

"You're mistaken." He shook his head. "I'm not homophobic. He lies. That's what he does." Again the irony and scorn in the pronoun.

"Not a man," he repeated. "I know how it sounds. But the first time we met, he was an Asian janitor who worked nights on the intensive care floor. My teenage daughter was in a coma. Five months, with a hopeless prognosis, but I tried to believe. I tried so hard. That's the interval."

He wasn't a reporter. She reevaluated his unshaven face, mussed hair, and wrinkled clothes. Michelle had made allowances for people's distress—of *course* they'd all look worried and frantic, black circles under their eyes as if they hadn't slept for days. But this guy was too comfortable in his crazed appearance; it wasn't a symptom of fresh grief.

"The interval. When you know something's bad, but you can't quite give up. You hold onto your faith, squeeze it close, but it gets weaker and weaker because you're smothering it. And *he* gets stronger."

Michelle wanted to walk away, but something in his manner held her fast. Perhaps she obeyed an unwritten etiquette for dealing with crazy people, especially after you'd confronted them. She needed to let him explain himself.

"An interval demon," he continued. "That's what I call him. He thrives on the interval between when people dread something, and when they find out for certain. At hospitals, of course. After natural disasters, after terrorist attacks. The more people, the more they wait in agony for terrible news, the stronger he gets. Do you understand?"

Michelle nodded, not caring what she agreed to.

"Yes, you can understand how this is a good one for him. Everyone in that room suspects someone in their family has died. But the airline dangles hope in front of them, draws it out. And the demon taunts people, walks around the room and gets them to talk about God and faith. That's how he gained power to perform his trick, flashing those images on the screen. He showed enough to ratchet up the fear, but not enough to demolish their hopes completely."

"I should get back to the room," Michelle offered. He ignored her and continued to spin out his twisted logic.

"These days," he explained, "cell phones and quick disaster response close the interval, making knowledge of tragedy more immediate. The demon has to sniff out places where the outcome will linger, uncertain."

Ridiculous. Even if she could accept the preposterous element at the center of his story—a shape-changing demon strengthened by human tragedy—how was this reporter (this hunter, as he fashioned

Interval

himself) able to follow the demon, much less identify it? This crazy guy was nothing more than a vagrant who stumbled into an emotionally charged scene, chose a scapegoat, and tried to stir up trouble.

"We have a connection," he said, sensing her skepticism. "Ever since my little girl died. That's how we sometimes end up in the same place." He swept the digital camera in a wide arc, taking in the outside wall of Office 2-C behind her. "The demon won't have gone far. It gains more energy the closer it is to the crisis." He stopped, pointed high above her to the right, and spoke in a birdwatcher's whisper. "The security camera."

Enough, Michelle decided. She wouldn't even look.

"There. In the corner."

And she *would* look—to humor him, and also to end it. She turned to where he pointed: the security camera, high-mounted over the baggage conveyors, its red indicator light steady over a wide-angle lens.

Nothing there. Since she'd already turned, she decided to keep going. Walk away.

"No," he said, insistent. "You have to look *here.*" The guy was right next to her, one hand on her shoulder and the other blocking her way with the raised camera, practically pressing the LED view screen into her face.

Michelle shrugged her shoulder free, raised a hand ready to slap the camera out of the way. She caught a glimpse of the view screen, its backlit image barely larger than a postage stamp. He held it steady, keeping the mounted security camera neatly centered, a silver and black rectangle appearing as tiny as a kernel of rice on the screen.

For the first time this stressful evening, Michelle laughed. This crazy guy was so desperate to show her his camera—and all the while his dumb, fat finger was over the lens. His fingertip was flat and out-of-focus on the top third of the screen. And what was so funny was that *he* was looking too: he stood right next to her, saw the same spoiled image, and still acted like he'd proven his point.

Out of focus, and yet pressed so close she could make out the tiny dark whorls of his fingerprint. So ridiculous the way it sat…it sat…

The way it sat right on top of the security camera. The blurred, lined smudge of flesh on the screen. It *perched*.

She realized now that he held the camera as before: from the side with fingers along the top, thumb on the bottom.

Even in that tiny image, she noticed shapes in the lines she previously interpreted as a fingerprint, the whorls twisting on an upraised lump to approximate a face. Shadows creased beneath wrinkles and folds, with dark blue veins scored over random, taut muscles.

"Right next to the wall, where it could be close to everyone's suffering." The reporter, the hunter, the vagrant—whatever he was—spoke with a detached excitement, happy to have solved his puzzle. "It hid above the security camera, so it wouldn't show up on the monitors. It can fool us, but not a camera."

Michelle had laughed at him seconds earlier. Now she felt her mouth tense into a grimace, the muscles in her neck stretching toward a scream.

Another scream came first, and another, a chorus of wailings from the other side of the wall. *Oh God,* she thought, *Wade told them. He finally told them about the plane crash.* And from the intensity of the reaction, he must have told them everyone onboard had died.

In response, something happened to the shape on the view screen. A pulse of red light and an awful flexing.

Michelle's hand, still poised to knock the digital camera away, twitched forward in a spasm. The camera fell from the man's loose grip, and as it spun away she thought she saw movement in the image. The man's camera dropped to the ground, and the *thing* dropped, too.

"It's gotten too powerful," he said in a panic. He dove after the camera. On all fours he scooped it from the ground and turned the shattered view screen towards empty air. He stood up, his legs unsteady, and he held the broken device in front of him like a talisman. "Where is it?" he said. "Where is it *now?*"

Frustrated, he threw the useless camera against the wall. What kind of hunter didn't bring a weapon? Perhaps the human forms of the

～ Interval ～

demon—an elderly janitor; a tall, frail gay man—seemed weak enough that he believed he could overpower them with his bare hands.

He waved his arms in front, scratching at the air the way someone falling down a cliffside would grasp for handholds.

Michelle backed away. The wails of agony from the next room were thick, as tangible as footsteps that drew closer. Beneath the human cries she thought she heard a moist crackling, like a scab lifted from a half-healed wound.

But she saw nothing now, and hadn't seen much before on that tiny screen. Maybe it had only been his finger over the lens. The man's insanity had influenced her, broken through a sense of reality already stretched thin by the tension of unannounced tragedy. She was susceptible.

Susceptible enough to see something now, too, a tear in the space between them, like the flashes of light before a migraine. It seemed to concentrate near the man's chest. His arms steadied, one hand wrapping in a fist. His face flushed and his feet lifted on tiptoes, chest heaving upward. The man's eyes glazed in horror, and his body trembled as if something were being pulled out of him—the strip of film she'd imagined earlier, ripped from a camera and overexposed to a shock of bright light.

Too much. Too much for him. He dropped lifeless to the floor.

"Thank you." The voice came from behind her, a familiar, slightly effeminate trill. Robert's friend was here, as he'd made himself appear previously, but seeming false now, too close to the stereotype of an older gay man. He smiled at her, and Michelle wondered what stereotypes would fit his true identity. His head should tilt slightly down, heavy from the weight of horns. The rustle of leathern wings and a forked tail should flow behind him, his long legs balanced above cloven hooves. Unpleasant as these images seemed, they were at least easier to grasp than the blurred mass of discolored flesh and muscle she'd glimpsed in the tiny camera display. Or the full-size version—invisible, mercifully—that had sludged its way across the tile floor.

"Another time, perhaps," he said. The man she had known as Robert's friend walked past her with a confident stride, his shoulders no longer slumped under the weight of feigned grief. Michelle did nothing to stop him. Instead, her mind flashed images of a sick mother in a hospital bed, her fingers curled through arthritis and clenched pain; in a similar bed, a similar room, a man she didn't quite recognize, his face handsome and soothing and the sight of his decline filling her with unbearable remorse; and a smaller figure in a glass-enclosed crib, the infant body wrapped in heavy blankets, and she wonders (then? now?) if God could be so cruel to let her finally carry a child to term, to name her, love her, only to watch her fall to sickness before the baby has even learned to walk. Michelle can never trust anyone in these hospital rooms—the doctors, nurses, other visitors to the intensive care floor—because she's learned that kind faces can lie, that even a frail, welcoming form can betray you. She wouldn't know how to identify the demon again, doesn't know his name or how to fight him, indeed knows nothing except to conceive of her life from this point on as an awful journey from one crisis of faith to the next, a series of horrible extended intervals of uncertainty in which she's feeding him, feeding him.

The Old Ways

"MAYBE your husband should buy this stuff himself."

Lisa tried not to bristle at the clerk's suggestion. She'd done fine on her own so far, her orange cart already half-filled with cans of wood stain and indoor-outdoor paints, brushes, replacement knobs and handles, screws and nails and tacks and duct tape. Twice already this short, thin teenager had asked if she needed help. He wore a store apron he'd probably wriggled into five minutes after a bell signaled the end of sixth-period social studies.

She held a chip of broken shingle to check it against display samples. "I'm finding what I need, thank you." Lisa didn't add: *I'm more than twice your age.* Or, *This isn't the first hardware store I've stepped foot in, kiddo.*

"Since he'll be doing the work and all," the clerk said, "your husband would know better what supplies to get."

No, Andy was good with words. If you could charm a hundred bucks from a hammer or talk a chisel into a year-long contract, he'd be good with tools, too. More likely, he'd smash his thumb, or twist crooked screws into the wrong hole.

Part of their agreement, when Andy inherited his mother's house, was that Lisa wouldn't find a job right away. Instead, she'd spend days fixing up the place, making the improvements his mother had refused to bother with, as if the woman knew her dilapidated house—mildewed and drafty, paint peeling, shingles sliding off the roof—wouldn't dare fall apart before she did.

His mother's town, Centreville, Maryland, had always seemed behind-the-times to her, an old-fashioned tourist stop with antique stores, a one-room post office, and a drug store with a soda fountain in back. More like a tourist *pause* than a stop, since people raced through Centreville during summer months, frustrated after Bay Bridge slowdowns and anxious to finish the 95 miles remaining before the crowded beaches of Ocean City. Gas and go, with the emphasis on go.

People who stayed in Centreville had stayed forever, like their families had, comfortable with the old ways, like porch-sitting and gossip and minimum wage, and maybe a little prejudice and chauvinism for good measure. Andy had argued the town wouldn't be as backwards as they feared. Television brought modern opinions into the most isolated homes, and the Internet made the world even smaller. What they couldn't find locally, they'd be able to order online: supplies *and* culture, as needed. Hell, Centreville got its own Home Depot last year, and a Blockbuster Video. And really, with the economy the way it was, who could afford to turn down a free house?

Yeah, he'd sold it to her.

So here she stood, her hand on a cardboard carton of roof shingles, the high shelf easily within her reach, and the clerk got all flustered, practically shouted, "Let me get that for you, ma'am." The shelf was too high for *him*, but the little guy brushed her aside, stood on tiptoes and stretched, red faced. The box teetered blind over his head for a perilous moment, then he swung it out and down from the shelf, and nearly heaved it into her cart.

"There you go, ma'am." He smiled like he'd rescued her from a dragon.

Lisa was furious that someone this young held such outdated opinions. She expected such foolishness from her neighbors at Sunrise Apartments, the senior community across the street from their new

The Old Ways

home. In that generation, gender roles were steadfast, ideas of strong breadwinning men and helpless women etched into their fossil brains. But young people should be more open. She wondered what they were teaching this boy at school.

Lisa had more things on her shopping list, but she decided she'd had enough for the day and headed for the checkout. Against her will, she let the boy load her purchases into her car.

~

SHE USED A paint-scraper to chip away at gunk that encrusted the rain gutters around the perimeter of the roof. Lisa fought with the stubborn, sun-dried substance of leaves and dirt and twigs, all baked into a burnt clay. It was a slow process: climbing the ladder, scraping at the layers of grime within reach, then climbing down to reposition the ladder against the house for the next segment.

A calm April wind cooled her forehead as she worked, and music helped relieve the tedium. Her radio was set to 98 ROCK, a Baltimore station—a faint connection to the city they recently abandoned. The music thumped heavy in her headphones, bass rhythm resonating through her body and adding energy to her arm as she chipped at crusted grime. Drum beats seemed to vibrate through the aluminum ladder, like footsteps.

Something tapped her heel. She was so startled, she almost lost her balance.

Lisa turned her head and looked down. An older man with a surprisingly muscular torso had climbed up the ladder beneath her, his eyes monstrous behind thick round spectacles. He held firm to the ladder with one arm, and waved the other wildly.

She screamed and instinctively clutched her paint-scraper like a weapon. She tensed, ready to scramble up onto the roof to escape him.

The old man clawed at the air with his free arm. He shook his round, gray-bald head; it was close enough for her to kick at it. The man's lips moved, but Lisa couldn't hear him over the radio.

The loud music—that would explain why he'd seemed to sneak up on her. She pulled off her headphones.

"Get down," the man said. "Get down from there." She heard urgency in his raspy voice, not malice. His words conveyed a warning, and Lisa wondered if there was a problem with the ladder, or if part of the roof was crumbling away.

"You shouldn't be doing this," he said. "Come down, and I'll do it for you."

Lisa couldn't figure out what he was talking about.

"Leave the tool there," he said, like a policeman asking a suspect to drop the handgun. "I'll get it, and finish up for you."

Now Lisa stifled a laugh. This old man had frightened her for a minute there, she had to admit, but only because he'd startled her. She realized now that he was at least seventy years old, and what she'd seen as a muscular torso was an illusion created by an out-of-season, down-filled jacket. He was already out of breath from his short climb and frantic arm waving: he looked like he'd barely make it up the ladder again, let alone have strength to scrape the gutters clean.

"I'm perfectly fine." Because the man was below her, and probably hard of hearing, Lisa shouted. "I know what I'm doing." Then she smiled, doing her best to hide the irritation. Honestly, was he *that* set in his ways? He couldn't imagine a woman doing any kind of physical labor—and so she needed a feeble old man to help her? Ridiculous.

He squinted his magnified eyes, and for a brief instant Lisa got the uneasy feeling he had read her thoughts. Then the old man's mouth twisted into a grimace—an awful, menacing expression. His hand shot up and grabbed her ankle.

His old fingers squeezed tight, and she was afraid he'd pull her to the ground. Lisa held onto the ladder and the roof; she tried to twist her body around, preparing to kick at him with her other leg. He yanked at her ankle.

"Chest," she heard him say. "My heart…"

~ The Old Ways ~

SOMEHOW, SHE'D MANAGED to get him down safely. First she had to break the man's terrified grip, then she had to practically climb over him, finding scant footing on the rungs his body had flattened against in panic. "Come down," she said, "I've got you." She couldn't trust him to hang on by himself, so she guided him, lifting one of his legs at a time and setting it on the next rung, her cheek and shoulder pressed against his back to hold him in place. If she had turned her head, his puffy winter jacket would have suffocated her.

An ambulance was there as soon as they'd reached the ground. But that was why she'd moved him: so she could get to a phone and call 9-1-1. How did the paramedics know...?

She looked across the street, where several windows of the Sunrise Apartments faced an open courtyard—and the front of her house. A few of the curtains fluttered. Some gray-haired ladies emerged from a side door and walked slowly toward the curb. One of them made stuttered steps behind a metal walker, wheels on the back and bright green tennis balls skewered beneath the front legs.

An on-call nurse pushed through the same door. "Ladies, ladies," she said, "step aside, please." She moved fast, dodging the metal walker and stepping past a tight cluster of two stooped women and one rail-thin man in an Orioles cap. The man's wooden cane looked thicker than his leg.

The nurse crossed the street to Lisa's front lawn. An iron-on patch depicting a sunrise adorned the front pocket of her jacket. She held a pair of rubber gloves in one hand, but didn't seem in a hurry to touch anything. Instead, she stood next to the two paramedics and watched as they lifted the man into a stretcher. "How's old Howard doing?" she asked.

"Probably another asthma attack," one of them answered. "We'll know more after we've checked him out."

"He'll be all right, won't he?" Lisa felt concern for this man, even after he'd frightened her. Not responsibility, though. It wasn't her fault "old Howard" had taken it upon himself to climb the ladder.

"Happens all the time," the nurse said. Lisa wasn't sure what she meant. People climb ladders all the time? People have heart attacks all the time?

The paramedics lifted the stretcher into the ambulance, shut the doors, and eventually drove away. They didn't use the siren, however, which made Lisa feel relieved: they must not think the man's condition was too serious.

"Back inside," the nurse yelled at the gathered crowd. "Give Howard his privacy." An odd thing to say, considering Howard wasn't there anymore. The nurse moved toward the seniors, and they turned their attention back to the apartment complex. She urged them inside, on crowd-control duty as they filed slowly through the door.

Except for one woman, who remained behind. She was dressed a little better than the others, with a more confident posture, and Lisa wondered if she weren't the manager for the facility rather than a resident. But as the woman crossed the street toward Lisa, it was as if she aged two years with each step. Her frosted blond hair was a wig; thick makeup over her pinched face couldn't quite disguise the wrinkles. The woman's confident posture seemed more brittle as she got closer, the overcompensation of someone suffering from chronic back pain.

"I'm Miss Teely," she said, extending her hand. Lisa shook it. The woman's fingers remained stiff, making no effort to return Lisa's grasp. "I wish I'd introduced myself earlier, before this…unpleasantness."

"I'm Lisa. Gladys Wittaker was my mother-in-law."

"Sorry for your loss," Miss Teely said. Her head dropped down slightly, as if uncertain what to say, and Lisa got the urge to help her through the awkwardness. She wondered if Miss Teely and Howard were close, and struggled with the right way to ask.

"Is Howard a friend of yours?"

At this, Miss Teely's head shot up, her eyes alight. "Of *course* he's my friend. He's not *much*—but then we haven't *got* much, have we?"

"I'm sorry, I was—"

"Don't flatter yourself. Young as you are, you don't need to be that pretty."

"Now wait a minute!" How did the conversation take *this* turn?

"I'm not trying to insult you. Simply stating facts. You haven't won any beauty contests—not lately, at least. But you got all of us beat, by a long shot."

It was as if the old woman spoke in a different language. Lisa deciphered the emotions behind it—a wounded pride, lashing back in cruelty—but the context was absurd. Here was a woman aware enough to dress herself, apply makeup, adjust a tightly styled wig. She'd lanced an angel pin, perfectly centered, through her lapel; its jade head and gold-wire halo sparkled, wings of frosted glass shaved thin as paper. The woman's elderly demeanor was precise and composed—but her words were from another realm.

"Younger than us," she continued, "than any of our men would see every day. The nurses don't count. Like harlots, they're paid to smile and to tolerate toothless flattery."

"Miss Teely, stop," Lisa finally had to say, "stop right there." The implications of "harlot" weren't lost on her, but she couldn't bother to take offense. It was more important to end the woman's misguided jealousy. "I didn't invite Howard over here," Lisa said. "I didn't ask for his help."

"You didn't have to," Miss Teely said. "You put yourself in his way, is what you did. You put yourself in his way."

IN CENTREVILLE, THE rumor mill was faster than cell phone connections. Andy returned her message in-between sales visits, and he'd already heard from a customer about the old man and the ambulance. Lisa told him about her encounter with Miss Teely, too, and by the end of the day he'd collected a handful of anecdotes to share with his wife over fast-food dinner.

"Well, I mean, she's *famous,"* Andy said. "Never was quite right in the head, and being older than dirt hasn't helped her disposition." He waved a french fry, impatient to bite into it, but too involved in his story to stop. "Clatch told me about some doodad ceramic bowl or something at the church rummage sale five years ago, and Miss Teely and his mom reached for it at the same time. Miss Teely *won,* and got the damn thing at a steal price, but she still held a grudge—against Clatch's mom for *daring* to want the same two-dollar bowl, against the woman with the cashbox who didn't settle the dispute fast enough to suit her, and maybe against the church, too, for letting the *wrong people* attend the sale." He bent the fry and stuffed it into his mouth, starting to laugh as he chewed. "Miss Teely didn't talk to his mom for a whole year over that. Some punishment, huh?"

It was Andy's gift, to weave a story that made things better. Here they sat in his mother's kitchen—still *hers* instead of *theirs,* since Lisa hadn't yet replaced the mismatched cabinet doors or added new countertops, hadn't pulled off faded wallpaper that curled away from the wall at the seams. Huge grease stains hovered over the broken stove, sticky with dust: atop the stove sat the single-coil electric burner Andy's mother had used to heat cans of soup in her last years. They'd bought a new microwave, but Lisa dreaded the many evenings of Lean Cuisine or carry-out meals before the kitchen would be ready for actual cooking. After that scare today with the old man, she had wondered—not for the first time—if she'd made a horrible mistake. The house would be a huge amount of work, basement to attic and every room between, the exterior walls a mess and a roof that might collapse with the next rainstorm. And even after months and months of work, they would still be in Centreville, their front door facing apartments full of elderly busybodies. There were some things she'd never be able to fix.

Despite her fears, Andy had made her laugh again. Miss Teely fighting over a beat-up ceramic bowl became Miss Teely fighting over a worn-out man, and maybe *Lisa* would be lucky this time and get the silent treatment over the next year or so. Andy winked at her, said she'd been tempting old men all day while he was at work, and it was funny again, *really* funny, and it was okay to laugh because they'd heard the old man was fine and already back from the hospital:

Oh, God, were you wearing those overalls? with the paint stains and the torn pocket? and that fetching corduroy work shirt from 1980, and your hair bunched up in a scrunchie? Well, no *wonder* old Howard couldn't resist climbing after you!

They laughed, then calmed down, then laughed again. The wax-wrapped burgers tasted greasy, over-salted, and delicious.

∽

THEY LAUGHED MORE that night, in bed together, and he promised not to mention Miss Teely's name while they made love. During the moment of her husband's release, though, Lisa thought of the older man's hand clenched at his chest, his expression twisted in agony, and Andy's face in the half-dark looked twisted, too.

She lay awake long after her husband had rolled over and drifted off. In the late hours, a storm rumbled in—the first big storm in their new house. She stared up at the unfamiliar ceiling and listened to the window frames rattle in the wind, then the gravel patter of rain on loose shingles. Lisa feared she would fall asleep with the house intact, then wake to water staining dark on the ceiling and plaster falling away like wet paper; and downstairs, a new rug soaked and ruined before it's been rolled over the floor, and the wooden coffee table warped and her magazines soggy as sponges; and the television and microwave and computer ready to explode in sparks once she flipped a switch. All the tensions of the move rushed back, banishing sleep.

Sometime in the night, a comforting dream finally answered these tensions. It was based on a fairy tale from childhood, The Shoemaker and the Elves. A beautiful story, as she half-remembered it: a family poised to lose everything, and some last hopeful order arrives for a hundred shoes. The shoemaker stays up late, tapping little nails into little heels, but he's old, and maybe sick, too, and he can't work fast enough to beat the clock. They'll lose everything: the rented house, the medicine his wife needs for her cancer; their son would be sold to the regiment and their lovely virgin daughter married against her will to a wart-faced fifty-year-old banker. If only he could make eighty more shoes before morning and earn the money to pay the landlord, the doctor, the grocer—but it's an hour later, seventy-eight more shoes to go, and he's ruined the leather on the seventy-ninth. His fingers are shaking, but there's no time to rest, he'll never finish anyway but he has to try, he *has* to…Well, that's the worst part of the story, but children know it will turn out okay: exhausted, the man falls asleep, and tiny elves whisper into the shop and go to work. They're gone when the shoemaker awakes at dawn, and—this is the beautiful part—there's one hundred perfect pairs of shoes all lined up on the counter. He thinks, *did I do this all myself?*—but it doesn't matter, because he can sell the shoes in time, and the family's saved.

That's the part she dreamt about: the lovely wish fulfillment at the end. Her house is finished, and dream-Lisa knows it's impossible, but everything's done exactly the way she would have wanted it. She races from room to room, smiling at the handiwork. The tub is refinished in the upstairs bathroom, and light blue tile glistens on the floor. Overnight the kitchen's been remodeled, with a shiny matching stove and fridge; and the living room carpet is in place, plush beneath new furniture, and fresh wallpaper brightens the whole room. Outside, dream-Lisa discovers the house completely painted, replacement shingles nailed expertly into the roof. A wooden railing encloses their front porch; someone has trimmed the unruly trees and bushes in the yard, and a neatly planted vegetable garden has appeared in the back.

The elves had been very busy. And they didn't want anything in return—the smile they imagined (but never saw) on Lisa's face was reward enough.

THE DREAM WAS pleasant, but not as relaxing as she'd have preferred. All that running from room to room, around the finished house—and she must have taken mental notes the whole time, getting decorator tips from her subconscious. She woke before Andy's alarm, restless again. She slipped into jeans and a pullover shirt, and headed downstairs to start the coffee.

What if the kitchen really had been finished in the night? (Ha, ha.)

Nope. Everything remained as it was when they'd gone to bed. She looked at the kitchen and what she really saw was a giant "To do" list, with pages and pages of empty check boxes. Every room had its own list.

Well, at least she hadn't discovered any leaks from the rainstorm.

Lisa poured water in the back of the coffee maker, scooped pre-ground Sanka into the filter and flipped the switch. She moved groggily to the front door to see if the newspaper had been delivered.

She turned the front knob and pulled the door toward her, but it didn't budge. Stupid house, she thought—but blamed herself also, because she'd forgotten where she was. In any normal house, the front door opened inward; here, you had to push the wooden door out, over the welcome mat and into the porch—and into anybody standing there, as the postman discovered when she almost knocked him over earlier that week. Yet another reminder of the tough work ahead: shoddy original construction, compounded by half-hearted (if that!) upkeep over the years.

The paper wasn't on the porch, and she didn't see it when she scanned the damp yard, either. Lisa did see something else, however: her ladder, against the front window where she'd been working yesterday.

Except, she'd put it back in the toolshed. After the mess with the old man, she'd decided not to do any more outside work that day. Had someone taken it from the shed...?

Old Howard. Sometime in the night, he'd snuck out here, moved the ladder against the house and climbed feebly up when nobody could see to stop him. He'd tried to finish the job she'd started—maybe even during the blowing rainstorm.

Her paint scraper was still clenched tight in his raised hand. His body curled around the base of the ladder, the jacket shiny from the last bit of rain. The skin of his face was an awful mix of gray and blue, and he stared right at her, not blinking at all.

Lisa ran into the house and grabbed the cordless phone to dial 9-1-1. She shouted upstairs to Andy at the same time, mixing up the conversations, yelling to wake the dispatcher, and whispering to her husband on the second floor, something about "the old man" and "I think he's dead," and maybe she was yelling across the street, too, because when she stepped back outside, the door to Sunrise Apartments had opened and a few gray-haired seniors started to amble out.

"Andy," she yelled, "Andy," praying he would get there before any of the elderly tenants crossed the street to question her. It seemed an eternity before he stepped out onto the porch, hair mussed and a terrycloth robe unfastened over his pajamas. He asked her questions about the ladder (Didn't you put that away?), about the man (Is this the same old guy from yesterday?), and Lisa answered him in a daze. By that point, seven elderly men gathered at the edge of the curb across the street, two of them in wheelchairs. Around them were nearly a dozen women. At different moments, some of the women cast angry, resentful glances at Lisa.

The ambulance arrived eventually. A different nurse in a Sunrise uniform strutted across the street, but she kept her distance from the body.

Miss Teely followed slowly in the nurse's path.

"I'm going to see if there's anything we can do," Andy said, and headed over to the paramedics. Lisa didn't think to stop him.

Miss Teely walked right up to her. She wore a perfectly ironed nightgown, and her eyes were red from crying. "It should have been *your* man up there," Miss Teely said in a harsh whisper. "It should have been *him* doing that work for you."

FOR LISA, THE rest of the day was awful. Andy had to go in to work—with a new job, he couldn't afford to miss any time. So her husband wasn't there to support her when the police stopped by that afternoon. Just a formality, ma'am, you understand—but still a strange

~ The Old Ways ~

accusation in their eyes, a leading emphasis to some of their questions: You've *no idea* why he would have climbed that ladder, ma'am? and, You've *never* seen Howard Millimet before today, err, yesterday?

While the squad car sat in front of the house, a few Sunrise residents wandered outside and gawked for a minute, then turned forlornly back inside. In the dozen or so facing windows, Lisa thought she noticed several curtains blink aside at different intervals. She wondered which of the units belonged to Miss Teely.

She couldn't work under such scrutiny. Certainly, out of respect for the deceased Mr. Millimet, she'd be expected to forgo outdoor work— for how many days: two? three? a week? Among her indoor projects, she decided to prioritize the large bay windows in the living room. Lisa left the house by the side exit, where none of her elderly neighbors could see her, and drove to Wal-Mart for curtains and hanging rods.

Once the new drapes were in place, she tested them, pulling the cord to reveal the clear view of her neighbors, no trees or telephone poles obstructing the facing apartment complex. Then she pulled the cord again, shutting the curtains tight for the rest of the day.

THAT EVENING, ANDY was sympathetic, said the right things. The french fry—crinkle cut, this time—waved in the air, and he said nobody could blame her for what happened; word on the street was that Howard was a bit of an odd duck, anyway; and Andy recalled his mother once mentioned the old guy in some pestering context or another. So, there you go.

He tried a bit of humor: "Give it time. I mean, Miss Teely and her cronies may be upset with you *now*, but they're in assisted-living, for Christ's sake. Won't be long before the next one pops off, and they'll have something else to worry about." His words fell flat. They'd had a relationship where they could joke about this kind of morbid thing, but *he* hadn't been home all day, facing months and months of cleaning and repairs in a dark, closed-up house that didn't seem such a bargain any more.

Each time, Lisa's "I'm not sure I can take this" tone was countered with Andy's "Give it time," making it an agree-to-disagree kind of discussion that left her angry and weary by bedtime. The night brought another storm, louder than before, and another fanciful dream:

The friendly elves are setting up to work on the house again, but this time she's determined to catch them before they start. She will thank them, grateful for the thought, then will graciously decline.

I'm not helpless. I can do my own work here.

I'm not even sure I want this house anymore.

Dream-Lisa tiptoes down the stairs, a child on Christmas morning hoping to steal a glimpse of Santa. There's a noise from the kitchen, a bustle and clank and clap of wood, and a stretched rectangle of light spills from the doorway. Her bare feet pad closer, and she peers around the door frame and sees...

Dozens of them, tiny as dolls or garden gnomes, moving in a cheerful blur. The kitchen has become a miniature city under construction. The elves have their own tools: bent sewing needles and fishing line, used to grapple themselves to the uppermost cabinets; a system of winches and pulleys to lift cans of paint and woodstain to the countertop. They have hammers as tall as they are, metal nails the length of their arms, and they loop the tools through thick twine and scramble up after them. They've made a painter's scaffold out of cardboard, and two elves in white overalls raise themselves to the air vent over the stove.

On the counter, two other elves balance a hammer across an overturned soup can, its claw-end positioned under a rotted cabinet door, and then their chubby friend jumps on the handle-end. The hammer pivots up, and the claw tears the door off its hinges. It's delightful how they've made things work!

Which makes it a shame she has to stop them. Lisa clears her throat, says "Excuse me" in a gentle girl's voice.

And they freeze, startled. One elf, in the act of guiding the broken-away door to the countertop, loses his grip. The cabinet door falls at an unpredicted angle, and another elf tries to dodge out of the way. His face is like Mr. Millimet, Lisa notices, and he wears a tiny puffy coat that isn't enough to cushion him as he trips to the side and falls from the counter, high as a cliff for him, and his round bald head breaks heavy against newly installed linoleum tile. In shock, some other elves rush to the edge, and some on the floor crowd around the tiny Mr. Millimet, and none of them attend to the hammer, which flips off the soup can in a new arc, the metal edge sailing like an anvil through the air to crack another tiny skull. The soup can starts to roll across the counter, heavy as an oil drum, and it flattens one of the elves. Another elf dodges out of the way, but slips over the edge; instead of falling all the way to the ground, he gets entangled in the rope and pulley system, the twine catching on his neck and strangling him.

"Stop it," Lisa yells in her dream. "Stop it. This is never what I wanted."

The elves—the ones who are still alive, at least—turn toward her. Several of them line up at the edge of the counter, level with her waist, and stare longingly at her. "We can't stop," one of them says. "We have to help you." His voice is ridiculous, like he's breathed helium.

It occurs to her now that they're all men. Tiny old men with gray beards, lacking the carpenter energy and elf-like, work-whistling spirit they'd exhibited seconds earlier. A few of them scrape across the floor in rickety, toy-sized wheelchairs.

She's so horrified that all she wants to do is get away. A group of them crowds around her, gathering under her feet like hungry kittens, and Lisa almost trips. Then her foot presses into something soft and warm that crackles and collapses beneath her bare heel, and oh God, where was Andy, where was Andy when she needed him…?

∽

WHERE *WAS* ANDY?

Her husband's side of the bed was empty when she woke. Lisa tried to shake the strange dream out of her head. It was after seven, early light breaking through the upstairs shades. The sunlight must mean the storm was over, if there'd been a storm at all. Perhaps the commotion was all part of her dream.

She heard something outside. Crying.

Miss Teely's voice rose above the somber silence of the morning. "Your husband should have done the work," she said. Her voice shook with sobs and age and anger.

Lisa pulled a robe hastily over her night clothes and rushed into the hallway. On the stairs, she again heard Miss Teely's accusing voice from outside. "We've no one left now. It's not right."

No one? There were twenty-five units in the apartment complex across the street. Lisa had counted at least seven men in yesterday's crowd of elderly spectators.

Before she got to the front door, she needed to maneuver through the boxes and supplies spread out through the living room. In the bay window, the risen sun illuminated the closed curtains she'd installed yesterday. The light hatched through the shadow rungs of a ladder.

No, two ladders. Three. At least three, and one against the side window as well.

She heard the sound of sirens in the distance, getting closer. Red strobe mixed with the colors of sunrise.

Lisa grabbed the handle and tried to open the front door, but it was stuck. That's right, she had to *push* instead of pull. Stupid house. Stupid—

But she *was* pushing. Something was blocking the door on the other side. Something heavy, like a rolled up carpet.

Outside, Miss Teely continued to cry.

Glue Traps

MY love, I've written the story you never want to read.

I have always wondered what would happen if I wrote a story that I knew would horrify you. What would I do with that story? Share it, publish it, tell you about it—all the while insisting that you couldn't read it? It's an interesting hypothetical puzzle.

Yet here I am, having to confront that puzzle. This story is the only thing that will explain why we've grown apart. You really shouldn't read it.

∾

WE HAD LOOKED forward to a good night's sleep at our hotel in D.C. I was in the chair by the window, reading the "Style" section of the newspaper to pick out what movies I could see while you attended the second day of your librarian's conference. The bed was still made: you stretched out on top of the comforter, recovering from a long day of panels about reference strategies and electronic cataloging. Then, out of the corner of my eye, I saw what looked like a moth fluttering quickly across the room.

"Is there something in here?" I said.

You sat up and looked around. "I think I saw something, too," you said.

Perspective can play tricks. It was actually a mouse. I saw it pause before it ran between my chair and the wall and scurried under the floor-length curtain. Its tail and small back legs stuck out from under the lace frill for a moment, then disappeared.

"It's a rat!" I said.

"What?"

"A mouse, I mean. A small mouse."

And I'm really sorry I said "rat" first. I know about your phobia. It's the reason we live in the suburbs, even though the city has better restaurants, bars, used bookstores, and theaters willing to show films with subtitles.

"We've got to get out of this room," you said.

So we went to the check-in desk, and you told the clerk about the mouse.

He acted surprised. "I'm sorry to hear about that," he said. "Would you gentlemen like me to send someone to look at the room?"

"You can do whatever you want with that room," you said. Your voice got steadily louder with each demand: "We need a different one. On another floor. On the opposite wing of the hotel." The clerk alternated between watching your reddening face and checking his computer screen. After typing a few quick changes, he produced a new key.

"You go ahead," I said. "I'll get all our stuff from the old room." I knew you'd be too afraid to go back there.

Funny how we can take on each other's fears.

I turned on all the lights when I got back to the room. Each time I opened a drawer, I stepped back before something could jump out at me. I scooped up all our clothes and pushed them into one of the suitcases. As I moved from one part of the room to another, I stomped my feet or clapped my hands to scare away the mouse. I stuffed everything from the bathroom into one of the plastic bags the hotel supplies for dry-cleaning. It felt like something was crawling on me the whole time. I didn't bother to check under the bed or behind chairs as I usually do

Glue Traps

to make sure I haven't forgotten anything. And I didn't go near the curtain where I'd last spotted the mouse.

I couldn't wait to get out of there.

We got a much better room out of the deal. Two beds this time, and a fold-out couch. An eighth-floor balcony overlooking a park, brick walkways winding through colorful flowerbeds. Two white bathrobes in the closet. If we had planned it that way, it might have been fun. But I knew you'd have trouble sleeping.

In my dream that night, I found the mouse and killed it. It was running around the floor, and I went after it with the phone book. I missed the first two times, but the third was a direct hit—when I picked up the book, the mouse was flattened to the bottom of the Yellow Pages.

There wasn't much blood. A mouse's skeleton is small and flexible—that's how they are able to sneak through small holes in the wall. The skin was intact, the body flimsy like a used teabag; the little bones had crushed inside the mouse, tearing through its inner organs and killing it neatly.

I remember thinking, in my dream, that I could hold this corpse up by the tail and show it to you now. You'd know the room was safe.

THERE'S SOMETHING I never told you.

Over a dozen years ago, when we first started living together, you knew about the mice in our apartment. You also knew about the glue traps. But there's one incident I never mentioned.

We lived then in a dingy studio apartment off Wisconsin Avenue, near the National Cathedral in D.C. The location was great—nearby shops, including a local dime store, and a nice safe neighborhood to walk in. But our apartment was in the basement of a converted house. It was all we could afford, especially with my small graduate-school stipend. I'd picked the place out, and felt guilty about it.

Because of the mice.

Glue traps were $2.39, four to a package. I bought them from the dime store because they were easy to use—no loud snapping, no blood. The box said they were non-toxic and friendly to the environment. The animal crawls onto the glue pad, and that's it.

There is no poison, which means the mouse is usually alive when it gets stuck in the glue. It didn't strike me as particularly humane, but it was convenient.

These days, it's pretty easy to find information online about how glue traps are really akin to torture. The mice struggle and starve on the traps, biting off hair, skin, even limbs, to try to escape. They soil themselves from stress and fear. The glue gets into their eyes and mouths, blinding and suffocating them.

That information wasn't easily available, then. Besides, I had no particular love for mice. I hated them because they frightened you. I was constantly afraid they would make you wish you weren't living with me. So I wanted the quickest, quietest way to deal with the problem.

I finished my classes by mid-afternoon. It was easy for me check the traps and remove the evidence before you got home from work. I carried any filled trap directly to the garbage bins in our gravel parking lot.

And for the most part I protected you from the situation. You knew, of course, but we rarely spoke about the mice. I think that made it easier for us both to pretend they weren't a big problem.

One day, however, I heard some plastic scraping against the kitchen tile under the refrigerator.

A large mouse was stuck on the trap. One back leg hung over the edge and scratched at the tile, a weak attempt to move the trap along the floor. The mouse had given birth into the glue. Eleven babies curled together across the trap, interlocking like pieces of a puzzle. They were delicate, their bodies the size of the top joint of a ring finger. Their eyes were closed, their hairless skin the pink color of flesh. Many of them were still alive, trying to breathe.

Until that point, the mice were the villains; simply by existing, they created problems for us and deserved to be exterminated. But now I felt

~ Glue Traps ~

like a monster. That helpless mother and her doomed litter of newborns brought home what I was really doing when I trapped animals, threw them in the garbage, and left them to starve.

How could I put them out of their misery quickly? I thought about stepping on them, but some of the glue was still showing, a yellow triangle on the upper right half of the trap. The whole thing would have stuck to my shoe.

I should take it outside, I thought, and find a large rock. I picked the trap up by the edge.

It's common wisdom that a mother will defend her young. But I wasn't thinking much, and the adult mouse had looked exhausted from her struggles with the trap.

I was just ready to walk outside when the mother's head lifted about an inch, strings of glue connecting it to the bottom of the trap. It seemed she could barely open her mouth; she let out a horrible, screeching wail before her head snapped back to the glue.

My arm jerked nervously, and the trap flipped up into the air. At the same time that I wanted to push it away, a strange instinct made me try to catch it. These conflicting impulses produced a muscle spasm that sent the trap whirling toward my head.

It stuck to the left side of my face, flat against my cheek.

I could feel the tiny animals squirming against me. I wasn't sure how to remove the trap from my face: should I simply grab one corner and pull, or should I reach underneath and scrape it off? Should I do it slowly, checking for progress as I went, or should I just yank it? The more I thought about what to do, the more unnerved I was by the struggling movements against my cheek. I noticed a faint perfume from the glue, beneath the awful sick smell of dying animals. I needed to do something fast.

I grabbed the trap from the edges with both hands and pulled it straight away from my face. Mercifully for me, most of the baby mice had stayed on the trap, along with the mother. But it's just like when you try to remove a price tag or a label—there's always a trace left behind. My cheek had a layer of sticky film, textured with hair and grime.

And two baby mice.

I could feel them. One was just beneath my cheekbone. The other was stuck near the corner of my mouth, and was trying to wriggle off.

In a queasy panic, I set the trap on the floor then pulled the two newborn mice off my face—first the one under my cheekbone, then the one near my mouth. Each time, the mouse stuck to my fingertips. The only way to get them off was to press them against something stickier: I had to push each one back into its original space in the glue trap.

I looked around frantically and found a section of newspaper next to the kitchen trash can. I tore off a large strip and placed it over the trap. Then I pressed down hard with my thumb and fingers to kill each baby mouse. It felt like I was popping bubble wrap.

AFTERWARD, I WASHED my face with hot water for what seemed like hours. The whole time, I knew I could never share this story with you.

That was more than a dozen years ago. It was horrible enough that I've been able to force myself to forget it. Or not quite forget: I could always remember that it happened, down to the last squirming, sticky detail. But the horror of it, the revulsion—somehow that got pushed back.

Perhaps not being able to tell you, then, kept it from affecting me. We were intimate; we shared everything, which meant that if we didn't talk about something, it wasn't real.

Over the years, I've been the strong one, able to warn you if they're showing commercials for *Stuart Little,* or if movie detectives are searching for a dead body in the basement of an abandoned house. "The squeaking has stopped. You can look now."

But last weekend's hotel trip, the way your own fear transferred to me, my dream that night—all of it brought the memories back, with new force.

And I can't get rid of them.

Glue Traps

This time, not being able to tell you has made it worse. Any conversation we have avoids the one thing I need to talk about. It's always present. I'm reliving it all the time.

So I've written it down, as if that might help. But you can't read this, even though you're the only one who could make any sense out of it. And it's the only way I could explain why our relationship has changed.

I can look in the mirror to convince myself that they're not there, but as soon as I turn away I can feel a slight sticky pressure on my cheek. It's as if the skin under my face is wriggling.

I look down at my fingertips, and they seem to breathe, to let out a squeal of air and pain.

How can I touch you with these fingers? How can I let you kiss my cheek?

The Quiet House

ON October 29, the decorations disappeared from the Myrick lawn. Rubber kitchen gloves, purple and stuffed with cotton, no longer reached hungrily from the lawn beside tilted Styrofoam grave markers. A faint autumn breeze no longer rattled the plastic bones of the full-sized skeleton that formerly hung from a leafless limb of their oak tree. From the Myrick porch, the motion-sensor eyes of a black ceramic cat no longer flashed red at children as they passed.

The only explanation came from a new decoration, expressing a similarly grave topic but without the spirit of holiday fun, this one affixed by the city atop a metal post, red letters on a white background instead of the seasonal orange on black:

QUIET
ZONE

DEATH
IN THE
FAMILY

Jeremy was pissed about it. His stepbrother, only three years older, benefited from the lenient rules of their shared father, but Mom was overprotective with Jeremy. He had only been allowed to go trick-or-treating under his parents' supervision, visiting barely a dozen houses on their stretch of River Street, then a pathetic consolation party at his elementary school. This party involved a few ring toss and broom race games in the gymnasium, some orange streamers and happy-face ghost cutouts stuck to the wall with masking tape. They had a costume parade, each grade lined up in turn, but no prizes since the losers' feelings might get hurt. At the end Mrs. Rubin would read from her *Children's Halloween Treasury*, lights on the whole time so kids could see the pictures, the story some saccharin fable about a monster scratching under the bed that turned out to be the family's new puppy, or one about a colonial-era ghost that helped a girl find her missing Barbie doll.

Jeremy hated those parties, and the takeaway plastic jack o'lantern with its mouth and eyes falling off in black flecks of cheap paint, a single-serve packet of candy corn within, some kisses and a couple "fun size" Three Musketeers bars—tiny, puffed with air and flavorless. How could this dollar-store giveaway compete with the dirty pillowcase his step-brother brought home late Halloween evening, overstuffed with full-size chocolate bars, packs of gum and mints, jelly snakes and rats, jawbreakers shaped like eyeballs, wax skeletons filled with colored syrup?

And the stories Sammy would tell, far better than those from Mrs. Rubin's so-called *Treasury*:

"We get to the Singleton house, and they have their shades down and the porch light off, no car in the driveway, so we're supposed to think they aren't home instead of hiding out, television turned down low or maybe reading books, for god's sake, letting us knock and knock and praying we'd give up and move along. Phillip squints through the front blinds, says he can't see them, and I'm like, it doesn't matter if they're home or not, what matters is that they're not giving us candy.

The Quiet House

Well, Chris is dressed like a mechanic, which means he carries his dad's toolbox, and he decides to unscrew the gate to their back fence. Phillip has an old clothesline in his bag of tricks: after I climb a tree that reaches to their roof on one side, he flings the clothesline up to me then loops it through a slat in the gate, and I'm pulling that fence door up through the lower branches, it's rustling and scratching as the whole tree shakes, and Roger starts to freak out a bit, in this lousy-loud whisper telling me to hurry up, if they're home they can hear me, hurry up... and it is kinda thrilling, the idea we might get caught, but then I think, what have we got to worry about? If Mr. and Mrs. Singleton are in the house, they're the ones hiding and scared. They can't rush outside to see what we're doing, since that would blow their cover. So I want them to hear me, to wonder what horrible thing I might be doing, and I shake the gate free of the branches then heave it toward their roof, and I'm telling you if they were home they must have thought the tree fell over and smacked into their house, or maybe they thought it was some kind of explosion or gunshot. I scramble down that tree fast, since Phillip and Roger and Chris are already running across the street, and I catch up out of breath from exertion and from laughing, and Chris says I can't believe you did that, and I'm like, it was *your* toolkit that started the whole thing, and we cut through the Garcia yard for some more trick or treating. Hey, Germy, you can have this Almond Joy if you want. I hate coconut."

And Jeremy would accept the unappealing candy bar the same way he resigned himself to the nickname—a grudging acceptance, better than being ignored.

"And listen, Germy, the Myrick House was even better than it was last year. You think the outside decorations are cool, but that's *nothing*. You have no idea what it's like inside, the way they fix up the whole first floor, kitchen and dining room and living room together converted into a real haunted house. They must spend a fortune: fog machine, spiderwebs, manacles bolted to a dungeon wall, a panel that slides open and a monster reaches out when you walk past. It's like being on a movie set. There's this cool trick with a mirror where you stare at your own face, but then there's a purple glow and it's like you're transformed into an old man and then a demon. They had the same gag last year, but I still can't figure out how it works. Then the floor moves, or the mirror does—it's hard to tell which—and you stumble into the next set up, a new one this year, like a crypt. There's this closed coffin and you hear knocking and scratching from inside, and I swear it feels like there's someone in there, then some moans, then a faint whisper, *Let me out*, then another moan, and you know it's a gag but can't help walking closer in case somebody really is trapped in there. Your hand reaches forward, your foot creaks against a floorboard, and then holy crap the lid flies open with a hiss of compressed air, lights strobe, and a corpse sits up, grinning through a mess of rotted teeth, skin falling off its face as it shakes, and its arm lifts slow, fingertips bloody where the nails snapped off from scratching. *Let me out* crackles over those rotten teeth, and then the strobe snaps off and the lid shuts, ready for the next guy to step on the floorboard to activate the trick again. It was awesome. I don't know how the Myrick's will top that one next year, Germy, but I'm sure they will. They always do."

Jeremy hadn't been old enough to visit the Myrick House. He'd simply been old enough to hear about it, and be jealous.

But this year, Mom and Dad had finally relented. He was in seventh grade, and if Sammy would agree to let him tag along, Jeremy could trick-or-treat with his older brother for a while.

"I dunno, kid. You'd mostly be in our way."

No he wouldn't. Phil and Roger and Chris wouldn't mind. Ask them.

"True, they do think you're kind of funny. Funny looking, that is. But you're a baby."

Only three years younger than you.

"Not just age. You have to be brave, to pull the kind of tricks we do. And you gotta keep your mouth shut, too. No running to Mom to tell what we did."

He wouldn't. He promised he wouldn't.

～ The Quiet House ～

"Maybe. I'm still not sure if we can trust you."

How could he prove it? How?

Sammy had a suggestion—*but you're not gonna like it, kid.* Double chores for the month of October. Triple, really, considering that Sammy's tasks were bigger than Jeremy's usual load. In addition to emptying the dishwasher and keeping his own room clean, he got stuck with tasks like dragging the vacuum cleaner over every carpet in the house. That, and countless loads of laundry, and scrubbing the kitchen and bathroom counters and even the toilets.

Amazingly enough, Mom and Dad approved of the bargain—as if it brought Jeremy and his brother closer, as if it held some fairytale lesson about earned rewards being sweeter than those granted freely.

One weekend, Sammy started the lawnmower then sat on the porch steps and sipped iced lemonade while Jeremy steered the heavy contraption over stubborn grass. "I'm supervising, which is actually hard work," Sammy said. He took another sip of lemonade, which Jeremy knew was tasty because he'd had to mix it himself.

~

AS WAS HIS custom in the last days of October, Jeremy took a roundabout way home from school so he could go past the decorated house. The Myrick house always stood apart, occupying its own blind lot, an unused, overgrown parking lot behind it, and the fenced-in remains of a long-abandoned factory. Previous years, the detour allowed Jeremy the fun of staring at the cat with its flashing red eyes, of waving at all the hands that waved back from beneath the ground. This year, those same decorations had been a promise of something more. Each day, the anticipation made all his extra chores, and his stepbrother's tyranny, worthwhile.

But now those decorations were gone, before their promise could be fulfilled.

Death in the Family? They didn't have children, so it must be one of the Myricks who passed on. He wondered which: Albert, round bodied and cheerful, with the carpenter and mechanic's skills to design contraptions to his wife Elizabeth's specifications; or Elizabeth herself, stick-thin and imaginative, the gardener who planted rubber gloves each year instead of flower bulbs.

Jeremy decided to knock on their door, tell whichever one who opened it that the other would want the tradition to continue. "Your wife wouldn't want you to disappoint this year's children." Or, "Your husband worked so hard to put those props together. Dedicate this year's exhibit to his memory."

He couldn't do it. Jeremy didn't know the Myrick family well enough. And that "Quiet Zone" sign achieved the same authority as a police uniform or the angry yell of a school principal. A knock would be too loud. The family did not want to be disturbed.

He felt he was being selfish, upset about his own petty disappointment when one of the Myricks had lost a long-treasured spouse. Here he was, pouting like a spoiled child, when he should have been respectful of their grief.

All the same, he'd worked so hard this month to make his Halloween into something special. It almost seemed as if his whole life had been leading up to this holiday. Now it was ruined.

How inconsiderate that one of them should die. What a cruel trick they had played on him.

~

"IT WAS A cousin's daughter who died. On Elizabeth Myrick's side of the family, according to what Chris heard."

A cousin's daughter? Jeremy had lots of cousins. Three of them lived in Kentucky, two in New Hampshire. Most of Mom's family still lived in Missouri, and he met about seven or eight cousins there during a summer trip two years ago. He didn't remember their names.

A cousin's daughter wouldn't require nearly the same level of grief as a spouse. There was still a chance the decorations would go back up. The house would open on Halloween, as tradition demanded.

The Quiet House

"Afraid not, kiddo. Apparently old Elizabeth Myrick is really close to this cousin, practically like a sister to her. And it was the cousin's only child. The whole family's broken up about it."

That sounds tough, Jeremy said, and he tried to mean it.

"Listen, kiddo. Since we're not doing the Myrick house anymore, it's kind of changed our Halloween plans. Chris and Phil and Roger think we should go to this party at Amy Bowler's house. Aw, don't get that look, okay? But I'll make it up to you. Besides, you still got your little Dracula cape, and those plastic fangs and everything. You can go trick or treating with your own friends instead, right?"

Jeremy didn't have those kinds of friends. He had school friends, maybe saw them occasionally as part of school-sponsored chess or film clubs. But he and his friends didn't do things after school together. That was studying time, computer time, television time. Not like Sammy and his friends who went to movies or shopping or just hanging out and sometimes getting into trouble. Jeremy was the good kid, the one his mother was proud of.

And look where it got him. Alone, tired from endless extra chores, and no payoff. He was angry at his brother for backing out of the deal, angry at his parents for allowing the deal to begin with—and for sending him to that baby party previous years while his brother had all the fun.

And as much as he tried not to be, he was furious at Albert and Elizabeth Myrick, at their whole sad family, and especially at that relative who didn't have sense not to have a heart attack or get smashed by a car or fall into a pit or whatever else it was that a stupid cousin's daughter died from.

Then he felt ashamed and hated himself most of all.

～

THE NIGHT BEFORE Halloween, Jeremy went for a late walk without telling his Mom and Dad. Let them worry for a while; that is, if they even noticed he was missing.

Barely thinking about his destination, he drifted into a familiar roundabout path that led him toward the Myrick house.

He expected the house to loom in the distance, a shadow of faded wood, dark glass, and jagged angles framed by tall, bare trees. The empty cul-de-sac and the abandoned warehouse behind it would add to the ominous effect.

Instead, the Myrick driveway overflowed with cars. A Ford Tempo was parked at the curb in front of the "QUIET ZONE" sign. Other cars crowded the rest of the street, with a few braving the cracked, bumpy asphalt of the old adjacent parking lot.

They're having a party, Jeremy thought—because the porch light was shining in welcome, and a murmur of conversation filtered through the bright front windows.

No, he corrected himself, not a party. A wake. It's a gathering. A quiet, mournful gathering where family and friends seek comfort in a time of need.

Judging from the number of cars, the Myricks had a lot of family and close friends. Jeremy circled the property, keeping his eyes on the front of the house. The shades were open on the lower level. As people walked past the window frames, ripples of black cloth flickered the interior light.

He stepped onto the old parking lot. The few cars here were trucks or SUVs with big tires, able to maneuver the uneven surface. His sneakers hadn't fared as well, and he almost tripped over a tree root that had pushed through a segment of asphalt. There were sections of tall grass here, thick with bristles. A boulder sat heavy at the lot's corner; pieces of it had chipped off to form smaller rocks at its base. Other junk littered the lot itself: food wrappers, cigarette butts, empty and broken beer bottles. Sometimes Sammy and his friends would hang out here. Those beer bottles or cigarette butts might have their fingerprints; Sammy might have been the one who kicked at that boulder to chip off the smaller rocks.

The advantage for his stepbrother was that cars rarely drove past the dead factory. Plus, the overgrown weeds and junk gave Sammy and his friends some privacy for their underage drinking or whatever. Still,

～ The Quiet House ～

Jeremy thought it was a stupid place to hang out. It was dirty. And if you stepped on a broken bottle, it could push through the sole of your shoe and cut your foot.

He turned back toward the Myrick house. The shapes in black cloth continued to flicker across the front windows, and their rhythm seemed predictable. It occurred to him that maybe the people inside were dancing.

He listened for the beat of a drum, for a soft series of notes tapped on piano keys.

Nothing.

Then a laugh like a clear bell rang out against the night's silence.

He'd barely spoken to Elizabeth Myrick over the years, but Jeremy was convinced the laugh belonged to her.

More laughter, a chorus this time, muffled by the closed windows. Someone had told a joke.

Maybe the joke was about a boy. A boy who loved Halloween and looked forward every year to the town's famously decorated house, yet never got to go inside. Isn't that funny?

This was not a house of mourning.

They were laughing at him.

He recalled his stepbrother's stories about families who practically invited a Halloween prank—the Singletons hoarding candy for themselves and hiding in their dark house while Sammy heaved part of their fence onto the roof. Served them right.

You're just a baby. You have to be brave, to pull the kind of tricks we do.

Sure, maybe somebody in the Myrick family had died, a *distant* relative, but it sounded like they'd gotten over her death pretty quickly. There was no reason for them to take down the decorations, to cancel their traditional haunted house display.

Quiet zone? He'd show them a bit of noise. Before the night was over, Jeremy would have his own trick or treat story to tell his stepbrother.

He went back to the boulder, kneeled and felt carefully for the chipped rocks at its base. His hand closed around one the size of a softball. He lifted it, tested the weight. It was heavy, but not too heavy to throw.

And he was running toward the house, dodging between the bumpers of parked cars, the rock a dead weight at the end of his arm as he raced up the lawn and toward a front window. He was silent, a wind of retribution, but he screamed in his head as he raised the rock behind his ear, arced his shoulder back on that side, still running, tensing the muscles of his arm, then launching it forward, his whole body behind the throw, fingers opening and the rock flying forward towards a top panel of the window.

What mischievous child wouldn't find some enjoyment in the sound of breaking glass? The rock smashed through with startling and satisfying force, and glass shards tumbled forward in a sharp sequence of high-pitched notes.

He'd brought music to their party.

Take *that* for ruining Halloween, he thought. A spiteful idea came to him that maybe he should have tied a note to the rock beforehand, some cruel threat misspelled in terrifying, shaky letters: YOUR NEXT, or GRETINGS FROM HELL. That would have been cool.

He backed up, ready to run like the way Sammy and his friends bolted from a house after a Halloween prank. But he paused, a scant ten feet from the shattered window, and hid in the shadow of a tree. He wanted to hear some reaction from inside. A gasp or curse word or cry of surprise.

The house was quiet.

What had he heard before? The window bursting inward, the melodic rain of glass. Something else, too. A thud like a dead weight dropped into sand, and the crackle of dried leaves crushed underfoot. Then this long silence, as if the house were holding its breath—

"Oh my God!"

A woman's voice, weak and raspy yet rising in surprise and horror, growing loud and cracking in the shrill, final syllable. Like the cry of a tortured animal, or of a person going insane.

～ The Quiet House ～

It was the most anguished sound he had ever heard.

Then other cries, too, a whole room full of people wailing in agony.

But he hadn't done anything, not really. He'd only thrown a rock. The way they cried out, you'd think Jeremy had killed someone.

That wasn't possible. Was it?

～

THAT NIGHT, JEREMY couldn't stop thinking about the agonized scream. He heard it each time he ran into the bathroom only to gag and heave up nothing, but he spat and wiped at his mouth while that woman screamed. He heard it while he walked into his parents' dark bedroom, clutched his stomach and told his mother he'd vomited, and she felt his clammy forehead and said, yes, you should stay home from school tomorrow, and Mom walked him back to his bed and tucked him in while the woman screamed and the other mourners answered.

As he tried to sleep, he'd thought about how he ran away, not knowing where that rock had landed, what it did, but wondering if its rough surface held his fingerprints for police to discover, and his memory of Elizabeth Myrick's cry would turn into a siren and flashing lights and an impatient knock at the front door.

Throughout the next day, Halloween day, Jeremy suffered new horrors as he waited, sick to his stomach, exhausted, still not knowing what he'd done. He listened from his sickbed as his parents and his stepbrother whispered at the breakfast table, but he couldn't hear them. Dad took the newspaper to work with him, and Channel 9 didn't mention the Myrick house during their noon report. All day he worried, guessing how hard he'd thrown the rock, where it might have landed inside.

He was ready to confess, just to learn the truth. Any punishment would be better than the torture of uncertainty.

Then Sammy came home from school. His stepbrother told him everything before their parents got back from work:

～

"SORRY YOU'RE NOT feeling so good, kiddo. I'll just sit at the foot of the bed here, if you don't mind.

"Mom thought I should stay away, so I don't catch that stomach virus or whatever it was that hit you last night. But I figure if I was gonna get sick, it would have already got me by now. Hey, we all had the same dinner, right?

"Anyway, I kinda wanted to apologize for being such a jerk about Halloween. I worked you so hard with those afterschool chores, and even made you mow the lawn last weekend and then, you know, let my friends pressure me to ditch you so I could go to Amy Bowler's party instead.

"I didn't feel so bad about it until today—which is funny, since now I've got a real excuse not to take you trick-or-treating.

"No, not because you're sick—though that lets me off the hook, too. Mom said you were pretty much awake all night, throwing up or feeling nauseous. I have to admit you look pretty green.

"Hey, you're half way to zombie-looking. You wouldn't even need any makeup if you went out tonight. But that's the tough deal: *nobody* in this town is going out tonight. It just wouldn't be respectful.

"Your mom didn't want to tell you, since you're not old enough or something, and maybe she didn't want to upset you while you weren't feeling so hot. But I think I should treat you a little better now, more like an adult I guess, after I'd been such a jerk these past weeks.

"Want to know the weird part? When Mom and Dad told me, I swear it was like they gave me the third degree: maybe not thinking it was me, exactly, but implying it might be the kind of thing Chris or Phil or Roger would do. I mean, seriously? If I believed any of my friends had done that—or even *thought* about doing that—I think I'd need to beat the crap out of him. I wouldn't want to be friends with him anymore, that's for sure.

"Okay, I see you getting anxious to hear what happened. It was at the Myrick's place. The cousin's daughter was named Jeannie, okay, the one who died, and she was about twenty years old. A college student, and really beautiful. They had a picture in today's paper, long

The Quiet House

blonde hair, pretty smile, and these wide-open eyes like she was in love with life, you know, and she wanted to take it all in. Now, people say nice things when somebody dies, no matter *who* they are, but for this Jeannie it was apparently all true. She did all her school work and got great grades, but she still made time with her church group to help poor people with, I don't know, canned food or second-hand clothes and stuff; and she helped out at the animal shelter, too, all volunteer work, so she was like the best-hearted person you could ever know. Jeannie met this guy her freshman year, really nice too, and they were what you call college sweethearts. Their wedding was scheduled the same weekend as graduation, so the families could attend both celebrations. Instead, they got together a bit earlier, for her funeral.

"Can you imagine? You plan for something really wonderful, and then that poor girl's life gets cut short. It's already the saddest story ever, right? But there's more.

"I told you about her work with the animal shelter. Well, she was such a loving and open person, and animals responded so well to her, so the rescue-folk didn't think twice about bringing her along for some of their call-in emergencies.

"In this instance, some stray dog had wandered into a family's shed, and it had given birth there. Nah, I don't know what kind of dog it was—Mom heard this part from Mrs. Singleton, so we don't have all the details. Maybe what you'd call a mongrel, or one of those ugly ones with the strong jaws. Well, apparently it had a litter of tiny pups, but when Jeannie and the animal control guys got to the shed, the mother had turned against one of her babies. That happens sometimes, when one of the pups is smaller or sickly, and the mother decides to cast it out or shun it. Except—and this part is kinda gross, so I hope it doesn't make you sick to your stomach again—well, when Jeannie opened the door of the toolshed, the mother dog was under a workbench and she had all these blind little newborns in a wet mess around her, and she had the runt in her mouth. It was dead, and the mother dog was... *eating* it.

"This Jeannie, she's not thinking of herself but about the other little pups, fresh in the world and blind, so they can't see what their mother is doing and figure out they might be next. Jeannie sees *for* them, since it's a rescue mission after all, and she's closer than the pros with their nets and shock-prods and padded gloves, and she reaches down to scoop those other babies away from their evil mother.

"Except the mother dog was only getting rid of the runt—since it wasn't going to amount to anything, you know, kind of putting it out of its misery. The mother wasn't planning to hurt those normal babies at all. So what does it think when this sweet, pretty girl starts grabbing at her newborns? Exactly. That animal or maternal instinct kicks in, and the dog jumps up at Jeannie, and its big jaws clamp right down on her face. She backed away and tried to stand up, and the dog was just hanging there off her face, jaws locked in place, its body dangling heavy and the legs moving, front paws scratching at her neck.

"Okay, here's a detail Chris told me about at school. I kind of wish I hadn't heard it. One of the rescue workers said she was screaming the whole time, but the dog's jaws were closed so tight over the girl's face, so it was like she tried to scream through a hot, wet rag—all muffled, you know? Pretty nasty.

"The guys tried to get her loose, I guess they zapped the dog or tried to pull it away, pressed their gloved hands against the side of the animal's jaws to loosen its grip, but it held on tighter and kinda shook its head back and forth, and those muffled screams kept coming...but no words, since the girl's mouth and tongue were getting messed up about this time.

"Dad said, he wished she would have gone into shock, since most people would have from this kind of pain. Even better if she'd died right away. Her family, they had to learn afterwards how much she suffered.

"She lived for a day or two. Long enough for her family to visit her in the hospital. It must have been really rough on her boyfriend, you know? The girl's head was all bandaged up, even her eyes and mouth covered. He didn't get to see her beautiful face again, or hear her voice.

"It was a mercy when she finally died.

⁓ The Quiet House ⁓

"Jeannie's grandparents used to own the house Albert and Elizabeth Myrick live in now, and the family burial plots are over in Gadsden, so it made sense to have the funeral here, and the wake at the Myrick home. They had to take down all their Halloween decorations, of course. I can't even imagine what that must have felt like—moving this plastic skeleton and fake coffin out of the way, to make room for a *real* body and coffin for the viewing.

"Yeah, it's part of their tradition to hold the viewing in a family home. Make some kind of party out of it, as best they can. Except *viewing* didn't seem the right word in this case, what with Jeannie's face being mauled and all torn up. It was going to be closed casket, all the way.

"But get this: the morticians in Gadsden must have been miracle workers. They had a lot of pictures to guide them, I guess, and ended up doing such a great job reconstructing Jeannie's face that it turned out they could have an open casket after all. They used wires to hold the mouth together and God knows what else underneath to fix the shape of her cheekbones. They'd put a marble or something in one of the sockets, then fastened the lids closed; you couldn't tell which of the eyes she'd lost. And they used a lot of makeup. A lot.

"Strange, if you think about it too much, but Mom says it gives a family a nice sense of closure to see the body one last time. Especially in this case, since Jeannie had been all bandaged and in pain before she died. They got to see her the way she always was: beautiful. Everybody said she looked so peaceful lying there in the coffin. Like she was sleeping.

"Last night, the fiancé kneeled by her coffin, and he sobbed quietly, saying how much he missed her already. I wish you could open your eyes, he said. I feel like you want to smile at me again. He was crying so bad, and the guy's parents were there too, falling apart like the rest of them so they were kinda helpless. Elizabeth stepped in. She moved next to the poor guy, put her hand on his shoulder to comfort him while he shook with sobs. Elizabeth was standing over the open coffin, right next to Jeannie's angelic face.

"Then some asshole threw a rock through the window. It was practically a cannonball, people said, glass flying everywhere, and the rock sailed across the room and straight toward the coffin.

"It landed on that beautiful reconstructed face. Smashed right through the mortician's meticulous, fragile work, and the face crackled like an eggshell. Bone and plastic, chipped teeth and twists of wire, wads of cotton and fleshy red clumps all spilled out the sides of her collapsed head onto the silk pillowcase. It gunked up her blonde hair. Some of it spattered onto her weeping boyfriend.

"The way Mrs. Singleton told it to Mom, everybody was just stunned. Nobody said anything. The house was so quiet you could have heard a pin drop.

"Then Elizabeth Myrick screamed, and it was like she gave the rest of the guests permission. Everybody started crying at once, and it seemed like they'd never stop.

"Can you blame them? That sweet-natured girl, taken so young and so violently. They must have thought: *this is as horrible as it gets; nothing else can compare.* Then the family comes together and grieves, and they're able to comfort each other a little, sharing nice memories of Jeannie, and they're so lucky the mortician did such a nice job, she looks so life-like, she's at peace—and maybe her loved ones can have some peace now, too.

"Then that rock comes flying in out of nowhere. That family had already been through *so* much. How could somebody do something so cruel? It's unimaginable.

"Wow, I see how upset you are, kiddo. Don't be ashamed to cry if you need to. I'm not gonna call you a baby. I got pretty choked up myself when our parents told me about it.

"Seriously, are you okay? Yeah, blow your nose and wipe at your eyes, all right? I'll still be around for a while if you need more tissues or water or maybe some crackers to eat. Just yell for me.

"Yeah, I'm still going to the party at Amy's. It's across town and we'll be inside, you know—so, not flaunting all our fun in the Myricks' faces like it would be if kids went trick or treating tonight.

～ The Quiet House ～

"Again, I'm real sorry what a jerk I've been to you lately. It's a bummer you're so sick, and on Halloween, too. Not that it would have been that great a Halloween anyway, but still.

"Hey, cheer up. Your Dracula costume will be just as cool next year, okay? And you'll feel better before you know it. I promise.

"Take care, Jeremy."

HE WOKE WITH a start, waiting for his eyes to adjust to the dark room. Jeremy had no idea how long he'd been asleep. Actually, after a second restless night in bed overcome by frightful, guilty thoughts, the possibility of sleep had grown foreign to him. And yet, exhaustion had eventually won out—at least in the short term.

Of course, now he was awake again. The awful memories rushed back, and he felt himself wanting to cry again. He turned his face into his pillow, so nobody could hear him.

If they heard him, his family would realize it was more serious than a sick stomach. He could never let them know. What would they think if they'd found out he was the one who'd thrown that rock through the Myricks' window?

Yeah. Right when his stepbrother was being *nice* to him for a change.

If I believed any of my friends had done that, I think I'd need to beat the crap out of him. I wouldn't want to be friends with him anymore, that's for sure.

They'd disown him. He would lose his friends at school, too. He wept into his pillow until his throat felt sore and dry. He wished he could forget—at least for a few minutes, so he might fall asleep again.

Then he realized he'd been too loud. His mother had come into the room to check on him. She sat at the end of his bed where Sammy had been earlier today. Her hand rubbed his leg through the bedspread, comforting him.

Maybe she hadn't heard him crying. She only thought he was sick. Jeremy sniffled, then gave a small cough. She patted his leg a few times.

He noticed the outline of her hair in the darkness. His mother kept her hair tied up during the day, but loosened it when she slept. She always looked different at night.

Her hair seemed brighter than its usual brown. Almost golden.

She slid closer up the bed. Her hand lifted up to test the temperature of his forehead.

He sat up in bed and tried to distinguish the features of his mother's face. Was her expression loving? Was she sympathetic, or suspicious?

He couldn't find her smile or her eyes. Her face was blank, as if she wore a dark mask.

There were bumps on the mask, like the chips and shadowy protrusions on a rock. A heavy rock, the size of a softball.

He remembered Elizabeth Myrick's scream again. He saw what had made her scream.

Wire and chipped bone poked through either side of the collapsed face. The blonde hair was matted with patches of wet cotton and gristle. A tooth rolled off one side and dropped onto his blanket.

Her hand swept the air between them. Her index finger curled and pointed at her ruined face and the rock he'd put there.

What did she want? A confession? If she'd come to his room, she already knew what he had done.

Even so, Jeremy couldn't speak his crime aloud. He couldn't tell anyone.

Her hand made a slow circle around her face, around the stone embedded there.

What could she want? This good-hearted girl, generous to the poor, kind to animals... Why had she come to him?

She grabbed his wrist. It was a gentle grasp, coaxing. She lifted his hand, guided it toward her face, and he understood. She was giving him another chance. A chance to take back what he'd done.

The Quiet House

His hand closed over the rough stone. That shape, so familiar in his hand the previous night, a match for the curve of his fingers. The stone was cool, then; tonight, its surface was warm, as if something tried to breathe through it.

Take it back, the ruined face breathed through the stone, and the heat tickled his palm. *You can take it back.*

His fingers tightened. He thought of the shattered horror beneath, and he wasn't sure he could bear to look into the exposed face.

He pulled the stone forward, and the head moved with it, coming closer to him. Jeremy wanted to push it away, but the whole awful shape slid closer to him in the bed.

In a sudden fit of revulsion, Jeremy thrust his hand forward, his fingers locked in the grooves of the heavy stone, and he screamed and twisted his wrist, back and forth, back and forth, like grinding a halved orange into the metal wedge of a juicer.

Jeremy screamed again and he battered at the young woman's corpse, hating her for dying, for being in the coffin beneath his blind throw, for visiting him tonight in some ridiculous gesture of forgiveness. He hit her face again with the rock, repeatedly hit her shoulders and her chest, screaming out, losing himself in the attack, and then his mother *was* in the room, his father in the doorway too, and Sammy behind him in the hall blinking out surprise, the bedroom light on overhead, the ghost and the stone gone but Jeremy's fingers holding that stone's shape, tensed for the next throw as he screamed at nothing, screamed how he couldn't take it back, how life didn't work that way, how he knew he could never take it back.

7 Distance

ON the day of his brother's death, perhaps at the very instant of Denny's bizarre (to some people, at least) accident, Scott again recalled the terror rides of his youth. The first time, after a late trip to Phil's Pizza & Liquors, Denny veered off the lamp-lit highway into twisting backroads. The flat cardboard square warmed the top of Scott's thighs, hung over the edge of his knees, and glass bottles clinked on the floor beneath his dangling feet, clinked louder as Denny urged the truck over unpaved dirt and gravel, steered fast into tight curves, while the box trembled hot in Scott's lap. Then his brother flipped off the headlights.

Hold on tight, Denny said. Scott didn't have a shoulder strap belt to clutch like he did in Dad's car, so he held the sides of the pizza box, praying he wouldn't squeeze so tight that cheese would stick to the lid, making his brother angry. *Look how dark,* Denny shouted over wind through open windows, and there was nothing to see, nothing, not even light on the dash, yet Scott's brother steered confidently over the missing road. Denny didn't say *Trust me* or *Don't worry,* but laughed at the exhilaration of it, or maybe laughed at his passenger who tried to pretend it was like flying and held his breath as if that would keep the car on course, fighting against shameful tears because he knew the road might produce obstacles not recorded in Denny's memory—a deer, a log fallen off a truck, a newly abandoned car with its rear bumper jutting into their path…or some driver from the other direction who, this night, played the same careless game.

The ride was forever. Scott closed his eyes, but that made the darkness worse, the sensation of movement more perilous. The breeze over his face and arms carried the warmth of engine grease and cigarettes and dry dirt that scratched the back of his throat. He lost count of the turns. He lost count of each tree he imagined Denny's truck smashing into.

Then the truck slowed, came to a gentle stop. *You with me? Still here, little brother?* The headlights remained off. Denny patted Scott's head, his hair already mussed from the wind.

His brother finally clicked on the lights, so bright that Scott couldn't stop blinking. The road ahead was empty and familiar. *Let's check the pizza, okay?* He moved Scott's hands away from the box (his fingers and thumbs had pushed small dents into the cardboard) and lifted the lid. *One slice. A small one.* That's when Scott realized he'd passed some kind of test. The pizza wasn't for him, and he was nine years shy of legal drink from one of those bottles at his feet—all intended for big brother and his school friends, with little Scotty tagging along for the delivery run. This was a special reward. He lifted a meager slice, then separated and pushed the other pieces together to disguise the missing portion.

Scott's mouth was dry. Denny's friends could never agree on toppings, and were too cheap anyway, so the pizza was plain cheese. He bit into the slice. "It's good," Scott said. His voice cracked a little, as if he were lying—but he had escaped death, which made things taste better.

⁂

THE PATTERNS OF his adolescence clicked into place—bumps and curves and the unpaved textures of each stretch of road. There wasn't any police tape marking the accident site, but it was easy enough to find. He had asked his father, *Where? Where did it happen?* —and he

Distance

hadn't needed much detail before he could picture the exact spot. *The dip and then the leaning elm? Got it.*

He clicked off the ignition, turned to his wife. "You getting out?"

"You want me to?" She didn't like it, and every gesture and tone of voice would remind him she didn't like it. But she was here. This was Sophie's way of being supportive.

Scott didn't answer. He unhooked his seatbelt and stepped out of the Jetta, expecting her to follow shortly. She hadn't appreciated the way Scott treated his father: in her view, it wasn't proper to ask a grieving man to give directions to where his eldest son died. What was the point, anyway? What was there to see?

A few stray twigs and clumps of leaves overlay the dirt road. Unlike paved streets, this road changed from day to day. He could follow the tread of his Jetta behind where he'd pulled off the road, but the marks of his brother's last ride had long been erased by rain, wind, and the infrequent passage of other vehicles. Dad said a rainstorm caused the problem that night: made the road muddy, and filled the dip at hill's bottom with rain water. Denny lost traction, skidded into a tree.

The thick-trunked elm was one of the markers that told you how far you'd gotten from town. First right after the leaning elm and you were headed to Braddon's farm; keep straight then veer to the left then right again, and you'd find the Nelson place.

Its trunk was scratched where the tree faced the road, bark chipped off at the height of a truck's bumper and grill. Where the wood was revealed, someone had painted black tar to help the tree heal. The tar shined like it was still wet. Scott touched the wound, thinking it would be sticky and warm like fresh blood, that it would rub off to stain his fingertips. But the tar was smooth, already becoming part of the tree. He traced around the flayed bark, imagining the impact. Head on, perhaps, glass shattering and metal bending to hug the curve of the trunk—and Denny curving too, until things snapped or punctured and bled out.

He heard the open and close of the passenger door, followed by the scuff of Sophie's feet on dirt then on dried leaves. "You okay?"

"I know this tree," he said. "Exactly the same as a dozen years ago. Same angle even, the way it leans slightly over the road." With both hands, he pressed against the trunk as if to straighten it. No surprise: it didn't budge.

Sophie kept her distance. She treated the area like a fresh grave site, not meant to be tread upon. "He was probably drinking," she said. "It was late at night."

"That doesn't matter." She completely misunderstood why he was here. He hadn't come to investigate, as if the road and tree would explain why his brother died. He simply came to see where it happened, to grasp at the same gift of closure his parents might expect from tomorrow's funeral service. So far, the pilgrimage wasn't working.

"Of course it matters," she said. "I know you and your brother weren't close, but..."

"That's not exactly true." He phoned Denny about twice a year, and spoke with his parents on major holidays—nothing like Sophie's weekly calls with her sister Karin, the every-other-weekend dinner with her parents upstate and their generous babysitting evenings whenever he and Sophie needed someone to watch Ellie. Scott didn't schedule his family affection the way his wife did, wasn't obvious about it—so it wasn't as genuine to her. But he loved his brother as much as anybody could expect.

It was a love built on trust. A trust that Denny had sometimes betrayed.

Scott pushed the tree again. He was like a jogger leaning into an isometric stretch. Probably he should hit the tree with his fists instead, scrape his knuckles and cry and lose control. That would prove something, wouldn't it?

He straightened. "Good thing it's not a dog." When Sophie asked him to explain, he said: "If a dog attacks someone, they always put it to sleep. They don't do that with trees: they patch them up, keep them healthy for the next victim."

"Other cars ran into this same tree?"

Distance

"Oh, not that I know of. I'm just thinking how we blame the dog, you know, even if the guy or the little kid or whoever was equally at fault—for taunting the animal, maybe. Asking for it."

For a while Sophie didn't respond. "Do you think…? Do you think your brother might have…?" She couldn't bring herself to say it.

"No," he told her. "No, I don't."

C'MON, LITTLE BROTHER.

An invitation—at the dinner table, maybe, or in the TV room, where the audience to *Full House* or *Facts of Life* laughed at the same jokes every week. Scott would excuse himself and, if the season required it, get his jacket or winter coat. Mom and Dad were always pleased, because most brothers would have groaned about a younger sibling, ignoring the "kid" who was nearly ten years younger. Denny was better than that. They'd raised him well.

Sometimes, Mom and Dad didn't know. A whispered wake-up, a hand on his sleepy shoulder. Scott would pull his jeans over his pajama bottoms, slip feet into untied shoes.

C'mon, little brother. I won't do it this time.

Sometimes he didn't. Most times. Nothing but a simple drive over backroads, Denny telling jokes or smoking or cranking tunes. These were their best moments, often spent in aimless silence, with Denny occasionally sharing wisdom about girls or school or friendship. Scott didn't care if his brother wasn't entirely with him, half-occupied with casual glances at the speedometer, the weight of his foot tested on the accelerator, the angle of a curve matched to hands on the steering wheel, and the changing feel of each stretch of road translated into some mysterious inner calculus. All that mattered was that they were together, Scott alone with the big brother he looked upon as a hero.

Yet on some of the darker nights, Denny would grow quiet and thoughtful, seeming to drift further and further away. They might return home without incident, or just as easily Denny might say, as if the idea suddenly occurred to him, *Tonight. How about tonight?*...and Scott knew he wasn't invited to express a preference (as if he'd have nerve to whimper, *Let's go home* or, *You promised not to do it this time*), but should simply brace himself, wait until Denny found his starting point—wherever it would be that night—then revved the engine and clicked off the headlights.

A dozen times, roughly, yet it seemed more frequent in Scott's recollection, the various rides longer than the minute or half-minute they must have taken in reality, memory and fear extending the roads with new curves and imagined obstacles.

They stopped when Scott turned fifteen—the calm trips and the terror rides alike. He never understood why, and never asked. Scott went to college in upstate New York, then married and moved to the city, where the idea of outdoor darkness slowly became impossible to him. Still, he thought about those rides often over the years, and many times imagined confronting his brother about them.

Well, too late now. He couldn't complain to Denny's closed casket about betrayed trust. Besides: he'd gotten in the car willingly each time, hadn't he?

THEY ARE HEADING home after the funeral. This has been Scott's family crisis, so he's taken the wheel out of guilt, even though he's probably more exhausted than Sophie.

She hasn't talked to him, that he can recall, but the light from her cell display illuminates the interior of the car. She dials their home, talks to her mother.

"Oh, as well as can be expected." Is Sophie explaining her own feelings, or has his mother-in-law asked after him? He never hears the other half of Sophie's family conversations—but perhaps that's for the best. "We've been driving a couple hours. Should cross the state line in a bit. No, nonstop. You know how Scott is. What's Ellie doing? Can you put her on?"

Distance

Then Sophie's cooing in baby talk, and eventually she says, "Your father's driving. He says Hi." Ellie's only three, too young to understand her uncle's funeral—which is why Sophie insisted they should leave her home. He wishes he could hear Ellie's side of the phone call, the child's trusting voice, a sweet jumble of nonsense sounds and real words.

He hears Ellie laugh, as if she's in the car next to him.

She is. In the passenger side, shoulder straps secure Ellie's car seat, which faces toward the back. A silly position, but supposedly the airbag will otherwise suffocate her if there's an accident. Her legs kick in the air, a swimmer doing the butterfly stroke.

Where is his wife?

He turns to the back seat, but it's too dark. "Sophie?" Keeping one hand on the wheel, he reaches behind, patting along the seat.

Nothing.

When he faces forward again, Scott begins to panic. An empty highway stretches ahead, the dotted yellow line clear in the arc of his headlights. For some reason, he's supposed to memorize the road. He wonders how far he could travel without the lights.

Ellie laughs again, but Scott can't take his eyes off the road. Both hands tighten on the wheel.

Tonight. How about tonight?

"Denny?" In the distance, the yellow line curves up into the crest of a hill. "Denny, you promised. You said you wouldn't do it this time."

Look how dark.

The road starts to fade. His headlights begin to dim.

You with me? Still here, little brother?

No. He hasn't memorized the road. He's not ready. The world is with him in the car. His whole world.

~

SCOTT WOKE IN an unfamiliar room. The nightmare wasn't entirely banished: he was still in the dark.

A hotel room, he remembered, because there wasn't space at his parents' house. Sophie had booked them in the Holiday Inn the next town over. These places had heavy lined curtains, blocking light and even sound from outside. Even so, he could sense the ceiling far above him, space around him on either side. Much larger than the bedroom in their city apartment.

The bed was larger, too. He reached for the comfort of Sophie's shoulder, but she'd rolled to the far edge of the king-size bed. The room was so dark and quiet. She might not even be there.

He thought about the nightmare, and also about the sadness of his brother's last days. The previous year, Denny lost his filling station job. He lost his wife somewhere along the way, too, then moved back with Mom and Dad—to save money, to try to pull himself together. He must have felt terrible. Scott knew he would himself, in a similar situation.

God, the hotel room was dark. He might as well have been on a road at night. Life was like that: a strange road you've memorized. You brace yourself for collisions you know will happen.

He wished he could wake Sophie up and talk, but he knew how she needed her sleep. Tomorrow was a long day: the funeral, time with his family, then several hours to drive home.

He imagined turning on the light, making her sit up. "I do think my brother killed himself," he would say. "Don't tell my Mom and Dad, okay?" He'd hug her there in the bed and finally start crying, his face pressing into her shoulder, and Sophie would let him, holding him close, not saying anything except maybe some nonsense like, *Don't worry,* or *Go ahead, let it out. You'll feel better.*

And that would be enough.

AFTER THE SERVICE, they stayed into the evening. His parents kept wanting to talk, unwilling to part from their son. Sophie was anxious to leave before dark, but he couldn't quite manage to get away.

∼ Distance ∼

After their third good-bye, they walked to their car at the end of his parents' long driveway. His mother waved from the lighted porch.

Their suitcases were already in the trunk. They added the leftovers his mother made them pack for the trip. The food would spoil before they arrived home, but it hadn't been worth arguing about.

"I'll drive." Scott said. "You always drive when we visit your family."

"You sure? It's a long trip."

"Yeah, I'm sure." He shut the trunk.

"We'll stop halfway and switch."

"That's all right."

They settled into the car, clicked the seatbelts into place.

I won't do it, he promised himself, as he always did before driving. *I won't do it this time.*

Then he started the engine and drove into the night.

The Shell

(A Zombie Approximation)

MY first year after college, my best friend Maddie headed out of state for two weeks and needed someone to watch her cat. I couldn't do it because of my allergies, but recommended that place your sister used a couple times for Nisha: a nice family, so the cat would be in a home instead of a cage at the local "Pet Hotel," and they were easy on the budget, too. When Maddie got back in town there was a message on her home phone. The woman said something along the lines of, *don't be alarmed when you get here, your cat's lost a little weight,* and Maddie just freaked out. Two weeks? How could Tab lose weight in two weeks? Why didn't they call sooner? —that kind of thing, and I had to go with Maddie to pick him up because she was in no state to drive. The whole way, she worried me with questions: I'd given them the number for my vet, so why didn't they call him? What could have happened to Tab, bad enough for a stranger to notice? What if *I* don't recognize him, Jay?

"You will," I assured her then. "Look in his eyes."

We parked at the curb, and Maddie got the plastic cat carrier from the back seat of my Escort. The carrier had been too big to set in her lap as we drove, because Tab was a sweet, fat thing and needed an oversized case: it actually had a Labrador's picture on the product sticker, but that's the best fit she could find in those days when people our age bought most everything at Target.

The house was pleasant enough, split level with lots of shade trees on the property, and a fenced-in back yard. Dogs barked from that area as we approached, different breeds from the sound of it, and I wondered how many animals the family boarded on a given day.

The empty carrier bounced against Maddie's right hip as she walked out of balance up the stone pathway. I stepped ahead of her to the porch, opened the screen door and rang the bell. Another variety of barks responded, then the cautious opening of the main door—not for fear of a strange visitor, but from worry that some animal might hurry out. A teenage boy stared past me at Maddie, saw the carrier at her side, and shouted *Mom!* without turning his head. He had a leash looped in each hand and he stepped between us, dragging his charges outside to fertilize the lawn. The smaller dog could barely keep up: the boy looped more of that leash over his palm, nearly pulling the well-groomed Yorkie off the ground after him.

I didn't really want to go inside the house, but we couldn't stand there with the door open. The smell of Glade stick and spray fresheners hit me immediately, not strong enough to cover the musk and litter box odors. The skin along my exposed arms started to itch, and I imagined I could see pet dander floating with dust motes, ready to tickle my breath into a fit of sneezing. Not yet, though. I held it back, for my friend's sake.

Maddie set the cat case on the braided rug circle—multi-colored tubes of cloth stitched together, worn down by sneakers and padded feet, soon to be cut in strips and knotted for a dog's growling tug-o'-war.

The empty case. I feared she might not have something alive to put in it.

Some doors opened and closed upstairs. "You must be Madeline," a voice said above us. Her shoes echoed like wooden clogs along the uncarpeted stairs. She cradled a bundle in the crook of her right arm. A towel was wrapped around what would have seemed a human baby, if it weren't for the orange ringed tail that hung limp out one end.

~ The Shell ~

"I left you the message." The woman spoke as she descended, the voice of a mother from a distant room warning her son to wash up before supper. "Your guy hasn't been feeling too well. Came on all of a sudden."

I sniffled a little, the dander starting to agitate me, and Maddie sniffled too. She was holding back tears, of course, and I thought for sure that woman was delivering Tab's corpse in a rag-scrap blanket.

More clog steps, and that booming voice didn't get quieter. "He'll get better, sweetie. Get him home."

She wouldn't say such things if Tab had died. The tail twitched slightly.

"Too small," Maddie said between sniffles. "Too small."

There it was. Now, I hadn't spent much time around Tab. Maddie usually came to my apartment, and for my brief visits to her place she'd vacuum the hell out of the living areas and shut the cat in her bedroom for the duration. Still, I saw him now and then from a distance, galumphing behind a door or, more likely, a furry orange and white smear sprawled atop the down comforter on Maddie's bed. Tab was a heavy cat, even with the diet kibble Maddie got from her vet: he just ate more of it. An animal that big, and this woman—with, well, a cat-lady's physique, short and a little flabby, none too strong—she clomped down the stairs with him cradled in one arm, effortless.

She reached the landing, held the bundle out for Maddie to accept. "You can keep the blanket, dear."

The cat was all covered up, including a flap of cloth over his head. "Look in his eyes," I whispered to Maddie.

She took the bundle. Surprised at how light it was, she burst into tears. Maddie reached to lift the flap.

"Look in his eyes," I repeated. "You'll recognize him."

I kept saying that, even as Maddie kept crying, as she stared daggers at the woman—who had the nerve to mention the balance due after the deposit, and I wouldn't let Maddie pay, practically threw two twenties at the woman to keep her from asking again—as Maddie lifted the flap of cloth, saw her beloved pet's frail thin head, the animal weak but still alive; as she opened the carrier and placed Tab inside, along with that woman's stupid blanket, and the cat so small in his big container, sending Maddie into a fresh burst of tears.

Look into his eyes.

Later, after she'd taken him to the vet's office, and Tab died there the same night, Maddie spoke to me about her first look beneath that blanket.

"I did what you said. I looked in his eyes. He wasn't there."

I HAD THAT same thought when you came back to me.

AT SOME POINT or another, everybody has a sampling of what it's like to be in a long-distance relationship. A college girlfriend spends a semester in Italy; a spouse attends a week-long training conference or visits an ill relative for a fortnight. *Go ahead. I'll be fine.* Maybe playing up the sympathy a bit, a ploy for better treatment when the other half returns home. All the while secretly thinking: This might be fun. I'll have the apartment to myself, won't need to clean or follow his schedule, can indulge in fast food dinners without her disapproving glances. I'll catch up on my *Newsweek*s or finish that shelving project in the garage. And here is what actually happens: you begin in optimism, the temporary bachelor days planned full of activities, but the first day you do nothing, and because it's strange sleeping alone, you read in bed until 3am. You're exhausted the next day, practically sleepwalking at work, and accomplish nothing of note that evening. That night, sleep will again be difficult. You simply miss him or her too much.

At least, that's how it always was for me.

So when SureTech needed you in India to supervise the IT installations for their new branch office, I began with my usual optimism.

The Shell

"I'll fix up the home office, like I've been meaning to do."

"Good idea," you said, clearing our plates from the table. I hadn't finished my asparagus, but you chose not to comment.

"Keep myself busy."

"Oh, don't pout Jay."

Was I pouting? I wasn't aware of it. "The news is a little sudden, is all."

"Jennifer was supposed to go," you said, heading into the kitchen. "But then her—"

"Her son." Easy enough to predict, since the same thing had happened before, on a smaller scale—emergency pick-ups from daycare, sudden doctor visits, custody issues with her ex. I'd have been more sympathetic if you weren't constantly making excuses for your lax co-worker.

"Kid's got an infection." You put the dishes in the sink and ran the faucet over them briefly, speaking over the running water. "The doctor prescribed a course of antibiotics that might produce side effects. She can't leave the country right now."

"Of course not."

I stared at the table where my plate had been, while you turned off the faucet then walked back into the dining room.

"I'm sorry, Jay. But this is a good leadership opportunity. I was lucky they were able to change the plane tickets into my name."

So, it had already been decided. "I guess you couldn't ask them to change it back."

"It's a month. Tops."

"Jennifer could take the kid with her. Don't kids fly for free?"

"Now, stop." You stood behind me, grabbed the back of my chair and gave it a gentle shake. I stretched my arms up toward your shoulders, ran my fingers along the creased fabric of your workshirt.

"I guess it won't be so bad," I said. "It's not like you'd be going off to war. I know you'll come back."

I stood up and hugged you—tight but quick, like one of those movie hugs at a train platform.

There were other consolations, you assured me then. It wouldn't be like low-tech separations in the previous decade, when we'd had to schedule brief, expensive calls from the hotel room. There were cell phones now, and plus, part of your job in India was to set up video-conferencing software: no reason you couldn't use that same system to connect with our home laptop, and then we'd be able to see each other.

"Great," I said, recovering some of my initial optimism. When you said the four weeks would be over before I realized it, I didn't contradict you.

The cell phones and emails would help, and the video feeds as well. I hugged you again, felt my arms around your torso then stepped back to run a hand along one side of your neck. For a moment, my palm would smell like the spice and sandalwood residue of your aftershave lotion. But it wouldn't last.

WELL, WE SPENT a nice week together before you had to head out. Two meals at neighborhood restaurants, a movie on the weekend, and a lot of quiet evenings at home. I won't do it here, but I really could write pages and pages of minute details—that's how carefully I memorized those days, so I could summon them later during your absence.

I went a bit too far in that respect, I'll be the first to admit.

THE VIDEO CONFERENCING wasn't as easy to set up as you expected, so it was about a week before you got it running. There was a slight lag in the Internet connection, so a couple times we interrupted each other, said sorry, then did it again. I wanted to chime "over" after each sentence, like truckers did in CB radio days.

"It's really you, isn't it," I said.

"In the flesh." Your face blurred when you moved, and there was a slight fishbowl distortion, but it was amazing to see you as we

~ The Shell ~

talked—so animated and responding to my comments. You wore a suitcoat and tie, more formal than your usual work attire to indicate your management status. The wall behind you was a clean white, with no paintings or other decorations.

"Show me the rest of your workspace."

Some loud clicks and the muffle of a hand over a microphone as your image jerked out of my view, then a blurry pan across the office floor.

"Were those cubicles?"

"Tell you the truth, I'm not really sure." You clipped the camera back into place, framing yourself and the bland wall behind. "Some of those might be markers for actual walls." A stage whisper: "They can't seem to make up their minds."

I took this as code to mean: you might be there longer than anticipated.

"Hey, is that *me* in there?"

At first I didn't realize what you were saying. The technology was still new to me, so I didn't quite register how much you could see.

It was tomorrow morning for you, from the time difference, but eleven at night for me. I'd set up the laptop in our room, giving you view of the bed, my legs over the kicked-down covers, my back slumped into the headboard. I hadn't been thinking, or I would have hidden the pillow that I held against me when I tried to sleep.

"Just one of your shirts," I said, embarrassed and pushing the shirt and pillow out of camera range. It might have looked like I shoved you out of bed. "I'm kind of a slob today, but I promise the place will be clean when you get back."

"No worries," you said. Then you told me more about the mess things were in at the new site, basically three bosses with different ideas of what should go where, and language barriers, too, and the culture so different from that of an American office. You whispered as if afraid to be overheard, and instead of a normal eavesdropper paused around a corner, or with ear to a cup held against the opposite wall, I imagined a security tech in headphones, huddled beneath a bank of computer monitors, typing commands to isolate the frequency of your voice.

"Hey, the cab drivers here are crazy."

"Really?"

"Maybe worse than New York. It's like I'm taking my life in my hands to get to work." A blip froze the image for a moment and your face became completely still. You stopped talking, but there was other audio: the grind of equipment, a metal door sliding open, a sledgehammer swung into a piece of drywall.

You coughed, and it seemed to jar the image back into motion. "Sell any new policies today?"

"I worked from home." Fidelity Life is good about that: no need for me to go into the office every day, as long as I call in and keep my accounts updated. "Went out for a quick lunch at Panera's, to escape the apartment for a bit." Burger King, actually, but you wouldn't have approved.

"That sounds pretty good right now. There's an odd spice to things here, whatever I try. Maybe it's the water." You raised a clear plastic glass to your mouth and took a long drink. The glass was smudged on the outside, or there's something in it, or it's some stupid pixilation from the compressed video. "Miss you."

I smiled as big as I could in response—to make sure you could see it. "That's what I like to hear."

There's a whistle, like storm wind rushing through a cracked window. It rose into a teakettle siren, then cut off. Microphone feedback, most likely.

"Love you," I said, and from your image it looked like you said the same thing and our words cancelled each other out. You told me you'd check in later from your hotel room.

I closed the laptop, putting the computer into sleep mode.

If only I could put myself in that mode so easily. I kicked the loose covers towards the foot of the bed then swung my legs over the edge and stood.

～ The Shell ～

When I walked to rescue "you" from the floor at the other side of the bed, it struck me how the half-dressed pillow had landed, the shirt sleeves twisted at odd angles as if the arms flailed in the air during the fall. If there had been a head on this improvised body, its neck would have broken.

※

WE TALKED USUALLY twice a day, once via video chat and once over the cell phones, with countless emails between. It was a good pattern, keeping us connected—but in isolated doses. I felt like my words and manner were somewhat forced: saying I missed you, and meaning *that* of course, but with a false cheer to the rest of it. As I think about it, a relationship isn't built on scheduled bursts of conversation but on little gestures or meaningless breaths—things you wouldn't bother to share in an email or repeat with some special emphasis, but you don't *have* to, because you're both in the same room. It seems to me, the real intimacy lies in those throwaway moments. Half-registered as they happen, but missed terribly when they're gone.

When you're gone.

So maybe I shouldn't have been so embarrassed about the pillow. I'm guessing a lot of people do this, when they're used to someone else in the bed: cuddle instead with a blanket or pillow, maybe even an article of clothing that reminds them of the person who's missing.

Would it be so strange to talk to these bits of cloth as well? Small observations: a comment about work or the day's weather; a reminder about the rent check or an overdue library book. People talk to themselves all the time, so how is this different? It's a comfort.

※

ONE OF THOSE nights—a rare night, when I fell soundly asleep—I dreamed that you were dead. It wasn't exactly a nightmare, though all the trappings were there: a fogged cemetery, a tombstone carved with your name, a hand clawing up through grave dirt.

Instead of being frightened, I step forward and clasp the hand, not bothered by the cold gray fingers, dirt and blood beneath the chipped nails, and I brace my feet and pull, helping you out of the grave the same as I'd help you off the couch after a weekend nap. A flash of lightning highlights your figure, and there's smudges on your clothing, and clumps of dirt in your tangled hair. I brush soil off your shoulders, pat at wrinkles in the dress shirt and try to smooth a rip in the pants leg. I comb my fingers through your hair to push out the dirt.

"They did a good job on you," I say. "You've held up pretty well."

Your head has fallen to the side, like you're listening to me. I lift it upright, but it tilts back over.

"The striped shirt was a good choice," I say. "Goes well with your gray skin tones. It makes you look thin, too."

I reach to hug you, and you let me. A few of your joints crack, so I don't squeeze too tight. I nuzzle into your neck for a moment. There's an earthy smell, like fresh fertilizer, along with some chemical undertones. "That's a different aftershave, isn't it?"

I step back, tell you how good it is to see you again. I'm so glad you could pull yourself away from those other obligations to make time for me.

And then I start blathering away about myself, the self-help book I've been reading, a local news story about a missing puppy, and a joke email Dean at work forwarded to me.

When I woke, my face was buried in the collar of your shirt, and I breathed in faint traces of spice and sandalwood.

※

IF I TELL you.

If I tell you how you passed...

Those details, the cold *facts* of them. An official phone call, an impossible formal explanation, then cruel logistics: your body in a box on a plane, the usual ceremonies of funeral and grieving.

The Shell

I can't illustrate such moments for you. They'd teach you too much about what happened, maybe make your death real again.

It would undo everything.

HERE IS HOW I brought you back:

Prayer is a kind of wish that hopes to influence the world. Through repetition, it sometimes gains traction.

In theory. I've never quite believed in prayer—in the proper, religious sense. At the same time, I've never let go of the idea that a person's imagination could make things happen. Self-help books about positive thinking, or the idea of a "guided visualization" leading people to *see* their life goals, and then tease them into reality—to me, such concepts have always seemed reasonable and right.

There's a power to negative thinking, too: the classic idea of self-fulfilling prophesy. My brain waves are naturally wired to worry—to ask, continually, *What's the worst that could happen?* I've got a gift for passing similar worries to others—which is why I'm good at my insurance job.

So whenever we were separated for a time, I wondered if I'd never see you again. What different scenarios would prevent your return: the temptation of newfound love in a foreign land; a bout of food poisoning that slips from dehydration into dysentery; a slight cough that later hacks blood into a Kleenex, or pops a blood vessel in your brain; an auto crash, or some stray cinderblock dropped from the roof of a high-rise or out the trash chute of an orbiting satellite.

If something were to happen to you during our lengthy separation, odds were good I'd have imagined it in advance.

And then I'd blame myself for it.

If my worried thoughts could anticipate your death, my grief could bring you back. Is that too huge a leap in logic?

There's power in grief, in the sincerity of tears. After your passing, I continued to hug a shirt-covered pillow at night, weeping over the stiff-ironed fabric and softening it. Your cologne continued to fade from the cloth, but some slight residue of your presence stayed with me. I added more articles of clothing: undershirt, pants, socks, arranged on your side of the bed as if ready for you to fill them. In my happier night-time moods, I could stretch out my hand and pretend to touch you.

In darker moods, my hand in the dark felt an abandoned pile of clothing, and it was like the swell of a grave mound.

Each night, I would lie beside your grave, one arm forlorn over the pile of dirt. I listened for the sound of your fingertips against coffin fabric, the tearing of puffed silk, the scratch of nails against wood. Beneath the bed as I slept, your stiff hands would cup and dig through packed soil. You scratched at coffin and bedframe, earth and mattress alike.

The mound of clothing rose like a filled stomach. A gasp of rotten breath clouded the air where you used to sleep.

A TERRIBLE WISH, certainly, but not without its share of beauty. Who could blame a wish born of love and grief?

There's a similar theme in some favorite tale from your childhood: a prince's kiss breathing life back into a glass-coffined beauty; a clay golem roused by loving touch or ritualistic words of cabbala; a parent's wish over a magical fragment of taxidermy, summoning a lost child's return. Such tales are common across different time periods and cultures.

I don't know which of these tales, specifically, caught your fancy as a child. I didn't know you then, obviously.

Mostly I knew about our eleven years together—from my perspective, and what I assume about yours.

I hoped that would be enough.

NOW I'D LIKE to tell the story of my own death, if it were to happen before my work with you has finished:

~ The Shell ~

Outside the apartment door, my supervisor from Fidelity Life says, "No, Jay hasn't checked in for at least a week. Some of his accounts need updating. He's never let things slide before."

Knocking on the door.

"See? No answer. His Saturn's out front, so he should be home."

More banging on the door. Hello. *Hello?*

"I'm not authorized to—" Mrs. McKenzie from across the hall. He cuts her off.

"Well who *is?* Get the landlord here. Or the police."

Numbers punched into a cell phone.

"And that awful smell—like a dead animal. How could you not notice?"

"Been like that for a while," she says. "Jay told me not to worry about it."

The doorknob rattles. Pick one of these: A credit card slips into the door frame. A shoulder slams into wood. A flying kick. The landlord arrives without ceremony. Mrs. McKenzie remembers she has a spare key. The door is already unlocked.

They step inside and immediately know something is wrong. The smell of death overpowers them. Mrs. McKenzie covers her mouth and kneels, says "I think I'm going to be sick."

In the living room, light filters through squinted slats of the mini-blinds. I'm stretched out on the sofa, eyes shut and dried spittle at the corners of my mouth. My pallor is deadly gray. I've soiled myself. An empty prescription bottle lies overturned on the coffee table.

They can't know, but the guilt has finally overwhelmed me. I wished for something I hadn't a right to, invented my own prayers and rituals until they worked a kind of magic. The result wasn't what I expected.

They step past me into the kitchen. *Hello?* And suddenly my supervisor, who I never thought liked me, yells my name and rushes forward to where I'm curled up on the floor. My face is contorted in agony, hand clawing over a stilled heart. "Oh how sad," Mrs. McKenzie says. "How terribly sad. You know, his partner died not too long ago, when—"

"Nothing here," my supervisor says. He heads into the hallway. My feet dangle a few inches above an overturned chair. A thin rope is tied around an exposed support beam in the ceiling. My face is purple, and my tongue has swollen to the size of a grapefruit. Mrs. McKenzie insists this time she is really going to be sick. My boss pushes me in the chest, making me swing back and forth. When I'm at my furthest arc, he ducks under me and continues down the hall.

He steps into the open bathroom. The shower curtain is pulled aside revealing my nude body in the tub. Most of the water and blood has dripped past the imperfect rubber stopper, but a long rust-colored spray falls from my wrist down the outside of the tub to the stained bathmat.

"Don't come in here," my supervisor warns, but Mrs. McKenzie is already peering over his shoulder, preparing a scream.

Whichever of these scenarios, they all end the same. My former supervisor points out that "The smell isn't the worst here" (meaning in the living room, the kitchen, the hallway or bathroom). "The worst is coming from behind that door."

The closed door to our bedroom.

He lays his palm flat against it, as if the inanimate piece of wood could have a heartbeat at its center. He takes a steadying breath, twists the knob then throws the door open.

You are quicker. Many things I'd taught you—about our casual calm moments, the thoughtless patterns of our life together. *This is what it means to be human*, I said. *This is what it means to be in love.* So much was missing, still: the years before we'd met, countless hours you spent without me at work, with your own family, on an evening walk alone. Any thought you had and didn't voice, or I misunderstood—I had no way to fill these in. I could only share my idea of you: wonderful and loved, yes, but incomplete.

Some things I was afraid to share. That awful month last year that almost broke us up. Trivial arguments over money or household chores, my list of tics or habits that annoyed you.

~ The Shell ~

Anything about death: what it means, how it happens, why it's designed to be permanent.

So you're angry about these gaps in your knowledge. You're bored and frustrated at having been brought back to an incomplete life. And I've abandoned you.

You know nothing about the desires of the revived dead, those shambling hungry creatures from books and movies. But some instinct kicks in: a hatred of these fresh bodies of blood and breath and consciousness.

Your fingernails have continued to grow, and your teeth haven't rotted as much as the rest of you. My former supervisor from Fidelity Life doesn't have a chance to react: you lash out, palming each side of his face, and one thumbnail presses into his left eye socket. He wriggles and turns his head away, exposing his neck, and although you can't see the blood that thumps and rushes beneath his jugular you find it anyway, your teeth gnashing and twisting at healthy skin that makes you jealous even as you shred and chew it.

He fights back, but you are strong and I never taught you to feel pain. He grows weak from loss of blood, and slumps to the ground.

You have finally learned about death.

Mrs. McKenzie is sick and half-frozen with surprise, but she breaks her stupor and turns to run. Perhaps she bumps into my hanging body, or trips over the chair in the hallway. You go after her.

I also hadn't taught you that the revived dead are supposed to walk slowly. You might be quick enough to catch her.

∽

YOU UNDERSTAND MY dilemma?

I'm so happy you're here. It's what I prayed for. But when you first dug your way back to me, I'm sorry I wasn't as grateful as I should have been. I mentioned that long ago situation with Maddie and her sick cat—when I insisted that recognition would begin with the eyes. I looked into yours, and couldn't find you.

Well, I guess it was like bringing a trauma victim home from the hospital. There would be a lot of work before you'd be back to your old self. I led you by the hand around the apartment, re-introducing you to the world.

—This is a couch. We can sit on it together.
—Here is a glass of water. Hold it to your mouth, like this, then pour it over your lips. Oh, hold on. Let me get a towel.
—Another shirt, much nicer than the one you've been wearing. Your arms go in the sleeves. No, take the old one off first. I'll help you.
—This photograph shows the two of us together. Yes, that one's you. I know you don't quite look the same anymore.

You were definitely listening to me. I saw a kind of inquisitiveness there, and some frustration, too. I sensed that you trusted me.

But, forgive me, you still seemed like an empty shell. How could I fill you with enough memories? I told you about us, put our lives into words to help you remember yourself. I wasn't sure it was possible, but I was determined to keep trying.

YOU SENSE IT, don't you? That it's not working fast enough.

Time passes. I have responsibilities at work, even with my flexible hours at Fidelity Life. I've got to find new clients: train them all to worry about horrible, unforeseen calamities.

I can't spend every waking minute with you—though each minute is a gift. It really is.

I'll admit you're not the same. Your skin is rough and dry and gray. Your neck has bruised and rotted on one side, and I can see through to the collarbone. I don't nuzzle so close against you anymore, because I'm afraid I'll hurt you. It's not the smell—even though it's gotten worse, I've grown used to it. Mrs. McKenzie has started to complain, but I don't mind. Who cares about her, anyway?

~ The Shell ~

Sit with me again on the couch. What shall I tell you about? How about this. Last year on my birthday, I thought the steakhouse dinner would count as my present. I certainly didn't expect anything more. As it turned out, that small envelope wasn't just for a card, but also contained plane tickets to New York for both of us. You'd made hotel reservations, too, and planned what tours and shows we would see. I've got pictures from the trip. I'll get them in a minute.

They'll help you see what we had together. What we could have again.

Yeah, I guess I am crying a bit. But I don't want you to get the wrong idea. It doesn't mean anything. I'm happy you're here.

It's just that…

I don't know what to do.

YOUR HAND REACHES out to pat my knee. You've made the gesture before, the way I've taught you. It's how you used to show affection while we sat and read the newspaper or watched television. These days, you mostly reach out like this at random moments, not quite in response to anything I've said or done—but now, it feels like a real effort at offering consolation.

The fingers are thin on that gray hand. There is dirt crusted on them and the nails are long and split in places. I'm afraid if I wash your hands, skin and muscle tissue will slough off with the dirt.

You make a kind of hacking sound. A grunt or growl. I look up to your face and see your cracked lips parting, a kind of straining at your neck—which makes the exposed collarbone even more visible.

The voice scratches through your vocal cords, but it sounds more like me—I guess because you've learned to speak again by listening to my voice. The sound doesn't matter. It's the beauty of what you say. The generosity of it.

I don't have to look into your eyes for recognition. I know it's you, finally.

"Tell me," you say. "Tell me how I died."

Burls

KENNETH argued against the Alcatraz tour—not forcefully, perhaps, but he stated his case clearly enough that Patricia should have respected his wishes. His private counseling practice was still small, and he supplemented his business with two part-time positions: Tuesdays at the Towson Juvenile Detention Center, and Friday afternoons at the East Baltimore Correctional Facility. Kenneth saw enough of prison environments during the year, and hoped their family's San Francisco vacation would steer clear of cement floors, iron bars, or high walls topped with curls of barbed wire.

Patricia remained neutral, which allowed their daughter's surprisingly passionate arguments to gain momentum. They were kid arguments: the tour would be "cool," an experience worth repeating to her friends back home, like visiting a movie set or an authentic haunted house. And how—Amy's clincher—could she *possibly* wear an "I Escaped From Alcatraz Island" T-shirt, if she didn't actually *go* there?

They'd stepped inside the corner tourist office after a pleasant morning stroll along Fisherman's Wharf. With giant hot pretzels for their walking breakfast, the family had alternately window-shopped and joined the tight crowds that encircled each street performance:

a man who juggled knives and torches; an energetic group of break-dancers who encouraged spectators to clap in time with their booming music; a woman dressed as a mime who balanced herself atop a 12-foot unicycle. Even though Amy, at eleven, was nearly too big to be lifted, Kenneth held her up for a better perspective on the juggler's fiery finale. And when they later walked along the wharf, Kenneth had put quarters in one of the bulky tourist viewfinders to give his daughter a closer look at Alcatraz Island.

That view should have been sufficient. The island was romantic on the waves, lovely from a distance, the prison itself like an exotic, ruined castle. Why spoil the beauty by stepping inside, passing into the harsh monotony of a prisoner's awful routine?

Now, posters of that prison on the tourist office walls completely captured Amy's stubborn imagination. She ignored the other tour packages—a bus trip through a park with California redwood trees, a ferry to the affluent shopping district of Sausalito, a scenic train through Napa Valley wine districts—and latched onto the one place she'd already seen.

"It's really not that impressive inside," Kenneth told her. He took the tri-fold brochure from the countertop and opened it. The largest pictures were from a distance, relying on frothy waves, island rocks, clear sky and seagulls. The prison hallways and cells were represented by small photos, grainy and underlit—probably stills from the old Clint Eastwood movie. "See?" he said, pointing to the darkest image.

A slender gray-haired man stepped closer and waved his finger in a circle above the open brochure. "It's quite fascinating, actually." His British accent gave an extra authority to his pronouncement. "We did that tour yesterday." *We* referred to his wife and himself, apparently. A woman smiled and nodded next to him, their shoulders almost touching. The two were slightly overdressed, as elderly tourists sometimes are: the man's dark blue sportscoat and his wife's lambswool sweater would grow uncomfortable in the afternoon sun, especially if they journeyed away from the waterfront's cooling breeze.

Burls

"The boat ride to the island is lovely," the man continued. Kenneth started to feel claustrophobic. The customer area of the storefront office was about twenty feet square. A dozen or so people filled the small space, most of them already in line to purchase tour tickets. His family was a captive audience as the British gentleman continued to sell the Alcatraz tour.

"As your boat gets closer and closer to the island, imagine you're a hardened criminal being taken there. Such a beautiful view—and it's your last taste of freedom."

Amy, wide-eyed, let out a small gasp. Clearly, Kenneth would never be able to talk her out of Alcatraz now.

"You climb a rocky island path, then step through the prison gates, which clang behind you with a somber echo—no one ever escaped, don't you know. The long, shadowy corridors of the prison are quite impressive. And if you ask, the guide might lock you up in a cell for a few minutes. Oh, and the stories: some of the worst imaginable criminals, and often their crimes continued even while they were under guard."

Yes, Kenneth thought, he could tell similar stories from his own experience. Inmates he counseled at the Baltimore prison provided lists of horrors—sometimes so extreme he'd think they couldn't be true, yet in his next thought he'd worry the prisoner actually held back the worst of his deeds. Kenneth never repeated these confessions to his wife, not out of respect for patient confidentiality—even at his most professional, he'd always held his wife exempt from that stricture; talking to her was like talking to himself, after all—but because he wanted to spare her feelings. Some nights after Tricia had drifted peacefully to sleep, he lay awake troubled by some awful image of ground glass or filed plastic pressed against sensitive flesh. Such acts of revenge were bad enough, but the common blur of expressionless faces was even worse. At the juvenile detention center, one 16-year-old boy admitted he didn't have a conscience: "I'm not sorry for anything. Sometimes I'm forced to apologize. But I've never said I'm sorry and meant it." That horrible, and honest, statement tormented him for weeks. The young boy's words predicted the bleak future of adult inmates Kenneth counseled each Friday afternoon. Then he noticed this lack of conscience in other teenagers, beneath the surface, unspoken. Patients who visited his comfortable suburban office began to display a similar attitude: deliberate and unrepentant sabotage of a coworker or theft from an employer; unapologetic physical abuse of a spouse; emotional trauma inflicted on children, then rationalized. Kenneth couldn't share this nightmare with his wife. Instead, the family vacation was a clean break, his needed respite from a consciousless world.

He refused to spend one minute of this trip inside a prison.

"Is the Alcatraz tour appropriate for kids?" Patricia directed her question at the British woman, as if she'd be the better judge of the tour's more sensitive moments. Kenneth felt a surge of hope as the woman pursed her lips in thought. Patricia was on his side, trying to find some way to budge their daughter's nearly unshakable enthusiasm for the prison tour.

But the husband answered: "Oh, certainly. Kids love it."

The argument was over, Amy tugging at his arm as if to coax his wallet from his pocket, then guide his credit card to the line of paying customers. The British couple watched him, as did several customers who had circled around his family while the older man described the tour. Patricia shrugged, helpless. Kenneth was an unwilling street performer, his audience waiting for the final trick.

The circle seemed to close in on him, pressing his decision.

"You guys can go," he said to Patricia and Amy. "I'll wait here."

Amy clapped her hands once under her chin, happy to win the argument, but unsure if she should pout and try to coax her father to accompany them. The spectators bristled, appalled that he'd even consider splitting up the family, however briefly. Amy, cute and awkwardly tall, clearly had their sympathy. No tips for this performance, Kenneth thought.

Patricia wavered, as if ready to cancel the tour for everyone. "If you feel *that* strongly…"

Burls

Yes, he did—not that he could explain himself in this public moment. Was there a law that said they needed to spend every minute of the vacation together?

"I'll be fine," Kenneth said. The crowd's disapproval thickened, almost choking him. Amy began to pout.

His rescue came from an unlikely source. "No need to wait behind," the British man said. "Other tours leave from the same place, and you can meet up afterwards." He opened up a different brochure, with the departure and return times listed in columns, along with the cost for each tour.

The crowd's sour mood dissipated, as did their interest. Kenneth took the offered brochure with thanks—realizing now that, all along, the man had only been trying to help—and he studied the times. He didn't care where he went, as long as it wasn't to Alcatraz.

Although the start times differed, one tour got back this afternoon very close to when Patricia and Emily's "deluxe" prison tour would finish. Kenneth chose this combination tour: a bus trip to Muir Woods to see the California redwoods, then lunch and afternoon shopping in Sausalito.

He wasn't terribly keen about the shopping, but the trees might prove to be interesting.

"WE'RE RUNNING A bit late," the bus driver said.

True, and it was the driver's fault. Kenneth and twenty-five other passengers had waited outside a locked bus for almost an hour before the uniformed driver showed up, out of breath.

Steep, serpentine roads up to Muir Woods National Park offered scenic views of lush California hillsides, but the turns were sudden and dizzying. The driver couldn't go faster to make up for missed time; already some of the older passengers had shifted from oohs and ahhhs to nausea.

When they arrived at Muir Woods, the driver parked the bus and told them they had only 40 minutes to explore. "You can go all the way to 'Bridge 3' on your map," he said, speaking through the vehicle's amplified microphone. "After that you should turn around and head back, so you don't leave the rest of us waiting."

None of the paying customers reminded the driver that he'd already kept *them* waiting for an hour, and he hadn't offered them a choice to stay longer at the park instead of spending the full afternoon in Sausalito.

See one giant redwood tree, you've seen them all, apparently.

Sadly, with all the extra waiting, Kenneth had plenty of time to read and reread the brochure for this tour, and he'd grown excited about these trees that stretched heavenward. His brochure promised that summer days brought fog to the redwood forest, with rich patches of wild azaleas, buckeyes, and other wildflowers. Sonoma chipmunks were common, and if he was lucky, he'd see some black-tailed deer. It sounded peaceful and restorative.

Thanks to the driver, he'd have to rush through everything.

"You see this intercom?" The driver waived the spiral-corded microphone above his head so all the passengers could see. "I'll make you sing a song for the whole group if you're late getting back." Several people laughed, with an especially hearty guffaw from the British woman who'd been so silent during her husband's tour office spiel. "I say that all the time, and nobody's ever late." More laughter.

He clicked off the intercom, then handed out entrance tickets as people filed slowly off the bus.

Most of the passengers gathered in a clump outside the vehicle, stretching their legs after the slow, twisting ride and clearly in no hurry to enter the park. Kenneth edged around them and made his way to the turnstiles to the left of the Visitor Center. Once inside the park he walked quickly, determined to out-distance the people from his bus.

Perhaps he'd arrived between tour groups. The dirt trail was uncrowded; most people headed toward him, leaving the park in leisurely procession. At the back of the group, a young married couple pushed a double-wide baby carriage. A twin baby was hidden in each compartment, entirely covered in blankets except for shadowed, bald heads. Rubber wheels scuffed awkwardly over the uneven path;

⌒⌒ Burls ⌒⌒

occasionally their well-trained toddler son ran in front of the carriage to kick aside a stick or large stone.

Once the carriage-family staggered past, Kenneth found himself alone at the apex of a sharp turn in the trail. He'd been so busy dodging the people that he hadn't taken the time to register the trees flanking the trail on either side. He looked up. And up.

He'd read enough about them to be prepared, but the redwood trees were even higher than he'd anticipated. He kept craning his neck back as he traced the height of a single tree, expecting the top of the tree to stretch into view at any moment. Instead, he ended up almost falling over backwards.

The tree was magnificent. Beautifully disorienting.

And there were thousands of these redwoods in the park, many certain to be even more awe-inspiring than this one he'd chosen at random. Kenneth leaned against a tree on the opposite side of the trail, both to keep his balance and to catch his breath. His palms pressed flat against the vast trunk of the tree behind him, fingers gliding against rough bark as if trying to read Braille in a forgotten language.

Kenneth looked up a second time. He remembered how as a young boy he would sometimes spin himself like a top on their front lawn, eyes upward, then would stop abruptly: the sky and the world kept spinning, and for a moment it was as if his brain shook loose and shifted in his head. The redwood trees now worked on him in the same way, like an optical illusion. At once, they seemed to rise in a straight line, while his sense of perspective made them shrink and curve in the distance. Patches of sky and sunlight appeared like the familiar opening at the end of a long horizontal tunnel, but the vanishing point was above him now. In a trick of perspective, the tree tops at the periphery of his vision seemed to move; they bent toward him like an adult stooping to hear the voice of a tiny child.

A section of the brochure told about John Muir, the philosopher-scientist this park was named after. He abandoned his university studies to attend "the University of the Wilderness." Muir became a conservationist, arguing for a greater sympathy between humans and nature. He believed humans had no priority over other life forms. All life was equally precious.

At this spot, in this moment, Kenneth could believe him. Maybe even go further: the wilderness wasn't a university, it was a *church*.

A girl's laughter interrupted his reverie. At first Kenneth thought the girl had somehow sensed the depth of his emotions and decided to ridicule them. But the sound came from around the bend in the trail ahead, high-pitched and distinct above the calm of insect buzz and the occasional chirp of birds.

Kenneth shrugged off his vague self-consciousness and followed the trail toward the happy sounds. The teenage girl aimed a camera at a boy her age. Clearly not her brother—the tone of her laughter told Kenneth that much, at least. The two of them, probably brought to the park against their will, had decided to make their own fun. The boy had stepped off the trail and climbed into the wedge formed by the merged trunks of three adjacent trees. He pressed his back against the farthest tree, arms and legs splayed against the other two trunks, and shimmied higher off the ground.

The brim of his blue baseball cap brushed against the trunk to his left; when he freed one hand to straighten it, he slid down several feet. The girl snapped pictures and laughed some more.

Then she noticed Kenneth. "Hey, uh, mister? One of us together?" She held the digital camera toward him, waited for his reaction.

"Yeah. Sure."

The girl's fingers brushed lightly against Kenneth's upturned palm as she gave him the camera. She ran towards the group of trees without looking back at Kenneth, then clamored into the wedge and intertwined herself with her boyfriend: one of his bare legs encircled her waist; she stretched one arm to wrap around his neck, used the other to grip his supporting leg.

Unlike the three trees, which had grown out of what seemed a single trunk then separated majestically into distinct but sympathetic redwoods, the young couple's union was fidgety and temporary. "Hurry," the girl said, anxious for Kenneth to take the picture before they tumbled out of the trees.

The trees didn't need such a record. A picture today or a hundred years from now would be essentially the same. Yet these teenagers will attend only to themselves in the developed photograph—in their young minds, only human presence gives meaning to the forest.

"Cheese," the boy said, his teeth close together. Kenneth snapped the photo.

He checked the frozen image in the inch-wide monitor. The girl and boy were a tiny jumble of bright cotton, hair, and exposed flesh. The tree trunks looked like three mighty fingers of a hand that rose from the ground. If those fingers closed into a fist, the teenagers would be crushed instantly.

The girl skittered next to him and retrieved her camera. "Cool," she said, looking at the picture in the display then rushing to show it to her boyfriend. Kenneth waved and walked away. Neither of them acknowledged his gesture.

Kenneth bypassed the first wooden bridge that spanned Redwood Creek. According to the map, two trails ran roughly parallel to the creek, connected at four separate points by the numbered bridges. Halfway between Bridge 1 and Bridge 2 was a black dot to indicate "Pinchot Tree," the oldest and largest redwood in the park. The dotted line of the trail bulged on the right side, presumably to make room for the tree's massive trunk.

He walked quickly. 30 minutes remained until he was due back at the bus, and he wanted time to marvel at this impressive tree.

As it turned out, Pinchot Tree was impressive for the wrong reasons.

∽

KENNETH'S HOPES SANK as he approached the area indicated on the map. Please don't let that be...

But it was. A log about twenty feet in diameter stretched horizontally away from his side of the trail, crossing Redwood Creek and flattening several smaller trees on the opposite bank. Other surrounding trees still showed signs of damage, deep scratches or missing limbs on one side from when Pinchot Tree fell—seven summers ago, according to an updated plaque.

The tree, over a thousand years old, was the victim of a lightning bolt.

On the ground, the tree's height seemed easier for his mind to grasp. He could never climb one of the upright redwoods, which gave an air of unreality to the trees' fantastic size. But Kenneth could imagine scrambling over the circumference of this fallen tree and walking its length, using it as a bridge to cross Redwood Creek to the parallel trail.

At its base, the tree seemed to have exploded. The trunk had not snapped cleanly; instead, it had bent like a hollow tube then burst outward. Scorch marks appeared along one splintered section of the rim.

Several gnarled burls, the size of basketballs, bubbled out along the base of the trunk. These protrusions, made of dormant buds, pushed from beneath and curled the vertical lines of the bark into whorls. They reminded Kenneth of knot holes in wooden furniture, where you could imagine faces or objects in the random patterns—except the burls were larger and three-dimensional, covered with warty bumps and crevices textured by shadows. The faces he imagined in these burls were monstrous.

His brochure explained how burls allowed redwood trees to reproduce. Unlike seed trees, redwoods mainly reproduced through sprouts that broke through these burls. Even a damaged tree, like Pinchot Tree, had a chance to reproduce if the trauma to the bark and tissue allows more sprouts to break through.

Ken kneeled to examine the burls on the area facing him. A thin stick poked through the largest burl, about where the eye would be on the imagined monstrous face. The twig was snapped off at the end, however, with no leafy greens to indicate a healthy bud.

~ Burls ~

Clockwise from this was a burl only slightly smaller. The left side was caved in, which he hoped was a sign that several dormant buds had been released. It would take a long time for these buds to come anywhere near the size and majesty of the parent tree, but it would be nice to know that Pinchot Tree lived on in some small way.

He peered into the hollow section of the hole, searching for hints of green.

The cavity was filled with garbage. Shining foil from chocolate bars. Empty boxes of Mike and Ike jelly candies purchased at the Gift Shop. Crinkled Twizzler wrappers. Several copies of the park brochure, abandoned by disinterested visitors.

There was more waste product than a single person, or even family, could produce. Obviously, one inconsiderate jerk made the first move; over time, others followed suit.

Before today, Kenneth hadn't been much of a naturalist. He made token efforts to recycle, when it was convenient. He appreciated the beauty of birds and flowers, yet only bothered to learn a handful of their names. But this park, these amazing redwoods, gave him a new appreciation of nature. The idea that people could be in this sacred place unaffected, that they could unfeelingly toss garbage in the ruined body of a magnificent tree—perhaps even smother its last chance to reproduce...

Kenneth was glad he hadn't caught anyone throwing their trash into that burl. Who knows how he might have reacted?

As he thought about it, his sense of causation began to blur. The plaque explained that lightning had caused the damage, and he had no reason to doubt the supplied information. And yet, he couldn't help but blame human agency—as if their neglect, their lack of appreciation, somehow authorized that random bolt to destroy Pinchot Tree.

He was overcome with a single thought: Other people ruin the world.

And other people were approaching from behind.

He could make out a thick accent—the talkative British gentleman, self-appointed as tour guide and embellishing the text of the park's brochure for the benefit of his no-doubt entranced audience.

Kenneth couldn't be there when they got to Pinchot Tree. He couldn't bear to watch them discover the tree had fallen. Somehow, he knew, their reaction would ring false to him.

So he ran.

<hr>

AFTER HE PASSED the second bridge, Kenneth rushed through another procession of dull tourists heading toward the park's exit. Their faces were animated by discussions about lunch, perhaps, or what they might watch on the hotel's cable television that evening. They might as well have already left the park, no longer registering the beauty of the giant redwoods towering on either side of the trail.

A fifty-something woman assisted her elderly mother at the rear of the procession. They both gasped as Kenneth ran toward them. Did they expect a collision? Or did they react to a wild expression on his face? No matter: he dodged to the left at the last instant, and kept running.

His arms swung recklessly at his sides. The trail was clearly marked ahead, so he couldn't really get lost. His only problem was time.

Bridge number three. He could turn around and make it back before the bus was scheduled to leave.

He gave himself permission. If he decided not to care, that was fine. If he enjoyed the park, it was his choice to stay. Adults are allowed to make these kinds of decisions.

He paused to catch his breath and look at the map. The distance to the fourth bridge was as far as the combined distance of the other three bridges. Branching away from the fourth bridge were extended trails, unpaved.

Kenneth ran deeper into the woods.

<hr>

HIS RUBBER-SOLED SHOES scuffed against the wooden boards of Bridge #4. Once he crossed the creek, the main trail looped around to

Burls

head back. But an unpaved trail beckoned to him from the side. A hint of fog softened the colors at the entrance; a spray of moisture brightened green leaves and added a glistening sheen to rough bark.

He stepped off the main trail.

Kenneth hadn't seen another soul since the third bridge, and he doubted he'd meet anyone here. The ground was overgrown, with no signs of recent footprints. He followed the vague and winding path, enjoying the notion that he entered forbidden territory.

Since the path never split, there was no point trying to map the twists and turns. It wasn't a maze: finding his way back would be a simple matter of retracing his steps. Better to focus on enjoying the moment: this was the world as he wanted it, empty and unspoiled.

Even, in an odd way, empty of nature. The buzz of insects and faint birdsongs faded into white noise, too familiar to register. Fog thickened in strange patches, sometimes low to the ground and adding needed moisture to the summer soil. Higher drifts obscured the tops of some redwoods, seeming to transform them into ordinary trees.

He paused to examine another grouping of three fused trees. The shared trunk pressed tight against the edge of the rough trail. A gigantic burl swelled out in the seat formed by the joined trees; a thin fissure split the front of the burl, curled over the top and expanded to almost a foot wide in the back. Kenneth braced himself against the front trees, stood on his tiptoes and leaned forward to peer down into the crevice.

No candy wrappers or other garbage. But no sprouting buds, either. Dry twigs, brittle pine needles, and chips of bark filled the rotted crevice. Kenneth reached forward to scoop aside a piece of loose bark.

It moved.

Kenneth drew his hand back as if he'd been bitten. The pile of rot and twigs breathed outward, and a small furry head poked through from beneath.

Only a chipmunk. Its front paws flailed and scratched at the mound; the edges of the pile shifted and crumbled as the chipmunk tried to pull itself out. Its torso wriggled through, but the dried twigs snapped and bent toward the animal as if trying to drag it back under. Finally, the back legs and tail broke free. The mound collapsed on itself as the chipmunk skittered away and escaped into the forest.

Kenneth turned from the fused trees, and he somehow managed to trip over an upraised root in the trail. He pitched forward, one hand stretching to brace his fall. The fog and leaves across the dry path created the illusion of a cushion, but the heel of his hand mashed against a sharp rock, and both knees hit the ground with a hard thump. He pulled his foot free and rubbed his ankle. The raised root looped at the perfect height to snag a traveler's shoe; leaves and twigs had disguised the root, almost as if it were a deliberate trap.

He rolled up the hem of his T-shirt and pressed his palm into the fabric to stop the bleeding. Then he stood, testing his weight on the sore ankle.

For the first time, he regretted his decision to separate from the tour group. His ankle wasn't sprained or broken, but if the fall had been more serious…Would anyone know where to find him?

Perhaps the bus driver's time restriction was intentional. With a scant hour at the park, his passengers would have less time to wander off and get lost. Or hurt.

None of his tour group had ventured this far, obviously. But no one else was here either—not even tourists with rented cars, free to make their own schedule.

Maybe it wasn't a good idea to be *this* alone with nature.

Kenneth looked at his watch. 12:27, which meant he was due at the bus in three minutes. Impossible, of course. But if he hurried he might make it in fifteen minutes or so. They might still be waiting.

He wondered what song the driver would make him sing.

~

KENNETH'S SORE ANKLE slowed him more than he'd thought—that, and the fear that he'd snag himself on another unseen root. Even so, he should have reached the main trail by now.

～ Burls ～

Possibly the fog had camouflaged an earlier fork in the path, or now tricked him into a side route he hadn't noticed during his approach from the opposite direction. Each winding stretch of trail seemed unfamiliar now. He tried not to worry—he hadn't committed his surroundings to memory, after all, and might still be headed slowly along the correct path. But it was so long since he'd seen another human, and the fog-shrouded woods were ominously quiet. A dusty, rotten odor hung in the mist, souring the faint perfume from sparse wildflowers.

Kenneth sighed with relief when he noticed the path widen slightly, expanding into an open area thatched with sunlight. He limped forward, ready to welcome Bridge #4 and smoother travel along paved trails.

Instead, he found himself in a barren clearing the size of a schoolyard baseball field. The earth was well-trodden, small stones and fallen branches packed into moist dirt. Redwood trees encircled the clearing, their roots raised along the periphery as if they wanted to step back from the flat, lifeless ground.

Opposite, near the entrance to another unpaved trail, a black-tailed deer lay on its side. Kenneth recognized it by its head, which raised and turned toward him, black eyes attentive to the human intruder. The deer's beige coat blended into the dirt floor, white spots along its body looking like pebbles in sand. Its ears stretched out on each side, rimmed with black fur and almost bat-like in appearance.

Kenneth stepped forward cautiously. The animal might be injured—though he wasn't sure what kind of help he might offer. It occurred to him that he didn't know what kind of sounds deer make—they weren't featured animals in his childhood nursery rhymes. Still, he knew the cry from this deer's closed mouth wasn't normal: a trembled bleating mixed with a low gurgle.

Kenneth lowered his palms to the ground as he moved closer. "All right. It's all right."

The deer pushed up on its front legs, twisting its body to keep its head toward Kenneth.

"Easy, there."

Then it stood completely, unsteady on all four legs.

"Looks like we've both had a bit of a spill," Kenneth said. The deer limped on its back leg—the one facing away from him. Its body leaned to that side. Kenneth stepped to the back of the animal for a closer look.

Another gurgled, closed-mouth bleat, and the deer circled away from him, keeping its injured side out of view. Its front legs struggled with the memory of graceful movement, while the deer's back haunches jerked and the rear leg dragged behind. From the motion, Kenneth deduced the leg itself was fine, but there was something wrong with the hip socket. He imagined he heard a faint sound of grinding bone.

"Let me see, fella."

Again the deer circled away, keeping the same distance between them as they edged to a different section of the field. The deer's back legs continued to falter, mimicking the hobbled gait of a child wearing an over-stuffed backpack over one shoulder.

Kenneth held up his hands and backed away. "All right. You win."

Another bleat, loud and scratchy, and the deer sprinted awkwardly to another unmarked path that led away from the clearing. As the animal exited, Kenneth caught a fleeting glimpse of the deer's right haunch. The hip was oversized and deformed—more likely a birth defect than from a recent injury.

He looked at the ground, a strange spiral overlay of footprints and hoofprints. To get his bearings he needed to trace the prints to the starting point, but the deer's dragged leg had smeared some of the tracks. Fortunately, he was able to locate the long smooth oval of dirt where he had surprised the resting animal. Now he could retrace his steps to where he'd entered the clearing.

But something about the deer's impression in the ground gave him pause. He moved closer to examine it.

The outline was normal: long torso and rounded belly; thin and angled impressions where the legs bent next to the body.

But a scooped impression appeared at the site of the injured hip. A half-sphere, wide as a dinner plate and pressed deep into the dirt.

~ Burls ~

With a face. The monstrous face he imagined on one of the treeside burls.

Lines in the dirt retained the whorled texture of twisted bark. Two bumps indicated the eyes, with a scalloped vertical indentation for the nose. A twisted horizontal slit represented the mouth.

Kenneth grew sick at the image: a burl attached to the animal like a tumor, the deer pressing its hip into the dirt in some vain attempt to suffocate the awful face.

An insect buzz rose up from all sides. Why had it been so quiet until now?

He wasn't sure where to go. Kenneth looked up, hoping to gain his bearings from the position of the sun. But he couldn't see anything clearly—only the dizzying redwoods all around, each one straight and tapering to a point high above. He got disoriented again, and staggered sideways, tripping over one of the peripheral roots.

He caught his balance against the trunk of the closest tree. His hand rubbed the soft bark of a knotted burl.

It pushed back. Like when his wife was pregnant with Amy, and he felt their baby's kick through the soft belly.

What horrible pregnancy was this? He imagined the curled fetus of an advanced ultrasound, crusted over with bark and tearing into the world with wooden teeth. Or the gnarled and squat face of a burl itself, dropping fully-formed from the side of a tree and seeking an animal host.

All the day's musings came back to him: Muir's concept of man's sympathy with the wilderness, his own newfound intuition that nature itself expressed a vague sense of purpose or will. In addition, his underlying fear of the inmates and patients he counseled, and the strain their remorseless confessions placed on his view of humanity—causing a strange distance between himself and Patricia, and even with Amy. He realized he'd barely thought about his family since they parted ways this morning.

Instead he'd been consumed by hatred for the visitors to this park—their inattention and disrespect to the majesty of nature. These angry thoughts still pounded in his head, thrumming amid the steady buzz of wilderness insects.

And another sound, continuing to gain momentum. The gurgled bleat of the deer, of several deer, echoing from all sides of the clearing.

Except he knew now it wasn't the deer. The deer's mouth had been closed.

Another mouth had faced away from him, open, forcing out each scratched bleat with an undercurrent of softly grinding bone, or sticks being rubbed together.

He sensed their monstrous faces staring at him from the shadowy periphery of the clearing. The low growl of the burls matched Kenneth's thoughts and encouraged them. They absorbed his deep disappointment with humanity—a process that began, he was now certain, the minute he stepped foot into the park.

In his mind he said good-bye to Patricia and Amy—though he was not yet sure if he'd doomed them or himself.

He closed his eyes and waited as the sound continued to rise. Soon, their voices might get louder as the circle of burls closed in around him, one awful parasite, then another, attaching to his body. Or they could reject him, flinging themselves toward a multitude of deserving hosts. A chorus of growls would fade into the distance, a new procession leaving the beauty of Muir Woods behind, planning to sprout new births from the ruined shells of conscienceless humanity.

Beneath Their Shoulders

(An Odd Adventure with Your Other Father)

> It was my hint to speak; such was the process.
> And of the Cannibals that each other eat,
> The Anthropophagi, and men whose heads
> Do grow beneath their shoulders. This to hear
> Would Desdemona seriously incline.
> —Shakespeare, *Othello*

"CELIA, I'm always happy to tell a story about your other father. The best ones involve you, of course—those calm sweet days when we'd settled down at the yellow house on Birch Street. But I know you're asking for one of the adventures—the more what you'd call *sensational* stories from our younger days, during that strange year of travel after college.

"We drove Jack's punch-red VW Beetle across the country for 13 months in the mid-eighties, a trip funded courtesy of an extravagant journalism prize Jack won as a graduating senior. I had the journey planned in advance in a meticulous organized folder of maps and triptychs from Triple-A. My idea was to hit all the highlights, those cities and monuments you were supposed to see before you died. I was excited at the chance to check them all off during a single, extended roadtrip.

"Except Jack kept driving us off the edge of the maps.

"In Jack's mind, Chesapeake University gave him that award before he'd written anything noteworthy. He needed to *live* more, to find his great subject…and he always said that would never happen if we stuck to the main highways, visited the usual tourist spots.

"Considering our old Beetle wasn't the most dependable car around, I would have preferred we kept within easy distance of Motel 6 and a well-lit filling station. But Jack was in the driver's seat. I was along for the ride.

"The ride got pretty bumpy now and then.

"Here's another case in point:"

THE CAR'S DOME light never worked, so I aimed my flashlight at the fold-out map—a real challenge in the cramped passenger seat. We hit another dip that grated my teeth together. My jaw muscles were getting sore. "Map says there's nothing here."

"It's not the best road," Jack said, "but it *is* a road. It has to lead somewhere."

Not true. Some roads led into construction sites or collapsed into sink holes; some wound in endless circles. Some roads led off a cliff. "I think we should turn around."

"Let's just try another mile or so." This was Jack's idea of a compromise. After a few minutes of driving nowhere, he'd stall again.

"Civilization," Jack said out of the blue. He hit the brakes, and I ground my teeth as gravel spun up from the unpaved road. He turned left at a handwritten wooden sign that was nearly impossible to read in the Beetle's weak headbeams. It said something like GAAORA, though some As and Rs might have been Bs. A thick line beneath the

Beneath Their Shoulders

name presumably once served as an arrow, but the directional tip had faded off from whichever side. Jack was taking a 50/50 gamble.

For an instant, I feared we actually *had* driven off a cliff. The forest road angled down in a steep slope, and a tree root suddenly lifted the passenger-side wheels in a jolt, threatening to tip the car on its side.

I told Jack to turn around.

"We can't," he said. "Not enough room."

True enough. Trees pressed close on either side, and an occasional cluster of branches scratched against our rolled-up windows. Eventually the slope grew less steep, but the nose of our car still tilted downward, its headlights projecting a dim fog of yellow light ahead of us.

Time and distance travelled are hard to judge, especially when you're lost, but it seemed like we'd been on that road for a mile and a half. Rough as this descent had been, puttering back up the same hill would be nearly impossible—that is, if we ever did find a spot to turn around.

The same thought likely hadn't occurred to Jack. He was good at driving us headlong into trouble, without planning an escape route.

Another car appeared on the road below, heading rapidly in our direction. Compared to us, all cars were big; this one looked big as a Buick or New Yorker. The driver didn't seem to notice us in his path, and there was no room for us to swerve aside. All Jack could do was stop the car and hope for the best.

I put my hand on Jack's knee to signal that I loved him. He pressed the horn and flashed his highbeams.

(Back then, Celia, a Beetle's horn meeped like a toy car. That would have been a pretty embarrassing note to go out on.)

THE OTHER CAR kept coming. It didn't stop until after it edged past us on Jack's side.

The local driver knew the path better than we did, obviously, knew where that massive car could tamp down underbrush to form an impromptu shoulder to the road.

Strangest thing, though: before the oncoming headlights had veered to the left, our own beams briefly lit the car's interior. It didn't look like anyone was sitting in the driver's seat.

"You okay, Shawn?"

"Yeah."

"Lucky I didn't crap my pants." Jack rolled down the window to stick his head out and crane his neck toward the other car—a Dodge Royal Monaco, I guessed, dark blue with a leather hard-top roof.

The Monaco door opened a crack, and the driver's arm slipped through and waved. "I'm fine," he shouted. "I didn't hit you, did I?"

"We're fine, too," Jack said. He looked at me to confirm, and I nodded okay.

"Where you headed?"

"Garora," Jack answered. "Did I pronounce it right?"

"Close enough." The arm slipped back inside the car, but his door stayed ajar. Although he yelled to Jack across a darkened road, there was a casual lilt to his words, like a neighbor speaking over a backyard fence. "Got a place to stay?"

"Not yet. You have a recommendation?"

Silence for a moment. Then the stranger said, "Mrs. Bittinger puts up lodgers now and then." The arm came out again as he shouted a few directions, index finger hooking to indicate each turn.

Jack thanked him, the arm withdrew, and the Monaco pulled away up the hill.

"He seemed nice enough," Jack said, "for somebody who almost killed us."

"Yeah. I wonder what he looked like."

"I considered sending you a picture, but you were already so stressed out…"

"Thanks."

(It was one of my rules, Celia, that Jack couldn't send me images while we were in the car. Even if I wasn't driving, I wanted to be able to *believe* in whatever I saw through the windshield. Technically, since we'd stopped, I guess Jack could have bent the rule—but I'm glad he didn't.)

He leaned over and kissed me on the cheek. "Let's head into town, see if we can find Mrs. Bittinger."

A TOWN AT night, even a small town, should at least seem brighter than the dark forest road we'd traveled through. But there were no streetlights. All the buildings we passed were dark.

"It's only 10 o'clock," I said.

"Yeah. Like a ghost town."

"I wonder where the main street is."

"Hate to tell you, but I think we're on it."

We followed Monaco's directions easily enough, even in the dark. There weren't that many places to turn.

"Some light down there." Jack pointed to a side street, with a distant glow of neon. "Maybe a diner or tavern window. Might be worth investigating later."

I made a mental note.

"There's the gas station he mentioned." Jack turned at the landmark and we followed a narrow road, searching for a brown house with green shutters.

In the dark, all the houses looked the dull brown shade of old, wet wood. All the shutters appeared black.

"It's this one. I think." Jack turned off the engine.

Maybe it was the right house, but it was as dark as the rest of them—and with no "ROOM TO LET" sign in a front window. I was uneasy about knocking on the door at this late hour. It would be one thing if it was our usual dingy motel with a night clerk on duty. This was somebody's home.

We had a bit of a tense "discussion" in the closed car. I said I'd rather sleep in the Beetle than disturb some stranger in the middle of the night. He countered that it *wasn't* the middle of the night, I could stay in the car as long as I wanted, but he wanted a bed. We sat there in the dark, and I guess I was still tense about the near-collision on the road into town, so I blurted out more frustrations: *Why are we here, anyway? What's the point of this kind of trip? You follow some weird hunch and we end up here in a ghost town or*—referring to his previous excursions off the map—*one of us gets kidnapped or attacked, and I see things that* nobody *should ever have to see.* I ended with a little whine about how we were supposed to visit Mary in Providence, and she would've had a nice guest bed for us.

Jack didn't respond for a long while. I couldn't read his face in the dark. Then he said, "I'm going in." He left the car and walked toward the unlighted porch.

I sulked for half a minute, then followed him.

(Because I loved him, Celia. I liked being with him, no matter what.)

~

I FELT VINDICATED when nobody answered. Jack kept trying, though, getting a decent clang from the door's thin brass knocker, then adding knuckle raps on the door and on the panel glass.

Whoever answers is gonna be really pissed off, I thought. I was ready to head back to the car, when a latch clicked and the door drifted inward.

"Mrs. Bittinger?" Jack said to the dark interior. "We're here about a room."

"Give me a minute." An old woman's voice. Her shadowed shape struck me as peculiar, but I couldn't entirely make it out. An odd roundness to her torso, and the head too small and possibly deformed. I wondered why she hadn't turned on a light to lead herself to the door.

Her hand found a switch on the wall and flipped it. At once, I understood my mistake: what I'd taken for her head was actually a swirl of gray hair, tied up in a loose, round bun. The bun sat just above the height of her shoulders, with the head hunched beneath.

She had the worst case of osteoporosis I'd ever seen. Her neck had disappeared; her spine curved and her shoulders shrugged up, forcing her chin into the ridge between her collarbones. As she stepped aside to let us in, she had to turn her whole body to keep looking at us. "Just the one night?" she said.

"I think so," Jack answered. "I'll let you know tomorrow if we decide to stay longer."

The house seemed cozy enough. Hardwood floors with fringe rugs in the entryway, and a small sitting room to the left, just visible in the foyer light: a long couch and two wing-backed chairs, a coffee table with magazines. A staircase led upward, slight depressions visible on the left half of each wooden step. The oak railings were thick, with patches of the wood-stain scratched and darkened. The old woman had clutched this railing to guide her to the door, I figured—that's why she didn't need a light. A service bell sat atop one of the flat newel posts. Mrs. Bittinger tapped at it, and three sharp dings sounded.

"Flora, my daughter, will fix up the room," Mrs. Bittinger said. "I hope you fellows don't mind sharing a double bed. The cot's a nuisance to set up."

"Sharing a bed will suit us fine," Jack said. There was a kind of wink in his comment, which I guess only I was supposed to notice, but it seemed a bit obvious.

"We're pretty worn out from travel," I said. "I'm sure we'll fall right asleep."

Slow footsteps sounded above, then a silhouette appeared at the bend in the staircase. The daughter leaned close to the banister as she descended, both hands on the same rail.

Then I realized Flora wasn't exactly leaning. She was a hunchback, like her mother. It wasn't osteoporosis after all, but some congenital defect.

(I suspected maybe this was Jack's doing, to get back at me for my little rant in the car. It fit his dark sense of humor, to hobble the daughter to create a matching set with the old woman. But the clomping of Flora's steps confirmed the image. Jack couldn't transmit sounds.)

I guess the daughter was about thirty-five or so. Her face would have been pretty, if it hung a little higher. As it was, she wore the depressed mask of a spinster, with no hope of romantic prospects in this secluded, unambitious town. She'd live at home, waiting to inherit the paltry business of her family's bed-and-breakfast.

Flora nodded at both of us, then ambled up a side hallway to our room at the back of the house. Jack gave Mrs. Bittinger forty dollars in cash for the room, then stepped out to gather our luggage from the car.

"Not a lot of rules here," Mrs. Bittinger said. "Bathroom's down the hall on the right: no shower, but a nice enough tub. Breakfast is at 8 o'clock tomorrow, if you want it. Please don't lie on top of the bedspread: lie underneath it, or take it off and set it in the chair."

(I never could make sense of the bedspread rule, but I swear she repeated it verbatim when Jack returned with our suitcases. Places have arbitrary rules like that—you know, like how Aunt Charlotte is with her bath soaps.)

Flora was smoothing the corners of this precious bedspread when we brought our luggage into the room. I unpacked my suitcase right away, filling the top two drawers of a thin wooden dresser. Jack dropped his case on the floor, asking what people in Garora did for excitement on Friday night.

"Nothing much," she said.

"I thought I saw a bar or something on the way in."

"Oh, I never go there." At the thought, she shook her head back and forth; the shoulders pivoted along with it.

"We should call it a night," I said. "We don't want to wake the house to get back in." Mrs. Bittinger hadn't given us a key to the front door.

"You didn't wake us. My mother hardly ever sleeps." She smoothed out one pleat in her dress with the same attention she'd given to the bedspread. "You could leave the front door unlocked, if you'd rather."

"Thanks," Jack said. "And thanks for fixing up the room, Flora." His kindness produced an appreciative smile. Then her eyes fluttered to the ground, a motion typically accompanied by a shy lowering of the head—unnecessary, in her case. I got the impression nobody had ever spoken to her with any degree of tenderness. Her mother had been officious and abrupt, ringing the bell for a servant and barely acknowledging her daughter's slow descent to the foyer. Perhaps Mrs. Bittinger resented this ever-present reminder of her own condition. And the men in this town—how did they treat her? I assumed the best she could hope for was their indifference, rather than active cruelty. Was it any wonder that she never visited the local tavern? I hoped her recent years were better than what she must have experienced growing up.

(Here, I was thinking back to my own troubles in high school. We didn't have anti-bullying initiatives, or Days of Silence to encourage tolerance. Even before I'd accepted my sexual orientation, I was teased about it—almost on a daily basis—to the point where I tried to hide whatever it was that made me different. Of course, Flora Bittinger didn't have that luxury.)

"What was it like growing up in this town?"

Jack's question was the exact one I'd been thinking about, but didn't have the nerve to ask. Then I realized why he did: it was a potential interview, gathering anecdotes for a human-interest story. He was being nice to Flora, yes, but that was also a common interviewer's strategy: flatter the subject, flirt a bit, in the hopes that she'll reveal details about her personal life. I worried that he might exploit her for the sake of a story. "Small Town Misfit Yearns For Normal Life and Love"—that sort of thing.

She glanced up at me first, then at Jack. "Same as anywhere else, I expect."

"You've been here your whole life?"

"Yes."

Good, I thought. Stick with short answers. Don't give him a story. Jack pressed onward. "The people here. What are they like?"

"Like people everywhere," she said. "Some decent folks. Some not so." That was an opening. Jack would follow up with, *Tell me about some of those indecent folks, would you?* But she cut him off with a question of her own. "Tell me why you're here, Mr. Jack, you and your friend. What do you expect to find?"

"We're traveling," I said. "We got a bit lost tonight."

"I wouldn't say we're lost," Jack told her. "I'm always interested in new places. New people. I'm a writer."

"I wouldn't mention that to anybody," Flora said.

"What, they don't like writers? They don't read?"

She rubbed a finger across her upper lip, thinking about how to respond…

(And I don't want to keep harping on her appearance, Celia, because it's not like I stared rudely the whole time. But it's hard to convey how strange she looked. Sometimes, a person might have a scar or a patch of discoloration on their cheek, and you notice it when you first meet. But the more you get to know the person, that physical detail becomes unimportant. You grow used to it. It's almost invisible.

With Flora, the physical deformity got more obvious the more I looked. As I mentioned, she was pretty: nicely pronounced cheekbones, a soft pale complexion, and beautiful blue eyes; although her hair was an unremarkable brown shade, it had a thick wavy texture that gave it life. I figured that her beauty was part of the problem, seeming so…misplaced. This isn't nice to say, but her head reminded me then of one of those hunting trophies—a deer's head mounted on a wooden plaque.

And there's this other awkward matter: when a man speaks to a grown woman, he's supposed to look directly into her eyes and *never*, um, beneath her shoulders, because that meant you were staring at her breasts.

Yes, Celia, gay men worry about that, too.

Subtle details had a similar effect—like the fact that, when Flora touched her hand to her mouth, she barely had to raise her arm. Little things like this were very disconcerting. It's hard to explain.)

…her hand dropped to her chin, cupping it. I had this crazy idea that she could push up, hard, and lift her head to where it belonged, simple as raising a jar of pickles to a higher shelf.

"Maybe Mr. Shawn is right," she said. "Maybe you should stay inside tonight."

~ Beneath Their Shoulders ~

WELL, THAT AS much as sealed our fate. Whenever somebody advised Jack *not* to do something, it was a sure bet he wouldn't listen. So, less than an hour later we began a late-night stroll to the tavern we spotted during the drive into town.

Aside from the lack of streetlights, Garora wasn't much different from other small towns we'd visited. Mostly two-story single-family homes, big yards with lots of trees, wooden fences here and there, an occasional "Beware of Dog" sign next to a metal mailbox on a post.

"Hey, that car's familiar." Jack pointed to a Dodge Monaco parked in a driveway to our right.

"Different roof," I said. A lush maple shaded the driveway, masking the car's color, but the car that nearly side-swiped us earlier had a leather roof. This one was metal, its paint job matching the rest of the vehicle.

We saw a few other cars in driveways. They were all Monacos.

"Must be a Dodge dealership in the next town," Jack said.

"They need extra horsepower for that steep hill out of town."

"Good point."

From behind we heard the soft rumble of one of those luxury engines. How ironic that a powerful car could practically sneak up on you, whereas our weak little Bug puttered loud as an 18-wheeler. We stepped out of the main road and onto the curb, giving the car room to pass. It beeped on the way, a kind of greeting I guess, rather than a complaint. Monaco #3, I'll call it, followed down the road then turned left, and I figured the driver was heading to the tavern.

In the darkness I couldn't give full credit to my clarity of vision, but when I squinted through the rear windshield, I once again got the impression that a moving car didn't have a driver.

WHEN WE GOT to the Tavern, its modest parking lot was half full. Pretty much all Monacos, though I noticed one or two other cars—older, but still luxury models. Probably quite a few people walked, too, as Jack and I had. The town was small, and it would be easy enough to stumble home after too much drink.

When we stepped through the door, it was almost like that scene in a classic horror movie when the visitor enters an English pub—all the locals stop what they're doing, glasses raised frozen to their mouths, and they turn their heads to look at the stranger.

They turned their heads all right. Their shoulders moved with the heads.

To some degree or another the people in their booths or at the barstools, or playing a friendly game of pool or darts, all displayed a version of the spinal affliction we witnessed at the Bittinger home. A few had merely a slight stoop and drooping of the head; most heads hung as low as Flora's, with maybe a slight tufting of hair reaching above the shoulder line.

A mounted deer's head hung above the line of bottles at the back of the bar. The bartender apparently stood on a platform so he could see over the bar. The top buttons of a white dress shirt were open, allowing his bald head to fit through; the Oxford collar fit loosely above his ears, roughly in the position of a classical laurel wreath.

"What can I get you?" His voice had a smoker's rasp. I considered how smoke might travel through a bent esophagus, getting stuck the way hair and grime clog the elbow pipe of a bathroom sink.

Luckily, Jack stepped up and ordered us each a beer. I'd stood frozen, trying too hard not to telegraph the shock of my observations. Legends told of small towns cut off from the rest of the world, their inhabitants marrying with neighbors or even within their families, the gene pool growing stagnant, spinning out a signature mutation: a Neanderthal ridge above the eyes in one town; another where webbed skin stretched between the fingers and toes of each inhabitant. But this was 1985. Such isolated towns, if they ever existed, were part of a distant past.

And yet, we'd stumbled into a community of hunchbacks.

⁓ Beneath Their Shoulders ⁓

"Thanks," Jack said, accepting our beers and placing some bills on the bar. He leaned close, the only way to be heard in a crowded bar with loud music. "Keep the change." When he pulled away from the bar, he didn't stretch to his full height. Jack was about 6'3", so he must have felt even more out-of-place than I did. Or maybe it was that phenomenon that often occurred during travel, where you unconsciously mimic local behaviors—developing a slight stoop in Garora, same way you'd slip into a Boston or Baltimore accent.

Jack handed me a beer, the glass cool against my fingertips. The bar was pretty much packed. I wished there was an open booth where we could sit privately. The other patrons mostly stopped staring at us, but I still felt uncomfortable.

"This is a pretty interesting place." Jack leaned close to talk. "Let's stand against the wall over there. I need to scope out some locals to interview."

"Be careful." I thought about Flora's comment, that he shouldn't mention to anyone that he's a writer. They probably mistrusted strangers, certainly wouldn't appreciate the publicity and gawking tourism a magazine article would attract.

"I'm always careful."

I took a quick sip of beer and handed it back to him. "I gotta find the restroom."

"That beer works pretty fast."

"Ha ha," I said, deadpan. "Wait for me before you start any trouble."

Kind of a wishful-thinking comment, but I wasn't planning to be gone too long.

⁓

TWO THINGS I hope for in any public restroom: that it be reasonably clean, and that it be empty.

I got one of my wishes, at least.

The men's room was behind the bar, in a tight corridor that led back to another, darker section of the tavern. The music played louder from back there—some classic rock tune, in the days before they called it classic. Either Free or Bad Company, I think.

The restroom was empty, but the floor was wet—water, one would hope. The lone toilet stall had a loose door, covered with smudges of greased fingerprints. There were two urinals on the same back wall. One was a standard model with a small pool of filthy water at the bottom. In typical bar fashion, it would never flush completely—if your own stream stirred too vigorously in the soup, you'd smell several weeks' worth of visitor waste.

That's the one I had to use, because the other one seemed broken. It was in the usual position of a kids' urinal, lower to the ground—but you wouldn't need one of those in a bar, it occurred to me. Instead of an "Out of Order" sign, they'd placed a slanted sheet of clear plexiglass across the top half of the urinal—kind of like a sneeze guard at the salad bar.

Graffiti covered the walls, as expected. The usual "Kilroy Was Here" drawing made its appearance—a face like a sun peering over the horizon, nose resting on the ground. In this version, the face was lower, the horizon aligned with the top of the scalp. A "For Good Head" advertisement, with phone number, seemed in particularly poor taste.

While I was taking care of things, I heard the door bang open. Music from the back room followed the guy in briefly, along with some heated conversations I couldn't make out. He went to the sink first, splashing and muttering under his breath. Then he headed into the stall.

He flushed the toilet immediately, growled something about *inconsiderate pigs*. His voice boomed from the small gap at the bottom of the stall.

Then, with a sound like a gunshot, the metal wall next to me bulged out in the shape of a fist. The whole stall shook from the impact.

I finished up and got out of there fast as I could. Truth was, I'd been holding my breath almost the whole time, and even the smoky bar would count as fresh air at this point.

I left the bathroom and walked straight into hell.

~ Beneath Their Shoulders ~

THE CORRIDOR WAS an inferno, flames stretching from the back room of the Tavern. A wooden beam had snapped and fallen from the ceiling, one end bright like a giant torch. Dark human shapes waved their arms in a dance of agony.

I thought maybe I was still holding my breath, since I didn't smell anything burning. I listened, and there wasn't the crackle and roar of fire; none of the burning people bothered to scream. Nothing but a guitar solo from the jukebox, and maybe a faint moan of pleasure.

Jack grabbed me by the arm, steered my attention to the front room. I should have known.

The same crowd of locals, their heads beneath their shoulders, arms lifting beer glasses a short distance to their mouths. Nobody in the front room was panicked about the fire. They didn't see it.

"C'mon," Jack said. "We gotta run."

"Are you kidding me?" I twisted out of his grip, started to turn around.

"Don't look back," he said. "Trust me."

And we fast-walked out of the Garora Tavern.

"OKAY, WHAT WAS the point of that fire?"

"Keep moving," Jack said. We were across the parking lot, a faint glow from the bar's neon sign lighting our way. "I'm sorry, it was the best I could do on short notice."

"Why?"

"I saw something in the back, okay. I wanted to protect you from it."

(Jack's gift was always kind of spur-of-the-moment. This ability... *glamour* I guess is the technical term...always came to him easily, but I was the only one who saw the images he conjured. Jack said it was a tribute to our relationship—we were on the same mental wavelength, literally. Since the communication was one-sided, and Jack's images always tended toward the gruesome, I often wondered if it wasn't more of a curse. Or, at least, one of those things about your partner that you can't change, so you resign yourself to accept it.)

We crossed the street, and Jack led me between two houses. Some kind of shortcut, I guessed.

We were half a block away when the Tavern door burst open. Jack ducked behind the nearest house, pulling me after him. He pressed his back tight against the wood siding and indicated I should do the same.

"Faggot," a man shouted to the night. "Faggot, where did you go?"

Jack pressed a forefinger over my lips to signal silence, then whispered a quick explanation. "I insulted him. By accident. Stupid, 'cause he's kinda strong."

His footsteps sounded strong enough, I admit. Heavy, drunken treads on the road.

Getting closer.

I wanted to look, but didn't dare.

The footsteps paused near the alley we'd ducked into.

"Inconsiderate pig." The voice was so near I almost cried out. I recognized it as the guy from the restroom stall.

A mucus sound, the gathering of spit—I thought again about a twisted esophagus—and the guy hocked onto the road. "Faggot," he said again. "Pig."

A nervous wheeze crept into my breathing. My asthma was never frequent or serious enough to warrant an inhaler—what I usually did was gasp for a minute or so until the attack passed. Psychosomatic, most likely, brought on by fear. It was loud.

"I see you, pig." This couldn't have been true since we were blocked by the house, but Jack wasn't waiting for him to round the corner. He pulled me by the shirt to guide me through the back yard, and my panting breaths were like a homing device for the guy to follow.

His heavy boots scraped the pavement, then crackled against dry grass. I turned and saw him—or, more accurately, his shadow, a short distance away. His head was already down, of course, and his shoulders were incredibly wide. He was charging at us like a bull.

A drunken bull, which gave us a slight advantage. That, and the dark. If only I could stop breathing, he'd lose our trail.

"Back to the road," Jack said. He knocked over a garbage can as we rounded to the front of the house. When we hit the asphalt, he steered me back toward the Tavern.

"Wrong way," I said. The words squeaked out, shrill in the night air.

"We can't lead him to where we're staying. Keep moving."

Jack was taking us off the map again.

∽

WE STAYED ON the road a while, and we gained a bit of distance. I think it took the guy a moment to realize we'd doubled back—plus, in his drunken state he had more trouble running a straight line than we did.

The Tavern's neon lights shone faint in the distance behind us. I could barely make out the bull's shadow, small and still. He'd given up the chase, but he kept watch.

"This way," Jack said at a cross street, again taking us in the opposite direction of the Bittinger home. The bull wouldn't be able to find our lodgings—but I wondered how far we'd stray before we headed back.

At least we could slow down a bit. I caught my breath, and the wheezing stopped.

Once we were a mile or so from the Tavern, I asked what had happened. "Seriously, Jack, I was only in the bathroom a minute or two."

"You know how when a straight guy walks into one of our bars…?"

It sounded like the start of a joke, and I said so.

"Bear with me," he said, which was my signal to sit down on the curb. Jack joined me. "This straight guy walks into a bar. He thinks it's one of *his* places. He doesn't notice right away, because most guys like to drink, and they have these sports bars where a bunch of manly men can sit close together and high-five each other or whatever when their team scores on the television. Seems normal, and maybe he's ordered a drink already and he's looking for the pool table in back or a bare patch of wall to lean against, and he passes this guy making out with his girlfriend. He checks her out, since that's another thing guys do, and she's got long straw-blonde hair and her pants are tight, and he walks past to see how the face holds up..."

"And she's got a beard."

"Exactly. So what does he do?"

I wanted to say the straight guy would be gracious. Finish his beer and step out quietly. But in those days the guy usually made a huge fuss—gagging maybe, saying "That's disgusting," or "I can't believe I walked in *here*," overcompensating for fear anybody'd think *he* was gay, God forbid. That bit of straight-guy theatre was pretty familiar, as was the frustration that somebody could feel free to step into our establishment and insult us.

"Right," Jack said. "And that's kind of what I did."

I didn't follow…

"So, we're in this local bar, and it's a *freak* bar, basically—you gotta admit it." He noticed my distaste at the word, but kept going. "The whole time we're in there—and you were doing it too, Shawn, don't lie—I'm trying *so* hard not to react at how odd the people look. I mean, all of them stooped over, their heads low, that bartender with the collar above his friggin' ears. Hard not to laugh or shudder or simply *say* something about it, you know, but it wouldn't be polite. So I'm kind of proud of myself for keeping my cool. 'Cause it's *their* place. They don't deserve to be insulted in their own place."

He attempted an ironic laugh, hoping to comfort me before he continued. That weak laugh scared me as much as anything we'd experienced so far. His voice dropped to a whisper—a reminder that our friend from the Tavern might lurk nearby in the surrounding curtain of darkness—and he continued:

"So when you headed to the restroom, I followed behind a bit, stealing discrete glances around the main room to find someone who might be approachable—maybe a good-natured couple laughing, or somebody lonely enough to welcome strange company. As I wandered past the bar, I saw the restroom sign and the hallway you'd ducked into, and I noticed how the hall led to a totally separate bar at the rear of the building.

"A few couples huddled against the walls of this hallway, keeping mostly to the darker patches. We have the same thing in some of our bars: kind of a 'make out' area where people kiss or rub against each other—a preview of what might happen later, or a bit of fun in its own right. If you're not there for similar action, the polite thing is to keep walking.

"Which I was doing, since I wanted to check out that back room. It was darker than the front of the tavern, the music was louder; more smoke clouded the air, making the room seem out of focus. I got closer, and the cloud started to clear.

"Then something in the hallway caught my attention. It was a girl about our age, with that same slouched head we've seen all evening. She was in an aggressive and flirty mood, and she'd backed this slightly older, kind of muscular guy against the wall. Her hands were on him, searching...

"That kind of behavior doesn't bother me, of course. I'm no prude. People can do what they want as long as they keep to themselves.

"Then I realized what I was really looking at..."

We still sat on the curb, our knees almost touching. It was so dark, I could feel his shudder easier than I could see it.

"I held two beers, pretty much both full since I'd barely tasted mine. I dropped them both on the floor.

"Remember, I'd put a cork in my reaction all this time. I was so good. But man, what I saw *really* shook me up, and the cork popped. I gagged, said something like Oh My God or What the Hell.

"I might have said *freak* once or twice.

"The beers had splashed on that couple, already a pretty rude thing to do, and here I was firing off the insults. In *their* bar, you know? But I was so shocked.

"By the time I recovered myself, it was too late to take it all back. An apology wasn't going to cut it. The guy called me a few choice names himself, including *faggot* like you heard, then stormed off to the restroom.

"If he saw me again, there'd be serious trouble. I knew you were in the bathroom too, but I didn't dare go in after you.

"I waited, thinking Hurry Up, Hurry Up, Hurry Up. One of the make-out couples had gone back to what they were doing, but another couple glared at me disapprovingly. A guy came from the back bar, and that couple stopped him, talking excitedly, doing that weird head-and-shoulders lean to nod in my direction.

"Timing was going to be tight. I couldn't stop to answer your questions.

"That's why I cast up that fire image—to help us get out quick, and to keep you from seeing what I'd seen.

"You finally came out, and I grabbed your arm, guiding you away from the glass shards on the floor, pulling you from the hallway.

"Pulling you out of the fire."

(What did Jack see in that hallway? I asked him the same question, Celia. Didn't think it could possibly be worse than a building on fire, seeing trapped bodies writhing and crisping in the flames. Jack said he'd explain later, after we'd circled back to our lodgings. It would be better to learn this part of the story in a bright, cozy room.

I don't know if he was right about that. You decide.)

EVEN SMALL TOWN roads will twist in odd ways, and not all the signs were clear. I didn't know which way was up, though Jack was confident we'd eventually stumble onto a familiar path. The whole time, I was afraid that guy could catch our trail again: he'd jump from behind a parked car, or his muscular arms would burst through the slats of a wooden fence.

Beneath Their Shoulders

I can't tell you how relieved I was to find that filling station and know we were close to the Bittinger home.

Our red Beetle, parked in the street, made it easy to spot the right house. A dark blue Monaco with a hardtop leather roof filled the Bittingers' driveway.

We passed the car on our way to the porch. Jack cupped his hands on either side of his face and peered in the driver-side window, but it was too dark to make anything out. He circled the car, inspecting it. He called my attention to the front grill.

Next to one headlight, a section of the grill had fallen off—the same side of the car that had brushed past us on the wooded road. We hadn't actually collided, but maybe the Monaco's bumpy detour had jostled something loose. Or maybe the grill was already damaged, and I hadn't noticed as it headed straight for us.

As Flora suggested, we'd left the door unlocked when we headed out for the evening. It was locked now, though. Nearly 1:40 am, but I was so exhausted and desperate for our quiet room that I overcame my scruples about waking the house. I lifted the brass knocker and gave it a few hard raps.

Flora answered the door. After the evening's drama, I was grateful to see a friendly face. A happy realization washed over me. Earlier, I commented how Flora's physical deformity grew more obvious the more I looked at her, as if I'd never get used to it. But I was used to it now. I'm not going to say she looked normal to me, but her appearance was no longer disconcerting.

We stepped into the foyer, and Flora asked about our stroll. Jack gave a vague response.

A television blared from the sitting room, dark aside from the gray and white flicker. Some late-night movie: I'd like to say it took place in Paris and starred Charles Laughton or Lon Chaney, but it was one of those black and white cheapies where third-rate Martin & Lewis knockoffs ran through an old castle. Lots of suspenseful music, not much suspense.

With the click of a remote, the television went silent. An arm waved from one of the wing-back chairs. The rest of the person was obscured by the angle of the chair; I assumed it was Mrs. Bittinger, but the bare arm had a masculine shape.

In a flash of panic, I thought it might be the man who chased us from the Tavern. He figured out where we stayed—how many bed and breakfasts *were* there in Garora, anyway, and with a sore thumb VW Beetle out front? He got here first and waited in the dark, sharpening a knife, polishing a loaded rifle.

The hand reached under the shade of a floor lamp and toggled the switch. A man, definitely a man, though he faced away from us. He struggled to rise from the chair.

"Oh Daddy," Flora said. "We've got paying guests. Put your shirt on, for goodness sakes."

Well, I knew Flora had to come from *some*where, but I'd assumed Mrs. Bittinger was a widow. The way she projected ownership of the house was part of it. The other part, well…she was a brusque, unattractive old woman, so I didn't expect anybody'd stay married to her.

"We've met already," Mr. Bittinger said. He rose to full height, stepping away from the chair, but his back was still to us. It was an old man's back, the bones of his bent spine making a mountain ridge down the middle. Freckles dotted his shoulders, and random patches of age spots darkened the pale skin. A few irregular moles, too, one of them big as a bullethole.

A fleshy smoothness ran uninterrupted from one shoulder to the next. From our vantage point, it looked like he didn't have a head at all.

Then he turned around.

Jack waited to tell me what he'd encountered back at the Tavern. It would have been less disturbing in a well-lit room, he thought. Well, the parlor and foyer were bright as can be, but that clear view didn't make it any easier for me to grasp what lumbered toward us in the parlor.

No head between his shoulders. Lower down, beneath his nipples sprouted semi-circles of dark hair that I recognized as…eyebrows. Blue eyes blinked beneath, one on each ribcage and large as lemons. The nose was puffy and red, like an alcoholic's, and it pressed out from the slight bulge of his stomach. The hair underneath was waxed in the shape of a handlebar moustache. And just above his waist, where the belly button should be, was a wide, toothsome mouth.

Smiling.

This is where I wish Jack had prepared me better. It's one thing to meet such a creature in a dark bar or chasing after you in the night, its teeth bared in malice. It's another thing to encounter one in the bright light of a sitting room, extending its arm in a friendly greeting.

Between mine and Jack's first encounters, I think I got the worst shock. I felt sick. It's like my whole world and everything I ever understood was wrong. I didn't scream and curse like Jack apparently had back at the Tavern, but I had to hold onto the wall to keep from fainting.

Jack stepped forward. "Nice to formally meet you, Mr. Bittinger." They shook hands.

My turn was next.

~

WELL, YOU KNOW, you have to do what's polite. I kept my composure, best I could, and shook Mr. Bittinger's hand. "Call me Simon," he said.

Nice guy, once you talked a bit. I felt a little better after he put a shirt on. A little.

(Since you asked again, Celia, here's what Jack saw at the Tavern—though you might be sorry to hear it.

As Jack described it to me later, that shall-we-say amorous young lady had the muscular guy pushed against the wall in the hallway. One of her hands rubbed at his pectorals through his shirt. The other went lower. She'd undone the last button of his shirt and slipped her hand inside to drag her fingers over the soft hairs of his stomach. Then Jack detected an odd slurping sound. When the young lady pulled back her hand, a string of drool trailed from her fingertips to the opening.

Yes, Celia, a tongue down there. As Jack realized this, his gag reflex starting, he also noticed openings beneath each of the chest pockets in the man's shirt. Large eyes stared out those openings. That's when he dropped the glasses of beer and started cursing.

You think that was worse than my experience in the Bittinger foyer? You might be right.

In the commotion, a few of the patrons walked in from the back bar, adding to Jack's surprise. As he figured it out, that wasn't simply a make-out hallway. It was the meeting ground between two groups: people like Flora and that amorous young lady, with their heads beneath their shoulders, stayed mostly in the front room; the back tavern was for folks like Simon Bittinger and the muscular man who chased after us—no heads at all but with facial features giant on their chests.)

JACK GOT HIS interview after all, but not with Flora. Simon talked to him at length, on condition that he never mention the town's location in his article. Not too many people knew about Garora, of course, and the residents made only rare visits to one adjoining town—with the Dodge dealership, and a group of open-minded friends Simon visited for a regular Friday night bridge game.

He told us about a legendary tribe called Blemmyae who supposedly lived in ancient Africa. Othello mentions them as one of the travel narratives that captured Desdemona's fancy: "men whose heads / Do grow beneath their shoulders." In *Naturalis Historiae* Pliny the Elder wrote about them much earlier than Shakespeare: about 75 AD. These were never confirmed accounts, however, and Simon didn't believe there was a direct lineal descent from Blemmyae to the inhabitants of his own isolated community. He only said, "We've been different here as long as anybody can remember."

Before Jack and I left Garora, he showed us the interior of his car: a mirror and lens device stretched through the dashboard and beneath the hood, allowing him to see through the missing section of the front grill. "It doesn't work so well on hills," he said. "That's why I almost ran you guys off the road."

(Simon gave us this souvenir, too. An old one—he was going to throw it away, or use it as a rag. Take it. See the holes here, cut beneath the front pockets? Gives you an idea how big their eyes were.

He also drew up a map to another strange town he thought Jack and I might want to visit. But that's a story I'll save until you're a bit older…)

The Man Who Could Not Be Bothered To Die

TONY didn't hear the first knock. He wasn't expecting anyone this Tuesday evening, certainly not so late on a work night, but Barker scrambled to the front door, tail wagging and head raised in expectation. Tony saw his sister through the spyhole, and he opened the door to let her in. Then a few more people swarmed onto the porch. His step-dad. Kevin from work, and Rachel. His regular doctor, plus the hygienist from his dentist's office, and the trainer-specialist from his gym.

They all jostled through his front door and crowded into his living room.

If Tony's family ever decided to give him a surprise birthday party, this was better than the guest list he'd expect. Unfortunately, they weren't bearing gifts, and they weren't wearing funny hats. He wished a few of them would smile.

His step-father made a hesitant step forward, as if he wanted to give Tony's shoulder a reassuring pat. He stopped himself, the well-meaning impulse suddenly distasteful. "I know I'm not your real father," Martin said. "But I pride myself on treating Ellen's kids like they're my own. Even after your mother died, I've always considered you and Jill part of my family. You may not think I've earned the right to say this, but here goes. You need to end it, son."

Tony looked at Jill, whose head was down as if she couldn't believe what she was hearing. This no doubt was supposed to be a happy occasion, and their awkward step-dad screwed things up once again, as he often had during Tony and Jill's childhood.

But Jill said, "My turn. We're supposed to use 'I' statements. So here goes: When you continue breathing, I feel sad."

Brad, who'd sold him a lifetime membership to MidTown Fitness, assured Tony that he wasn't trying to cheat him out of remaining years on his policy. "Hell, do the math. You've been a member for 6 years. Yearly dues are $250, so you've already more than recouped the cost of your lifetime plan. I think you should just face the facts."

Doctor Maddox said, "I've taken the Hippocratic Oath, so I can't really speak frankly. But we all know why I'm here. I support your family and friends, and think you should listen to them."

The dentist's hygienist says, "We don't care anymore if you floss. We really don't."

That's when Jill totally lost it. "Look at him," she screamed. "He's not listening to us. He's going to keep going, regardless of what we feel. He's so selfish."

His step-father, as usual, assumed the weak role of mediator. "Look what you're doing to your sister. I want you to think about this."

◈

HAD THINGS REALLY gotten this bad? He was only 35 years old. How had he reached this point?

◈

AT THE DENTIST'S office two weeks ago, he'd experienced a familiar disorientation as the chair tilted back, raising his legs unnaturally higher than his head. He tensed up.

The hygienist seemed more than usually hidden behind her surgical mask. He imagined her nose crinkled up behind the paper. She wasn't talkative. She didn't push the small mirror into his mouth to

The Man Who Could Not Be Bothered To Die

angle for a better view of his teeth. All the years he wished the dentist visits would go more quickly—that the hygienist wouldn't scrape and scrape at his teeth, pressing metal tips into spaces between, poking at his gums then asking him to rinse blood out of his mouth. Now, the process was quick and painless, and he should have been happy. Instead, he felt insulted.

The hygienist stretched a span of floss between her fingertips and reached into his mouth. Floss pressed into his loose gums like a wire through warm cheese.

On the way out, he stopped at the front desk to schedule his six-month return visit. Instead, the receptionist just looked at him and shook her head.

Tony tried to be cheerful. "Is your computer down? I can call you tomorrow."

"No," the receptionist said. "Just…no."

~

"I THOUGHT YOU were gone for the day." Kevin's chin rested on the back wall of Tony's cubicle. This was how he often saw his co-workers: heads on the partition wall, lined up like tin cans for shooting practice.

"No, just 90 minutes for a dentist's appointment. I don't want to waste too much sick leave."

"But you're *supposed* to waste it. I woulda gone home to rest up—after all that drilling or whatever."

"I like to save it. Might need it later."

"Might need it now," Kevin said. "Honestly, you don't look so good."

Great advice, coming from a disembodied head.

"Thanks," Tony said.

"Don't mention it. Hey, you think those guys in the collapsed mine will get out today?"

"Dunno. It's Day Nine, isn't it?"

"Ten. But who's counting?" Every news program and website, for one. And the office pool. Kevin had two bucks riding on Day Thirty-Six.

173

Later, Rachel-head drifted by and told him about donuts in the break room. The chocolate-frosted ones were gone by the time he checked, but maybe he'd have better luck next time.

That afternoon, Alan-head asked for a donation to his son's uniform drive. "I'll try to bring my checkbook tomorrow," Tony responded.

"Now might be better." Alan-head jiggled the donation box over the top of the cubicle, and coins rattled against cardboard. "Anything you can spare, 'cause…tomorrow might not work out for you."

In retrospect, that last remark seemed ominous. Other people noticed something, but Tony was oblivious.

He was always the last to know.

AFTER WORK ON Mondays, Wednesdays and Fridays, Tony went to the gym. Mostly he used the treadmill or the bike, sometimes one of the weight machines.

There were rules posted for the machines. At the bottom, in caps and highlighted in yellow, each instruction sheet said: PLEASE WIPE OFF THE MACHINES WHEN YOU ARE FINISHED.

Such an unpleasant reminder. It made Tony think of germs and fluids, a smeared stain left behind as a back pressed into vinyl, or calloused palms scraped over a metal bar, leaving behind flecks of dead skin.

It was rude to stare at people while they exercised, so he found himself absently reading and rereading the instruction sheet—while his own body, like a squeezed sponge, left its impression on the equipment.

The phenomenon wasn't unique to exercise equipment. Every surface you pressed against absorbed a small piece of you. Life was a constant, tedious leprosy.

But that Wednesday night, two weeks ago, should have been a cause for celebration. Tony had reached his target weight—the last ten pounds seemed to melt off effortlessly. And he'd finally achieved the body-fat ratio recommended on his exercise card.

The Man Who Could Not Be Bothered To Die

He took the card to the gym's resident trainer. The card was hatched with weights and dates annotated in Tony's meticulous handwriting, most of the ink smeared by months of fingertip sweat. Brad accepted the card from him, then gave him a new one with slightly different goals.

"This *might* help," Brad said. "More cardio. More weights to strengthen muscle tone." He seemed skeptical.

But now Tony had new goals. Something to live for.

So he did.

∼

LATER THAT SAME day, he watched *Crime Spree: Tuscaloosa* on channel 43, sprawled on the sofa and tossing a few random pretzel sticks to Barker during the commercials. Maybe sometime during the final segment…maybe that was another moment when it almost happened. Maybe Tony's heart had *almost* stopped.

But there was too much going on in the episode: the rusted key hadn't yet been matched to a bank deposit box; the numbers and symbols on the first ransom note hadn't yet been decoded; Detective Ajax still hadn't discovered the fourth victim's body, and his partner still needed a date for the Governor's Gala (would she ask him?). Too many loose ends, and only five minutes left.

Dammit! It was a two-parter.

Which meant he'd *have* to wait until next week.

And the next, too, if it was a longer arc.

∼

SOME THINGS WERE worth looking forward to: vacations and weekends. Going to the movies. Walking Barker each night after dinner. Reading in bed and eyes getting heavy until he set the book aside and drifted to blissful sleep.

But just as many tasks were tedious. Waking and showering and getting dressed. Brown-bagging a lunch. Driving to the office. Then work itself: a series of repetitive tasks, laced with the stress of artificial deadlines.

At his cubicle, Tony often caught himself staring at a blurred computer screen, not remembering what task he was supposed to complete. He'd check his email, and find a large list of "New" messages, many of them marked with a red exclamation mark.

Urgent. Funny how so many things could be considered urgent…

Last week, for example, a window popped-up to inform him that his "Virus Definition File" was 30 days out of date. He could fix the problem now, or click on "Remind Me Later."

He'd clicked "Remind Me Later" each day since. It only took a few minutes to update the file, but the reminder always popped up while he was in the middle of something else. Like, while he was entering figures into the budget spreadsheet, or replying to a memo about the new reimbursement policy (receipts, in triplicate, for anything over $10). Or when he was checking CNN and Fox for information about the trapped miners (still trapped), or checking his Match-up website for potential dates in his area (he was planning to click "Interested" on a few of them, but wanted to finish reading all the profiles first. More profiles were added each day—it was impossible to keep up).

"Day Twenty," Kevin said from his cubicle on the other side. He wasn't standing and peering into Tony's area, so his voice sounded muffled. Possibly, he also had a hand cupped over his nose and mouth.

"You might win the pool," Tony told him. "I'll be curious to see how this turns out."

"Yeah, if you outlast them."

"What's that supposed to mean?" His co-worker's voice was still muffled and nasal, so Tony might have misheard.

"Nothing," Kevin said.

"You know, it's kind of cruel that you picked such a high number—like you wished they would stay down there longer."

"Just playing the odds. The guys in Chile were stuck for 69 days."

"Even so, you'd be profiting from their discomfort." Tony thought about germs and fluids, scraped skin and body waste and foul breath—

The Man Who Could Not Be Bothered To Die

the constant, tedious leprosy of existence. "All of them stuck in that tight space. Can you even imagine the smell?"

"Yes, I think I can," Kevin said.

He didn't seem to want to talk further, so Tony turned back to his computer monitor. A new profile, added today: Kristin R., 42. Likes: Dogs and Cats. Favorite movies: *Fight Club* and *Gone with the Wind*.

His finger slipped on the mouse button as he clicked for the next page. There was a slick gel on the button, in the shape of his fingertip. He clicked in the navigation bar then typed in a new web address. The letters on the keyboard felt soft and wet.

⁓

THESE RECENT DAYS, the heads seemed to float more quickly past his cubicle wall. Rachel-head didn't tell him if donuts were in the break room; people avoided getting into the elevator with him.

Still, Tony's job performance was fine. At the end of each year, his boss checked the "Meets Standards" box on the review form. Tony continued to meet standards.

Yet when he phoned his sister for their usual Sunday chat, she mentioned some of his co-workers were concerned about him.

"Kevin, most likely," he said, and Jill didn't deny it. "What kinds of concerns? Why is he calling *you*, instead of talking to me directly?"

"Some topics are difficult," Jill said. She proved her point by not elaborating.

"Okay, I've been feeling a little weak lately," he admitted. "I overslept some mornings, and maybe didn't dress as carefully as I usually do." Or showered, though Jill didn't need that detail.

Seemed like she already knew, though: "There's kind of a bare minimum. An expectation for what's worth…um…"

"I should take better care of myself," he said, finishing her argument.

"That's not quite what I meant."

Silence.

They typically spent most of their Sunday talk complaining about their step-dad. This was getting a little too personal.

So he changed the subject. "How's your husband?"

"Fine."

"How are the kids?"

"They're fine," Jill said. Usually she had lots of stories—cute dinner-table remarks from Janey, or Adam's latest score on a math quiz.

"I bet they miss their Uncle Tony. I should visit more often."

"Actually, Janey's got a flu bug," Jill said. "Adam's coming down with it, too."

"I wasn't talking about visiting *today*," Tony said.

"Oh."

"I thought you said they were fine."

"Yeah, aside from the flu." He heard Jill's hand smother the mouthpiece as she yelled into the distance. "What's that? You need mommy? You think you're throwing up again?" Another scratch against the mouthpiece, then Jill spoke in a normal voice: "Time to go, Tony."

She hung up before he could say he'd call again next week.

~

HE VISITED INSTEAD. That same Sunday. His sister's house was a quick twenty minute's drive.

Jill wouldn't open the door.

"I'm not feeling well," she shouted from inside the house.

"I thought the kids were sick, not you."

"The kids? They're not here."

"Jill, come on." He resisted an urge to kick at the door. "Let me in."

Eventually he heard the latch chain jangle, and his sister opened the door a crack. Jill peered at him over the taut chain. She had pulled the collar of her T-shirt over her mouth and nose. "I can't let you in. Don't want to give you this cold." She lifted a hand and fake-coughed into her T-shirt.

∼ The Man Who Could Not Be Bothered To Die ∼

In the background, he heard SpongeBob's theme music. "You watching cartoons?"

"No, that's..." Her eyes darted uncomfortably to the side, then back. She spoke to his left shoulder, rather than to his face. "I just left it on. You know how, sometimes, you keep things running."

"I guess."

"It's not good though. A waste." Another fake cough.

"Of electricity."

"Sure."

He heard Janey's distinct laugh in response to one of SpongeBob's antics.

"Tony, you have to leave," Jill said.

Even then, he sensed his sister was doing more than chasing him off her porch.

She closed the door.

∼

TWO DAYS LATER, that crowd of people muscled their way into his house. Jill must have organized the whole intervention—which explained why she got so out-of-sorts after he didn't respond as she'd hoped.

"You're putrefying!"

It wasn't a terribly polite thing to say. His sister recently gained back all the weight she'd lost after a recent diet—and then some—and he'd been courteous enough to keep silent.

Martin placed a gentle hand on Jill's shoulder. "No insults," their step-father said. "That won't get us anywhere."

"You're right," Jill said. As far as Tony could recall, she'd never agreed with Martin before. As a matter of fact, it was odd that she didn't shrug his comforting hand off her shoulder.

Doctor Maddox stepped forward, his arms raised toward the living room ceiling. "Walk into the light."

There wasn't an overhead light in the living room, so Tony didn't know how to respond.

"Oh God," Jill said. "I don't think he *knows*."

She looked ready to cry. Tony suddenly wanted to hug her, but his sister's body language told him the affection wouldn't be welcomed.

They all kept their distance.

Even Barker. He could see that now, the way his dog jumped up at Kevin, delighting at a simple scratch behind the ear, licking his co-worker's hand then sniffing at his crotch. Barker hadn't acted like that in quite a while. Lately, the dog stayed in separate rooms; he pulled to the furthest end of the leash when they went for their evening walks.

"Of course I know," Tony said. "I'm not blind." He thought about how he'd dressed each morning. He would pat his hair gently with his hand, afraid a comb would pull out clumps of hair or wet scalp. When he checked his appearance in the bathroom mirror he focused mostly on one shoulder or another, as Jill had when he visited on Sunday.

Tony always knew this would happen eventually, but he was only thirty-five. It should wait until he was in his seventies, in a nursing home bed. His loved ones would gently ask to unplug the machines. He'd let them.

"So why didn't you…?" Jill couldn't quite bring herself to say it.

Tony shrugged. "I don't know. I've just been…busy."

Jill snorted. "Busy? Doing what?"

How could he respond? His sister ran her own catering business, raised two kids, kept the home spotless for her whole family. What could he say that would satisfy her: Walking the dog? Watching television? Waiting for chocolate-glazed donuts?

"It's hard to find the time," he said.

"Oh, listen to you." His sister raised her voice; he didn't want to hug her any more. "It's like you couldn't be bothered."

"No, it's not that." He had work to finish. He wanted to date someone from the Match-up website. He wanted to plan a vacation cruise for next summer.

"What is it then?"

The Man Who Could Not Be Bothered To Die

Something about the concern in Jill's voice struck him, making Tony feel unbearably sad. "I hadn't realized how much I was hurting all of you," he said finally, giving in. "All the people I care about." He felt strangely charitable, as if he loved everyone in the room—even his physical trainer.

Jill's eyes lit up. "So you'll do it?"

"Yes. Yes, I'll try."

His step-father scolded him. "You need to do more than try, son."

"Okay. I'll do it."

Soon. He really meant it.

This had been a difficult intervention for him, and he realized it was tough on them as well. Especially Jill. She'd planned the whole thing, must have agonized over how things would play out. She'd done it all out of love.

As the gathering dispersed, she was the last to leave. Before she stepped outside, she turned and looked directly into his eyes.

"Thank you," Tony said, and she nodded.

He closed the door behind her, exhausted. This would be the perfect time to let things take their natural course.

He wandered into the front room. His dog whimpered from the kitchen, and Tony sank into the couch. He lifted the remote and aimed it at the television, surfing the channels one last time. Maybe there was news about the trapped miners.

He stopped on channel 13. No harm in watching for a few minutes. The first episode of the latest *Survivor* had already started.

He wondered who'd make it to the end of the season.

The Everywhere Man

THE video camera focuses on a young woman as she struggles past a crowded bus stop. She's bundled up in a puffy jacket, and a walking cast covers her right pant leg. Snow has been pushed away from the sidewalk, gray-white piles on both sides along the curb and storefronts, but portions that melted during the day have frozen again over sections of concrete. The woman negotiates over random patches of ice, and the rubber heels of her crutches lose traction in unpredictable jolts.

"Stop filming," she says. She waves one crutch in the air as a mock threat. The action makes her lose her balance, and she nearly falls. "I mean it, Ian. Stop filming!" Then she laughs.

The picture darkens and halts for a moment, and a bright halo illuminates a man further up on the sidewalk. A yellow cartoon arrow appears near the top right corner of the screen, above his head, and follows him as the scene resumes motion.

The woman stops to catch her breath. She puts one hand under her long brown hair to lift it away from her coat collar, then rubs gently at her neck.

The computerized arrow fades away as the man steps next to her on the sidewalk. He is short and stocky, with a tan jacket that flaps open in the chill night air. His sandy blond hair is curly and unkempt. He has stubble on his face; instead of a beard, it appears like a strange skin condition, as if his face is grainy or out of focus.

He grabs one of the crutches and hooks its cushioned end under the woman's chin. A quick shove knocks her into the brick front of a used clothing store; a turn and jerk of the crutch sends her sideways into a large pile of snow.

The man pulls the arm cushion off the top of the crutch and tosses it aside. "Stop filming," he says as he swings at the woman's head with the wooden crutch. After the first two blows connect, the woman covers her face with her hands and moves her one good leg in an attempt to stand. Her foot slides on a patch of ice.

"I mean it, Ian," the man says as he continues hitting her. "Stop filming!"

The cameraman moves closer. The frame jerks each time the crutch batters at the woman's arms, body, or head. Her coat absorbs some of the force, but one of her sleeves tears from the impact. Blood glistens between her fingers, which are interlocked to cover her eyes. It is not clear if the hands are damaged, or if the blood flows from cuts on her forehead.

Viewers wonder why Ian is silent, why he continues filming. It may be shock. They should also remember that he watches through a viewfinder, which can give the unfolding action an air of unreality, as if it is part of a movie or a television show. On another level, he might think that capturing the event on film will provide important evidence that will help police to identify the attacker.

We can clearly hear the whistle of air through the slats of the swinging crutch, the muffled thump as it lands against the puffed front of a winter jacket or cracks against the bones of an arm or hand. Voices from the stunned crowd at the bus stop start to assert themselves: "Look over there." "What's that guy—?"

And Ian does move closer. Not just for a better angle, we hope, but to separate this lunatic from the woman. He transfers the camera to

The Everywhere Man

his left hand; his right arm appears close in the frame, gigantic, as he reaches out to grab the man or to take away the now-bloody crutch.

Then he slips.

The camera falls with him, and lands to the side. The rapid pan halts and becomes a still shot that frames a streetlight and the starless sky beyond. The image is essentially useless now, but the audio continues.

A pair of footsteps gets louder, alternating with one foot on the sidewalk, one crunching into the hardened snow.

A female voice rings clearly—"Help her!"—and we hear the shuffle of onlookers moving to surround the beaten woman.

In the foreground, the footsteps stop. The whistle of the swinging crutch resumes, louder, with hard splintering sounds as each blow strikes.

Then an awful silence. A slight murmur from the crowd, with no distinguishable phrases. Three quick beeps from a cell phone.

"Ian?" the woman says weakly. Her cry is faint; the name appears in white subtitles at the bottom of the still, black picture.

A shadowed scruffy head appears. It is startling because nothing has moved for so long. It is startling because the man is smiling.

His face gets larger as he moves closer. He looks into the camera as if deciding whether or not to take it. He leans close to the lens and grunts. A cloud of frozen breath smokes out of his mouth.

∽

NATALIE WHEELED CLOSER to the television and pressed the off button on the front of the set. When Jason made her rent the chair, she should have insisted they splurge for an electric model—one with a built-in cup holder, maybe even with a storage pocket for the TV remote to keep her from misplacing it all the time. The layout of their apartment didn't help matters. Wheels don't work well on carpet, and she soon wearied of bumping over the frilled edges of the oriental rug in their main hallway.

It could be worse. Some people have to live their whole lives in a wheelchair, but Natalie's situation was temporary while she recovered from the accident. The collision had almost totaled her car, but she practically walked away without a scratch. Except she hadn't walked steadily: her right heel and tendon suffered damage, partly from the accident itself, and partly because she foolishly pulled her wedged foot out from under the bent brake pedal without waiting for the paramedics. The corrective surgery was successful, but her recovery was taking its time. Natalie was surprised that such a localized injury could seem, almost on a whim, to shoot unexpected pains up her leg, could cause problems to her whole body on the worst days.

Both literally and figuratively, a foot injury was a real headache.

The routine that worked best was to spend most of her day in the living room, with all her books and papers spread out on a fold-out card table she could reach easily from the chair. She was actually able to get some work done—although the television loomed large in the room, an easy distraction.

Most of the daytime shows were about the video.

At first she didn't recognize all the talk show hosts. Back when she wrote her master's thesis (on "Representations of Women in Daytime Television"), Donahue, Oprah, and Geraldo were the big names. Oprah was still around, but there were several new faces: an actor from a cancelled sitcom, the spouse of a music star, a former game show host. This week, each show covered the York Road video in a similar fashion, with police experts, pop psychologists, advocates against violent crime, and long segments of emotional reactions from studio and call-in audiences. The national news had picked up the story, with daily updates on Ian Patton's status in the hospital, on funeral arrangements for his girlfriend, and on the so-far unsuccessful attempts to find any trace of the attacker.

The incident happened last week in a nearby suburb, so Natalie also suffered through local coverage from the Baltimore stations. A few days earlier she got the idea to write a conference paper about the recent media frenzy, including a comparison of local and national perspectives. A timely topic, it provided a handy justification for the hours

The Everywhere Man

she spent watching television during her winter break. The presentation might even grow into a scholarly article. Her teaching position at Catonsville Community College didn't require that she publish regularly, but she liked to stay active.

She looked over the notes she'd written. Although Natalie usually wrote directly into the computer, it was easier in her current situation to write things out on legal pads. The different routine, she found, encouraged her to be more creative. Her first attempt had been an objective description of the York Road video—a warm up exercise for the critical piece she envisioned. Reading it over, she decided that the flat tone, combined with the present tense required for an academic summary, somehow made the description more immediate and disturbing.

Natalie noticed, also, that she'd allowed some commentary to slip in toward the end of the description: speculation about Ian's silence during the attack, comments on the killer's appearance in the final seconds of the video. Well, with this kind of subject, that impulse was understandable. As she saw on all the television shows, everyone had a strong reaction to the video.

The central argument of her presentation would condemn the media for perpetuating our obsession with violence. On a separate tablet, Natalie had drafted the opening paragraphs:

The York Road video was horrible, the first time.

After repeated viewings, it became worse.

Most people in the country had seen the video several times before the end of the day. By the time the week was over, the average U.S. citizen had seen it nearly a dozen times. This average includes children, unfortunately.

As a nation, we spend too much time reliving awful scenes, burning them into our memories.

"UGH," JASON GRUNTED. "What a face to greet me after a hard day's work." He hung up his coat in the hall closet and walked into their living room.

"Thanks a lot," Natalie said.

"I should think you've had enough of him by now." Jason approached her chair from behind and draped his arms around her shoulders. He kissed the top of her head. A large freeze-framed face leered at them from the 32-inch television screen.

Natalie pressed "stop" on the remote (she'd found it earlier under pages of notes) and the recording clicked off. By coincidence, the local news program underneath the recorded image was in the process of repeating the same video. The man took his first swing with the wooden crutch.

"We've *all* had enough of him," Natalie said, then pressed the power button to switch off the television. "That's the point of my essay."

"Hmm…" Jason edged around the card table, moved a stack of books aside to clear space on the couch, then sat down. Natalie rolled back the right wheel to turn the chair to face him.

"How was the meeting?" she asked.

"Great." Jason slouched down and stretched his legs towards her. He tapped one foot gently against a metal footrest on her chair. "They like our guy for the campaign. They wanted a celebrity at first, but Simon convinced them to go with an unknown. He argued that a new product needed a new face. Besides, with all the print ads, billboards, television and radio spots, we'll be *making* the new kid into a celebrity."

Natalie had known Jason since college, where he had been a drama major. Now he worked as an agent representing actor/models, typically for commercials in the cosmetics industry. With her own background in women's studies, Natalie couldn't entirely approve of her husband's promotion of vanity—but at least he kept a sense of humor about it. The latest product was a new perfume called "Whisper." The scent, Jason told her, was supposed to be subtle and enchanting. "Is it?" she had asked. "Eh, what do I care," he had shrugged. "I just sell the talent."

It was good to know that he had closed an important deal. Natalie didn't mind when Jason worked long hours during the school terms—her own schedule of classes, preparation, and grading papers kept her pretty busy herself. But the isolation of winter break, worsened by her limited mobility, was making her stir crazy. She'd be happy to have reliable company in the evenings ahead.

And Jason looked exhausted. His tie hung loosely around his unbuttoned collar, and his thin, straight hair stuck up in stray wisps—a clear sign he'd driven home with the windows rolled down (which was, itself, a sign he'd needed to relieve stress).

"Writing going okay?" he asked.

"Oh, I'm still working things out." Natalie didn't go into too much detail, because she knew that Jason's inquiry was largely out of politeness. He supported her work, but didn't buy into all her theories, didn't approve of the pop culture venues she examined. Jason particularly hated the daytime talk shows, and would leave the room if she ever clicked over to Jerry or Maury or Montel on one of his rare days off. He didn't like the way those shows depicted humanity—though, of course, their audience was the same people he helped encourage to buy perfume.

He should watch more. It would be good market research.

Last night, Jason was especially annoyed when a celebrity news program repeated segments from the video, then followed up with a story about a New York street vendor who sold the killer's image on T-shirts. "This is the best story they can come up with?" he'd shouted at the screen. Was it moral indignation, she wondered, or professional jealousy? Someone infamous—Michael Jackson with child molestation charges, an O.J. or some other killer of the week—could get an incredible amount of free, if unattractive, publicity. It was Jason's job to get people to *pay* for that kind of exposure.

All the things that irritated Jason about the video, however, made it an ideal case study for her kind of media study. Each day, despite the lack of anything new to report, different channels found some way to force the same video clip into their programs.

Neither the police nor the reporters had come up with any leads. In the first days after the story broke, the expectation was that repeated broadcasts of the same clip would bring forward a viewer to identify the attacker. Recent on-air speculation emphasized how strange it was that this identification had never happened. No one seemed to know who the man was.

The police didn't have his real name, and the media was having trouble inventing a catchy label for him. The "Bus Stop Killer" seemed a likely moniker, until they realized it sounded like someone who attacked wooden benches rather than people. When the story went national on the second day, there followed a brief attempt to localize him as the "Maryland Maniac," but that name lost momentum quickly (much to the relief of locals who, excited about the national attention, nonetheless wanted to avoid the stigma of that label). The different outlets eventually settled on a quick reference to the street where the violence occurred. But they usually didn't bother: in the current media saturation, just mentioning "the video" was enough.

Natalie had her own name for him. But she'd save that for her essay.

"I'd like your opinion about something," she said to Jason now. "Why do you think, in the video, he says to 'Stop filming'?"

Jason ran his hands through his hair before responding. "I don't know, Nat. He's crazy. I try not to figure out crazy people."

"No, seriously. At first I thought he was just repeating the same words Sharon said to her boyfriend. But is he mocking Ian—or is it a *dare*?"

"What, like 'I dare you to stop filming me while I brutally attack your girlfriend'?"

"Yeah, that's what I'm thinking now. A taunt, as if he knows that, if what he's doing is horrible enough, it's hard to resist filming it."

"Then showing it over and over on television?" Jason continued. A throwaway line, as if he thought her argument was silly.

The Everywhere Man

"Exactly," she said with a steady voice. "Exactly. The more I see the clip, the more I'm convinced that, whoever he is, he knows just how this whole thing is going to play out. He knows he'll never get caught. And that's the way it *is* playing out. Eight days, and they still can't find him. Nobody's ever seen him before. It's as if he doesn't exist outside the video footage."

JASON CHECKED THEIR apartment before bedtime. He clicked the deadbolt into place on the front door, and secured the lock and safety bar on the sliding glass door in the kitchen.

Natalie was back in the bedroom, already under the covers. She seemed more calm at the end of the day—relieved to be out of the chair, he guessed. The recovery was hard on her, and he wished he could be around more to help. She got upset at dinner when he mentioned he'd be home late again tomorrow. Simon wanted him to be more hands-on with the rest of the "Whisper" campaign. This was good news, because it meant he was closer to getting a promotion—but it also meant he'd keep working long hours, and he'd have to travel out of town for a location shoot in a few days.

Jason looked through the glass door at the back yard of their apartment complex. The night was calm and quiet; a faint dusting of fresh snow covered the patches of browned grass that had briefly been visible since the previous storm. He turned off the porch light.

He was a little worried about the essay Natalie was working on. He didn't always agree with her arguments, especially when she pulled in feminist and popular culture theory to support them. But the more she talked about this current project, the more she seemed overly involved. True, she was writing about media obsession—but did she have to get obsessed herself?

The last argument she'd built up to was particularly disturbing. She granted too much intelligence to the man in that damn video—as if his eyes showed some awareness of what effect he'd have on viewers. Natalie had practically convinced herself that he had supernatural powers.

That was, Jason told her, a common feeling you got from watching any lunatic. *Remember the television interviews with Charles Manson? And that videotape left by that crazy cult leader, Martin Applewhite?—that guy spoke so calmly about a spaceship behind the comet Hale-Bopp, then he and his Heaven's Gate followers poisoned themselves with a cocktail of applesauce, vodka, and Phenobarbital. People like that seem to have a strange, charismatic power because they're doing something that makes no sense to any rational person—and they believe in it utterly.*

He stepped into the living room. It was no wonder Natalie couldn't maintain cheerful thoughts. She was stuck in this same room for most of the day, and the television set was her main window to the outside. The card table filled the center of the room, and there was barely space for her to turn the wheelchair around.

They'd both be in better shape in a few weeks when she was up and around again. He couldn't remember when she'd looked forward so enthusiastically to the start of the spring term.

Jason looked at her handwritten notes spread out across the card table: three different legal pads with rolled back pages of writing, stacks of three-by-five cards, and countless loose sheets. There were only a few scattered patches where he could see the table's fake vinyl top.

One page in particular caught his eye.

He slid it out from underneath a stack of note cards. The handwriting seemed less controlled, a cursive that sprawled over the page rather than fitting neatly on the lines. Jason had once described her cursive as "regular print with the letters connected." But the writing on this page had a random flow that almost looked as if it were written by another person:

You look into the camera, intense.
A squint, and you stare at the mechanism
Of the camcorder you've discovered.

Or do you stare through the screen
Across space and time
Searching for me...

Jason dropped the page back onto the table. He couldn't bring himself to read the rest of it.

Jesus.

Natalie didn't write poetry, but that's what this looked like. A love poem to the creep in the video.

∽

SHE HAD MORE ideas the next day.

Jason worked late that evening, but Natalie worked late also. She wrote pages and pages of notes.

Beneath the heading of technology, she wrote about how television made it possible for people to be in many places at once. Distance education allowed teachers to project themselves into remote classrooms. And as digital cameras got more portable and more prevalent, nearly every moment had a chance to be captured and replayed. It could change our conception of time: every moment was potentially tangible, rather than transient.

Beneath the heading of mythology and belief, she wrote about different traditions of omniscient and omnipresent gods. She put a sinister spin on the holiday tradition of Santa Claus: "He sees you when you're sleeping..." What does it mean that we train our children to grow up under constant, ominous scrutiny?

Beneath the heading of delusion, she wrote about someone from her family, great-aunt Helen on her father's side, who was afraid to undress in front of the television: she thought the people in the set could see her. In a separate column on mass delusion, she wrote about mothmen and kidney stealers, witch hunts and ritual satanic abuse. What, she questioned, was the catalyst that could take an individual perception and bring it to life for the general populace?

THEY RELAXED AT the kitchen table after dinner. It was dark outside, so the sliding glass door worked like a mirror. With the porch light on, though, they could see partway into the snow-dusted back yard, where their reflections floated, ghost-like.

Natalie sat in one of the kitchen chairs closest to the glass door. Her wheelchair was next to her, and they used it now to hold discarded sections of the newspaper.

Jason folded around the first page of the Sports section and absently pinched the crease. "I like the newspaper better than television," he said. "You have more control, and can fold the page over if you decide not to read a story." The room had been quiet for a while, but this may not have been his best choice of words to break the silence. When Natalie earlier steered their conversation to her latest theories, he reacted quickly and told her he didn't want to talk about "that video" at the dinner table. Now, maybe she thought he'd folded *her* out of the way, like *she* was a bothersome newspaper article.

Jason looked briefly into the backyard, then looked at Natalie. He hoped she would look up and see him smile. She would know then that everything between them was fine.

Natalie did look up, but not at him. She looked at the sliding glass door. She had a transfixed expression, like that of a child who watches a television cartoon.

Jason followed her gaze.

The man was already halfway through the open sliding door. It was open only about eight inches and he was squeezing through, one arm and one leg into the apartment.

He wore the same tan jacket he wore in the video; his curly hair was stiff and unruly, just as Jason had seen it countless times before. Jason wondered why, having gotten the door part-way open, the man hadn't opened it all the way to make it easier to get inside. It was strange that Jason latched onto this detail, rather than on the terrifying coincidence

The Everywhere Man

that the man had appeared at their home. Jason also registered in the back of his mind that there wasn't enough time for the man to have opened the lock and gotten this far inside. Their backyard had been clear when he looked a brief moment earlier. No approaching footsteps were now visible in the snow on their porch.

This was the way time jerked forward in a dream, or in a badly edited movie.

Jason jumped out of his seat and ran to the opposite side of the sliding door. He pushed hard against it, trapping the man in the opening. For leverage, he pulled down the safety bar to help him push harder against the edge of the door. The man leered at Natalie, and reached for her. There was dirt, or dried blood, under his fingernails.

Jason turned his head away from the man and looked at Natalie as he continued to apply pressure on the door frame. She remained motionless in the kitchen chair, inches away from the man's groping arm.

There was a sickening crunch, like the sound of a heavy boot spiking into a chunk of hard snow. Natalie screamed. The door closed all the way.

And the man was gone. Or maybe Jason saw a faint after image, from persistence of vision—a surprised expression on a grinning face that split down the middle, then disappeared.

Jason breathed hard from the excitement. He rushed to hug Natalie, and placed his body between her and the door. He was surprised at the violence he was capable of, as if he had lost his mind in the moment of trying to save his wife.

THERE WERE MANY sightings of the man that evening. Reports came from all over the country. This time, nothing was captured on film.

The stories could not be true. He couldn't be everywhere at once. But local and national newscasters counted off the reports as they came in.

In most of the alleged appearances, the man was seen by both a targeted victim and a loved one. In all of the reports, the target had limited mobility: a woman on crutches, as in the video, or in a wheelchair; in a few rare cases, a disabled man.

Some people had died. Had the man from the video, or someone who looked like him, been the murderer in each case? Or did some unintended damage occur as a loved one became hysterical and desperate to defend the intended victim? Apparently, there was no clear evidence at any of the crime scenes. The reports were so emotional and unbelievable that it was impossible to say anything certain.

Like many couples who shared a similar encounter that evening, Jason and Natalie hugged each other as they watched the television.

Inevitably, because the different stations lacked new footage, they all rebroadcast the original video.

Natalie would swear the man's expression had changed in the footage. His smile was more sinister, and he seemed more aware of his power.

JASON OPENED HIS eyes in the dark.

He and Natalie had talked for almost two hours in bed before they tried to sleep. She admitted that her fascination for the video had gone beyond scholarly detachment. She feared it had worked like a mystical summoning, one that gave shape to her worst fears and literally brought them home.

He couldn't agree with her, even if he'd wanted to. Natalie seemed to need some simple explanation, some set of rules that tell you when the world is safe, and when it's not—like the silly expectation that monsters attacked only at night, or that witches were more dangerous on Halloween. As if you could split your day into good and bad, carve up the calendar like a pie and toss out slices that seemed rotten.

If you must blame someone (he'd said to comfort her), blame the television shows: that's the monster we've created, demand-driven and out of control. The media has to top itself, become more sensational with each new story.

"Media?" she had said. *"You're* the media." And instead of talking rationally about this impossible thing that had happened to them, to others, they fought an old fight, an academic battle that had no immediate relevance. What a hypocrite he was, she said, then pointed out how his job involved manipulating the public, creating desire and need out of nothingness, exploiting people's fears of inadequacy.

As he tried to steer the discussion in a safer direction, she became more angry. When he stayed calm, that seemed to deny her fear, to suggest that nothing had actually happened. (He didn't dare hint at skepticism, the possibility they had both suffered a dreadful hallucination). Eventually Jason resorted to a mantra: *We shouldn't fight. We need to be strong together.* There was nothing more to say.

It was a long time after that before he fell into an uneven slumber.

Now, he'd wakened in the middle of the night. Natalie was motionless next to him. She always slept on her side, turned away from him.

Jason lifted his hand to find her shoulder in the dark, but paused before he touched her.

He sensed another presence in the room.

"I am the Everywhere Man," a voice whispered. The voice had a hollow echo; it seemed as if it spoke to him, and to more than him.

The smell of the man's breath was like stale coffee. Jason could feel its awful warmth on his face.

He heard a quick gasp from Natalie's side of the bed. The horrible whisper, he knew, had been in her ear at the same time.

"Jason, help me." It was clearly Natalie's voice. But it was scratchy and distant, as if he listened to her over a bad telephone connection.

He heard the cry for help again. But this time, he was no longer certain it was Natalie's voice.

Jason lashed out at the sound with his fists.

∽

"WE HAVE TO warn you of the graphic nature of the footage you are about to see."

Jason stared blankly at the television.

A "Breaking News" banner scrolled across the bottom of the screen. The news anchor continued: "Not all details are in, but this does look to be the same man we've seen in the York Road video."

The footage played. In it, the man attacks a pregnant woman. It is worse than anyone might expect, Jason thinks, even after the news anchor's warning.

The footage will be rebroadcast later, countless times. Everywhere.

Control

HE couldn't get that subway girl out of his head. A college student, judging from the young face nested under a knit cap and multi-colored scarf, and her two male friends, one of them wearing a Terrapin jacket with the team mascot hovering beside the university name, the other boy casual in a rugby shirt, as if November wind didn't chill the world outside the tunnel. They started teasing her, the good-natured way that friends do, pushing the cap askew or untwisting the scarf and tucking one end in her coat pocket, wrapping the other around her wrist, stepping back to admire their handiwork. She smiled, a beautiful smile playing along, and a laugh too, but inaudible over the screech of a southbound train on the opposite tracks.

Barry had left work early, so the platform lacked its familiar rush-hour bustle. This was a rare, empty world: he was free to study the group of college friends, rather than jostling them aside to reach an empty seat then bringing a tightly folded newspaper to his face to shield against inevitable, inane chatter. In this calm moment, the girl was charming. She did a quick little rag doll dance, and one frilled end of her scarf rippled like streamers in a breeze. He was tempted to smile at her, then, or maybe a slight nod, but stopped himself—their age difference, for one thing, besides his not wanting to intrude. Instead, he glanced at his feet for a moment so he wouldn't appear rude.

Let them enjoy their frivolous moment in private. Perhaps some professor got sick and their Thursday afternoon class was canceled—that's why they're so happy. A pleasant scenario, as opposed to one he might imagine for later this evening on the same platform, a similar young woman frail beneath a bundled coat, and two strangers approaching from opposite sides; the empty platform is dark instead of spacious, and smiles signal a threat as surely as knives pulled from the front pocket of a hooded jacket.

He snapped out of his reverie, looked up to ensure himself nothing had changed. The girl was still happy, permitting the boy in the rugby shirt to bend up the sheepskin-lined collar of her coat. Her friend in the Terrapin jacket laughed and held his hand up as if to say, No, no, let me try—then he tugged down the brim of her knit cap, nearly covering the girl's left eye, and she kept smiling, and he grabbed one arm and bent it to rest her fist on a swiveled hip, and the boys both pointed at her new pose and laughed good-naturedly, and…

…and she was crying. Barry couldn't pinpoint the moment when things changed, but his awareness was a step ahead of the two boys, one of them reaching out to readjust her scarf and stopping only when he realized her whole body was shaking with sobs. Barry wanted to comfort the girl, but that was the role of friends—and they clearly were her friends, the way concern and confusion washed over them and they huddled close to her as she nearly collapsed to the ground, friends unaware if they'd done something wrong, or if some random thought had burst like a blood vessel in her brain.

The Terrapin boy had pulled off her cap and, nearly in tears himself, was patting her light brown hair. For Barry, it was one of those moments when he had to look away out of embarrassment, had to pretend not to notice even though it's obvious he had. Luckily the northbound train arrived; he found a crowded section, far away from the once-happy girl who did not even get on the train, her sobs growing distant as doors slid closed and the cars pulled north, other passengers pressing their faces to windows trying to figure out what tragedy had occurred.

He didn't look. He gave her a meaningless sliver of privacy.

Now, he couldn't stop thinking about her. He sat in the living room and flipped through his usual programs—Weather, Headline News, Sports Review—and even paused on some of the daytime "Judge" shows he rarely had opportunity to watch. But he couldn't concentrate on the television, instead wondering how a girl's mood could shift so thoroughly from joy to anguish. What in her life could be so traumatic? A recent death, he supposed, and her friends had helped her forget for a few stolen moments. Or past abuse laid its grimy hands on her again, a familiar touch twisted into violation.

Barry indulged the strange sensation that he had caused her distress—not by staring (he'd been discrete enough), but by imagining a violent mugging on that same platform. As if his dark thoughts could project into her mind, manipulate her mood as easily as her friends could bend her arm or drape a scarf over her wrist.

At some point the Headline News cycled to the top of the hour. The same warehouse burned again, the same soldier died and the Dow Jones dropped the same amount.

A key rattled in the front bolt, and Joan stepped into their apartment. "You're home early," she said, surprised, but neither pleased nor annoyed to see him. She shut the door, shook her hands as if to brush off the cold before taking off her coat and hanging it in the closet. He told her he hadn't been feeling well at work.

"Well, where's your water?" She stepped into the kitchen and turned on the tap. "You need to drink your water." He hadn't said what was wrong with him, but water was Joan's cure for everything from headaches to influenza. If his leg was broken, she'd tell him to drink more fluids. In Barry's case, the advice was usually legitimate: he suffered from kidney stones about once a year, and drinking more water would help flush them through his system more easily.

She stepped into the living room, recounting some workday outrage. "Those internists can be so immature, not ready to be doctors by a long shot. Though the doctors are just as bad sometimes, encouraging them by laughing." Instead of placing the water on the end table next to his chair, she pressed it into his hand, curled his fingers to match the curve of the cool, wet glass.

BARRY DIDN'T TELL her the reason he'd come home early. A little difficult to explain, really. He'd filled out the onscreen forms, as usual, but the program was behaving differently. As he moved from one record to the next, the computer didn't always display the usual prompt: "Do you want to save your changes? [Y/N]". He was on automatic pilot, perhaps. In moments of tedium life becomes an out of body experience: we let the world wash over us instead of interacting with it. Whatever the case, he gently asked Amy why the onscreen prompts had changed, why the program stopped saying "Please press [Enter]", and why it didn't always wait for his input. When Amy looked blankly at him, he told her how the computer didn't say please, it didn't say please—and maybe he shouted it a third time, pointing back towards his desk and then daring her to disagree with him.

Before he knew it, Mason's hand was on his back, leading him to his station. His boss touched him the way you touch somebody who's just lost a loved one. "Maybe you better take a break, go home and lie down or something." Mason held up Barry's sports coat and guided his arms into the sleeves.

WHAT ARE YOU doing?

His eyes asked the question, but of course Joan couldn't see him in the dark of their bedroom.

She answered him anyway. "I'm just touching you," she said.

Control

But it was more than that. Her hand had brushed over his head while he slept, smoothed the side of his cheek. Next she'd held his wrist and moved his arm under the blanket, then pulled the bedspread tight to his neck. An affectionate gesture. But he wasn't a child. Not a child needing to be tucked in.

Now he understood why the girl cried on the subway platform. Relationships were like that: you love the attention at first, smile and play along and let yourself be controlled. But at some point you lose yourself. It isn't funny anymore.

And he's in front of the television again. His hand is on the remote control. Still, the channels change without his effort, clip past the shows that used to interest him and pause on the wrong programs—spirituality, finance, cartoons and blaring snaps of commercials and music videos. He is in a large room, and others are deciding what to watch. "Damn interns," Joan says under her breath. He feels a draft as if he stands near an open vent, wearing only a gown that doesn't fasten properly in the back. He hears distant laughter. Someone grabs his arm, lifts it, bends the elbow joint and smacks his stiff hand against his forehead, posing him in a soldier's salute.

The Transfer Student

NOBODY from the English Office bothered to warn me. Midway through the first month of winter trimester, this kid shows up unannounced to my morning Composition 102 class and hands me the bottom carbon of a schedule printout. The class is already full at twenty-five students, but my name and section number are on the form, with the secretary's initials pressed through in faint purple, and an empty box marked "Instructor Approval"—as if a lowly graduate assistant has any say in the matter. This means another essay in the stack, an extra half hour of grading each week when I should be finishing my dissertation (Representations of Masculinity in Wordsworth's *The Prelude*). The kid waits, eyes down, never introducing himself except with the name, Samuel Arthur Reece, atop the yellow form. I realize I'm not his teacher: I'm the train conductor with the hole punch; I'm the flunky who tears tickets and says "Third screen on your left" to cinema patrons. I scribble my initials into the box, return the form to him, and start my class.

It's supposed to be discussion-based, but it's 8:30 a.m. and my students are always tired. I do all the work, speaking from notes I type up and practice the night before: two hours' worth for an hour-long class, since I worry I'll run out of things to say. I tell myself the notes will make it easier the next time I teach the course.

Samuel fits in pretty well with this quiet bunch, except the other students will occasionally make eye contact. Straw-colored bangs fall over his eyes, especially when he leans forward over his three-ring notebook. If he ever looks up, he must do it when my back is turned, while I'm at the board writing up character names or providing a sample outline for this week's essay.

At the end of class, I mention to Samuel that he'll need to turn in his essay on Friday, same as the rest of the class. I'm talking to the top of his head, but he seems to get the message before he stands to leave the classroom. I tell the back of his shoulders that he's welcome to visit me during office hours for extra help, an offer I extend to all my students.

They almost never take me up on it.

WHO COULD BLAME them? Our graduate student offices sit deep in the basement of Glaser Hall; visitors must locate an underlit hallway at the south end of the main floor, slide open a metal door, then follow concrete steps downward, holding the wall for guidance. I wouldn't visit my office, either, if I weren't being paid.

I should point out, "paid" is somewhat of an exaggeration. My office-mate Alicia did the math, and we make about seven percent of what an average full-time faculty member would get for teaching the same course. That is, *if* any of them would lower themselves to teaching freshman composition, a required course students resent because of the high number of essays each term…and which teachers resent for the same reason. So, graduate students get stuck with the assignment. I'd avoided the job until recently, benefitting from a long-term fellowship that carried into my dissertation year. At this stage, unfortunately, my project is apparently neither as brilliant nor as finished as my advisor had hoped. Hence my demotion to the

The Transfer Student

job officially designated as "Teaching Assistant"—although, as Alicia says, "Someday I'd like to meet the guy I've been assisting. I'm doing all his work."

Yeah, I'm doing that hypothetical guy's work too, and it's killing me. I taught 101 in the Fall, with two sections of 102 this semester—hours of new preparation, weekends and evenings surrendered to essay grading, and all for a monthly paycheck that amounts to several hundred dollars less than I received in my fellowship years. Don't even ask about my dissertation. Teaching is so all-consuming that I haven't written anything new since August. Really. Not even notes.

It makes me wonder if I'll ever finish.

Which is why I have no sympathy for a guy like Samuel Arthur Reece. Here I am knocking myself out to get through each day, and he can't summon motivation to crank out a simple two page essay—not his first week, and not the second week, either. Tomorrow, his third one's due. I mark papers down 10% for each day late, no excuses, so we both know he's headed toward an "F" for the term.

That's what I'm thinking—and honestly, I realize I've been giving more thought to this student than he's likely been giving to my course—when I look up and he's standing in my office doorway.

I barely recognize him. First, because I'm not expecting a visitor. Next, because he looks taller in the doorway than he seems in my classroom. I've grown used to seeing him from a distance: he's either tucked behind a back-row desk, or slouched over and scurrying to the exit without turning in his overdue essays.

The other reason I don't recognize him is that he's brushed his hair off his forehead. He's actually looking at me.

He knocks on the doorframe. "Professor Braddock?"

I have to correct him: I'm not a professor, since that's a title people earn after they finish their Ph.D. and get hired in a tenure-track job, and there's actually stages from Assistant- to Associate- to Full Professor. Alicia is grading papers at one of the other desks in our cramped, shared office. I can tell she's half laughing at me, but I let it go.

"Come on in, Samuel. Take a seat." I borrow a chair from Ben's desk—his office hours don't overlap with mine and Alicia's.

"I go by Arthur." He leans his backpack against the bookshelf then sits, back straight and hands cupped over his knees. "That, or Artie."

I feel bad about using the name Samuel when I call attendance, and I say as much.

"Oh, that's okay. I mean, that's my name, too."

"Fine. I go by Glen, by the way." I'm only ten years older than my students; it seems silly to insist on the formality of "Mr. Braddock."

Arthur points to the stack of half-graded papers on my desk. "I haven't finished any of mine yet. That's why I'm here. To explain. I'm not making excuses or anything, and I can't ask for special treatment. But I want to explain."

In the space of a scant minute, the kid's spoken more than in nearly three weeks of class meetings. Not just words, but the openness of his expression: a wry half-smile, eyes bright without the early morning drowsiness. I don't let him fool me, though. I'm sure he's here to negotiate his grade.

He looks past me at Alicia's corner of the room, then scrapes his chair a little closer. I expect he's going to whisper so that my officemate can't overhear, but he speaks at a normal volume. "I've always been pretty good at deadlines and stuff. No problems in high school, and I did fine in English at Chesapeake last semester. But I've been having trouble since I transferred here."

The speech has got to be rehearsed to some degree—no point visiting your teacher if you don't have some idea what you're going to say—but his delivery is natural. It has the ring of truth. And now he pauses, as if he needs my help to continue.

"Something's changed," I say as a prompt.

"Well, at Chesapeake I was living at home. Here, I'm in the dorms, and…"

"Lots of distractions," I finish for him. "More things to get in the way of work."

The Transfer Student

"Yeah." His eyes get even brighter, as if he thinks I'm some kind of mind reader. He doesn't realize: even though this is my first year of teaching, I've already heard the "adjustment to college" excuse more times than I can count.

"There's too much…" He lifts one arm and waves his hand like he's painting circles in the air. "Temptation," he says finally.

It isn't the word I was expecting. At least, not the way he says it, with (to my mind, at least) an inappropriate connotation, as if he's sharing sexual conquest stories with a frat brother. On reflection, the hand gesture, too, seems a bit suggestive—though I can't exactly pinpoint how it could be construed that way. Probably all my imagination. My face flushes, and I look away.

"I can't explain what it's like for me now," Arthur says. "I was always the reliable one. The one teachers were proud of. You know?"

Of course I know. More than I can tell him. My first year of graduate school, I was the star student. Teachers would write on my papers, "You could get this published," or, "This could be the starting point of an interesting study"—as if fishing for the honor to oversee my eventual dissertation. Each year my peers got teaching assistantships, and I got extensions on my fellowship: free money, essentially, as long as I kept impressing my professors. Turns out I did, at least in the classes. When it came time for my dissertation, I chose my favorite English Romantic poet, pitched a trendy topic to the department's most prestigious professor, and immediately got to work on the book-length study. But so far, everything I've written has fallen well short of expectations. I don't know if something's wrong with the topic, or with me.

"What are you going to do about it?" As I ask, I get a strange consciousness that this kid is on the verge of an answer for himself. Probably something simple like, *Work harder* or *Get organized.* Some epiphany about how larger tasks, broken into smaller steps, won't seem as intimidating. Waiting for his response, I forget my sense of superiority to an eighteen-year-old, forget my earlier notions about college students having simple lives, with no excuse for missed deadlines. All because I have an overwhelming sensation that *his* answer…will be *my* answer too.

His lips tighten while he concentrates. I wait.

"I don't know," he says.

And I want to laugh at myself for wanting more from him. I'm so angry I contemplate being a real asshole—the way some teachers get all puffed up, as if a missed deadline is a personal insult. Something like, *Your work is late. I'll no longer accept it. Please leave my office.*

What stops me (other than common decency) is the kid's expression. He looks helpless, like he's about ready to cry. There's fear, too—almost like he's afraid of me. Ridiculous, because I have no real power. The worst I can do is give him an "F" for the term. Next semester he'll take the same class over, and replace the failing grade. That's how things work around here.

"Life's a lot more complicated than I realized," Arthur says. "I'm having to confront things about myself."

He's struggling over what to say next, and I know I should prompt him. But for some reason, the situation's awkward for me, too.

I say nothing.

The student takes a deep breath. His head starts to drop a bit, his shoulders begin to sag—as if he wants to sit at the back of the classroom, face buried in a notebook instead of looking at me. He shakes it off, straightens up in the chair. "I'm having these images. Mental pictures. They're really disturbing."

He doesn't describe these images. I don't think it's appropriate for me to ask.

"That's why I'm having a tough time finishing those papers," he says. "It's because of what I see in my head."

He waits for me to react. Or perhaps he simply wants me to rescue him from speaking further. I maintain an interested silence.

"I guess I'm not doing such a great job of explaining," Arthur says. Then his eyes grow bright with inspiration: "You know how you think you're one kind of person? Your whole life you think this? And then,

The Transfer Student

you realize maybe you're *not* that person anymore? That's what's been happening to me. It's really disturbing."

In an instant, his predicament becomes clear. Everything makes sense—including the odd connotations I registered earlier. I know *exactly* what this kid has been going through.

And I'm sympathetic towards him, finally. I tell him he can have extra time on the papers, even provide some tips on how to write them—same advice I'd already given during class, but perhaps it gets through this time.

It's important to me that Arthur leaves my office feeling better about himself.

∽

"I ONLY WISH I'd figured it out sooner."

Alicia turns her chair slightly. She asks "What?" in a distracted way, and I'm worried she'll pretend she hasn't overheard.

"Isn't it obvious?" I repeat a few of my student's phrasings, with air quotes to emphasize *"disturbing images"* and having to *"confront things about myself."*

Alicia plays dumb. She puts the cap on her red pen, afraid the ink will dry up in the brief time she talks to me.

"The kid," I tell her. "The way he was struggling. He's trying to come out of the closet."

"Hmmm." She does this little "thinking" pose, crossing her arms over her chest. It's a teacher's strategy, pretending to consider a comment before disagreeing with it. "That's not what he said."

"Well, of course he didn't *say* it." I think back to my own difficulties in college—a quiet loner, wanting desperately to fit in, so confused about my sexuality I didn't dare name it as an issue. One of Arthur's lines really resonates with me—the one about spending your whole life thinking you're one kind of person—and I recall how tough it was for me to throw away those ideas of marriage and 2.5 children and whatever else it was that society and my parents expected from me. "He probably hasn't even admitted it to himself yet." Alicia's still skeptical, so I get exasperated and challenge her: "What *else* could it be?"

"Just about anything, really. Maybe he got drunk, or smoked pot for the first time. Maybe he had a bad dream. Or a *good* dream. Maybe he's been having all the fun college kids usually have, and it's caught up with him—and *that's* what's scaring him right now." Alicia smiles. "It's natural to read your own issues into what he was saying, I guess. But be careful not to assume anything."

I want to challenge her again. I wasn't assuming anything. Still, Alicia's been teaching for five straight years, and I always thought she had a good sixth sense about students.

It irritates me that she might be right.

I SPEND A lot of time worrying about Arthur. If I'd jumped to the wrong conclusion—putting him in my shoes, instead of vice versa—then careful, sympathetic attention should give me a better sense of what is really going on.

I've taken to moving around the classroom a bit more as I lecture. Sometimes I pace the aisles between desks, occasionally venturing as far as the back row where Arthur, his hair over his forehead and covering his eyes, slumps over his open notebook.

Images, he'd said. *Disturbing images.*

I can't seem to manage a clear view, but I realize now that Arthur doesn't take notes on my lectures. He's drawing pictures. Some of them seem like random geometric shapes, overly shaded. There's a scratchy quality to them, and they're surrounded by hatch lines—similar to those directional streaks that convey motion behind a running cartoon character.

I remember those teachers of my childhood who could act on the merest suspicion of impropriety. Kids might be passing notes and laughing, and the teacher would swoop between them and grab the offending piece of paper—read it, maybe share the contents with the class if they

The Transfer Student

were sufficiently embarrassing, then call for a parent conference that evening. If only I had a similar authority. I'd snatch Arthur's notebook before he'd any chance to protest. *What are we drawing, Mr. Reece?* The pages would make loud snaps as I riffled through them. *What is this supposed to be?* pointing to a shaded cylinder that seems alive enough to breathe. *Doesn't seem to relate to our discussion of "Politics and the English Language," does it?*

But we can't do that kind of thing to college students. They have privacy rights.

Although you'd think Arthur surrendered some of those rights when he spoke to me in my office.

I have another talk with Alicia, to get her thoughts about confidentiality issues. Is a teacher's office like a confessional? Should I cast myself in the role of a priest, forbidden to repeat a confessor's remarks unless he seems likely to inflict harm on himself or others?

She calms me down. Arthur doesn't seem like one of those kids who'd go on a shooting spree (I nod in agreement); and nothing in his words suggest that he's suicidal (True. But what if he *is* suicidal. Isn't there someone I should notify?).

"He's missed a few deadlines, and he's nervous about his grade," Alicia says. "He gives you an excuse serious enough to win your sympathy, but keeps it vague enough so you won't question him further."

"Calculated."

"Don't worry about it. I mean, keep an eye on him, like you would with any of your students. But don't get too worked up about it."

"I'll definitely keep an eye on him." I convince Alicia that her advice has helped me. I'm no longer overly concerned about Samuel Arthur Reece.

Because *concern* or *worry* aren't quite the right words anymore.

Something worse: curiosity.

Maybe he was just making up a story to fool his novice teacher. But what if he was as honest as he seemed to be? If I assume that he wasn't struggling with his sexuality, and that the images weren't the product of homicidal or suicidal impulses…what other disturbing possibilities remain?

I think about what those images might be. I think about them all the time.

OH, AND NOW he's turned in three of his essays.

THEY'RE DISAPPOINTINGLY AVERAGE. Nothing distinctive about them, but all passable. He'll likely get a "C" in my class.

As I grade them, I read between the lines. For these papers to have been so difficult to write, there should be more sweat and agony behind simple observations such as, "Young Goodman Brown doesn't know who to trust" or, "Sonnet 20 is about love and disappointment."

I follow my usual procedure. After the initial read-through of the papers, I pick up a red pen. On the first pass, I make only grammatical or diction corrections: commas inserted or deleted, unnecessary phrases crossed through or suggestions offered to replace imprecise words (teachers can usually tell what students *mean* to say, even when they don't say it effectively). My second pass, I mark the paper's content. For example, *True?* to question an inaccurate statement; or *Provide supporting examples,* if the paper needs textual quotations to develop its argument. The strategy is to get students to realize that their first drafts are never good enough. Their ideas aren't fully formed; they need to write and rewrite, to complicate their response to literature. English teachers don't just teach students how to write: we teach them how to think.

Of course, I spend extra time adding comments to Arthur's papers. He came to me for help, so I'm giving it to him. For example, I painstakingly underscore each instance where he oversimplifies the moral and social implications of Hawthorne's story. For the sonnet essay, I call attention to Arthur's naive generalizations about love, and clarify

The Transfer Student

the dramatic situation regarding the "fair youth" Shakespeare's narrator addresses. I also place the poem in the historical context of male friendship during the English Renaissance period—a rather lengthy notation which barely fits in the left margin of the second page.

Likewise, his personal experience essay gets exhaustive, detailed annotations.

When I'm done, red ink weaves in and out of the black typeface. It's late at night, and I take off my glasses to rub my eyes. In my nearsighted blur, Arthur's essays look like the drawings he produces during my lectures: geometric shapes and frantic hatch marks, a strange representation of movement. I've scraped my own marks into the shallow, ordinary typeface, exposing muscle and arteries beneath.

If I stare long enough, I think I see the pattern of those disturbing images Arthur complained about.

～

I RETURN ESSAYS at the end of Monday's class. Most of my students turn quickly to the last page to find the letter grade, ignoring my comments.

Arthur, of course, gets three essays returned instead of one. I've put his papers in the middle of the stack—not first or last, which might seem as if I've singled him out in some way. As I hand back the remaining essays, I try to judge his reaction. Does he appreciate all the effort that went into my comments? It's hard to tell, since I'm moving around the room, matching faces to names, careful not to trip over backpacks or laptop extension cords. He's leaning forward, with the attention that he usually gives to one of his drawings.

Margie G. distracts me for a moment with a question about tonight's reading. Before I realize it, most of the students have filed out of the room, including Arthur.

I find all three of his essays in the recycle bin in the hallway.

～

I SHOULD PUT this into perspective. The important thing for him was to finish the essays. My grade was what mattered, rather than the comments. I shouldn't feel bad. It's no surprise to learn he's no different from any other student.

Except he *is*.

⁓

IT'S ALWAYS AWKWARD when you run into a student outside the classroom—at the laundromat, the grocery store, the mall. Usually, as a favor to them, I pretend not to notice them.

Later this week, I notice Arthur in a side booth at Lantern House. I'm picking up my carry-out lo mein, and he's with three other friends. It's a double date, clearly, and a girl snuggles against him, her fork darting at items on his plate. They act like they've known each other a long time.

At the very least, I now know Alicia's reading was correct: he doesn't seem confused about his sexuality.

Arthur laughs, and the girl laughs too. I think he noticed me at the counter. I think he whispered something to his girlfriend about how easy it was to trick his English teacher into giving him an extension on his papers.

My face flushes. I pay the balance and stuff the change into my pocket without putting the bills in my wallet. I'm headed out the door when the cashier yells after me: "Sir! Don't forget your food!"

I go back and grab the brown bag by the stapled rim. As I turn to leave, I'm so nervous I almost drop the bag. Arthur and his girlfriend laugh again.

Walking home, I'm afraid the lo mein carton will leak and soak into the bottom of the bag, weakening it until it bursts. I support the bottom of the bag with my left hand. Through rough paper the food feels warm, like a living thing.

⁓

～ The Transfer Student ～

THERE'S ANY NUMBER of explanations for how my distraught student managed to cure himself. The most obvious would be the completion of his overdue papers: once they were turned in, the burden was lifted from his mind.

But I think it happened earlier. The visit to my office was the cure. That's when the disturbing images left him.

He passed them along to me. For weeks, while Arthur wasn't writing those simple essays, I wondered about those mental images he complained about. What visions could be terrible enough to warrant the frightened and helpless expression the boy exhibited in my office that afternoon? What visions had greeted him when he closed his eyes at night? What shadows stretched into sunlit paths, threw dark ribbons across every surface? I wondered what after-images flickered onto blank pages—needing to be crossed out, imprisoned behind hatch marks and inky swirls. As a literature scholar, that's what I've been trained to do: I get inside the minds of characters, study an author's psychology, stare at vague poetic phrasings until an elusive meaning shimmers to the surface.

And as I struggled to intuit *his* disturbing images, my imagination produced its own awful variants.

No wonder Arthur couldn't write his essays. It's worse than any nightmare, and it never ends. I've tried to take control through these journal entries, composing scattered reflections about Arthur, about myself, about what's happening to me. But the images, *my* images… they're so horrible, I can't even begin to write them down.

My best attempt is impressionistic. Take some simple idea of physical discomfort—at the dentist, for example, or some memory of childhood pain, a fingernail on a blackboard screech and then the nail snapping up like a lid, and underneath there's another nail tearing through red raw skin, tearing like a tooth growing back into inflamed gums—and you're at the dentist again, and your own teeth are the drills. Well, that's just one example, and I've only begun to hint at the worst. It's a complex recipe, and we'd all spice it differently. Add a pinch of loss or regret; sprinkle in your favorite phobia to taste.

Can you imagine?

Can you, Professor Lowrey?

OF COURSE YOU can. You trained me, after all.

Even before I gave you that brief, inadequate sample of what's been torturing me lately, you must have started to construct your own theories. That's one of your gifts, always being one step ahead of the author.

I know you're still reading, Professor Lowrey. My time in your classes, and in those shaming office conferences, gave me countless opportunities to identify the patterns of your great mind. I can't duplicate these patterns—you never ceased to remind me of that sad fact—but at least I can identify them.

The timing may not be exactly right, but I'm 99% sure these steps are in the right order. First, you pull these pages from your faculty mailbox, see my name in the upper right corner and set it aside for later that evening. Another dissertation chapter, you think—another chance to wield such demoralizing phrases as "this simply won't do, Mr. Braddock," or "perhaps you should begin again from scratch." Later that evening, you're surprised to learn it's not a dissertation chapter after all, but more like an autobiography, an extended complaint letter against the department, against *you* (How dare he!). Or…a confession.

You should stop there, but you want to see how deep a hole I dig. When you reach the narrative of my student's office visit, you might exclaim, *Why, Mr. Braddock is as inept a teacher as he is a critic!* Possibly I'm setting myself up for a negligence lawsuit, if the student attempts suicide. More likely, as my comments become increasingly obsessive, I'm venturing into sexual harassment territory.

And he's put it all on paper, the fool!

You're ticking off my errors in judgment with Arthur, then you reach my expressions of self-doubt—pleased with, to your mind, the uncanny accuracy of the observations. And you notice flaws in the writing itself: why a present tense narrative, when the story is clearly

~ The Transfer Student ~

composed in retrospect? These surface details are specks of gunpowder you can't wait to ignite during our next conference—*What were you thinking, Mr. Braddock?*—but at the back of your mind (because you can't help it), you attend to the *story,* to the dilemma of my student's disturbing mental images.

I tried not to overplay that element. If an idea's too obvious, your clever mind won't care to grasp at it. A hint here and there, and you fill in the shadows—but you attended mostly to the elements that could help you to humiliate me.

Am I right?

Like yourself, I think like an English teacher, trained to read symbolism into every object and gesture. Arthur's confession in my office represents a passing along of his burdens. I didn't deserve to have my nights disturbed by terrible dreams, my days overcome with images of agony and despair handed to me like some horrible gift. But Arthur's situation symbolizes something larger: that continual push and pull between student and mentor; the fine line between constructive criticism and the withering, malicious discouragement you practice so well.

The same moment that interpretation occurs to you—most likely somewhere in the previous section, a few paragraphs before I mention you by name—you might also wonder if there really *was* a Samuel Arthur Reece who transferred into my class a few weeks ago. You could check registration records at the office tomorrow, but it doesn't matter. What matters is what he made me think about in these pages; and, through these pages, what he made *you* think about.

I'm certain your own cruelty kept you reading, Professor Lowery, unable to resist fresh and plentiful opportunities to belittle your inferior student. While you delighted in my foolhardy confessions, these pages purged me of the most disturbing images my mind could conjure—and passed them along to a more deserving recipient. And, I'm still willing to grant, your mind is far more original and creative than my own.

As disturbing as my images were, yours are bound to be much worse.

Enjoy them as my gift.

The Thing With Feathers

HE could fly in his dreams.
His earliest memories were of flight, a graceful arc past his bedroom window, a weave through wooded trees, an easy glide in cushioned air above the school yard.

The same school yard where, during waking hours, other boys would push him aside on the soccer field or dance mockingly past him on the basketball court.

He longed to soar above this world of taunts and disappointments. Rather than play with other children during recess, he found escape in books—about the history of flight, the lives of pilots and astronauts. New dreams included his own innovation in aeronautical design, a patent that would make him rich and surround him with a throng of loyal, adoring friends.

Hope gives some substance to a child's dreams. And wasn't there a law of compensation—that a person's physical awkwardness was always balanced by an uncanny intelligence?

Not in this case. His mind was unexceptional. Just enough to imagine a better life, but without the ability, on any level, to produce it.

So each dream faded. His hand-eye coordination was barely enough to get him a driver's license, certainly not sufficient to carry him through the rigorous tests and training required for a pilot. After struggling through his freshman year, he dropped out of college—ending the fantasy of a successful career, a rich man with his own private jet and a pilot on his company's payroll. He took a job in retail.

Such was adult life: watching the dreams fall away, peeled back like flakes of sunburnt skin, scratched through to raw, weakened muscles; fat and gristle; the dry, brittle bones beneath.

Dreams peeled away like a wet label off the side of a beer bottle—a lazy diversion for a man who drinks alone, waiting for something that will never happen.

Waiting for a world where he will have grace, where his motions will be fluid and poetic.

FEATHERS WERE AVAILABLE in bulk via the Internet, priced by weight. His order arrived tightly packed: gray mallard duck feathers spilled over the top of the opened box when he punctured the vacuum-sealed bag; the hiss of escaped air brought a scent of plastic and disinfectant, with a hint of earthiness.

A separate package contained an assortment of smaller plume feathers.

He fashioned the end of one quill to make a hypodermic syringe, then added several notches above the tip. It would slide in easily, then catch like a fishhook.

He prepared all of the quills in the same way.

When he was finished, he began to press each point under his skin. Quills pierced the dermis, drilled through nerve fiber and fatty tissue. They speared the folds of a muscle; the notches hooked beneath tendons. In time, quills twined together, forming clusters.

Soon, his entire body was alive. Wind from the open window wove through his feathers and stirred the quills beneath his skin.

He became the poem. With hope of flight, he jumped.

~ The Thing With Feathers ~

~

LIKE MANY POEMS, this one is about poetry itself.

~

CLAIRE WANTED TO be a doctor, but her then-boyfriend, Lonnie Belvins, could barely face the simple dissections of high school biology. The worm already made him uneasy, a gray strand, wet and cool to the touch. Lonnie helped her pin it to the dissection board, then handed her the scalpel and took notes from Claire's dictation.

Afterwards, she teased Lonnie about how he barely looked at the opened worm. He'd held a forefinger beneath his nose to mask the smell of formaldehyde, like some delicate Victorian gentlewoman who covered her face with a perfumed kerchief while her carriage jostled through a city slum.

And hadn't they previously shared a laugh at Francie Piccolo's expense—the girl a year ahead of them whose parents had forced the school to offer equivalent dissection exercises with a plastic model or color diagram. The family raised such a stink that the story got picked up by Channel 13. Their daughter's "moral objection to this treatment of a dead animal," etc., etc. Dead animal, meaning worms and frogs, for Christ's sake. Not only that, they noticed Francie eating a hamburger in the cafeteria ("that carnivore!"). Francie didn't have a moral issue about animals—she just thought dissection was icky, and wanted to avoid the work.

Besides, there was no equivalent to an actual dissection. A diagram, no matter how detailed, wasn't the same as the rich unfolding when you peeled back the specimen layers and peered at the wonders inside. The whole point was to go *beyond* what you could read in a book or point to on a dull, predictable model—to see the actual insides of a once-living creature. As much as Claire liked to criticize their high school, with all its useless classes like gym, social studies, and "language arts," the AP science classes were one thing they did right.

She couldn't wait until next marking period, when they got to dissect a frog.

Claire was fearless then, lifting the tiny heart with tweezers, cutting open the frog's stomach to see traces of digested food. Lonnie took notes again, a passive lab partner. But he had to excuse himself from the room several times.

Lonnie seemed less impressive to her after this display of squeamishness. Their relationship ended a few weeks later.

Ironic, really, because a different animal specimen might have revealed Claire's own squeamishness.

It came out later. But not in biology class.

~

SHE NEVER DID the readings in advance. What was the point? For the novels, Claire just waited to see which parts got mentioned in class—those would be the only sections covered on the test. For a poem, Mr. Stansbury would recite the whole thing aloud, and you could follow along in the literature textbook. If you did your homework, that spoiled the surprise, making class all the more boring.

They were in the middle of a unit on Emily Dickinson, and Claire wasn't too fond of her. She was a scared little woman who wrote tiny, insignificant poems: sing-songy lines that tried to address all the "deep thoughts" that only an English teacher could love. Teachers loved her *too* much, if you asked Claire.

The treat for today was titled, "#254." Apparently, Dickinson couldn't be bothered to give her poems proper titles, so they just had numbers. The textbook listed the word "Hope" in brackets in the table of contents, but Stansbury informed them it was also an "editorial convention" to refer to Dickinson's poems by their first line.

When Stansbury reached the end of that first line, his flat, booming monotone pausing just before the final, upsetting word, Claire began to feel uneasy.

The Thing With Feathers

"Hope is the thing with…*feathers.*"

#254 ["Hope"]

Hope is the thing with feathers
That perches in the soul.
And sings the tune—without the words
And never stops at all.

And sweetest in the gale is heard;
And sore must be the storm
That could abash the little bird
That kept so many warm.

I've heard it in the chillest land,
And on the strangest sea;
Yet, never, in extremity,
It asked a crumb of me.

THEY WERE JUST words. They didn't have any power.

Poems were supposed to produce images in the reader's mind. As much as Stansbury would gush—"Do you see it? Do you *see* it?"—they'd never had that kind of influence on Claire.

But now she was getting the picture—and she couldn't shake it.

As Stansbury droned on about the poem's controlling metaphor—the inspirational idea of hope as a constant comfort, sweetly represented by a fragile but resilient bird—Claire fought back the image of something sinister.

A *thing* that perched in your *soul?*

Claire had a phobia about birds—robins, starlings, peacocks, ducks, chickens. Anything with feathers. No surprise, then, that the poem bothered her from its opening line. But the poem literally got inside her.

References to "chillest land" and "strangest sea" resembled descriptions from the awful realm of an Edgar Allan Poe story.

The "tune—without the words" brought to mind some horrific, unpronounceable chant, a summons to an unnamed demon.

Something unrelenting, inescapable ("And never stops at all").

It was inside her body. Perched in her soul.

Claire tasted bile at the back of her throat. She pushed her chair back loudly and lurched toward the front of the room, ignoring the sign-out sheet, crossing in front of the teacher (still lecturing: "Hope represents Dickinson's artistry. This poem is a small bird. Like many poems, this is a poem about poetry itself…"), rushing into the hall where she could almost breathe again.

The nausea persisted. She pushed her way into the girls' restroom, kneeled in the first stall, then vomited into the toilet. Her whole body shook as her stomach muscles spasmed. Claire felt a feverish chill when she finished, then a faint tickle grew in the back of her throat—a signal that another wave of nausea would surge upward. The tickle made her think of a feather, stuck in her esophagus. She whimpered, but her vocal cords were raw from the vomiting. The sound came out as a high-pitched squeak.

From inside her, like the whistle of a small bird.

A PHOBIA, BY definition, is an irrational fear. You cannot talk yourself out of it. Even if you have a mind that hates poetry, that prefers facts and the reproducible results of science and medicine.

For some people, a phobia appears out of nothingness—it's just there, fully formed. Other people are able to trace their phobia to a specific memory, a trigger event that originates or intensifies the fear.

Claire had three such memories:

∽ The Thing With Feathers ∽

I.

WHEN SHE WAS six years old, her family took her with them to the county fair in Gaithersburg. Claire loved the kiddie rides, especially the merry-go-round and the dolphin boats, and she wasn't too annoyed that her brother was tall enough to ride the Ferris wheel while she waited with Mom and Dad at one of the picnic benches. There was enough magic to carry her past the dull stretches: the smell of cotton candy and roasted peanuts; occasional sightings of a clown, a juggler, or a mime on stilts who teetered carefully through the crowd.

After she finished eating a corn dog ("Nature's perfect food," her father had joked), they all visited the animal exhibits. A large tent housed a petting zoo with sheep and a weird square-eyed goat. Her father lifted her so she could reach over a fence and scratch the ear of a small pony. The whole area smelled of straw and hair and manure, but Claire enjoyed it.

The next tent was a farm exhibit. Claire couldn't see much through the crowd as they approached the entrance, but she heard clucking sounds.

Then a shocking green blur passed in front of her.

"Chicken on a stick! Chicken on a stick!"

The dry, muffled voice came from beneath the felt and rubber and plastic of a chicken-head mask. The body was tall and broad, covered with green, brightly-painted feathers. Across the front, the performer wore a yellow apron with the words "CHICK'N STIX, $2.99" printed in red letters.

The giant green chicken began to dance in front of her, hopping from one foot to the other.

A rubber hand reached out to grab her arm. The fingers circled her wrist; brown talons bent back where the rubber nails mashed together. A poor imitation of a squawk rose rhythmically from behind the mask.

The chicken head leaned closer to Claire's face. A whisper came from inside it, like the sound of a man trapped behind a door. Or the sound of someone suffocating.

The chicken said: "Hi there, little girl!"

Claire heard: "Help me. Let me out."

She yanked her arm away with a high-pitched scream.

Claire looked at her brother and her parents. All three of them were laughing.

As she stepped back, two teenage boys ran at the chicken from either side, practically tackling the green monstrosity.

Had they come to her rescue?

"Mr. Chicken!" yelled the boy on the right. He had greasy, slicked-back hair and wore a Black Sabbath T-shirt and a goofy grin.

The other boy gave the chicken an exaggerated hug. "Quick, take our picture," he yelled to someone in the crowd.

"No, wait." His friend wrapped one arm around the chicken's neck. "Look at me! I'm chokin' the chicken!" There was a quick flash of light, and Claire blinked. The giant chicken pushed back from the teenager and began to sway, a drunken version of its earlier dance. Or was it little Claire who was swaying?

"You kids! What's the matter with you kids?" An older man dropped a pair of metal serving tongs and stepped from behind the nearby concession booth. He said "kids," but he directed most of his words at the boy with greasy hair. He grabbed the collar of the boy's T-shirt and pointed at the chicken. "There's a person inside there! A person!"

Of course.

Claire knew that.

But it was odd to hear someone say it.

2.

THE SUMMER AFTER her fourth grade, Claire and her brother visited their aunt and uncle's farm near the Pennsylvania border. She was excited about the two horses, and her dad promised she'd get the chance to milk a cow. The kids would stay at the farm for five days while their parents went on a brief vacation of their own.

The Thing With Feathers

Claire had met her aunt and uncle before, but only briefly at a crowded Christmas gathering. Uncle Frank had rough hands and a gentle voice. Aunt Pearl had a hearty, booming laugh, but Claire got the impression from cousin Danny that she was a bit strict as a mom.

The first day, her brother and Danny worked with Uncle Frank in the field. In a division of labor that struck even her ten-year-old mind as stereotypical, Claire stayed behind to help Aunt Pearl with the cooking.

Which might not have been so bad, except Pearl had gotten it into her head to cure her niece's bird phobia with a bit of home-spun immersion therapy.

"Come on in." Aunt Pearl held the wire gate open just wide enough for Claire to slide through. "Hurry up! We can't let any of the chickies out."

She stepped inside the coop, and Pearl fastened the gate latch behind her. Claire stomped her feet firmly on the ground, hoping the noise would scatter the chickens. Instead, they moved in random patterns, sometimes heading straight for her. She wished there was a chair or bench she could climb up on. Or better, that she could go back outside the coop and watch from a safe distance.

"Atta girl. Now, which one do you like?"

Claire didn't like any of them, so she kept quiet.

"Suit yourself," Pearl said. She picked up a thin metal rod that was stuck in the ground next to the gate. It was almost as tall as Claire; one end was bent into a small crook.

"This critter seems to like you," Pearl said. A fat white chicken with dirty black spots had paused at the girl's feet. Claire stepped back, and the chicken moved the same distance closer.

Before Claire knew it, her aunt had hooked one of the chicken's feet with the metal rod, swooped the bird up, then flipped it upside down. Pearl gathered both its feet together with her right hand, the bird's wings flapping furiously all the while, then removed the animal from the hook and speared the sharp end of the rod back into the ground.

She flattened the wings and body under her left arm, still holding onto the feet, and the chicken seemed to calm down.

"Get that metal bucket, dear, and follow me. We don't want the other chickies to see this part."

Claire swung the bucket by its handle as she walked behind her aunt on a gravel path and into the barn. On one side of the barn, opposite three empty horse stables, a thick twine noose was draped from a hook on the wall. Pearl pushed the chicken's feet through the loop, pulled it tight, then let go of the bird. It swung away from her and hit the wall with a hollow thunk. Upside down, the chicken began to cluck and wave its wings, as if it had woken from a sound sleep.

The wings disturbed the air. Claire saw flecks of dust in the bars of sunlight that shone through slats in the wooden wall. She smelled hay and sawdust and feed and sweat, mixed with a faint vanilla perfume from her aunt.

Pearl patted down the front of her overalls and pulled a pen knife from the wide pocket across her chest. "Now you'll see why I wasn't wearing my best clothes this mornin'."

She pinched the fingers of her left hand over the beak and stretched its neck away from the chicken's body. "Hold that bucket up underneath. Right there."

Claire did as she was told, using both hands to extend the bucket in front, level with her shoulders.

"It's not so bad, honey. Look away if you want."

Claire watched. Her aunt's hand flicked quickly across the chicken's neck. At first nothing seemed to happen, then she noticed a red line on the neck, followed by a gurgle of blood.

The chicken messed itself when its throat was slit. Her aunt used the edge of the knife to flick the poop off the chicken and into the bucket, which Claire held steady to catch the draining blood.

Did the slow red drip make the bucket heavier, or were Claire's arms just getting tired? Either way, she was grateful when her aunt finally took the bucket from her hands. Pearl smiled and patted her

The Thing With Feathers

niece's head, as if she had passed some kind of test. And it really hadn't been that bad—even with Claire's fear of birds, she didn't give way to panic while inside the barn. She was a spectator, able to separate herself from the task her aunt performed.

Claire didn't do as well with the second portion of the test. The "hands-on" part of the immersion therapy.

Pearl held the dead chicken over the bucket and motioned for Claire to follow her to the house. She shouldered the front door open, then asked Claire to shut it behind them before they walked to the kitchen.

Her aunt set the bucket on the counter top, draping the chicken across the bucket's lip to keep it from soaking in the blood and grime. She turned the kitchen tap to hot, and got a large saucepot from the cabinet under the sink.

Her aunt filled the pot with hot water, then submerged the chicken. "Just a few seconds," she said. "Otherwise the skin turns yellow."

Pearl lifted the chicken by its feet, then shook it over the pot to get some of the water off. "Spread that newspaper on the table, sweetie. And have a seat."

She unfolded the papers neatly while her aunt rummaged in the utility drawer. Claire sat down and tried to look attentive—her back straight, her hands on her knees—waiting for Aunt Pearl to take the seat across the table. Instead, Pearl dropped the chicken with a wet smack on the newspapers directly in front of her.

"I did the hard part already." Aunt Pearl held out a pair of needle-nose pliers. "Now it's your turn to work."

Claire stared blankly, her mouth closed in a tight line.

"The pliers," her aunt said.

She felt the rubber grips of the handles as Pearl pressed the tool into her hand.

"Makes it easier." Pearl nudged her, then nodded at the bird. "Go on. Pull 'em out."

Claire looked at the chicken. It was on its side, legs close together, wounded neck twisted so the head faced her. One eye remained open;

the other eye was closed in a drowsy wink, as if the left side of the bird had died more calmly than the right.

She wasn't sure what Aunt Pearl expected her to do.

Pearl shook her niece's shoulder from the side, as if the girl had fallen asleep. "Pull out the feathers. Don't have all day, sweetie."

Claire waved the pliers over the dead bird for a moment, then opened the tool with both hands like she was holding garden shears. She stayed as far from the dead bird as possible, pinching the tip of a spotted feather that stuck out from the wing. Claire moved the pliers slowly, and the wing stretched toward her; she raised her arms, and the wing stretched above the table. The chicken's body lifted slightly, the newspaper sticking to one side, but the feather held fast.

"No, No!" Pearl grabbed Claire's left hand and slapped it on top of the chicken. "You gotta hold it down. Dig in, girlie!"

She shivered at the unexpected texture of the dead bird. The feathers were soft along the edges, but stiff in the middle like the bristles of a hairbrush. The bird was wet and warm—not at all like the cold, packaged meat she'd seen in their kitchen at home. The warmth reminded her the chicken had recently been alive.

At her aunt's urging, she tugged and twisted with the closed pliers. Even with her left hand holding it down, the whole body of the chicken shook from the movement. The chicken's head bounced three times off the table before she finally worked the single feather loose.

There were hundreds of feathers all over the bird—an impossible task. And as much as the chicken scared her, she was even more bothered at the thought of how unnatural it would look once the feathers were all plucked away.

She pushed back from the table and tried to stand, but she felt her aunt's hand firm on her left shoulder, anchoring her to the chair. "On the farm, we all contribute. The boys are out in the field with your Uncle Frank, and we're fixing the dinner."

Claire started to cry.

The Thing With Feathers

"Now, no time for that," her aunt said. "Hot water loosens the feathers, but it doesn't last. The slower you take, the harder it's gonna be."

And that was true. Claire had trouble with the first feathers, having to twist and pull, but it grew even more difficult with time. The feathers began to hold fast, as if something gripped them from the other side. Claire recalled the time she accidently bent back a piece of her own fingernail—that awful, against-the-grain tearing; the sharp pain where the nail hinged into the red pulp of flesh along the cuticle.

She tried to move faster, each tug more violent than the last, her vision blurring from tears. The chicken's head thumped and its talons scratched at the newspaper as she moved the body around. The wet, musty feather smell stuck to her fingers, an earthy gore she could actually taste in the back of her throat.

Although the pile of plucked feathers next to the bird got taller, the bird's body was still covered with plumage. It seemed like the job would never end. Claire cried and said "I can't, I can't," but her aunt's firm hand pinned her to the chair.

Finally, with the feathers thinned and the chicken half-plucked, her aunt took pity on her and excused her to wash up at the big sink. Claire scrubbed her hands with the scratchy bar of soap, then rubbed in some of Pearl's vanilla-scented lotion to mask the smell of the dead bird. While the water ran, she kept spitting into the sink.

During dinner, seated with the "men folk" at that same table, she pushed food sullenly around her plate. Aunt Pearl told everyone that Claire had helped with the preparation. She lied and said Claire plucked the chicken easily, all by herself. "She's a strong little girl," her aunt said, then winked at her, like it was their secret.

~

"YOU'RE STILL SCARED of birds, aren't you?" her brother asked that night, and she wouldn't answer him. Not in front of Danny, since the three of them were crowded into the same bedroom. The boys had sleeping bags on the floor, and Claire got to use Danny's bed—which her cousin may have resented, just a little.

In the middle of the night, Claire's hands were sore, as if someone pinched them tightly over and over.

She had fallen asleep on her side with her hands folded together near her face. Her cousin had brought a duck into the bedroom. While she slept, the boys had poured bread crumbs over her hands.

3.

AND THE HIGH school incident with the Emily Dickinson poem.

DURING HER FIRST month as a family practitioner, Dr. Claire Morland sent away two boys who brought a stray cat into the waiting area. The animal had been in a fight, one ear torn and bloody, and a large scrape along its right hind leg. Her receptionist looked at Claire as if she were heartless: "Couldn't you make a quick splint for the leg, at least?"

Through the glass door at the front of the office, Claire saw the two kids sitting outside on the curb. The blond boy held the cat in his arms and rubbed its neck gently. His friend looked down at the cat, and occasionally turned a pleading expression to the receptionist. "You may think this is something a small town doctor should do, Amie. But this office is for sick people. We can't expose them to unclean animals."

Amie waved at the empty waiting area. "I don't think our current patients would mind."

"Call the vet for them if you want. Or one of the parents. But they're not coming back in here."

Claire had to be firm. It wouldn't harm her reputation as a doctor to be fastidious about cleanliness—certainly not as damaging as a

The Thing With Feathers

terrified reaction to the next well-meaning child, if he brought in a pet parakeet or a rescued fledgling.

That was four years ago. Claire had set the right tone with Amie, and there hadn't been any problems since.

She survived college the same way, controlling the variables wherever she could. The worst obstacle in her Pre-Med curriculum was a required course in animal physiology. Claire finally felt some sympathy for silly Francie Piccolo: she found herself wishing for a plastic model instead of the wet, cold, ruffled thing she accepted with gloved hands from her professor. She forced herself—this one time, this one time—and managed to get through enough to pass the assignment, before excusing herself from the biology lab.

After she graduated, Claire attended University of Michigan, one of many medical schools in the U.S. that did not use animal dissections in their training—no great loss, since in her opinion animal anatomy didn't really teach how to treat human patients.

And now, in her personal life, she avoided long-term relationships. If people got too close, they started making demands, suggesting romantic walks through the park where an overhead flap of wings, a musical chirp carried in the wind, or a sudden rustle of feathers would be enough to trigger a small panic—rapid breaths, quickened heartbeat, cold sweat along the back of her neck and on the tops of her hands.

We cannot choose what frightens us. Claustrophobia, for example, would be much easier: learn to leave a room when it gets crowded; take the stairs if the building's elevator is too small. But birds could show up at any moment.

Claire's phobia conscripted her life, and she could not imagine a future where that world might expand. Her medical practice was in a one-story office complex in the same town where she grew up. The complex had once been a strip mall, but the shops went out of business shortly after the attached supermarket closed. A large stretch of parking lot surrounded the professional offices—no shade trees in sight, no forked branches to cradle nests or invite random perching. Claire's space ("Physician's Parking") was right in front.

She would drive even for short distances, her life a series of tense movements from one protected space to another.

IT STARTED AS a typical evening at work. Claire stayed late, dictating notes about the day's patients, and stacking folders atop Amie's chair as she finished with each one. She paced the waiting area as she spoke into the tape machine. Sometimes she paused to check her scribbled notations on a chart, tilting an opened folder downward to catch the last bit of natural light through the glass storefront of the office.

A shadow fell across the page, a dark cloud blocking the sun.

The thump against the door almost made her drop the stack of folders.

Before she turned, Claire subconsciously analyzed her memory of the shadow. She had thought of a cloud, because the shape couldn't be human. Not quite. More like the strange approximation of a human form that a child might notice in a cloud: the same general shape, but ghosting on the edges; whorls and bumps where they shouldn't be, spoiling the figure's outline.

And there, framed in the doorway, backlit by the setting rays of the summer sun:

A large shape, red and dark brown, with tufts of dirty white and black and gray curling outward in unnatural yet strangely purposeful patterns.

A man, puffed out and distorted.

At first Claire thought he was wearing a heavy winter coat, out of season—that he had been in a car accident, and the coat had shredded with him through a windshield, tearing and mixing with flaps of his skin, feather-down insulation bursting through the cloth and matting to his torso.

But the puffed distortion affected his entire body, not just the torso. He looked like a man who had fallen from a great height into a pile of feathers, the impact pressing them into his skin. Blood would have sealed the feathers to him, working like hot tar in the infamous lynching technique of olden times.

The man weakly lifted an arm to drop it against the door, a wet thump followed by a smear and squeak against the glass.

He wanted her to let him inside.

This fear that haunted her life, now literalized on her doorstep.

The thing with feathers.

I.

HER HEART RACED, nervous sweat began to build, and she felt the tremors and uneven breaths that accompanied her usual panic. This man, whatever happened to him, now embodied her worst fears, gave them a horrible shape.

He had come to her office, of all places. The door was bolted, the object of her fears safely locked on the other side—but she could *see* him through the glass.

Claire knew she should call 911—leave him to the paramedics and the emergency room. She should run screaming in the opposite direction. But Claire's life-long efforts to control her phobia seemed to culminate in this moment. There was something awful and inevitable about his appearance here: a horrible destiny that she couldn't escape.

She exhaled loudly, and noticed that her next breaths fell into a normal rhythm.

Claire would help him. That is what doctors do.

She set her folders and voice recorder on a nearby end table, then unlatched the door.

The man lumbered into the dimly lit waiting area. He walked like the victim of severe sunburn, his legs spread wide and arms bent down at right angles to keep his limbs from brushing against each other. Claire attempted a clinical, emotionless glance at the man's warm, raw body. He was naked, covered only by layers of blood and feathers.

She couldn't bring herself to touch him—not from fear or revulsion, surprisingly, but because there was no surface on his body that wouldn't be sensitive to pain. Claire motioned him to the hallway behind the receptionist's desk, the examination room on the right, waving her arm to encourage his slow movements.

Then his hand shot out and grabbed her arm. The fingers locked around Claire's wrist, feathers scratching her. She stifled a gasp. There was desperation in his grip—like the hand of a dying man urging a visitor not to leave his bedside.

She understood: he expected her to guide him. His hand had found her wrist in a swift clarity, but his eyesight was obscured, lids swollen into a squint through the gauze of feathers and dried blood, flares of pain bursting across his field of vision.

Claire walked slightly ahead of him, urging him forward until they stepped inside the examination room.

After a few clicks and flashes, fluorescent light hummed steadily over clean white countertops, steel instruments, and the cool olive vinyl of the raised examination table. In this new light, her visitor left the shadowy realm of nightmare, his colors brightening into a shocking parody of a cartoon character. Dried blood brought rich brown highlights to the feathers. Fresh wounds supplied a bright glaze: blotches of red reflected off medical instruments, mirrored in the distorting curve of a glass jar or the wedged blade of sanitized scissors.

Claire now realized the feathers were not stuck to the surface of the man's body. Their quills reached under his skin. Deliberate. Like a costume.

She could barely locate his eyes beneath the feathered mask of gore. Swollen lips parted slightly. His hand, still tight on her wrist, squeezed with the two whispered syllables:

"Help me."

~ The Thing With Feathers ~

Claire recalled the suffocated voice from her childhood visit to the county fair.

She thought also of her training, the insistence that she remember each patient is a living being, not just a statistic or example of disease, not merely a nameless challenge to her medical skills.

A reminder in her head: *There's a person inside there.*

2.

CLAIRE UNROLLED A fresh strip of sanitized white paper and draped it down the center of the padded examination table. The wax coating crinkled beneath him as he lay back.

She put on a fresh pair of latex gloves. She decided to test one of the feathers on his arm. She tugged the feather gently, but it held fast. His arm lifted off the table as she pulled—like the wing of the chicken on her aunt's kitchen table. The man made no sound, not even a moan of pain. She read encouragement in his eyes, and continued.

Claire held the arm down on the table with her left hand, pinching the quill where it emerged from his skin. With her right hand, she gathered the feather and tried to jostle it loose, working it back and forth. She was a gardener, uprooting a stubborn weed.

The feather finally tore free with a wet scratch. She looked at the quill and noticed how it had been sharpened and notched. The feather was specifically prepared to hook itself beneath his skin, to tangle with neighboring quills and form an interlocking mesh—a web of agonizing sensations.

She looked into his eyes, and she knew he had done it to himself.

Claire now realized why he did not cry out. It wasn't that he was in stunned shock, or that his body had produced natural endorphins to numb his pain. No: He had made a choice, and he wanted to be fully aware of what he had done.

As she worked on him, Claire saw his past despair, his striving for something miraculous. She sensed his hope for the release of flight: the determined preparations; the excruciating, meticulous insertions. She imagined his leap of faith, then the awful disappointment when he fell to the ground.

She considered what tall building might be nearby, what cliff or highway embankment. How could he have walked here without being seen and stopped?

Claire kept working. After a while the quills broke through the latex of her gloves, so she removed them. Her touch became more direct, more intimate.

Blood soaked through, weakening the firmness of the wax paper beneath him. Random bristles tore at the wet paper. The quills and plucking had done the same thing to him, tearing his skin easily.

It was a job she would finish this time—not half-done, not done through tears.

3.

FATE HAD BROUGHT him to her, a sacrifice to cleanse her of her phobia. A perfect antidote: loosening each feather, unthreading it and pulling it from his body, Claire felt her own fears unravel.

She was a student again. She learned from him, as the best doctors learn to listen, to feel and understand each patient's pain. A perfect empathy, as if his soul opened up to her.

It occurred to her that he must have read the Emily Dickinson poem, had intended to recreate it. Maybe he was even in Claire's high school class, years ago, when she'd been so weak and had run from the room.

"What's your name?" Claire asked. "Do I know you?"

No response. His eyes were still.

Her miracle, her thing with feathers, had died.

Now there were practical issues: what to do with the man's remains, whether or not to search for relatives or friends, what story to tell the police. As grateful as she was to be cured of her phobia, Claire felt empty and uncertain. Perhaps she could find some way to pay tribute to his life, to the amazing thing he had done, to their rich, shared flight of agony.

A ring of pulled feathers surrounded him on the table. The rest of the feathers had spilled over, covering the floor. The man's body was red and raw. He looked like he had been turned inside out.

As if she'd torn him open, searching for something.

And Claire thought of another lesson from a long-ago English class, this time from her study of classical literature. She recalled the term "augury"—the ancient art of divining the future from examining the entrails of a sacrificed bird.

Claire gazed into his body, and read her future there.

Four Legs in the Morning

(A Dr. Sibley Curiosity)

FRESH air lured him from the musty interior of Dr. Sibley's cabin, and Leonard's bare feet tested the dry half-circle of dirt outside the porchless doorway. "There's plumbing and electricity," Sibley had told him, "but you'll have to bring your own comforts, I'm afraid." Leonard interpreted comfort as a coffee maker and a stockpile of vacuum-sealed bricks of caffeine—food supplies and warm clothing were almost an afterthought, so naturally he hadn't bothered to pack bedroom slippers. If he was lucky, heat from the metal carafe in his hand might eventually work its way down; in the meantime, he curled his toes and favored the outside arch of his feet to minimize contact with cold, hard ground.

This would be an academic's idea of "roughing it": no distractions from television or telephone. He brought his laptop, but would do most of his work the old-fashioned way, with notes on index cards, and chapters scratched in long-hand on stacks of legal pads. Sibley approved: that was how *he'd* written *his* textbook on Greek tragedy. A single book, not one that would merit tenure in the current market, but with good, close readings of Sophocles' plays. Critics at the time praised Sibley's depiction of classical performance: outdoor amphitheaters, choric dancers, stone masks over the actors' faces. Pretty standard historical background, actually, but influential enough in 1956 to establish Sibley's reputation. Even today, you couldn't write about the Oedipus trilogy and not cite Bennet Sibley.

Dr. Sibley. Leonard's department chair at Graysonville University. As a mentor, Sibley couldn't really provide helpful advice: he was too out-of-touch with recent scholarly trends. But he had the cabin, and generously offered it to Leonard for the full month between semesters. Enough time, Leonard hoped, to kick-start ideas for his second book. As a new member to the Graysonville faculty, he needed to make a strong impression.

He sipped his coffee, bracing against the January wind. Caffeine was his muse. He would linger with her a while in the chill outdoors, then retreat to the warm cabin, to his boxes of books and notecards, to pages of half-formed ideas he'd spread last night over a folding card table. Although he briefly considered driving into town for more supplies—surely there was *some*thing vital he'd forgotten?—Leonard resisted. He had to focus on his project. That's why he was here. And that's why he'd stepped outside without shoes, without his down-filled jacket: so he wouldn't be tempted to wander away from the cabin on a lengthy mission that was nine parts avoidance to one part exploration.

He didn't *need* to explore the area around the cabin. He needed to work.

Look at the text, Sibley had advised. *All the answers you need are in the text.* Easy for him to say. In 1956, critics didn't have to worry about new historicism, feminist or queer theory, structuralism and post-structuralism, and all the backlash against (and redefinition of) these same critical approaches.

Unconsciously, either from irritation or to keep warm, Leonard started to pace. He stayed next to the cabin, avoiding the stone-step path to the carport, and the line of grass and rocks and sticks that beckoned to surrounding woods. The cool dirt beneath his feet was

Four Legs in the Morning

packed tight, smooth as asphalt but with occasional bumps of buried stone or tree root. When he stopped pacing, Leonard backed one heel against a broken branch that was thick as a roll of pennies.

He barely brushed over it, expecting to roll the branch with his heel. Instead, he crushed the segment flat.

Startled, Leonard nearly lost his balance. Was it hollow? Rotted through? A sliver of bark stuck to his bare heel; without looking, he scratched it out with his fingernail.

He set his empty carafe on the ground and kneeled to examine the flattened branch. The bark was as thin as paper. The patterns along the segment seemed more fauna than flora. Hard to trace after he'd crushed the hollow cylinder, but it seemed like a repeating geometric design of dark lines and inscribed ovals. Beneath the design were faint ridges, like the whorl of fingerprints.

Probably, this was a segment of snakeskin. How did that work, exactly? The snake wriggled out of the sleeve of its old skin, emerged shiny and fresh—didn't it? Well, he was no expert on reptiles, wasn't certain what species were common to this region. Venomous or non-venomous? Either way, he hoped the skin's former resident had slithered far away by now.

Leonard peeled up the empty skin—brittle, like a piece of overcooked bacon—and brought it inside. He shut the door behind him, checked the seal between the door and the frame. Then he made a nervous sweep of the cabin's four rooms, looking under furniture, behind appliances, inside closets.

THE CABIN OFFERED no resources to help alleviate his uneasiness as the day progressed. No Internet access, no phone, and no books on Sibley's shelf titled *Deadly Snakes of Northeast Alabama*. As he sat in the main room of the cabin, several times he caught himself peering beneath the table to check his feet—now in socks and shoes, thank you, although he wished his pants were more snug at the cuffs. He considered fastening them closed above his ankles with rubber bands.

Again, the temptation to ride into town. He could stop at the General Store, maybe find some out-of-work locals huddled in a warm booth at the Gas 'n Dine. He'd show them his strip of bacon, get advice from old coots who'd survived wars and the depression, had hiked through years of Alabama woods, dodging snakes along dark paths. But, for all Leonard knew, his skin sample really *was* bacon—and how silly he'd feel, then.

The worst thing for an academic was to look like a fool. He'd take the risk of his silence.

Better to concentrate on his book. He'd chosen a creative deconstructionist approach—a mode of criticism mostly out-of-favor since the early nineties (and thus, Leonard gambled, due for a trendy comeback). At the very least, a deconstructionist approach would help him make original claims about an ancient, over-examined play. The idea was to take *Oedipus Rex* apart, ask questions that tore at the perfect fabric critics had admired since Aristotle's day.

Sacrilege! Bennet Sibley exclaimed when Leonard first mentioned the project. *You don't need fancy critical approaches.* Sophocles *will teach you how to read Sophocles.*

Sibley had too much respect for the text. It limited him.

The play was based on a riddle. Why not treat the play itself as if it needed a new solution?

He'd transcribed the famous Riddle of the Sphinx on the first sheet of a fresh legal pad: *What walks on four legs in the morning, two legs in the afternoon, and three legs in the evening?* The equally famous solution is "Man," since he crawls on all fours as a baby, walks upright as an adult, and needs the assistance of a cane in later years. But Leonard had scribbled notes over the page to ridicule the accepted answer. *Two arms aren't two legs! A cane is not a leg!*

Sophocles didn't invent the riddle, doesn't quote it within his play. But it's crucial back-story, the reason Oedipus fills the newly vacant seat as King of Thebes. And yet, why praise a man for solving an unfair

Four Legs in the Morning

riddle? Rather, grieve for the guiltless heroes before him, who stood their turn before a feather-breasted monster, half eagle and half lion, and tried to shape an honest answer to the Sphinx's trickery. What might these men have guessed, in days when such she-monsters could besiege a town? Did some say "Chimera," their voices rising in a fearful squeak? Perhaps some others made up an animal, in Seuss- or Swift-like fashion: "A bumble-glumph," or "Hurgle-whynn." Others, soiling themselves with fear, could have blurted out a desperate, hopelessly wrong answer: "A frog?" "A donkey?" Or maybe a few of them proposed the only reasonable response: "There's no creature in this world that fits your description."

The answers don't matter. The Sphinx kills them all.

When Oedipus offers his solution, it's over-elegant: an analogy of life-span to time-of-day, tucked inside other substitutions of *crawl* for *walk*, *cane* for *leg*. Legend asks us to believe the Sphinx is so upset by Oedipus's attack on her riddle—her monstrous sense of self so tied to that impossible one-question quiz show—that she immediately commits suicide.

Would that all monsters were this sensitive to criticism.

These were Leonard's whimsical musings, yet they supported his thesis about the classical unities of time, place, and action. In his argument, these rules actually weakened our ability to appreciate Sophocles's play. All those important moments from the past, all those bits of violence banished tastefully off-stage and reported by a weeping messenger—if these scenes were represented somehow, in a radical re-staging of *Oedipus Rex*, the audience would have an entirely new understanding of the central character. The usual interpretation presented Oedipus as an intelligent, well-meaning king (he saved the city from the Sphinx!), undermined by his tragic flaw (pride and impulsiveness... and that unfortunate accidentally-killing-his-father-and-sleeping-with-his-mother scandal). In Leonard's view, Oedipus's tragic flaw is not an exception to an otherwise noble life. Oedipus *is* his tragic flaw.

Abandon the classical unities. Imagine a production of *Oedipus Rex* where the Sphinx towers over the stage of Thebes, appearing in gruesome flashback when summoned by the Chorus. Or, as Oedipus recollects possibly the world's first instance of "road rage," show onstage his disproportionate reaction as he beats a man to death at a crossroads, simply because the apparent stranger (his father) refused to grant him right-of-way.

Perhaps such a staging would be impossible: too costly, too violent or inappropriate, a logistical nightmare. But his book could do the same work. A chapter for each of the unrepresented scenes, envisioned in a creative section, followed by serious critical commentary. The book would be controversial and attention-getting. Did it matter if the interpretations were "correct"?

Blasphemy! Sibley would say. *Greek theatre is like magic. There are specific rules you must follow, or the spell is broken.*

Well, he was planning to break a lot of spells. By the time Leonard was finished, Sibley would likely regret allowing him use of the cabin.

LEONARD WORKED THROUGH the day, mostly brainstorming and outlining, and the ideas came almost faster than he could write. The shift to handwriting rather than typing seemed to open new floodgates. He devoted a separate legal pad to each chapter; in different ink colors, he drew arrows from one idea to the next, spread new thoughts into margins or pinched them in tiny print between previously written lines. It was a strange and welcome reverie, his vague fear of snakes easily forgotten.

He nearly forgot lunch, too. At three o'clock he fixed a quick sandwich, smearing peanut butter on bread using a thick handled steak knife he discovered in a kitchen drawer. Then he worked past the winter day's early sundown, his pen scratches accompanied by the steady rumble of the generator that kept the cabin warm and lighted.

The generator sat in the utility closet on the other side of the small kitchen. Propane-fueled, it produced a noise similar to the rhythmic

Four Legs in the Morning

rattle of an old-fashioned film projector. Leonard fancied himself in a movie: the scholar, hunched over a table, frenzied in the formative stages of his most brilliant work.

Then the film jumped out of the sprockets. At least, that's what it sounded like: a metallic screech from the generator, like something got jammed in the mechanism. Leonard rushed to the utility closet out of instinct. The generator was his life-line, and if it broke down he'd have to return home—just as he was getting started, after his most-productive day in recent memory.

He threw open the closet door, and the generator rumbled even louder. This close, the sound was overwhelming. The machine shuddered as if trying to shake itself into pieces. Not that he understood the equipment, but Leonard studied the beige and copper engine, and all the screws and bolts and belts seemed in their proper places. The rumble was loud and steady, with no trace of the scrape and screech he'd heard from the main room.

Or, perhaps a slight screech, like an undercurrent. Maybe in the mechanism—maybe more distant, outside the cabin, an animal's awful cry of pain.

~

LEONARD HAD SLEPT well the previous night, exhausted after the drive up I-20, then side-turns down country roads into twisting, barely marked, gravel and dirt lanes to Sibley's cabin. He'd thrown fresh linens over the cot's thin mattress, fluffed his own pillow over the lumpy one Sibley had left behind, and dropped into calm slumber.

Tonight was different. The day's mental activity refused to abate; ideas tumbled through his head in time with the spinning gears and belts of the straining generator. The two bedrooms were each equipped with a working fireplace, but they were too much trouble to get started. He'd pulled the cot into the main room, where he could huddle close to the wall-mounted electric heater. As a result, he literally couldn't get away from the day's work: it loomed near his bedside, spread overtop the card table.

Now that the glow of inspiration had faded, Leonard began to worry that his day's work wasn't as good as he'd thought. Was he a victim of that dreaded malady Sibley called "Scholar's Delusion"? Even in Leonard's young career, he'd seen his share of the afflicted. Most recently, a colleague had grown so wrapped up in study of a minor 19th-century poet, that he convinced himself she was the greatest writer who ever lived. *Honestly,* Don had said to him in all seriousness, *I prefer Felicia Hemans's poetry to Wordsworth's.*

Had Leonard fallen into a similar trap of self-deception? His department chair would probably agree. Bennet Sibley's skeptical countenance floated before him in the dark, a bearded Tiresias eager to express the most awful prophesy of failure. *You're welcome to use my cabin, but…Why would you want to write that kind of criticism? Why would anyone want to read it?*

No, no, he had to remind himself. Forget Sibley and his outdated, reverent respect for the text. He wasn't writing to please Sibley. Indeed, he'd spent too much of his life trying to please people whom he didn't respect. The same problem plagued his romantic and family entanglements—which largely explained why he was free to spend an entire month alone in a secluded cabin.

Leonard wrote for a more sophisticated audience, one fully aware that drama was a living organism, no longer the author's property. You can't appreciate a text by ignoring its flaws. Oedipus's story relies on ridiculous coincidence: that a man should flee his adopted father, only to cross paths with the father of his blood; that a she-Sphinx kills each challenger, until one man twists out a solution to her torturous riddle; that a land should need a king, and one walks in. The drama finds its convenience in uncanny chance.

These were the kinds of observations liable to give Sibley a heart attack. But that's what the play was all about, wasn't it—the younger generation taking the place of the old? Harold Bloom said the same thing about writers in *Anxiety of Influence:* to make their reputations, authors had to reshape the works of their predecessors—kill the fathers of literary tradition, so to speak. The theory should hold equally true in the cutthroat world of academic tenure and promotion. Someday, stodgy old Sibley would have to retire as Chair of the English Department; in his place, Leonard would encourage the inventive scholarship and teaching Sibley hoped to suppress.

The film projector continued to rattle from the utility closet. Leonard's thoughts threaded through the sprockets: some projected a grandiose, satisfying future; others cast "Father" Sibley's vision of doom. He pictured the man's rich, fuzzy beard, with its neat convex shape—as if half a gray tennis ball were glued over Sibley's chin. And Leonard knew his thoughts had gone loopy now, from the day's excitement and subsequent lack of sleep. Sibley typically would rub his bearded chin with one fingertip as he conjured phrases—no insult intended, nothing more than observations, really—but phrases that might undermine a young teacher's confidence. If the old man had magical powers, they were centered in that weird tuft of beard. Push aside those stiff, overcombed hairs, and from behind would wink his third eye, the source of his prophetic insight.

These were Leonard's last semi-lucid thoughts before sleep finally overtook him. He was unable to rouse himself from bed in early morning, when faint cries again seemed to rise above steady mechanical thrums. He was on a train that passed between strange villages. The shades were drawn against the sunrise. In the fields, small animals lifted their heads in a shrill chorus, high-pitched yet also guttural, as if they gargled food, or they were being strangled.

SLIGHTLY AFTER NOON, Leonard staggered outside with his coffee. Thick clouds masked the sun, a diffuse gray light breaking through. Another abandoned fragment of skin lay, hollow and fragile, on the patch of ground fronting the cabin door. It was not a snake skin.

He kneeled on the ground to get a closer look. The same repeating design of lines and ovals around the circumference, the same ridges faint beneath, the texture of fingerprints. He hadn't crushed this specimen with his heel, so the cylindrical shape was preserved. It swelled thicker on one end, and bent at a right angle directly in the middle of the hollow tube. In size and shape, with a brown-bark dead-leaf color, it looked like a broken cigar.

The smaller opening was frayed in tiny strips; they curled like paper at the end of an exploded firecracker. Leonard brushed the side of his forefinger against the frayed edge, then pulled his hand away in surprise. The tiny strips were sharp, like pincers.

Without thinking, he pressed his finger to his lips, then bit down slightly where he'd been scratched.

Maybe he really should drive into town, find somebody who could tell him what the heck this thing was.

Then that animal cry again, familiar from last night, and from this morning's hypnogogic daze. He had trouble judging direction, here in new surroundings and with sound waves echoing off the perimeter of trees. But the noise seemed to come from the other side of the cabin.

This morning, his exit from bed had been more leisurely. He'd put on shoes and dressed for the day. The air was brisk, but not as chilly as yesterday. He could walk for a short while. Go exploring.

~

HE DIDN'T FIND any strange animals. But he found something equally strange.

Some evergreens grew close to the back of the cabin, giving the building year-long shade on that side. Past the edge of the woods, most of the trees were bare. Leonard found the obvious foot path, and followed it. A few yards in, the path sloped into a steep drop. Through thin, leafless branches, Leonard could easily distinguish a clearing far, far below.

At the center of the clearing sat an impossible, full-scale replica of a Greek amphitheatre.

Hidden out here? In the middle of nowhere?

Four Legs in the Morning

Leonard had to see it up close. He followed the path, keeping the outdoor theatre in sight. He felt dizzy after a moment, and soon realized the cause. It was a trick of perspective. The clearing wasn't as far below as it seemed, and the amphitheatre wasn't a full-sized model.

Once he corrected his erroneous impression, it took little time to reach the small clearing. He stood with his hands on his hips, an unlikely Gulliver. The amphitheatre was made out of stone blocks, as the originals had been, but they were set in a round cement foundation—about the size of a large dinner table. A rectangular stage occupied one ground-level section, with all the appropriate elements: the *parados,* aisles where choric singers entered from the sides; the flat *orchestra* area where dancers would perform between scenes; and the *skene,* the building that formed the backdrop to the stage, with three doors in place for the main actors' entrances and exits. The *theatron* itself, where the audience sat, fanned out from the orchestra area in rising cement steps, forming the main bulk of the structure.

Some people might lay down cement to build a barbeque area next to their wooded cabin. But Sibley, he built himself a miniature amphitheatre. From the looks of it, the model was old—showing some chipped decay, to echo the modern-day ruins of the real theatres in Greece. Leonard guessed it dated back to the fifties, from when Sibley was writing his one and only book.

He wondered if Sibley's wife ever accompanied him to the cabin. She might have sat there and watched him, knitting while her husband envisioned a miniature Oedipus or Creon or Iocaste pacing the puppet-sized stage; or pictured the *deus ex machina* contraption lowered from the top of the skene replica, like a tiny God from a tiny heaven.

Nothing currently perched on the roof of this skene—no serpent-drawn chariot for Medea to ride, no cut-outs of the sun for Apollo, the lightning bolt for Zeus. But the detail on the small building was remarkable. Faded paint over the rough concrete simulated the brick-pattern of a royal palace. Thin rectangular panels along the top border glowed with faint gold inlays. The three doors along the front of the skene looked like weather-worn wood, rather than concrete. They each had a small hook-latch on the front, as if they were actually functional doors.

Were they? Leonard bent toward the left-most door and tapped it with a knuckle. The answering sound was a wooden thunk.

He tried the latch. The rusty hook was stuck in the eyelet, and needed to be forced before it would lift. The door itself, in contrast, swung outward with little protest. Inside, the model skene was hollow and mostly dark.

Leonard put his mouth near the opening, shouted "Hello" to amuse himself.

No answer, which was just as well. He remembered the shrill cry he'd tried to follow, and cautioned himself not to upset some animal's nest.

Even the day's dim light was enough to reveal that, luckily, the inside of this tiny bunker was uninhabited. The building's floor was a continuation of the cement base, with a faint layer of undisturbed dirt overtop.

Maybe it was okay to try another door. Number two, in the center. He placed one foot inside the model, planting it on the flat circle of the orchestra stage. He rested his elbow on his knee while he reached toward the second hinge. This latch flipped up easily, and he pulled the door open.

A shape of lumped fabric lay inside the middle doorway. A dark-blue, flannel rag. It didn't seem like an article of clothing—there was no pattern to the cloth, no seams or pockets or buttons. Leonard brought his other leg into the dipped center of the amphitheatre, then lowered his Gulliver-giant rear onto the jagged slope of the theatron seats. Holding his hands to each side for leverage, he eased the tip of his right shoe into the doorway, giving the cloth lump a gentle nudge.

No animal growl or hiss, thank goodness. Only a slight clacking sound. It seemed safe enough to investigate further.

Four Legs in the Morning

It turned out to be a small cloth sack, cinched at the top with a threaded rope of yellow yarn. In earlier days, the yarn might have appeared golden.

He lifted it from underneath with one hand. The sack rattled, as if it were filled with tiny bones. He tugged at the yarn, and the soft flannel opened at the mouth of the sack. Again, a clacking rattle as the contents shifted over his supporting hand.

Leonard was disappointed by the contents. Empty walnut shells. Roughly two dozen, at first glance.

Then he looked more closely. The split shells had tiny markings on the surface. Colors. Carved furrows. Threads and faded tinsel.

They were masks. Half-masks for the chorus, full-face ovals for the main characters. Leonard picked up one of them: a miniature comic mask, the smile painted in a delicate red curl, pin-hole eyes drilled in careful symmetry above a natural nose-like ridge in the shell. The craftsmanship was amazing.

He lifted another from the sack. This one was clearly a tragic mask, mouth twisted in an agonized black line, a spiked tin-foil crown attached askew atop the head. Wisps of red thread were glued beneath blinded eye sockets, simulating blood. The shell had a thin elastic band looped around the back, as if to hold the mask on a tiny head.

On a whim, Leonard set down the bag and slid the Oedipus mask over his right thumb. He wiggled the thumb, and the small face shook on its new perch; from the motion, red threads waved faintly in the air, fresh blood streaming from the doomed king's empty eyes.

AFTER THE STRANGE discovery, Leonard accomplished little else that day. He'd spent some time admiring the skill that produced those small masks, many with painstaking details that helped him easily identify the characters: Antigone, her expression firm in quiet defiance of the king's law; Creon, face ablaze with self-righteous anger. Although the masks obviously had been designed to fit dolls or marionettes, Leonard found no such puppets in the hollow skene replica; a cursory search of the cabin similarly turned up nothing.

As much as he appreciated the meticulous artistry of those masks, the oddness of the project unsettled him. Similarly skilled fingers assembled ridiculous "ship in a bottle" models, popular with old men in a previous generation. Those ship models eventually became so common that they lost much of their charm. Something dusty and pointless, earning a curious glance then low bids (if any) at an estate auction. The people who built these ships were eccentric retired men with too much time on their hands.

Sibley had invented his own peculiar pastime, without the calming association of shared practitioners. A twisted version of an old man's hobby—but Sibley, obsessed with classical texts, would have been an old soul before his time. This state of mind surely explained his lifelong resistance to new ideas.

The man's headstrong resistance had seemed annoying to Leonard, maybe slightly affected or quaint. But now he wondered if his former teacher hadn't long ago left quaint behind, and crossed into more disturbing territory. Mrs. Sibley had passed on in the early 90s, yet the Doctor still spent summer months in his isolated cabin. Supposedly he was working on his second book, but that was decades overdue; when asked, he declined to state a title or clarify the topic. Looking for the marionettes earlier, Leonard had uncovered no evidence of scholarly work: no textbooks or journals or scribbled notes.

What did he do all summer: act out the plays with his walnut-shell masks, recreating his own festival of Dionysus at his miniature amphitheatre? Leonard considered the building where he'd found the masks, the roof of the skene from which a god could descend to resolve the play. In *Herakles*, the spirit of madness scratches at the roof, breaks through and forces its way into the hero's mind. Perhaps something similar had happened to Sibley.

Four Legs in the Morning

Phrases from Sibley's book gained new meaning. (But were they from his book? Or simply those expressions he repeated in class, in the faculty room? The sources tended to blur.) *Greek theater is like magic. The unities cast a kind of spell.*

And all that emphasis on masks. *The actors wore masks. They conveyed no emotion through their faces—it was all in the words themselves.* Sibley's face was expressionless whenever he said this.

Leonard tried to push these troubling thoughts away and work on his book, but ended up doing little more than pushing his notepads in new arrangements across the card table. Doubts overshadowed the productivity of his first day at the cabin: doubts about his own project, and doubts about the sanity of Bennet Sibley.

Which affected his sleep again that night. How frustrating to waste the day, then lie awake knowing that, without rest, the next day could follow the same frustrated pattern. A mechanical screech from the generator closet compounded the problem. Leonard was too exhausted to investigate, and the worrisome machine seemed to wail loudest when he teetered on the edge of sleep, startling him awake.

Sometime in the night, he must have gotten up to turn off the generator. The wailing mostly stopped, but the room grew cold. Leonard huddled under borrowed blankets, and another sound circled the dry dirt outside the cabin—a sound the generator's hum must have obscured the other two nights. It was something like footsteps. *Two small feet have a predictable rhythm,* he thought. *Three is two with an extra sound. Click click thump. Click click thump.*

◆

HE'D KICKED THE blankets away during the night, and the sweatshirt and sweatpants weren't enough to keep him warm. He lay in the fetal position, his arms hugged tight to his chest. Leonard wasn't sure he'd gotten any sleep. Certainly, he was awake earlier than he should be: only a faint morning light, and his battery clock indicating twenty minutes after six.

And that howl. That howl that was *not* the generator. A gargling, choking sound, like a human infant needing to vomit, but too young to know how.

Outside the cabin.

Leonard unfolded himself from the bed, stumbled in stocking feet to the door, then opened it in a quick motion to catch whatever was making that awful sound.

When he saw it, Leonard was unable to step closer. He held onto the doorframe for support, clenched the wood for a reminder of something solid and familiar.

The creature stood near the far edge of the dirt porch. It was about a foot tall, covered with scales like a lizard, but with a hard insect back. Its head was the size of a walnut; wire-like bristles sprouted out the top, approximating the appearance of human hair. Impossibly, the creature stood upright. A third leg, thicker than the other two, looked as if it had burst through the creature's neck, distorting its guttural growls. Flaps of skin, like the suckers of a lamprey, twisted and agitated against the throat-end of the leg. The howling sound whistled over these flaps, a wet and frantic wail.

As Leonard watched in horror, the third leg began to swing back and forth. The lamprey-flaps pushed and scraped until the skin of this thick digit began to slough off. The leg bent and wiggled, and the casing of skin slipped to the ground. The creature howled again through the opening in its throat, a faint hiss from its mouth joining the awful cry. As it screamed, the raw limb began to tear itself down the middle. Two newly formed legs stretched in opposite directions, then the creature's body shifted, and the new legs lowered to the ground. It walked on four legs in the morning.

What was it?

Bumble-glumph, Leonard thought. *Hurgle-whynn.*

No.

The creature studied him, its eyes black in a pruned and scaled face that expressed a terrible malice.

Four Legs in the Morning

Leonard backed into the cabin and slammed the door. He flicked the latch to hold it closed, noticing now that it was a similar hook-and-eyelet contraption to the three doors at Sibley's miniature amphitheatre. Next he heard a gallop of four legs, two of them untested and shuffling in the dirt. A hard crack hit the bottom of the door, as if a golf ball had been rolled into it. The wood shook beneath his hand. He heard a quick chittering sound, then the creature scrambled away.

Thank God. The thing was some weird hybrid, a chimera. Leonard's late-night musings seemed less preposterous after such evidence. Perhaps Sibley was some kind of magician after all, his studies of ancient texts uncovering dark secrets other scholars overlooked or avoided out of fear. Sibley had summoned this creature somehow—or he'd had some hand in its making, as surely as he'd crafted those bizarre, tiny masks that would fit perfectly over the creature's head. Leonard imagined this had been Sibley's real project all these years: not a second book, but a quest for new, literal truth in the Riddle of the Sphinx. A creature that transformed each day, its two front legs withering away to an upright noon, then a new thick leg tearing through the throat as evening fell. At night the throat would swell around a leg that choked each awkward step. By early morning this leg would itch and wriggle itself into agony: Leonard thought of his own hand, if the webbing between the middle and ring fingers were stretched until it split, then the palm ripped raw, the whole arm torn up the middle. And cursed to suffer this same metamorphosis each day? No wonder the creature howled. No wonder it looked so angry.

As if it blamed Leonard for its pain.

He heard the howl again: the throat gurgle and the hiss combined. A similar cry answered from the right side of the cabin. Then two distinct calls from the left.

Leonard slid to a seated position, his back supporting the door. Tiny feet scuffed in the dirt, the leader's gallop more steady. A patter joined from the sides, like rain, then a series of hail-stone cracks battered against the bottom of the door. Leonard's lower back jolted with each strike.

He couldn't hold this door forever. He wondered about other entrances. In the kitchen, the window was up high, over the sink; but in the main room of the cabin, the sill was a scant two feet above the floor. Those legs—the two back legs, constant through all the transformations, their muscles strengthened over time…How high might these creatures be able to jump?

A weapon would help ease his mind, and Leonard recalled the steak knife he'd used for yesterday's meals. He saw the wooden handle along the edge of the kitchen counter, knew he could retrieve the weapon in a few quick seconds. But he was too afraid to leave the front door unguarded.

The chittering noise grew louder, then the scuffle of retreat before a renewed assault. In that instant, Leonard realized he'd neglected the early part of Oedipus's story. King Laius learns that his son will grow up to murder him. To circumvent the prophesy, he instructs a servant to abandon the infant in an isolated place, where he would surely die.

In this formulation, Sibley hadn't loaned the cabin to Leonard out of kindness, but to remove a threat from the new generation of scholars. He struggled to remember Sibley's exact phrasing. *You're welcome to use my cabin. But I'm afraid no one will ever read that book.*

More patter of small feet in distant dirt, getting louder.

The words of these plays are like magic. They cast a spell.

Leonard concentrated, even as the feet grew closer, the steps more numerous. A word appeared to him, in Greek letters, but somehow beyond pronunciation. The letters enveloped him, out of focus. If he could grasp the letters, speak the word…

The creatures' heads battered against the lower door. The latch rattled with each hit, and he knew that soon either the wood would splinter, or the hook would jiggle out of the eyelet. To drown out the fearful sound Leonard covered his ears and shouted that strange word.

The spell. The name. The true answer to the riddle.

Four Legs in the Morning

The door ceased to move against his back. Leonard dropped his hands from his ears, and heard nothing. The creatures were silent. No chittering. No shuffles in the dirt as they moved away.

He stood up, then rushed to retrieve the steak knife from the kitchen counter. Dry clumps of peanut butter stuck to parts of the serrated edge, but the tip was sharp and the heavy wooden handle offered some comfort as Leonard returned to the windowless door. He wasn't ready to open it, yet he was certain the creatures had disappeared. They were banished once their name was spoken, the Riddle of the Sphinx solved after all these centuries. Leonard had accomplished something where Sibley, where even the mighty Oedipus, had failed.

Beneath that pride, Leonard worried he might have seen too much. The mask of his face must have held its expression, the curious look he'd worn all weekend, brow furrowed in the perpetual pose of a scholar's inquiry.

A rush of wind blasted through the silence, like the flap of large wings over the cabin. A hideous shriek sent tremors through the walls; the floor shook beneath his feet.

The old story was wrong. She wasn't suicidal: she was angry.

He clutched the knife's handle, certain that the Sphinx was ready to pose a new riddle, one he'd never be able to answer. Heavy talons scraped along the roof. Leonard felt the temptation of an itch behind each eye.

Invisible Fences

THERE'S an invention for today's dog owners called an invisible fence. It's basically a radio signal around the perimeter of the yard, and if the dog steps too close to the signal, it triggers a device in the animal's collar and delivers a small electrical shock. Perfect Pavlov conditioning, just like I learned back in ninth grade psychology class. But it seems a bit cruel to me. The dog's bound to be zapped a few times before it catches on. Dogs aren't always as quick as we are. Hell, growing up we had a mongrel lab that would probably never have figured it out: Atlas would have barked at air, then -zap!-. Another bark and charge then -zap!- again. I loved that sweet, dumb animal.

Still, I guess for most dogs the gadget would work eventually. Inflict a little pain and terror at the start, and then you're forever spared the eyesore of a chain-link fence around your front lawn.

"The Big Street"

WHEN I WAS growing up, my parents invented their own kind of invisible fence for me and my sister. All parents build some version of this fence—never talk to strangers, keep close to home after sundown, that kind of thing. But my parents had a gift with words and storytelling that zapped those lessons into my young mind with a special permanence.

My father taught Shop—excuse me, Industrial Arts—at Kensington High School, so I guess that's where he built up his skills with the cautionary tale: don't feed your hand into the disc sander, keep your un-goggled eyes away from the jigsaw blade, and other Greatest Hits. But listen to his rendition of that old stand-by, "The Big Street":

He walked me and my sister Pam to the divided road on the north end of our community. I was six, and Pam was three years older. He stopped us at the curb of McNeil Road, just close enough where we could hear the cars zip by, feel the hot wind of exhaust or maybe get hit by a stray speck of gravel tossed up by a rear wheel. A half-mile down, on the other side of McNeil, was a small shopping center: a single screen movie theater, Safeway grocery, People's Drugs, and a Dairy Queen, among other highlights. In the other direction visible from the top of this hill was Strathmore Park, with swings, monkey bars, and a fiberglass spider with bent-ladder legs. We could visit these wondrous places anytime Dad drove us there, but we were never, ever, to cross the Big Street on our own.

"Now, let me tell you about a boy who used to live the other side of the road," our father said. "About your age, Nathan. He crossed back and forth over this Big Street all the time." Dad swung his arm in front of him, parallel to the road. "Looks like a pretty good view of the road in both directions, doesn't it?"

We both craned our necks and followed the swing of his arm. Pam nodded first, and I did the same.

"Well, you'd be wrong. Some of those cars come up faster than you think." As if to confirm his point, a blue truck rattled past. "When you do something a lot, you get pretty confident. Over-confident. This boy, he'd run across early that morning without a hitch, like usual. On his way back, he was standing right where we are now. Looked both ways,

Invisible Fences

I imagine, or maybe he forgot that one time—we don't know for sure. What we *do* know..."

Dad dropped to one knee, the toe of his right sneaker perfectly aligned with the edge of the curb.

"See right there, where the gutter doesn't quite match the road? Not too close, now, Nathan." He stretched his arm out like a guardrail, and I leaned against it to peer over. The blacktop of the road had a rounded edge, about an inch higher than the cement gutter, but the asphalt was cracked or split in a few places. One spot, it looked almost like somebody'd taken a bite out of it. I guessed that was where Dad wanted me to look.

"His foot likely got caught in that niche, and the boy tripped into the road. The black van might have been speeding, might not. But it wasn't entirely the driver's fault, was it?"

I swallowed hard, my throat dry. I'd have loved a Misty or a dip cone from Dairy Queen, but I sure didn't plan on crossing the Big Street to get it.

"See that dark patch in the road?"

I leaned forward again, and my T-shirt felt sweaty where my chest pressed against Dad's outstretched arm.

"County trucks cleaned things up, best they could, but you can't always wash away every trace of blood."

A shadowy stain appeared beneath the rumbled flashes of painted steel, chrome, glass, and rubber tires, a stain wet and blacker than the gray-black asphalt, in which I could almost distinguish the outline of a boy, just my size.

∞

"I'D HEARD THE story before," Pam told me that afternoon. We had separate bedrooms in our small house on Bel Pre Court—a luxury a lot of our friends didn't enjoy—but I was in and out of my sister's room all the time. She even let me use the bottom shelf of her bookcase to store a few Matchbox cars, a robot, and a plastic astronaut.

"Really? Did you know the kid who got hit?"

"No, I heard it before from *Dad*. Two years ago."

Pam had fanned baseball cards in front of her on the bedspread. She'd invented this game of solitaire: traded players, constructed her own all-star teams, grouped them in batting orders, then shuffled the cards to start again. Often she waited long minutes between each shift of card, as if the game required intense, chess-like concentration. She never could quite explain the rules to me, but I didn't mind: I wasn't that keen on sports like Pam was, and I was happy she still managed to talk with me while she played.

"The kid wouldn't need to cross the road," Pam said.

"Huh?"

"All the good stuff's already on his side. Movie theater, playground, burgers and ice cream. Why cross?"

I hadn't thought about that. "Maybe he had friends over here."

"Nope. The friends would all be visiting his side, where the fun stuff is. They'd be the ones who got whacked by the *black van*."

She said "black van" in a sing-song voice. I didn't understand why she'd make a joke, go so far as to imagine more kids killed while crossing McNeil Road.

"I saw the stain on the road," I said.

Pam switched two baseball cards, then flipped another one face down. "Probably a car broke down on the side of the road, leaked a little oil. Check our own driveway, and you'll find a few stains there, too."

"Not like that stain," I said.

"Okay."

"He showed us where it happened, Pam."

"Okay."

Pam had pretty much destroyed our father's story with logic. She was three years older, obviously a little more worldly than I was. But I don't think I was naive to side with my dad. More than logic, it was the *story* that convinced me. The confirming details of the cracks in the asphalt, the boy-shaped stain on the road, summer's heat and the rushing cars making me dizzy—just like must have happened to the careless young pedestrian in Dad's account. Maybe it wasn't true, okay, but it could be true if somebody didn't follow the rules. Accidents happen. We may not all have friends who've chopped off a digit or two with the buzz-saw in Industrial Arts class, but if a couple circles of red marker on the shop tile, scrubbed into faded realism after hours, help the teacher point the next day and shout, "There! There's where the fingers rolled off and bounced like link sausages onto the floor!"—well, strictly true or not, such lessons are worth learning.

No way was I going to cross the Big Street on my own.

"Dope Fiends"

THE NEXT SUMMER, Mom staked a claim to her own span of our invisible fence. Dad came up with most of the stories, so in retrospect I'm grudgingly proud of Mom for thinking this one up.

A deep stretch of woods formed a natural barrier behind our house. Dad had a few gems about kids getting lost, bitten by snakes, or swollen and itchy from a patch of poison ivy—all of which generally kept us from setting up camp in there. We wandered into the woods sometimes, peeling bark off trees, flipping logs to look for ants or pill bugs, poking a stick at a rock to make sure it's not a bullfrog. As long as we didn't go near Stillwater Creek, we didn't get in trouble. The creek had its own persuasive power: it was muddy, shallow, and stank of sulfur, so Pam and I steered clear without being prompted.

But Mom, overcautious, decided we shouldn't venture into the woods at *all*. One rainy day, she called us into the living room where she typically sprawled out on the sofa and watched her "plays" on CBS. "Turn down the television, would you? I've got something serious to talk with you kids about."

With the rain outside, and the shades pulled down, the living room was pretty dark. The main light source was the television, which reflected a kind of campfire glow on Mom's face as she talked. "There are dope fiends in the woods," she told us. "I heard about them from Mrs. Lieberman."

~

I HAVE TO explain a few things about my Mom before I go any further.

When I was three years old, my baby sister was born. I remember playing with her, in particular a game where Pam and I lined up plastic bowling pins around the rim of Jamie's crib. She'd wait for us to finish, then knock them over with her tiny fists, and laugh and laugh. That's mostly what I remember, the laughing.

Jamie had to go to the hospital when she was about fourteen months old, after a really bad cough developed into something more serious. Apparently they put her in a croup tent, a plastic covering that kept away germs and allowed doctors to regulate her oxygen. I never visited her in the hospital, but my parents later told me how much Jamie hated that tent. I imagined her beating at the plastic covering with her fists, but too weak to laugh or even breathe.

I don't remember what my parents said the last night they returned from the hospital. I know they must have agonized over how they'd break the news to us, my Dad no doubt holding back his natural tendency towards the grisly, giving us the soft version of Jamie drifting painlessly off to sleep and never waking up; how babies were innocent and always went to heaven, so she's with God now, and we'll always have our memories; Mom convincing us that *we're* all right, that *we'd* never get that sick, and Mommy and Daddy would always be there to protect us, and nobody's dying, not anytime soon that's for sure, we promise; and all the time both of them trying not to cry themselves, knowing if they messed this moment up it could haunt me or Pam for the rest of our lives.

I know they worked really hard on what to say, and I'm sad I don't remember any of it. But I was only four, and memory keeps its own protective agenda for a child that age. Just the bowling pins, and the laughter.

～ Invisible Fences ～

There's a Polaroid of me and Pam taken the day of Jamie's funeral. Pam's in a frilly peach dress, holding a small bouquet of daffodils. I'm wearing a tan suit—a handsome little gentleman, in a heart-breakingly tiny clip-on tie. We're standing next to the grave marker, which has a hole in the center where Pam will soon place the daffodils. According to my father, before Pam had the chance to fit the stems into the grave marker, I kneeled down to peer deeply into the hole. "Jamie's down there," I said, then waved. "Hi, Jamie!"

BUT I WAS talking about my mother.

After Jamie's death, not right away, but gradually, my Mom became more and more withdrawn. She didn't have a job, and never learned to drive, but she used to go shopping with my father, or went with us on day trips to visit relatives in Silver Spring or Tacoma Park. She also maintained a small garden out front, and played bridge twice a week with neighboring housewives. After the tragedy, she told Dad she didn't feel like talking with family about Jamie, not for a while at least, and somehow that ended her drives to the grocery store, as well. The bridge games slipped to once a week, and then just the gardening. And then not even that.

Agoraphobia roughly translates to "fear of open spaces," but that's not exactly right. It's a kind of depression that, in my mother's case, at least, was more about avoiding interaction with other people. Dad and Pam and I were the notable exceptions. She didn't want to see anyone else, and she didn't want anybody else looking in—which explained why she lowered the living room shades, even during the middle of the day. Eventually she refused to leave the house for any reason—certainly not for the psychiatrist visits that probably would have helped her, if people hadn't frowned so much on therapy in those days, or if my Dad had been strong enough to force her into treatment. His version of "strong" was letting her have her way, adding cooking and cleaning to his breadwinning duties, with Mom on occasional assist with the child care when absolutely necessary.

But more often than not, it was us kids doing things for her. Mom spent most of her time on that sofa, to the point that it's hard for me to recall her in motion. Certainly she must have moved from the bedroom to the living room on occasion, definitely needed to use the bathroom like the rest of us. But mostly things were brought to her: a cup of water with ice and a bendable straw; Diet Rite Cola in the tall glass bottle; two peanut butter and banana sandwiches for lunch, the crust removed; and a small plate of Oreo cookies with a mug of milk for her afternoon snack. She had a remote for the television, but mostly watched the soaps and local news on channel 9, and if either Pam or I were passing nearby when she wanted to switch, she'd have us turn the channel.

Mom's other entertainment was newspapers, with a special fondness for the crossword puzzle and the Word Jumble. She stored the day's puzzle folded over like a napkin on her TV tray, next to a plate of food, and worked during the commercials or during an especially slow-moving plot on *As the World Turns* or *The Edge of Night*. Some days she didn't finish the puzzles, or didn't skim her way through the rest of the newspaper sections. Stacks of newspaper piled next to her beside the sofa, beneath the TV tray, and at her feet. Mom could never keep straight which stack was the most current, so when Pam asked for today's Sports page or I wanted to read the comics, we each had to choose a pile to sort through.

Dad taught summer courses. Even between terms he went to school on a nine-to-four schedule, and used their shop equipment for woodworking projects he solicited via purple, mimeographed ads stapled to telephone poles throughout our neighborhood. All for the extra money, of course, but just as likely because the day-dark house bothered him in ways it wouldn't bother little kids who didn't know much better.

At least, not usually. But that overcast, rainy day when Mom told us about the dope fiends, the bleak, shadowy living room gave her words the chilly certainty of a midnight-whispered campfire ghost story.

Invisible Fences

"THE POLICE FOUND needles in the woods," Mom said. We stood next to the couch and Mom sat up, a striking change from her usual horizontal posture. "Just thrown on the ground where kids like you could step on them in your bare feet. They found rubber tubing, also. These dope fiends tie tubes around their arm to make the veins stand out, then use the needles to inject drugs into their bloodstream." She lifted her crossword-puzzle pencil and mimed jabbing it into her forearm.

Due to my twice-yearly doctor visits, I was already plenty scared of needles. I never escaped without some vaccination or another—for German measles, smallpox, tetanus, whatever. After losing Jamie, Mom wasn't taking chances with me or Pam. I hated the awful tension when the nurse squirted a faint arc of fluid over the sink before she plunged the stinging needle beneath my rolled-up sleeve. The needle was too long and thin; I worried it could snap off inside my arm and hurt forever.

The idea of tying a tube around your arm sounded complex and painful to me. Who would do something like this on purpose?

Fiends, of course. A much better word than "addict" for kids. The word addict scares adults, because it's all about loss of control—our fears that we'd drink or gamble or screw against logic, throw money we don't have into greedily programmed machines or wake up late mornings with a monstrous hangover and an even more monstrous bedroom companion. Kids don't fear addiction (they don't have much control over anything to begin with). Better for them to visualize some tangible bogeyman, like the monster *under* the bed or evil trolls who live beneath storybook bridges.

"I know you kids would never be foolish enough to try drugs," my mother continued. "But if you run across a group of dope fiends, they may force their drugs on you. Chase you down, and whoosh!" She jabbed her pencil in the air towards Pam for emphasis, then towards me; I jumped back in nervous reaction.

"The police haven't caught any of the dope fiends yet, so they're still out there." She pointed at her main sources of information: the television, in its rare moment of flickering silence; disorganized towers of newsprint; and the end table telephone, her daily link in epic half-hour conversations with her two remaining friends, Mrs. Lieberman and my Aunt Lora. "If I hear anything more, I'll let you know. Until then, I want you both to stay out of those woods."

I nodded first, without waiting to see Pam's response.

This was before a president's wife told us to "Just Say 'No'," before "Your Brain" sizzled sunny-side-up in an MTV frying pan. But even then, in the post-hippie 1970s, drugs were dialed pretty high on a kid's panic-meter. I was too young to grasp the concept fully, of course, and stirred my own fears into the mixture. When my mother mentioned the "paraphernalia" found in the woods—hypodermic syringes, rubber tubes, empty glass vials of medicine—she may have said something about medicine caps. Or maybe the "dope" idea was suggestive enough. My third grade mind somehow latched onto caps, conflated it with the image of a cartoon child in the corner of a schoolroom, a pointed dunce or dope cap rising from his head. I imagined predatory older boys donning these caps as the proud symbol of their gang. They patrolled the woods behind our house, seeking new initiates—would toss syringes like darts at your exposed arms or neck, then would force you to the ground and press their ignorance into you, lowering it like a shameful cap onto your struggling head.

Ignorance was even more terrifying to me than needles. I was a slightly overweight boy, uncoordinated at sports and generally unpopular at school. To be stupid—to be unattractive and awkward and picked-on *and* stupid—was the worst fate I could imagine. Smart was all I had.

AND YET I was stupid enough, later that summer, to let Aaron Lieberman and my sister talk me into visiting those woods to search for abandoned needles.

Sunday Morning

THE AGONIZING STRETCH between 10 am and noon every Sunday morning was without doubt the most mind-numbingly boring interval of my childhood.

Dad preferred not to go to church alone. With Mom's stubborn agoraphobia, that left me and Pam as potential company. Neither of us liked church: the wooden pews were uncomfortable, and the monotonous Catholic mass lacked for us the religious significance our father so evidently derived from it. Worst of all, the final service of the day was a 12:15 "folk mass" at Saint Catherine's, that church's desperate attempt at "hip"—as if bad singing and silly acoustic guitar arrangements were enough to spark young people's faith. The folk mass was the one Pam and I usually got stuck with, if we ended up going at all.

Here was the odd thing about Dad and church: he wouldn't drag us out of bed and make us go. I guess he thought we should practice religion willingly, or it wouldn't be meaningful. If we were up and around, though, he'd ask us to get ready for the next scheduled mass, and in that trapped interchange, neither Pam nor I would have the heart to say we'd rather stay home. The only sure church-avoidance strategy, which Pam and I developed independently and practiced with varying success, was to make yourself sleep past noon.

Seemed easy enough. We'd stay up as late as we could on Saturday night, watching horror movies introduced by Count Gore de Vol on Channel 20, or switching to Ghost Host with the snowy reception of Baltimore's Channel 45. No matter if the creature feature lacked a creature—like that Japanese mushroom-people flick with no Godzilla to stomp the cast into oblivion, or the "old house" mysteries from the 40s where foolish people ran from room to ghost-less room. Sometimes the films portioned out a few decent scares between the "Hair Club for Men" commercials, enough to distract us while we waited for the night to become our own. We watched television in the den, on the other side of the kitchen from Mom's living room. During the first feature, Mom disappeared to join Dad in their bedroom (did we ever see her go? At some point we'd look past the kitchen doorway to the other end of the house, her couch empty against the far wall). To extend the night past Ghost Host's nonsensical farewell ("Here's blood in your eye!"), we'd play a game of Life, steering blue- and pink-pin families in plastic cars over plastic hills or, even better, Monopoly—the full version, not the quick cheats with dealt-out properties or "Free Parking" windfalls. The longer we stayed up, the easier it would be to sleep late on Sunday morning.

In theory. I could usually drowse past the departure time for the 10 a.m. mass, easy, but eventually I'd hear Dad fixing himself breakfast in the kitchen, the murmur of Sunday news programs from the living room. With a hopeful stretch I'd grab my metal-band watch from its place around the bedpost, certain it was nearly noon, and see the phosphorous hour hand aimed squarely between the ones in eleven. No matter how hard I tried, I couldn't get back to sleep: I'd toss and turn, check the watch again, distinguish a few stray words or commercial jingles from Mom's TV, rearrange my pillow, check the watch again (only 11:15!), and, defeated, resign myself to a hard wooden seat and the latest strummed arrangement of "The Lord's Prayer."

Seems silly now, all that effort. Church itself couldn't be any more tedious than those endless minutes of feigned sleep. But even in summer, when every day was free of school and schedule, I still fought to avoid that single hour in church. Maybe it was a competition with Pam (who "won" more mornings than I could count, Dad and I leaving for church without her). Maybe it was an early instance of childhood rebellion, a passive battle against a father I loved but subconsciously blamed for my mother's infirmity. Whatever the case, those hard-won mornings where I did sleep long enough were sweet victories. The day was mine: a quick slip into fresh underwear and yesterday's shirt and blue jeans, and I'd escape into noon-day sun with the whole world open to my explorations.

Within the accepted boundaries, of course.

~ Invisible Fences ~

ATLAS HAD WRAPPED his rope around the tree in our front lawn again. He panted against the trunk, collar stretched tight and his water bowl temptingly out of reach.

"Retard," I said, and the dog barked in agreement. I pointed to his left, made a "go 'round!" motion with my hand, but all he did was twist his head, brown ears flopping stupidly.

"C'mon, boy. I'll show you." I walked counter-clockwise around the tree, and Atlas followed me. If I stopped, Atlas would have stopped too, not grasping the concept of the wrapped leash. I had to go all the way around for each of the six twists.

The ground remained spongy beneath my feet. Dad had tied Atlas's leash to the porch banister, since the wooden spike wouldn't stand firm in the lawn. We'd had a week of off-and-on heavy storms, thunder and loud downpours that rattled like gravel tossed against the windows and aluminum siding. Mom watched the televised weather reports from the safety of her sofa. "You wouldn't catch me outside in that mess," she said more than once.

July 18, 1971. That Sunday morning's victory over church and time and weather was cause for a special celebration—maybe even a little mischief.

I heard the screen door screech open and bang shut. "Wasn't sure I'd make it this morning," Pam said, then she bounced down the three cement steps. "I had to fold one end of the pillow over my eyes to block the sunlight."

She picked up a gray tennis ball, muddy and matted with dog drool. "Ready, dummy?" She moved the ball back and forth; Atlas followed the motion, as if shaking his head in the negative. "How about now?" This time, with Pam moving the ball up and down, Atlas nodded "yes."

No matter how dumb the dog, you can teach it a trick or two. You just have to figure out the right kinds of tricks.

"Here," Pam said, and she tossed the tennis ball straight up into the leafy oak. Atlas stood under the tree and barked as the ball bounced slowly down, ricocheting from limb to limb. It took an unexpected hop before the last drop, but Atlas caught the ball in his mouth after the second soggy bounce.

"Your turn," Pam told me.

I didn't much care for this next part. Atlas was a gentle dog, not at all intimidating. He wouldn't give up a toy easily, though. Pam and Dad both liked to grab a ball or rag or bone in Atlas's mouth and try to pry it free, tugging and making fake growling noises to taunt answering growls from Atlas—deep yet playful, almost a parody of canine anger. His lips snarled up over the gums, yellow teeth gleaming large and slick. Atlas was a big dumb dog, but he was Atlas, so I wasn't scared he'd bite me. But big dumb dog mouths produce a lot of drool: I didn't want that smelly, slimy stuff on my hands.

Pam was watching, though, so I went through the motions. I pinched the ball between the tips of my finger and thumb, tried to tease it out gently, but Atlas nudged his wet nose into my palm then shook his head back and forth, slobbering on the inside of my hand. With my other hand, I tried to pinch his jaw at the hinge; Atlas opened his mouth, the ball shifted, then Atlas clamped down on it again. I tried a tighter grip on the ball, my pinky rubbing against the dog's slimy tongue, and I felt the jaw start to slacken. The instant I pulled the tennis ball free, Atlas let loose a head-shaking, lawn-sprinkler-style sneeze.

"Yuck," I said while Pam laughed. "You can have your nasty tennis ball." I dropped the ball at the dog's feet, then held my right hand away from my body and shook it in the warm air.

"Hope you don't catch Atlas's cold," Pam said. Funny thing: neither of us tended to get sick in the summer, but we suffered more than a few fever-less headaches or stomach cramps during the school year. Mom was sympathetic to any illness, and didn't question us if we somehow healed miraculously once the school bus pulled away from our street. Still, some of Mom's germ phobia rubbed off on me, especially when I thought of a dog's bad breath heating up its thick, sticky drool. Not bad enough for me to run inside and wash my hands with soap and water, you understand, but enough to make me feel icky for a little while.

"Let's see who else is around," I said. We liked to do a sweep of the back yards in our neighborhood—better than calling people on the phone or knocking at their doors, since you could see right away who was around, and if the other kids were having any fun. If you just drop in on a group, it's easier to leave if you get bored.

The Liebermans, directly across from us in the cul-de-sac, was a popular stop. They had a decent play set in their back yard, with two swings and a slide. There was a fun element of danger to these swings: if you arced out too high in front, the whole metal frame would lean after you a bit, its rear legs lifting slightly out of the ground. They'd thump back in place as you swung back, a satisfying rhythmic drumbeat over the squeal of metal chains. Lots of fun, as long as Aaron's sixth-grader brother wasn't around: he was a swing-hog, and rude on top of that, adding a "y" to the end of mine and Pam's names to emphasize how much older he was compared to us. "Hey, Natey and Pammy," he'd say, "you here to pway with widdle Aaron?" I couldn't figure out how him talking like a baby was supposed to make *us* look childish, but it seemed to work that way.

That afternoon, their back yard was empty. I could see why: the ladder-and-slide end of the play set hovered a foot over the lawn; the swing-seat on the furthest side lay on the ground, its chain hanging slack.

The rain must have softened their ground even more than ours. Pam started laughing.

"What?" I said. We had visiting rights for this play set. As far as I was concerned, this was a tragedy.

Pam stopped laughing long enough to explain. "Big shot David must have been in for a shock when he sat his fat butt in that swing!"

And I caught Pam's joke. David pushing his brother aside in a race to the swings this sunny morning, heaving himself into the seat, and then the whole side of the play set sinking to the ground beneath him. If that wasn't exactly what happened, that was how I wanted to picture it.

"What's so funny?"

My face flushed at the high-pitched voice, and I turned expecting to see David's rude expression. Instead, it was Aaron, his natural voice closer to his brother's mocking lilt than I'd previously realized. Aaron had quietly opened their kitchen's sliding glass door and regarded us from the Lieberman's cement porch. He held a half-eaten strawberry Pop Tart, and wore the same green shorts and blue-striped shirt he favored for summer months. He was an okay kid, but he tended to dress in seasons: the winter outfit was brown corduroy trousers and an orange wool sweater; spring brought out the blue jeans and a button-down denim shirt; the autumn collection was tan corduroy and a red lumberjack-flannel shirt. I thought maybe he had identical pairs of the same clothes, but one winter Monday he tore a hole in the right knee of his corduroy pants. It grew slightly larger in the same place each passing day, until the knee was covered by a patch on Friday.

Of course, kids my age didn't always pursue things to their proper origins: Aaron's wardrobe was more a sign of his parents' (in those pre-liberated days, his Mom's) laziness, not bothering to dress the kid nicely until he'd reached the age when such things mattered (whenever that was). Or maybe a sign the family wasn't as well-off financially as their fancy backyard play set would indicate, and they'd cut corners with the clothes and laundry budget. I never actively teased Aaron about his wardrobe, which is some comfort to me now, but I remember having the vague impression my friend was like a cartoon character, Charlie Brown in every single panel with the same shirt, black mountain-peak stripes across his chest.

"Nothing's funny," Pam said. "What happened to the swing set?"

"Storm damage," Aaron said.

"Like what? Struck by lightning?"

"Something like that."

I couldn't look at Pam, but thought I heard her stifle a snort.

Invisible Fences

"You guys want a piece of toast?" Aaron asked, indicating his Pop Tart.

"Sure," I said, and we followed him into the Lieberman kitchen.

⁓

THE QUICK SNACK was fairly uneventful, but I ate gratefully, hungrier than I'd realized. The older brother stepped into the kitchen at one point to grab a can of root beer from the fridge, but fortunately David left without making a snide comment.

Aaron collected our napkins and empty milk glasses when we were finished; he shook the crumbs over the sink, then turned on the faucet to rinse the glasses. I only half paid attention, but he seemed to be standing in front of the running water longer than he needed to, his elbows lifted on each side in an odd stretching motion.

As Aaron returned slowly to the square kitchen table, he held both hands behind his back. Aaron veered toward the side of the table where I was sitting, then he lifted his right arm level with my head, fingers curled toward the ground. In one quick motion, he squeezed his thumb forward to meet his fingers.

A thin crystal arced from his hand. An ice-cold whip lashed my face and neck and I jumped back, nearly knocking the chair over as I stumbled from the table.

Cool water ran beneath the collar of my T-shirt.

Aaron smiled, and turned his hand over.

"Oh my God," Pam shouted. "Where'd you get that?"

In his upturned palm: a hypodermic syringe.

⁓

"I DON'T WANT my Mom to hear."

Aaron should have considered that before he squirted my neck with ice-cold water. He was lucky I didn't shout loud enough to bring the whole neighborhood running.

"Let's go back outside." Aaron used both hands to pull open the sliding glass door, then stepped onto the patio. We joined him, but nobody spoke until after Pam closed the door behind us with a heavy click.

Pam stepped forward with her hand out. "Let me see it."

"Sure," Aaron said. He traced a little path in the air with the syringe, treating it like a toy airplane. He made a buzzing noise then veered it in a mock crash landing towards Pam's hand. She didn't flinch, and I figured out why: the nose of the "plane" was flat, with no needle at the tip of the syringe.

Pam pulled out the plunger half-way, then pushed it back in with a faint hiss of air.

Thin black lines and small numbers marked the clear plastic casing. The syringe was thinner than I expected, about the diameter of a pencil.

Then Pam pulled back the plunger again, and twisted her face into a goofy wide-eyed expression. She placed the syringe above the bend in her left forearm, then pressed down hard enough that I saw her skin dimple beneath the tip.

"Don't, Pam," I said.

She drove the plunger home with her thumb, then screwed up her face in a farce of agony and bliss. I looked away.

Aaron was smiling. "Cool."

The next few minutes, Aaron used the garden hose to show us how to fill the syringe with water. Instead of pouring a thin stream of water through a hole, as you did with a normal squirt pistol, the trick was to put the tip of the syringe in the stream and pull back the plunger. Water dragged in after the retreating rubber plug, filling the cylinder like magic. I was the last one to try it, and the simple motion made the syringe less threatening. That, and its relative ineffectiveness as a squirt gun. You only got one shot, and the aim was unpredictable—a dot of metal remained in the plastic tip where the needle had been broken off, misdirecting the arc of water.

I took a "revenge" shot at Aaron, and mostly missed. Maybe a little on his sleeve.

"We should put cherry Kool-Aid in this thing," Pam said.

"Blood, huh?" Aaron pondered the idea as he took the syringe back from me. I wasn't sorry to give it up, but I was glad the syringe had lost some of its power to frighten me.

"Yeah," Pam said. "You could jab it in your arm, then scream like you messed up. Blood everywhere!"

Great. And now I wondered about the missing metal point—if, as my mind sometimes pictured it, the needle had broken off in somebody's arm, a metal splinter tearing along a vein, the blood flow's force pushing it further inside, tumbling like a whisk through fat and muscle tissue until it reached the heart. With each heartbeat, the lodged needle would scratch at the chest from the inside—an endless, painful metronome.

Or something like that.

Pam looked at Aaron. "Where'd you find it?"

"Where do you think?"

"Any other needles? Could you take us there?"

He shrugged, answered a single "maybe" to both questions.

Pam's eyes lit up.

"But what about…" I had to speak. "What about the dope fiends?"

Even as I said the words, rich with all the haunting connotations conjured up in the dark of our mother's living room, the phrase sounded foolish. Fiends, in our quiet suburban neighborhood? Proof stared us in the face, a hypodermic syringe apparently used to initiate a crazed drug binge. And yet, Aaron had tamed that horrible icon, needle broken off the tip and the stupefying drugs chased from the plastic cylinder with cleansing streams of water. An unspoken childhood dare hovered over us, as well: Aaron, the small boy whose mother also warned of dangers in our woods, had ventured into that wilderness and returned unharmed.

One additional comment about Sunday mornings: my Catholic upbringing designated this as a "day of rest," which might be another reason why Dad chose not to wake us for church. It was intended as a thoughtful, reflective day, a religious day. But for me and Pam, when our ploy to oversleep succeeded, the sweet freedom made it more of a stolen day. We'd tricked Dad—maybe even tricked God in the process—and that gave us some extra license. If we were ever to break a rule, Sunday was the day.

And so…

The Woods

MY LEFT TENNIS shoe squelched in mud, and I almost lost my balance. The woods had suffered the same week of heavy rain as the rest of the neighborhood, and now the dense trees overhead kept the sun from drying the ground.

"Maybe…over here." Aaron was supposed to be leading the way, but he had a tendency to drop back slightly. Pam overtook him a few times, then stopped and glanced over her shoulder for Aaron's guidance.

It was hard to tell where we were headed. We'd passed our usual area at the perimeter, with its familiar landmarks: the double-trunk tree that split like a wishbone; the heavy boulder Pam always tried, unsuccessfully, to roll; the pile of abandoned lumber, too rotten to inspire dreams to build a secret clubhouse. Now we traveled strange ground, doing our best to locate naturally formed paths that wove between trees.

Enough sunlight filtered through leaves to help us see, but it seemed darker the further along we got. The air smelled of dust, humid and misting along my exposed arms and legs, prompting sticky sweat along my shirt collar and behind the bends of my knees. The throbbing buzz of insects seemed to thicken the air as well, adding to my confusion.

"That tree looks familiar," Aaron said. The tree he pointed to had no distinguishing features at all. He might as well have said "eenie, meanie, miney, moe" to choose our next turn.

I checked my watch. 1:15, which meant we'd been in the woods about ten minutes. Time to worry not about where we were headed, but how we'd find our way back. I'd have to trust Pam's sense of direction; I couldn't keep the twists and turns straight in my mind.

I tried for a heavier tread, to press more obvious footprints into the muddy ground—an improvised version of Hansel and Gretel's breadcrumbs. "How much farther?"

"Close," Aaron said. "I'm pretty sure."

He'd said the same thing two minutes ago.

Eventually, a sulfurous smell wafted into the hot mist. A faint murmur mingled with the steady thrum of insects.

"Did you go as far as the creek?" Pam asked.

⁓

THE MURMUR GOT louder with each step, the only obvious path forcing us down a slick slope toward the rising smell. I wanted to cover my nose, but needed to keep my arms out for balance.

"You don't know where we're going," I said to Aaron. "I don't think you've even been here before."

"Maybe to the other side of…that tree." He pointed at another identical oak or maple or whatever. Pam charged ahead, her momentum fueled by the path's downward slant. I paused every few steps to secure my footing, which made it hard for me to keep up.

Careful as I was, I slipped and fell next to a puddle. My hand sunk into stagnant water, and a mush of brown clay oozed between my fingers.

My face flushed, and I prepared myself for the laughter and scornful pointing that usually greeted one of my pratfalls. Instead, I heard only the rumble of the nearby creek. The path in front of me was empty.

I got up, then with quick steps and slides I followed the curve of the slope.

Pam and Aaron stood motionless after a sharp bend in the path. But they weren't waiting for me to catch up.

They were looking at the creek.

Today, more like a river.

The Log Bridge

PAM AND I had always avoided the creek, so we didn't have an obvious point of comparison. Even so, recent rains had clearly caused the creek to rise higher than it should have.

About a dozen feet ahead of us, creamy brown water rushed past, the roiling surface flecked with swirls of heavy tan foam. Although fresh rain should have diluted the creek's tell-tale odor, the extra motion seemed to have unearthed new offenses, stirred them and mixed them and carried them foully through the air.

Instead of the muddy, pebbled banks you'd expect beside a creek, the waters reached to a line of trees on either side, and weaved among slightly submerged trunks.

It was as if a river had dropped here out of nowhere. I couldn't trace the original creek path beneath it.

Most amazing of all, the constant rain had weakened the foundation of a large tree; its roots and trunk had split from the bank and the entire tree had fallen on its side. It now formed a perilous bridge over the rushing water.

"No," Aaron finally admitted. "I've never been here before."

I remember thinking about the log bridge in *King Kong*. The ship's crew ran from a man-eating dinosaur, rushed over a fallen log, only to have their escape blocked by a giant, angry ape. Kong lifted the trunk from his side, and shook the men off the log one by one. They each fell screaming into the pit below.

Practically in our back yard. A lost world.

"Oh my God," Pam said, her voice pitched to a shout over the roar of water. "What happened to *you?*"

She'd turned around and was pointing. Aaron turned as well. Against the wondrous backdrop of foamy dark water and fallen tree, they stood and pointed and laughed.

~ Invisible Fences ~

I looked down at my shirt, ridiculously splattered along the front. My right hand wore a brown glove of mud, with long chocolate smears on my shorts where I must have wiped off the excess.

"Did you crap yourself?" Aaron asked.

"I fell."

"Uh, no kidding." Pam snorted, more than she had at her earlier vision of David's humiliating swing-set disaster.

In an instant, the magic of the moment was gone. I wasn't on some movie set or in a storybook fantasy land. I was where kids often ended up: in an embarrassing situation, with no exit to slink through.

Did we ever miss an opportunity to be cruel? Even with siblings, especially with friends?

Let me tell you about friends. I didn't have many. Aaron was my best friend by default—proximity in the neighborhood, his Mom friends with my Mom, and at school we suffered a fairly similar level of peer tyranny. I was the third geekiest kid in our grade level; Aaron was second. How did I know this? Well, whenever Aaron was absent from school, I got picked on twice as much by the other kids. The two of us, together, sometimes picked on Ralph Fancy, our grade's number one geek (and yes, his last name was part, but far from all, of Ralph's problem).

Now, as Aaron joined my sister in booming laughs at my misfortune, I hated them both a little bit. But I hated the predicament more, my clothes soiled and the rancid odor of the risen creek asserting itself anew.

"Where'd you find the syringe?" That would get him. I knew he didn't have an answer.

"Nowhere," Aaron said. "I get allergy shots each month, and the nurse sometimes breaks off the needle and gives it to me." His voice, loud over the rushing water, expressed a kind of confidence he'd never had before. "I just wanted to see how far you guys would go."

I was ready to run at him, head butt him in the stomach and knock him into the brackish water. See how funny *that* was. Pam, I knew, would be furious about the wild goose chase.

But she laughed again, not bothered at all. "Doesn't matter." Pam waved an arm over the water. "Look what else we discovered!"

Two against one. I was supposed to play the role of "good sport," no matter how much I wanted to rush home and ditch these uncomfortable, mud-soaked clothes. No choice but to stay, really. I didn't know my way back through the woods.

"Let's look at the tree stump," Pam said. She used other trunks to support her, staying a few feet from the water's edge as she walked to the fallen tree. Pam didn't look back to see if we followed her. I let Aaron go first.

The trunk was gigantic—half again as tall as Pam. Its gnarled roots stretched in several directions like the tentacles of a desperate octopus.

"I wonder what sound it made when it fell," Aaron said.

Pam smiled. "No sound, since we weren't here to listen."

On one side, the roots dipped below the surface of the water. The rushing creek splashed loudly against the trunk and the clumps of disturbed earth. A Pepsi can rattled against the side, and a cardboard carton had hooked strangely on an extended root, just above the water line.

"Hand me that branch," Pam said, her feet anchored against the dry edge of the trunk.

Aaron figured out where she pointed and grabbed at the long overhanging branch on a nearby tree. He tried to snap it, but the wood wasn't brittle enough. He had to bend it back and forth, then tear it from the tree like it was a drumstick torn from a roasted chicken.

"Here you go." Keeping his distance, he passed the branch to my sister.

Her feet steady against the trunk, her right hand tight around a thick root, Pam extended the branch past her left arm and poked at the trapped carton. Her first few movements misjudged the distance, but she finally caught one of the side flaps with the stick and lifted.

Aaron leaned forward, but only slightly. Like me, he was too timid to approach the water's edge.

We couldn't quite see inside. Pam tried again with the stick, this time lifting up a second flap then pushing the entire box away from the root. The box floated back, caught a spin in the current, then ducked under the tree and sailed out of sight down the creek.

Nothing. In the movies, a severed head might have fallen out, or at least a dead animal.

"This is stupid," I said.

"No, it's not." Aaron maintained an undeserved pride in the scene. Sure, he'd led us here—but by accident. And now he was letting Pam do all the dangerous work.

"I dare you to walk across," I said to him.

∼

WELL, WHY NOT? The fallen tree really did span the risen creek. Maybe these woods were like our neighborhood: all the good stuff on the other side of a Big Street we weren't allowed to cross. Maybe we really would find abandoned needles on the other side of the creek. Or something better: an empty clubhouse; a bird's nest of speckled eggs; a thick, rubber-banded stack of dollar bills we could split three ways.

The tree would be wide enough to walk on for the first part of the crossing, a fairly straightforward balancing act. Further across, as the branches and leaves sprouted in different directions, it would be a simple enough task to find your footing. Just like climbing a tree, except you'd be climbing across, which was better than the increasing threat from gravity if you climbed straight up.

I dare you.

But he wouldn't. Aaron would be too chicken to make the attempt, and that would end it. Humiliated, he'd agree this was stupid, and we should head back home.

"Worth a try," he said. Before I could stop him, he slid down near Pam and reached for the dry roots on the right side of the trunk. The roots were spaced almost like a ladder, and he stretched an arm toward one high over his head.

And: "Faked you out!" he said. He spun around laughing. "No way I was gonna do—"

Then it was Aaron's turn to slip and fall.

IT WAS ALMOST comical, the look on his face. He'd spun around to laugh at me, and one foot just kept moving. His leg went sideways, like he'd swung at a football and missed. Then his body did a little ballet wiggle: his arms grasped in the air at roots that weren't where he expected them, then he twisted back and the ground wasn't where he expected either, then water was, beneath him, his body caught in a strong current that was ready to pull him away.

(Now you might understand the significance of the box from earlier. We needed to see the empty box spin its perilous path along the rushing current. That set up the suspense—established the danger Aaron was in now, if he followed that same path out of sight.)

Like Aaron before the splash, the moment itself twisted in the air, suspended between tragedy and comedy. I imagine my younger self with muddy hands raised over my mouth, either to stifle a gasp or hide a smirk. What saved the moment—and Aaron, of course—what made it okay to smile and maybe point and laugh and think, "You got what you deserved for fooling around, for fooling us," was…

For all its rushing force, the creek wasn't really that deep.

Aaron wasn't swept away by the current; he didn't sink beneath the surface, a trail of bubbles leading to a murky unknown depth. Instead, he stood there in the creek, a few feet to the right of the fallen tree, about six feet from the raised bank where Pam and I watched him. Aaron's arms and head remained safely above the water line, five of his shirt's horizontal blue stripes clearly visible. His hair wasn't even wet.

He swayed for a few seconds as the water foamed past him. He balled his hands into fists. The spray misted the lowest of his visible stripes into a rich, dark blue.

Then he started to walk. His elbows winged out to each side, his fists nearly touching in front of his chest, Aaron swung his shoulders back and forth. If we could see beneath the water, we could have watched him lift his legs, knees high and feet lunging forward.

But he made no progress. He was like one of those stupid mimes, doing the standard "walk in a windstorm" routine.

Pam yelled out to him. "Are you stuck?"

"No," Aaron said. "The water's too strong in front of me." His voice cracked with a tremor of anger and humiliation and fear. "And the ground's slippery."

He stopped moving and looked around for a minute, as if he could read an answer in the ripples of the water, in the gnarled bark of the fallen tree. "I could try moving sideways, I guess. If I reached the tree, I could pull myself along."

More swinging of the arms and shoulders, but Aaron was still a mime in a windstorm.

He stopped, and looked at us.

"You might still be able to swim," Pam said. "If you push yourself forward with enough force…"

Aaron nodded his head back and forth, his lips tight.

Pam had moved closer to where Aaron had fallen in. She tucked the toe of her left foot beneath a sturdy root, and leaned forward. Her torso swung out over the water and she stretched out her arm, but her reach was too short by about three feet.

"Nathan, maybe if I hold your arm real tight, you can wade into the water and pull him in."

I wished Pam hadn't spoken so loudly. Aaron heard her, brightened up a bit, said "Yeah, Nathan!" and waited for me to dive in. Two against one, again.

My earlier pratfall was still on my mind, the slime of mud and puddle water damp on my skin and my shirt and the seat of my pants. The creek water was far worse: loud and stinking of filth and whatever awful decay the recent rains had unearthed and stirred into a foul broth.

"Swim," I said. "Why don't you swim?"

Aaron knew how to swim. The Liebermans, in addition to their backyard swing-set, owned summer memberships to the municipal pool, and took yearly vacations to Ocean City.

With Dad's summer school job and woodworking projects, he'd never taken us to the pool. We'd gone there a few times with our cousins, but always stayed in the shallow end. I hated getting wet—even there, with water that was clear and smelled only of bleach and the vague threat of other children's pee. A couple times I breathed water up my nose by mistake, which led to fits of gasping coughs, and bleachy soreness at the back of my throat. It surprised and outraged me that my nose and throat were connected: smell and taste were different senses, after all.

"Just push yourself forward," I told Aaron. I stayed back a few feet from the water's edge. "We can grab you from here."

Then Aaron started getting mad. He waved his arms and screamed at me. "This is serious, Nathan!" The language he used next, if I transcribed it here exactly, would not have the proper effect: we were elementary-school kids in the seventies, in the years before cable television brought "fuck" and "shit" and "asshole" into everybody's homes. "Retard" or "homo" or "pussy" were about the best we could manage, but those childhood insults no longer parse. "Poo-head," historically accurate, provokes a giggle; I need the anachronistic shock of something like "motherfucker."

Not simply to convey Aaron's rage—which was considerable, his hands scooping the surface of the creek and splashing rancid water toward us. But to convey how it felt to me, to be called these names by my friend. Not in the joking way friends spoke sometimes, not even how your enemies might taunt you in the hallway between classes. Aaron threw these ridiculous names at me, and he meant them.

Still, I refused to wade into the creek. His shouts and stirrings made the water all the more unappealing, and I stepped a little behind Pam to keep out of splashing distance. I could hear the names he called me, though.

~ Invisible Fences ~

That's when I solved the problem.

I picked up the branch Pam had used to dislodge the cardboard box. It was about three feet long, probably enough to extend her reach to Aaron.

"Use this," I said, and handed it to Pam. The branch had been too stubborn to snap when Aaron tried earlier to break it off the tree. It would be just as sturdy as a rope.

Pam poked the stick forward, just as she'd prodded earlier at the cardboard box. She had the advantage this time of using her right arm, so her aim was better. She slapped the end of it at the water next to Aaron, then held it steady for him to grab.

Which he did. His right hand caught it, then he heaved his left hand and shoulder over. That branch was all he needed: Aaron moved now with an effortless grace, making his previous helpless flailings all the more ridiculous in comparison. A few simple hand over hand motions and he'd pulled his whole torso out of the water. Two steps now, legs high and feet lunging like I'd imagined them earlier, and he made it to the ledge.

Aaron sat cross-legged on the ground, his arms in front and curling into the mud as if afraid he'd slide back into the water. Even over the steady rumble of the creek, I could hear his heavy, gasping breaths.

I held out my hand to help him up.

He raised his head, his mouth a thin line and breaths coming loud through his nose. He pushed my hand away, and stood.

"I could have drowned," he said, a calm steady voice that gained strength as he continued. His voice had a raspy quality that sounded less like my friend and more like his older brother. I stepped back from him, edging closer to Pam, beside her, then putting her between us as he invoked the names again, the curses and insults of a child, then a new insult, "coward," with the added threat that he wanted to kill me.

I turned and ran back through the woods.

THREE SETS OF footprints marked the path, making it fairly easy for me to retrace my steps away from the creek. I scrambled up the muddy slope, steering wide of the puddle where I'd fallen on the way down. Even in my haste, I sought solid footholds: dry patches of ground, or buried rocks or tree roots that jutted from slick mud.

When I'd nearly reached the top of the slope, I heard footsteps behind me, splashes and heavy wet slaps of someone taking less care to study the ground as it rolled beneath. I imagined Aaron closing the distance between us, his anger urging him up the slope. He'd dive at my legs to tackle me, climb onto my back and push my face into warm, swampy ground.

Any other time, I wouldn't have run from Aaron. We were the same height, but my chubby build gave me the advantage over his thin, gangly body. If we'd ever had cause to fight, I'd have won. Of course, I never expected we'd have reason to come to blows, and my surprise at his anger, at the venom in the words he'd spoken earlier, gave the situation a nightmare quality—as if my friend had been transformed into a rabid animal.

I worried that panic would cloud my judgment, send me blindly down the wrong fork in the path, one early mistake compounded by each subsequent turn to twist me further and further into unfamiliar territory. The path ahead looked different in reverse; the ground was smeared in both directions, no clear sign which way we'd traveled earlier. I took the fork on the left.

Perhaps I'd chosen this route simply because it seemed brighter and easier to follow. Shadows from overhanging limbs hatched the dirt, and I hurried from one lighted island of ground to the next. Still, my pursuer edged closer. I heard the slide and slush of sneakers through mud, a quicker pace than mine and accompanied by forceful exhalations of breath I could practically feel on the back of my neck.

I turned to face my pursuer.

Pam.

"Keep going," she said as she caught up alongside me. Her left hand reached out to rest on my shoulder, urging me forward. "This way," she said next, and steered me into a nearly hidden path between two trees. A low hanging branch brushed along the top of my head. I didn't remember ducking beneath this branch when we'd approached from the other side, but I trusted Pam's sense of direction. Whatever happened, at least we'd still be together.

Then, under the comfort of Pam's guidance, I decided to worry about Aaron. I didn't want him to catch us, obviously, but I also didn't want to abandon him to wander the woods all alone.

"Aaron won't get lost, will he?"

Pam stopped and leaned against a tree, surprised I'd care what happened to my friend after the way he'd spoken to me back at the creek. She waited a moment, closed her eyes and tilted her head to help her listen, then squinted at the path. She pointed the way we'd come. "He's right behind us," she said.

I saw him in the distance. Aaron's clothes were so covered with mud they blended into the green and brown like a military camouflage uniform. He was bent over slightly, hands on his knees as he paused to catch his breath.

Initially, Aaron's proximity prompted us to move faster through the woods. As our track grew more twisted and confused, however, I continued to worry that he'd lose his way.

"Where is he?"

"He's right behind us," Pam repeated.

And he was. Aaron kept a deliberate distance. When Pam and I got tired and slowed down, Aaron slowed as well. If he caught up, he'd have to follow through on his threats and the two of us would get into a fight we'd later regret. If we kept our distance now, in a day or two we'd be back to normal. From my experience, childhood friends never stayed mad at each other for very long.

Eventually we reached the pile of abandoned lumber, then the unmovable boulder. Aaron could thread his way through these familiar landmarks—no need for us to glance over our shoulders to see where he'd paused with heavy breaths at the latest turn in the path. We sprinted ahead, burst out of the woods, then raced over safely mowed suburban grass toward home.

Home

ATLAS YAPPED AS we turned the corner into our front yard. I had hoped to get into the house quietly, sneak past Mom who may have fallen asleep on her living room sofa, and change into fresh clothes before she saw me. "Quiet, retard," I said, but Atlas stood next to an overturned water bowl and continued to bark. Pam kicked the tennis ball toward him, which distracted him for a moment.

Our mother kept the house locked at all times, as if we lived in what newscasters called a "high crime area." Flecks of dried mud fell like scabs from my hand as I reached into my pocket for the house key. I opened the screen slowly then eased the key into the knob, twisted, then pushed in the door.

"Nathan? Come here."

We barely had time to shut the door behind us before she'd called out. From the living room, Mom couldn't see which of us had stepped inside, but she often asked for me specifically. My sister was more independent, more likely to respond "Just a second," then need to be prompted again five minutes later.

Pam slid past me to the hallway that led to our bedrooms. I wiped my feet quickly on the foyer mat, brushed at the front of my shorts and headed into the living room.

The afternoon was still sunny, but the closed shades and curtain might be enough to mask the stains on my clothing and smudges on my hands, knees, and face. If I was lucky, Mom wouldn't look at me at all: she often kept her eyes on the television screen while she talked to me or Pam.

"Where you kids been?"

"Nowhere. Goofing around with Aaron."

"You weren't at their house." Not really a question: obviously she'd spoken with Mrs. Lieberman on the phone while we were out.

"No. Their swing set got broken from the rain." I kept my right hand, the muddiest one, behind my back. She turned her attention to me for a moment, but seemed to stare only at my face instead of at my clothing. A commercial for Promise margarine played in the background. Brightness flickered from the screen, and I imagined waves of color tracking over me like spotlights in a prison yard.

"Make me a sandwich," she said.

"Okay. I have to use the bathroom first."

"Wash your hands when you're done," she yelled after me.

The Swings

IT WAS A while before I gathered up the nerve to visit Aaron. That, and I actually managed to catch a rare summer cold—provoked, no doubt, by the teeming cocktail of germs and smells of the creek. For a few days, Pam had the dubious honor of caring for me and Mom at the same time.

I headed over alone, approaching the Lieberman's back yard with cautious steps. The play set had been repaired, and Aaron sat on the furthest swing. His legs hovered over the ground, and his arms grasped the chains on either side. His older brother stood next to him near the support post.

When he saw me, David walked quickly in front of Aaron and blocked me from approaching. "What do you think you're doing here?" he said.

"I wanted to talk to—"

"You little shit." David drew closer, a tight fist raised near his chest. He was about a head taller than me, thin like his brother, but with an unpredictable anger that added an air of menace. "You could have helped him."

"I did," I said. It had been my idea to use the stick to pull him out—though obviously Aaron's version of events had emphasized my cowardice.

"You left him there," David said.

"No. He was right behind us. We went slow, so he could follow us out of the woods." I kept looking around David's body, past his raised fist, at Aaron. My friend sat sullenly in the swing and stared at the ground. He wouldn't even look at me.

"Tell him the truth, Aaron," I said. And David hit me.

I'd always been scared of getting into a fight, of getting beat up by larger, older kids. Now, the blows that landed on my shoulder and my chest weren't as painful as I'd feared. But the idea of getting hit still frightened me, and I cried out.

Loud enough that Pam came running. Somehow I'd ended up on the ground, curled into a ball with my hands over my head. David punched at my back a few times before Pam stepped between us.

She was closer to David's age, closer to his size, but he didn't try to fight with her. It was still taboo for a guy to hit a girl, even if she was a tomboy.

"Come on, Nathan," Pam said, and motioned me ahead of her toward home.

I picked myself off the ground. When I glanced back briefly, David held his arms straight against each side, fists clenched. Aaron looked up finally, his face blank and accusing.

AARON NEVER SPOKE to me again. The way he managed to represent the story to his family, I had masterminded the visit into the woods. I'd dared him to climb on the log bridge (true, as I've already admitted). I'd refused to help him from the water after he fell in the creek, then ran out of the woods with my sister—abandoning Aaron deep in the maze-like paths.

~ Invisible Fences ~

He'd arrived home covered with mud, and he turned me into an enemy to escape his punishment. No blame for my sister, the eldest and most responsible in our group: I was the friend, and should have looked after Aaron more carefully. Aaron's parents ordered him to stay away from me.

Me. Weak, uncoordinated, overweight. The third nerdiest kid in our grade at school. Somehow I'd become a "dangerous influence."

Don't go near that evil, scheming, friend-deserting Nathan, or…-zap!-

I'd become part of another kid's invisible fence.

MOM'S FRIENDSHIP WITH Mrs. Lieberman didn't last much longer. They had a few phone conversations, but only five minutes each compared to their usual half-hour gossip sessions. Mom barely spoke during these calls: just a few interjected agreements while Mrs. Lieberman's voice buzzed from the phone's tiny speaker in an angry monotone.

The summer just didn't feel right anymore, and I wasn't looking forward to going back to school. No doubt Aaron's mother had spread the news about me to parents of other kids my age. The "bad-boy" reputation wouldn't match my physical appearance, and I'd just come across as a jerk, a laughing stock. I'd knock Ralph Fancy out of his number one spot, and that geeky kid would be making fun of *me* soon enough.

So I wasn't terribly upset when Dad announced the family was moving at the end of August to Alabama. He knew a school principal in Graysonville, and could get a job as a Special Education teacher. Dad also told me and Pam that he needed a drastic change from the house in Maryland: "Too much of your mother's papers here, and she won't let me throw anything away. If some of it gets lost in the move, well, that can't be helped."

A good story, like a lot of Dad's stories. But I always thought the move was because of me.

PART TWO: CAUTION

A Promise

LIKE MOST PEOPLE'S superstitions, mine are selective and irrational. I don't believe in any form of good luck: rabbit's feet, lucky numbers, rubbing the belly of a Buddha statue. Superstitions about bad luck, however, have more emotional truth for me. I'll avoid black cats and the underside of ladders, and will pinch spilled salt and throw it over my shoulder.

Because the one time I crossed my Mom's warnings and wandered deep into the woods behind our house, it turned out my best friend would never speak to me again.

As an adult, I follow most rules to the letter. Not because I respect the rules, necessarily, but because the one time, the one time I edge over the speed limit or underreport my taxes or leave a door unlocked for five minutes, I believe that something terrible will happen.

Consider which of these scenarios is more likely: 1) someone wins a contest the first time he enters; or, 2) the winner, jumping for joy with his lucky ticket, drops dead of a heart attack. My luck, I'd be the second guy.

Terrible things may still happen to me, but I won't seek them out. No bungee-jumping or skydiving for me. I am not the leather faced eighty-six-year-old woman who dares cancer by smoking two packs every day of her long life. Neither am I the wild partier whose slowed, overcompensating reflexes somehow swerve past deserved late-night collisions.

I'd rather be overly cautious.

I want to coast into my tragedies.

~ Invisible Fences ~

~

ALL THIS TO explain why my life might sound rather dull.

I've stayed in Alabama since we moved here in the early seventies. Pam and I went to a poorly funded elementary school, followed the same small groups of kids through junior high to high school. Pam left Alabama after she graduated, but I went to a small state-run college. After that, I took a job with the local library branch, housed in a former post office, and I've worked almost twenty years in the same position.

Forty-two years old, and I've never been in a romantic relationship. I'm fairly average-looking, almost like the movie stereotype of the spinster librarian. Except, of course, I'm a guy. I don't know if that makes me a sadder case or not.

Most years, the biggest excitement in my life is when the "theft detector" goes off. Bookmobiles in other states have a better selection than Graysonville Public Library has in its catalog, but we still have a decent security system: not much stuff, but we want to keep it. I'd planted metal stickers in each book myself, small magnetized strips hidden in the binding or beneath the card holder or in the crease between two pages. Libraries have used this technology for years—an early version of the invisible fence designed for dog collars.

People have this "zapped" look on their faces when the warning buzzer goes off, and it's easy to tell that they're shocked. They're not professional thieves—just absent-minded. Most often, it's adults who forget to check out their books before passing through the security gates. Kids usually remember.

~

PAM HAD STRAINED against the confines of small town life. She was wild in high school, smoking with friends on the front steps between classes, parking with boys in the lot behind the Fruit of the Loom factory on weekends. As soon as she turned eighteen, she left for a job with a New York software firm. We talked on the phone now and then, but not in much depth. Five years ago, I was surprised to learn she'd broken up with a live-in girlfriend.

Myself, I grew to appreciate the small town calm, and things seemed to get easier each year. Once you were fixed in people's minds as the librarian, as the "confirmed bachelor," they pretty much left you alone.

Except, of course, for Dad, who wanted grandchildren. I was closer, so I bore the brunt of his teasing and cajoling. I was also the "go to" person in case of any emergency, and was expected to visit Mom on weekends while my father immersed himself in woodworking projects. "You're not doing anything else," Dad would say. "You don't have a date, do you?"

SOMETIMES I THOUGHT of my parents as a burden. A continual source of bad luck, perhaps, like a gypsy curse. Other children feel this way too, I know, so it's not a particular source of guilt for me.

It's difficult to express how strange it was to grow up in their home. First, for all Dad's remarks about needing a drastic change from our Maryland home, the house on Jackson Lane was uncannily similar. It was a single-floor building, since my mother refused to go up and down stairs. The L-shaped layout was the main change, but otherwise it had the same number of rooms. The furniture from the Maryland apartment followed us, and took its place in roughly equivalent positions. After only a few weeks, my mother had accumulated enough newspapers to reproduce the familiar towers around her living room couch. The same dark green curtains hung over the windows, shutting out light and protecting her from imagined mobs of prying eyes.

For me, it was as if the new house in Alabama was haunted by the house in Maryland. My mother, especially, added to this impression. I don't have many memories of the move itself, but I imagine her packed into the dark cab of the moving van, riding the 800-mile distance lying on her couch and facing an unplugged television, at ease amid the crowded stacks of inanimate objects. Over the years, my mother aged like a piece of furniture: instead of wrinkles, her skin warped or cracked like a badly varnished surface; her pallor went from indoor white to a muted gray, as if she were covered by a thin layer of dust. She was a voice from the darkness, a controlling presence that projected from the living room into every corner of the house.

Even when I visited my parents as an adult, familiar objects from my childhood, shifting piles of junk and strange plays of light and dark, and my mother's voice through it all, combined to give their home a haunted atmosphere.

I'D MENTIONED HOW Pam and I, as children, stayed up late each Saturday night in an attempt to sleep through Dad's visit to church the next day. As I'd pointed out, we watched a lot of late-night television, with particular scorn for the "fake" horror movies: ones that didn't show the monster, or haunted house stories that turned out not to have any real ghosts.

When I speak about Mom and Dad's house on Jackson Lane as haunted, and it's only a metaphor, that's the kind of cheap literary device that really angered me and Pam as kids.

Be patient.

Before it's over this story will, I promise, summon up a real ghost.

Likes and Dislikes

"HOW'S MOM?" I could tell Pam didn't want to ask the question, but she knew why I'd called.

"The same. Fever of 102, and trouble breathing."

Pam sighed. "She should be in a hospital."

"I agree."

"You should make her go."

"Easy for you to say. You're not here."

"Okay, then. Dad should make her go."

"They're stubborn. Mom cries and wants to stay home. I tell Dad she won't get better on her own, and he says he has to 'respect her wishes'."

"He's always done a little too much of that. He should dial 911 and let them decide."

"I think he's embarrassed about the house. The paramedics would need to clear a path through all the junk."

"God, I can't even picture it." Pam hadn't been to the house in almost ten years, but I'd given her a pretty good idea of the condition. The main change was due to the Home Shopping Channel and Mom's convenient couch-side telephone. I think some of the operators at HSC knew her by name. She had more electronic gadgets and kitchen appliances than anybody in Graysonville, some still in the UPS boxes they'd been shipped in. And Joan Rivers jewelry—ones where you could snap out the glass "jewels" to match the colors of different outfits (many of *those* still pinned in flat, laminated rectangles, never to be worn).

"I'll come down if you think I could help," Pam said.

"Come down if you want to see them."

"Yeah, maybe I will. I'll probably call Dad, see what he thinks."

"Good idea."

Dad would never invite her down. He'd say not to worry, Mom was getting better.

Then she'd get worse, then it'd be too late, and then Pam would *have* to visit.

WHEN I WAS twelve, Aunt Lora stayed with us for a week. Dad cleared out the guest room, basically by moving everything into the garage. Lora was technically my dad's sister, but she'd been my Mom's closest school friend since the eighth grade, so I tended to think of her more as from my mother's side of the family. Aunt Lora had an amazing obsession with neatness, so it was fun to see her navigate our home. In addition to the guest room, she cleaned the kitchen, the hall bathroom, and the area around the living room chair closest to Mom's couch. Each of these clean spots were her sanctuary against encroaching clutter—but to her credit, she never complained about the house, and cheerfully sat with my mother for extended in-person versions of their daily phone sessions, and running commentaries on *As the World Turns* or *Love is a Many Splendored Thing*.

She also cooked for us, which was a tremendous change from peanut butter sandwiches and Dad's package-mix dinners. The thing I complimented Aunt Lora most on, though, was a lemon layer-cake she'd made from scratch. At the time, I'd thought there were only two kinds of cake—chocolate and "regular," with corresponding brown or butter-cream frosting. I liked the cake partly from novelty, but the novelty wore off when Dad made his own version of lemon cake for each of my subsequent birthdays. At one point I tried to tell him I needed a change, and he gave me an incredulous look: "You *love* lemon cake."

He never let me grow out of my childhood likes and dislikes. Perhaps if I did something he recognized as "adult"—move out of state like Pam, join the Army, maybe, or get married and pop out the grandkids he wanted—maybe then I'd be allowed to change. But I did change, in more subtle ways than he was able to notice:

The simple pleasure I got from my low-paying library job ("Are you ever going to get promoted?"). My book collecting hobby, with a special weakness for Victorian novels in three-volume editions ("Can't you get a paperback for cheaper? It's the same book!"). And my modest apartment, large enough for me, one cat, and a lot of Dad's bookcases ("If you had a house, I could build you a dining room table and chairs." Or, less subtle: "I built a wooden crib for the Fergusons. Too bad you don't need one.")

Mom noticed, though. She kept the windows closed tight, but studied the world through her television screen. In the seventies she laughed at the gross innuendo of *Three's Company* and *Match Game '75;* she picked up street slang from *Miami Vice* and other cop shows in the eighties; and developed an edgier sense of humor as the nineties brought sitcoms like *Friends* and *Seinfeld*. Dad worked in the real world, while Mom lived through MTV's version. Ironically, the woman who was afraid to step outside her house had smoother, more adaptable social skills.

In her last years, I grew to enjoy my weekend visits with Mom. In addition, I'd often call at night to check in—usually after 10:00, once my father was already asleep. We'd talk about what was on TV, what movie I'd gone to see, who'd checked what book out of the library. Back in Maryland, it was my fault Mrs. Lieberman stopped talking to her on the phone. I'd like to think I made up for it, eventually.

One night we were talking over the late night news. I heard the local CBS anchorman in the background—Shane or Marv, or Frank-something. And she just said: "You're happy with your life." It wasn't phrased as a question—just a simple observation, not even prompted by anything we'd said before.

I could honestly answer, "Yeah, I am."

AFTER DAD RETIRED in '92, Pam and I would sometimes indulge in morbid speculations about which of our parents would die first. It wasn't exactly a game of choosing your favorite, but had more to do with practical matters.

— Who was healthiest? They'd both developed diabetes in their old age, but Mom tended to cheat by eating real candy, including *the largest Hershey bar I'd ever seen! Ten pounds, Pam. I don't know—I guess she ordered it off the TV.* Obviously our father got more exercise. *But Nathan, Dad's more likely to get in a car accident or fall down an elevator shaft.*

— Who had the stronger will to live? A tough one. After retirement, we worried Dad would go stir crazy. Instead, he found more woodworking projects, did substitute teaching, and played poker and

~ Invisible Fences ~

bridge games three times a week. *But Mom's got her "plays." God forbid she never find out if Laura recovers from amnesia or if Allison's twin sister fools the Addison family out of the inheritance.*

— Which of them would be hardest for us to care for? No question, Mom. She was okay during the day, but needed Dad to do everything once he got home: cooking, shopping, laundry, other essential cleaning. Dad was self-sufficient, but Mom would need full-time care. *And what's this "us" business, Pam? We know you don't have room in your tiny New York apartment. I'll be stuck with whichever one survives.*

— Who would be the best company? I had my answer, but Pam insisted Dad would be less bother. *You always liked him better. You went shopping with him and bought comic books at Drug Fair; interned with him two summers at Pelham Elementary. And those goofy stories which you loved: car crashes and poison ivy and sawed-off fingers. He was your lifeline, Nate.* True. But our childhood likes and dislikes can change.

First

MOM FINALLY ENDED up in the hospital. I called the ambulance myself, while Dad waved his arms and threatened to disconnect the phone.

He dressed Mom in one of the nightgowns she'd ordered from the Home Shopping Network, a cheerful floral pattern that struggled to offset the weak, dusty blue pallor of her face. Dad insisted we flank her on each side and practically carry her to the front door before the paramedics arrived. She wasn't as heavy as I expected—but then, she hadn't eaten much over the past few days.

Turned out her flu symptoms had developed into double pneumonia. On top of that, she had an irregular heartbeat—possibly congestive heart failure.

How strange it was to see her in a brightly-lit hospital room. A frail elderly man occupied the bed closest to the window (Dad's insurance policy only allowed for a semi-private room); the man kept the curtains drawn aside and the blinds open. Different nurses hustled in and out during my visit, and Mom seemed not to mind the attention.

I visited each of the four days she was in the hospital. If Dad was there, he'd go to the cafeteria for coffee or a snack, to give me time alone with her.

The day she died, she still had a clear plastic mask over her mouth and nose, with oxygen tubes to help her breathe. She had to move the mask aside anytime she wanted to speak.

I did most of the talking. I even switched TV channels for her, like Pam and I used to do in the old days. She'd nod and hold up a weak hand when I reached a program she liked.

After a while, I sat next to her quietly. She drifted in and out, her eyelids heavy. Then both her hands moved slowly to the plastic mask, and I turned the volume down on the television and leaned closer to her face. I could hear the strain of the elastic bands, the scrape of plastic against skin as she slid the mask aside.

"I'm sorry," she said.

"What for?" I responded. "You don't have anything to be sorry for." And I patted her hand and kissed her forehead.

PAM CAME DOWN for the funeral, of course, and Aunt Lora as well. Most of the Graysonville attendees were from Dad's school, or his group of card players. A little under twenty people in all. A respectable-sized crowd, I guess.

We'd had a bit of confusion about the viewing. Initially it was to be closed-casket, since Mom was such a private person most of her life. Then Dad saw the job the morticians had done, and he thought she looked good. "Leave it open," he said, which made me a little angry. I sat with Aunt Lora for most of the two-hour viewing period.

"Your mother was smart," she told me and Pam. "I used to check my homework against hers, and she was always right. And she knew electronics. When I needed to hook up my VCR, I called her and she

Invisible Fences

talked me through it better than the damn customer service at Best Buy. That picture is crooked." Aunt Lora leapt up from her seat after this last comment and crossed the viewing room to a framed landscape print. She nudged the bottom right edge of the frame to make the picture even with the hatched pattern of the funeral home wallpaper.

Pam and I looked at each other and tried not to bust out laughing.

~

"YOU KNOW, I promised myself I'd never step foot in here again."

"I figured as much."

Pam bent down and scraped her finished cigarette against the edge of the concrete porch. I hadn't let her smoke in my car on the way from the funeral parlor.

She'd emailed a few pictures, but it was strange to see her in person. Her hair was shorter than she'd worn it as a kid, but still thick, her natural curl matted with gel into shiny waves. The style seemed old-fashioned, almost business-like, to match her charcoal jacket over a blue open-collar shirt.

It was easier to talk with her on the phone. No awkward pauses, unsure where to direct my eyes.

"Where's...?" My voice trailed off.

"Sondra. I asked her not to come." She took a deep breath, exhaled loudly. "Let's get this over with."

"Sure." I pulled out a separate key ring with a tiny LED flashlight attached (a free gift after some over-$50 Home Shopping Club purchase). Turned out I didn't need the key: behind the screen door, the front door was unlocked. That never would have happened while Mom was alive.

I stepped into the foyer and held the edge of the door for Pam. She paused at the entrance, then put her head down and pushed forward. Her body trembled as she passed the threshold.

Then, nothing.

Pam was struck by it too, I could tell. The hollow atmosphere of a house that, for twenty years, had never for a single moment been empty.

I didn't want to leave the hallway, step into that awful, cluttered, uninhabited living room.

"She would have called one of our names by now," Pam said eventually.

"Yeah."

Our own voices seemed to break the spell. I led the way; my feet had worn a familiar path along the foyer tile and into the flattened green-and-mustard shag carpet.

The heavy curtains were pulled aside from the windows, shades lifted. Dust, surprised by sunlight, hovered like drunken gnats. Nothing had been cleaned or removed, but some of the newspaper stacks had been dragged away from the front of the couch and lined up against the wall. Several UPS boxes, pushed to the front of the room, covered the television screen.

The couch seemed untouched. Two cotton towels lay over the sofa's ridged fabric, which Mom had declared as too scratchy to be comfortable against her bare legs and arms. A memory of our mother's shape left a depressed outline in the cushions beneath the towels.

"Dad always blamed this clutter on her," Pam said. "We'll see how long it takes him to clean things up."

Mom's phone was still perched on the end of her rickety TV tray, with several outdated issues of *TV Guide* next to it. A yellow recipe card box held pens, pencils and Post-It notepads. A newspaper section was folded back on the Jumble page, circles filled in for three of the four words.

"Look at this," I said. Beneath the table were two small cartons made of rugged black plastic. They were snapped shut at the handle, like toy briefcases. Mom had written my name on a sticky-note attached to the top case, Pam's name attached to the other.

I handed Pam her case and lifted the plastic clasp on mine. It was some ridiculous thing called a "LightDriver": a flashlight with a tool-attachment node on the opposite handle. Snapped into compartments on the inside of the case were three rows of tiny screwdriver and wrench attachments. Even with my limited knowledge of tools,

I could tell the design was flawed. The flashlight would shine in your face instead of on the worksite while you tried to use the screwdriver at the other end. Peggy on Home Shopping would say how great it was to have all these tools in one convenient place, the "Items Sold" counter would click higher and higher, phones ringing off the hook in the background, and most people would think, "What idiot would waste money on something like that?"

I started to cry, and when I looked at Pam she was crying too.

∽

WE WERE THERE because Dad had asked us to stop by the house. He'd uncovered some of Pam's things—"Maybe worth something on eBay"—and gathered them in a box in her old bedroom (now better known as junk storage room #3).

As reluctant as Pam was to revisit our parents' home, it gave us a chance to get away from the funeral crowd. After the viewing, there was a reception at the house of one of Dad's card-playing buddies. We were expected to attend, but could use the house visit as a stalling tactic.

Pam walked down the hallway, carrying her tiny "LightDriver" briefcase at her side—a comic addition to her business-like attire. I followed her into her room on the left.

There was barely space for both of us inside the doorway. Pam's twin bed was still in the far corner, pointed away from the window, but it was impossible to reach it. Boxes covered the bed, some with paperback books, others with vinyl albums and cassette tapes. Examples of my father's handiwork covered the floor space—wooden shelves, dressers, and oversized storage chests shoved tightly together in an abandoned spatial puzzle.

Pam's box was balanced on the edge of an open-top wooden crate filled with kitchen appliances (including a toaster-oven, an old-style coffee percolator, and two waffle irons).

"Oh, these will make me a fortune," Pam said. She reached down and pulled out a shoebox, the bottom of it stained with water damage. Inside were her baseball cards. The ones on top were too worn to interest any serious collector; further down in the box, the cards were warped, stuck together, and coated with mildew.

Also in Pam's box were a few of my things from the Maryland house: matchbox cars (rusted), and my plastic robot and bendable Major Matt Mason spaceman.

"What a bunch of crap," she said. She tugged at a red corner of fabric tucked deep in the box, then pulled out and unfolded a wrinkled felt pennant for the Washington Senators. Pam had rooted for the team for a few years after we moved out of Maryland, but then the D.C. owner sold the ball club to Texas. She tossed the pennant and shoebox back into the larger box.

A gold-painted frame was flush with the back side, picture facing the cardboard. "Don't tell me..." Pam lifted it, and turned the portrait around. "I can't believe he put Jesus in here."

It was a "floating head" picture, Jesus with eyes slightly upturned, his face surrounded by a shimmer of light. In my youngest years, it hung in Mom and Dad's bedroom. At the end of each day Pam and I were called in to sit on the edge of their bed, fingers interwoven and facing the picture for our nightly prayers.

"I wondered whatever happened to this guy," I said.

"I think after Jamie died, Mom took it down." Pam slid the picture back in the box, the frame askew and one Jesus eye peering over the top of the shoebox.

"Remember the 'glow'?" Pam asked, miming quotation marks in the air with hooked fingers.

I shook my head.

"You were pretty young. Dad used to tell us if we did an extra special job of saying our prayers, the picture would glow. You know: a sign of Christ's approval."

I didn't fully remember, but as Pam spoke I caught the texture of a wish, a child's wonder.

"You asked me once if I saw the glow," Pam said. "I could tell you tried pretty hard for it: saying the prayer in the right order, concentrating on each word, remembering at the end to bless our relatives and neighbors and the babysitter. You looked disappointed, so I told you it was just Dad's trick to help us pray better. That pissed you off—at me, not at Dad. You always believed Dad's stories."

I thought then of my younger self, four or five years old, striving for some sign of approval from a dime store painting in a gilded frame. Would the halo shine like neon? Would Christ's entire face brighten, light stretching away like lines from a cartoon sun, heating the painted frame into red-hot metal? None of it happened.

"I was pretty gullible, I guess."

"Maybe," Pam said. "He let Mom die, you know." The comment seemed to come out of nowhere. I wouldn't normally expect Pam to stand up for our mother. Of the two of our parents, Mom did the most to push Pam away. Every weekend night of my sister's high school years, Mom yelled at Pam from the couch: she insisted Pam abide by an unreasonable 10 p.m. curfew, then screamed criticisms at her the instant she pushed in the front door after midnight.

"Blame me, too," I said. "We should have taken her to a hospital sooner."

"I'm not talking about now," Pam said. "All those years, ever since Jamie died. When Mom wouldn't leave the house. Dad was letting her die. It just took a while."

As Pam spoke, her words felt like the truth.

Soon, Maybe

A COMMONPLACE ABOUT long-married couples was that once one of them died, the other would soon follow. There was a morbid undertone to Pam's "See you soon, maybe," when I dropped her off at Birmingham Airport after Mom's funeral.

Actually, Dad seemed to bounce back easier than I expected. He added one extra day of card-playing to his weekly schedule, continued with substitute teaching, and plastered community bulletin boards with ads for his woodworking service (these days the flyers, supplemented with color Clip Art, were coughed out of his former school's laser printer).

Dad found lots of things to do, including a scratch-built wooden deck for the backyard. He never actually threw away any of the junk in the house, but he bought large plastic containers to organize things in, and a daisy-wheel label maker to mark each bin. The entire inside of the house was a work-in-progress, without any real progress being made.

He decided he wanted a dog. "Your mother wouldn't let me have one after Atlas. Too much trouble. Too many germs." Several weekends, I went with him to PetSmart or the Humane Society, but he never quite found one to suit him. In the meantime, he built several prototype dog houses of different sizes. Each time I visited, it seemed like there was a new dog house in the back yard.

I counted four of them back there the day of his stroke.

"DAD?"

His television's volume was turned up, making me strain to hear him. He was using a speaker phone that came pre-installed in his new living room recliner. I knew something was wrong: I usually initiated our phone contact these days, to the point where I suspected he'd forgotten my home number.

"Nathan, where are you?"

"My apartment. Right where you called me."

"No, why aren't you here?"

Maybe he only wanted me to meet him for some project or another. Another futile shopping trip for a new dog. "We didn't make any plans, Dad."

"It's Saturday. Your mother's expecting you."

His speaker phone caught a sudden blare of music from the television. A woman's voice drifted under the music, and I told myself it didn't sound like Mom.

"I'll be right over, Dad."

⌇

ALTHOUGH DAD DIDN'T scrub things spotless as Aunt Lora had, he followed her technique of clearing a path from one usable island to another. His bathroom, his side of the bed, one section of kitchen counter and one uncovered place setting at the table. The living room chair, and the woodworking station in his garage.

He was in the new recliner when I got there, and looked up at me with a surprised expression. The chair was gigantic, with thick arms and puffy cushions at the back, layered like rolls of fat. My father looked shrunken and weak in the new chair, his formerly stocky frame now thin after the removal of sugar from his diet. I wondered how he'd maneuvered the massive chair into the house.

He lifted an open package of sugar free caramels from the floor beside his chair. "Want some? Tastes just like the real thing."

I waved the package away and tried to speak gently. "Why'd you call me?"

"I didn't."

"You did." I pointed to the arm of his recliner. "The phone compartment's open."

"Oh. I don't really know how to work that darn thing yet."

Two blue plastic bins sat open on the couch, surrounded by newspapers. Tape labels stuck to each empty bin said NEWSPAPER. "You mentioned something about Mom."

He tilted his head as if he were thinking, then I heard the wet sound of him trying to unstick a piece of caramel from his upper palate. "Let me show you something out back."

Dad stood up, keeping his balance by gripping each arm of the chair. He started to head toward the kitchen, but his left foot seemed planted in the floor and he walked in a circle three times. Then he sat down again.

I pressed 911 on the speaker phone.

DAD TRIED TO talk over me while I spoke to the dispatcher. "I'm fine," Dad said. "I could drive myself, or have my son take me. *If* I needed to come in." I cupped my hand over the disconnect switch, and Dad's finger tapped on my wrist a couple times as I repeated the address to the operator.

I certainly could have driven him myself, but I knew I wouldn't be able to convince him to get inside the car.

"I'll call them back and cancel it," he said after I hung up. His arms pulled close around his stomach. In the large chair, he looked like a child.

"Too late," I said.

While we waited for the ambulance, I stepped into the kitchen for a moment of solitude. I looked out the back door, counted the dog houses.

THE ELDERLY GET prompt attention, even in a small-town emergency room. They hooked Dad up to an I.V. and a heart monitor right away. He fell asleep on the stretcher-bed, and I waited with him in the curtained-off area until the on-call doctor showed up.

"It looks like you've had a 'mini-stroke'," the doctor said. She looked mostly at me, but spoke loudly enough for my father to hear. "Probably nothing too serious, but we'll need to keep you overnight for more tests. Okay?"

I nodded.

WHEN I DROVE back to the hospital the next morning, Dad was gone.

That is, he'd checked himself out the night before. As soon as I'd

Invisible Fences

left, he called one of his poker buddies for a ride home.

He was back in the arm chair when I went to confront him.

"I was fine," he said. "I had a mini-stroke just like this last year."

"Last year? Why didn't you tell me? Or Mom?"

"Oh, I wasn't going to tell your mother. No need for her to worry."

I VISITED MORE frequently over the next few weeks. Dad was often lucid, but would sometimes drift into confusion. He'd pause over the kitchen counter, as if thinking about which cabinet he wanted to open. "Dad?" I'd say. "Dad?" No answer, but in a few minutes he'd be his usual stubborn self again. I tried to talk him into hiring a part-time nurse, but he said the house wasn't "ready," and argued he didn't need a nurse.

"Well, why don't you call a cleaning crew in here," I said. "Clear out some of this junk."

During a few of his confused episodes, I wondered what would happen if I started arguing back at him, saying every angry thing I ever wanted to say. After all, it wouldn't hurt his feelings: once he snapped back to normal, he'd already have forgotten what we talked about.

One afternoon as we sat at the kitchen table, he looked right at me and started to carry on a conversation with Pam. "Your brother doesn't understand," he said. "Nate thinks everything is so clear cut."

That's when I yelled back. "Pam's not here, Dad. I'm the one who stuck around. She left home because of you, because you let Mom sink into herself and almost drag the rest of us down with her. Pam's the one who blames you for Mom's death, not me."

Silence followed. He nudged his half-empty coffee cup and his eyes seemed to follow a gentle ripple in the dark liquid.

When he looked up, he was Dad again, as pleased as if I'd just arrived at the house.

"Hello, Nathan," he said. "Let's go in the garage. I've got a story to tell you."

SOME OF THE junk near the wall was pushed against the tracks for the garage door, jamming the mechanism so the door stayed half-open. A few boxes and RubberMaid tubs had forced their way into the driveway since my last visit. A wedge of daylight stretched beneath the opening, filtered by slats of unfinished wood, a bookshelf without a back, and an upturned Formica table. It was bright enough that Dad didn't bother to pull the metal chain hanging from the uncovered light fixture in the ceiling.

And dark enough to set the mood for my father's final cautionary tale. Aside from a few stripes of light across his legs, Dad's figure seemed gray and muted. Although his voice had a slight old-man tremor, its volume commanded attention. We stood amid the workshop tools that formed the subject of his story, and at strategic moments, he would rattle a toolbox, or shake the metal frame of an upright buzz saw. The tight quarters of the junk-crowded garage pressed me to stand close to him: we were the same height, but as his story progressed, my father seemed to lengthen slightly, like a late-evening shadow.

The first storyteller of my childhood was back, and I listened.

ONCE THERE WAS a young boy [my father began] who grew up in a neighborhood much like this one. He lived in a modest-sized home, full of many memories. So many, that they pushed him into a smaller space, almost like life had forced him into a box.

His big house became as small as the apartment you live in now, Nathan.

This boy was critical of everyone around him, but that meant he had to be critical of himself, too. He didn't always like himself.

That might be why he had the accident, as if he'd subconsciously decided to punish himself.

~ Invisible Fences ~

He went to his father's garage, where he'd been warned not to play with the electric tools. He turned on the drill press and the disc sander, and they made loud buzzing and screeching noises. Then he placed a fresh blade in the jigsaw, perfect for making careful cuts in thin strips of wood—the same machine people use to make the precise, interlocking pieces of a jigsaw puzzle. He pressed the red power button, and the machine roared to life.

But he didn't have a thin strip of wood to cut. Instead, he pushed his left index finger against the blade. Cut the finger off before he'd even registered what happened.

The finger wiggled on the work surface of the jigsaw. It rolled on its side, and the knuckles curled—either from reflex, or from the vibration of the saw's motor. The finger seemed to beckon him closer to the saw, as if asking the boy to cut himself up some more.

His screams were drowned out by the hum of the jigsaw, the buzz of the drill press and the screech of the disc sander.

The boy was sorry for what happened; he hadn't intended for things to turn out this way. So he turned off the machines, cleaned up the garage, scrubbed away every trace. He wrapped the severed finger in a paper towel and brought it into the house. He hid it where nobody could find it.

Then he forgot where he'd put it.

Do you see the point of the story, Nathan? We all cut parts of ourselves away, but we never lose them. Things stay with us—souvenirs with memories attached. We can't always choose what to keep, what to throw away.

~

SO ENDED MY father's only attempt at allegory. At first the boy in the story was clearly intended to represent me, a veiled criticism of my safe, sheltered life, with the finger-chopping as a clumsy Freudian jab at my decision not to have children. Then the story seemed a general meditation on regret, as Pam might regret leaving her parents' home at

18, or as those parents might cling to bitter-sweet recollections of their other lost child, Jamie. According to the moral my father supplied, it was also the story of a man who, near the end of his days, tried to explain to his son why neither he nor his wife had been able to throw anything away, each object in the house a potential container for a hidden, forgotten, yet precious memory.

The story's logic didn't hold up under scrutiny, but it had its own grotesque persuasive power. I believed in it, exactly the way I'd believed in all my dad's stories as a child.

His story complete, my father's head dropped slightly. He turned to walk inside, but then looked at me as if unsure where to go. "This way, Dad," I said, and pressed my hand gently against his shoulder to guide him into the house and back to his armchair.

"PAM. IT'S NATHAN. I need you to come home again."

I WAS THE airport shuttle for Pam and Aunt Lora. My aunt went to the Stoney Mill Inn, where she'd stayed seven months earlier, and Pam got the fold-out couch at my apartment. Sondra still hadn't come with her. "We broke up, I think," my sister informed me.

Dad's viewing drew a bigger crowd than Mom's had. A few former students showed up; several former and current teaching colleagues; a handful of his regular woodworking customers; the expanded circle of card players. About sixty in all.

As the on-site relative, I'd been responsible for most of the planning. Essentially, I followed the decisions he'd made for Mom: I used the same funeral home, the same priest, the same message on the prayer cards. Same style of casket, open during the viewing.

Some people I'd never met or barely knew came up to me and said what a good man my father was, told me he was proud of both his children.

∽ Invisible Fences ∾

Equally? Pam and I had fought on the drive over, since I didn't think she was doing her fair share of the necessary tasks. She refused to take any time off to help me get Dad's house in order. "I'm not stepping foot in that house again," Pam said. "I don't want anything. You can have it." As if there were some great inheritance to be found. Aunt Lora remained silent most of that drive. She clearly realized the cleaning job was too big, even for her.

At some point during the viewing, both of my relatives had vanished from the main room. I knew where to find them: at the side entrance of the funeral parlor, smoking.

Without energy for argument, I simply chose the sanctuary of familiar company. "Hey," I said.

"Your father has, *had,* a lot of friends." Aunt Lora balanced a long cigarette from a hand twisted by arthritis. She rolled ashes neatly into the ash stand next to the four-paneled exit door, and tried not to flinch when Pam tapped her own ashes over the sidewalk.

I stood between them, hands in the pockets of my black wool trousers. "The last time I saw him, I yelled at him about Mom."

"When you're old, you're used to getting yelled at," Lora said. "People think we can't hear."

I smiled. "For a while, he thought he was talking to you, Pam. Looked right at me."

"Wifty," Pam said.

"There you go. In one of your father's ears, out the other."

"I guess. He told me one of his stories afterwards. Remember Pam? Like in the old days."

"Did you *believe* him?" It was a taunt, but Pam seemed good natured about it. She probably didn't feel like fighting anymore, either.

"God, he did that to me too when we were kids." Aunt Lora crossed her arms in front, cigarette balanced carefully, and mimed a shiver. "Used to scare the wits out of me."

"I miss the old days," I said, and my throat started to feel a little sore. "It's so funny to think about that house in Maryland.

Our dumb dog, Atlas, with his rope wrapped around the tree. The Lieberman's swing set. And I miss my best friend, Aaron." Then I started crying. I couldn't yet manage tears over losing my dad, but I cried anew about Aaron. I wondered where he was now. What would my life be like if we'd remained friends, if our family had stayed in the Maryland house?

Aunt Lora reached out to hug me. "That was a long time ago, Nathan."

Pam studied me for a moment, then nodded her sympathy. She tamped out her cigarette in the ash stand and went back inside.

PART THREE:
EXCAVATIONS

I BEGAN WITH the hallway bathroom, one of the few places my father had kept functional. I'd need to use the bathroom myself while I was working there, so it only made sense to clear that space first. Besides, there wasn't much thought involved in sorting through bathroom items. Most of it I could toss immediately into one of the thick green trash bags I'd bought in bulk from Sam's Club in Gadsden. A dozen or so toothbrushes, large packs of disposable razors, four different electric shavers (including one that looked like it ran from a wind-up key). Nail clippers and trimmer scissors (one shiny of each type, the others tarnished or rusty). Lots of prescription bottles, some of them with Mom's name on the labels.

The kitchen next, with a priority on perishable items. Each sweep through the chill refrigerator air mixed a new wave of odors: curdled milk, the sweet vinegar of spoiled ketchup, a yeasty tang of dried bread in an unsealed package. Why hadn't I noticed things had gotten this bad? The answer, of course, was that fresher items toward the front gave a veneer of clean; expirations dates got older the further back I reached, where spoiled items were packed so densely they practically created an air tight seal until I disturbed them.

Some of the items in the vegetable bins had liquefied. I held my breath as I pulled the clear bags from the bin and tossed their sloshing contents in the garbage. The last bag stuck to the bottom of the vegetable bin and burst when I tugged on it: orange and brown and green sludge poured out in chunks (baby carrots?), and a horrible stench rose up, a chilled bile I could taste when I swallowed.

I stepped back, ready to douse the whole bin with Clorox and Sunlight detergent. Then I stopped myself. Whoever bought the house would surely install a new refrigerator—new cabinets, new tile and wallpaper, and a new stove while they were at it—so why waste time? I held my nose, pulled out the whole bin, and dumped it into the Hefty bag. I twisted the bag closed, sealed it with the locking-tie, then walked it to the end of my father's long driveway.

After three hours work, I'd placed four bags on the curb for tomorrow's trash pickup.

As a break from the kitchen, I decided to go to Pam's room. My sister and I had made peace, but I still resented her refusal to help—it might be cathartic to toss some of her junk into Hefty bags.

The box of stuff Dad had gathered for Pam was still next to the doorway. Everything remained exactly as she'd left it, except I noticed Dad had removed the Jesus painting—the only sign he'd been back in this room since the day of Mom's funeral. I shook the box, retrieved my toy astronaut for a moment. On both arms, bendable wires had torn through the rubber elbows. I dropped him back in, then tossed the whole box into a new garbage bag.

The appliances were easy to throw away—out-of-date, with black tape wrapped around worn sections of the electrical cords. The storage box was another matter, constructed of impractical heavy wood that pressed a flat rectangle almost an inch deep into the carpet. I'd eventually need to hire some help for the furniture, especially the stuff Dad had made. Maybe a yard sale, but the idea seemed a bit morbid at this point.

Some of the cardboard boxes were surprisingly light, unopened UPS packages filled with Styrofoam peanuts and bubble wrap and some small item Mom probably forgot she'd ordered. I cut into one and dug through crumpled newsprint to find a plastic yellow fan the size of an alarm clock, battery operated and with a wrist strap. No date on the receipt, but the battery still worked.

After placing three full garbage bags in the hallway, I could slide one of the bookshelves aside and get part-way to the bed. In with some of the record albums and Book Club novels, I found old issues of *TV Guide* in the digest format, plus the grid guides from the *Washington Post*. Mom had circled some of the programs she wanted to watch, and of course she'd filled in the crossword puzzles in the back. I also found two volumes of Pam's high school yearbook, which I set aside in case she wanted them. A separate box contained a French textbook and a stack of different-colored pocket folders, subject names written atop the front in Pam's bubble letters, and bored doodles scratched beneath—hatched lines, cones, shaded spheres. Graded tests were in a loose pile at the bottom, along with a few English themes, handwritten on notebook paper. A theme on *The Scarlet Letter* earned Pam 75% and lots of red marks. I wondered if Pam had saved these things herself, or if she'd just given them to Mom.

AS IT HEADED into evening, I decided to take a break and give Pam a call. I dodged the hallway bags and stumbled toward the recliner in the living room. When I sat down, the over-cushioned chair was a welcome comfort after a long day of stooping and sitting cross-legged on tile or worn carpet. The phone compartment was already open. I leaned over and punched in Pam's number.

She didn't answer on the first ring. The thought occurred to me that Pam would notice Dad's name on her Caller ID screen, which might be like seeing a ghost—one of those old *Twilight Zone* episodes about a call from the grave. I thought about imitating Dad's voice, just to freak her out.

"Nathan?"

"Yeah." I leaned closer to the open arm of the chair and spoke into a small circle of dots beneath the number pad. "I'm at the house. First day of cleaning."

"How's it going?"

"A lot of unidentified objects in the fridge. I'll have eight huge bags of junk on the curb by the end of the night. Only about a million more to go."

"Wow."

"Hey, check this out." I moved my arm over the microphone, the tiny fan hanging by its strap from my wrist. I pressed the plastic switch.

"What is that? A bee's nest?"

"One of Mom's prizes from the Shopping Club. A plastic fan about three inches square. It puts out more noise than air, though."

"Glad you're having fun."

"You know I'm not."

An awkward pause. I switched off the fan.

"Listen, there's a lot of your stuff here. A whole box of tests and papers from high school."

"Damn, Nathan, I was probably stoned when I wrote those. Toss 'em."

"What about your yearbooks?"

"Got nowhere to put anything. Apartments are small in New York."

"Okay. If you're sure."

"Throw it all out. I'll never miss it."

I twisted the fan from my wrist. It felt odd not to hold a phone to my ear. Sound projected from a speaker in the phone compartment, but Pam's voice seemed to fill the air of the room.

"There's just so much stuff here," I said. "Most of it's junk, of course, and I don't want it. But I keep thinking, somebody else might."

"Yeah, right. That's the same logic Mom and Dad used to keep all that crap around in the first place. Don't fall into that trap."

"I guess."

"Set some kind of limit. Save one thing from each room, maybe. If it makes you feel better you can pick something out for me—just one, though. Your choice."

"Okay."

"It seems like—I don't know—you've come to terms with a lot of things lately. Don't get sucked back in."

"Yeah."

"If it gets to be too much, don't feel bad about throwing in the towel. Sell the place 'as is'—let the buyer deal with all the crap."

"All right. Thanks, Pam."

I FOUND A half-dozen cans of Chef Boyardee mini ravioli in the kitchen cupboard, and opened one for my dinner. After that, I shifted to my old room for the rest of the evening. Just as much junk as in Pam's room, in no particular order at first, but as I plowed deeper into the room I found more items with a "Nathan" theme. Two boxes of my school stuff as well (in better condition, and with fewer red marks on the English themes). I also found a collection of old horror paperbacks and movie memorabilia—some of which I'd bought at a fan convention in College Park when I was in ninth grade. Lots of books by Robert Bloch and by the *Twilight Zone* writers: Serling, Matheson, Beaumont. Rolled-up posters and 8 x 11" stills from *King Kong*, and from Ray Harryhausen's dinosaur and Sinbad movies. I'd packed these away before I left for college—neatly, perhaps an early manifestation of a librarian's cataloging skills. They really might be worth something on eBay. Unless I decided to keep them.

I cleared off a corner of my bed and sat there to look at each item, returning it carefully to the box when I was through. I read a few short stories, paged eagerly through a "special effects" magazine and an issue of *Famous Monsters* with Chaney's "Phantom" on the cover. The evening got late without my realizing it: I'd lost myself in things I hadn't thought about in almost twenty-five years.

Many boxes still covered the bed, but I was able to balance most of them atop existing piles along the wall. Eventually I unearthed larger portions of a ridged tan blanket, and two pillows at the head of the bed. I patted the top pillow as forcefully as I dared, and was pleased that not too much dust flew out from the pillowcase. My mother hated dust and dirt and germs, but most of her life she was too tired to do anything about it. At that moment I knew how she felt: I stretched myself over the cleared sections of the blanket and allowed the back of my head to settle into the pillow. Beneath me the mattress was sunken and uneven; bedsprings creaked with each new shift in weight.

In the strange and familiar space of my childhood room, in the half-conscious moment before exhausted sleep, I lapsed into a childhood memory of prayer. Instead of looking to heaven, I cast weary eyes at a blank spot high on the opposite wall, where I imagined a framed portrait of a painted savior, still refusing to glow.

WHEN I WOKE, I didn't remember where I was. The overhead light was on, but I'd set my glasses somewhere. I tried to bring my apartment into focus, but instead saw tall stacks of boxes that seemed ready to tumble onto me. My feet stretched off the edge of a wooden bed, its shape similar to the one from my childhood bedrooms, the Alabama and Maryland houses conflated in a fuzzy blur. I held a shoebox close to my body; apparently I'd grabbed at it in my sleep, then hugged it near my chin as if it were a stuffed animal.

The shoebox was sealed with string, tied in a bow. I held the box close to my face. Mom had scratched "Jamie" on one side with a ball-point pen.

When I shook the box, it made an odd, hollow sound. I slid the string off one end without untying it, then flipped up the lid.

I recognized the colors first: red, yellow, green, blue, and orange. Two each, for a total of ten bowling pins. Beneath them was a pink, neatly folded blanket.

The bed's headboard had a thick flat ridge along the top. Without even thinking about it, I began to stack the pins in a neat line along the ridge, just as I'd stacked them on the edge of my little sister's crib.

The pins felt tiny, so frail I was afraid I'd squeeze them flat. When I moved them farther from my face, I couldn't see them clearly; my memory superimposed a crisper image over the blur of colors. There wasn't a bowling ball included in the shoebox, but Jamie never needed one.

I knew what to do.

I reached my hand next to the right-most pin, and swept through all ten in an even motion.

The sound of those thin hollow pins colliding together was like magic. In all the intervening years, I hadn't heard that distinct sound—it was packed away in a shoebox, muffled against the favorite blanket of an infant who'd died too soon. Now the past tumbled toward me with the tumbling pins. I was there again.

I could almost hear Jamie's laughter behind it all.

THEN I HEARD a snap at the window, like a flat palm slapped against the glass.

Old houses can settle and resettle, the wood expanding from humidity then cracking back into place. During the day the sound goes unnoticed, smothered in the hum of appliances and ventilations systems and human activity; at night, after a disoriented waking, the sound can startle like a gunshot.

Followed by a scramble and slide, footsteps in dirt and fallen leaves?

Maybe I really had heard laughter earlier—but not Jamie's.

Graysonville was a small enough town; neighborhood kids up for a dare would know the house of a man who'd recently died. The same house that, for years maybe, inspired whispered rumors of an unseen presence, a strange woman who locked herself inside its walls. Late on a chill November night, a group of children might wander there, be drawn to a lighted bedroom then laugh and run as the bravest boy reached to rattle the window frame.

I stood up, my legs pinched in a thin wedge between the bed and stacked boxes. I felt along cardboard edges, and eventually found my glasses balanced where the lip of one box jutted next to the headboard. I pushed the glasses onto my face, bringing the world back into focus.

The bedrooms were on the shorter leg of the L-shaped house. The window of my old room looked out on an alley of grass and a line of trees that insulated us from the neighbors on that side. The footsteps, if they were footsteps, seemed to skirt the rim of the house in the direction of the back yard.

I edged out of the room. On my way to the kitchen, turning on lights as I went, I stopped to open the only item I brought with me: a tiny plastic briefcase I'd dropped just inside the front door. I retrieved the main flashlight element from the LightDriver kit and headed to the back of the house.

Sliding open the glass kitchen door, I stepped onto the raised deck. It wasn't my father's best job of woodworking: instead of removing the previous deck, he'd nailed fresh boards onto the old ones. The kitchen light cast my shadow in front of me; it stretched over the boards in an uneven accordion pattern. As I walked to the edge of the deck, a few of the boards seemed to roll beneath my feet.

The night was quiet. From the raised vantage of the deck, I squinted over the yard. Five of my father's prototype dog houses formed two rows in the back half of the property. They looked like monuments: grave markers for pets he'd never owned.

The smell of sawdust overpowered the scent of grass and tree bark. I turned on the flashlight and aimed its beam. Dark triangles wavered in the grass behind each pointed roof; carved door-less openings swallowed the light, the small interiors deep in shadow.

Five stairs led to the ground, and I made sure to grip the banister as I stepped down.

I swept the flashlight over the lawn. One large poplar tree loomed over a tool shed on the left side. Both of the shed's doors were open, with a riding lawn mower spanned across the entrance. Behind the mower, boxes of junk and newspaper were stacked too tightly in the shed to afford any hiding places for mischievous children.

I aimed the beam of light at my feet. Just listened.

Nothing.

I lifted the light towards the house, brushing a faint glow from the garage end to the living room. I moved to the corner window.

As I pressed my face near the glass, I recalled my mother's voice: *I don't want people looking in here.* The curtains were open, but a shoulder-high stack of boxes partly obscured my view beneath the raised shade. Storage bins and papers covered Mom's couch. I moved my head and a ripple in the glass shifted the room, like a dry wind had swept over the abandoned papers.

I opened my palm and slapped it flat against one square of the window. The sound echoed slightly. Was it the same sound I'd heard earlier when the frame of the house had settled—or when a young trespasser had tried to startle me? The noise seemed different out here.

After I pulled my hand back from the window, I fogged breath over the glass. A wet outline of my hand appeared, fingerprints and palm lines clearly visible. Then the water evaporated around the edges, shrinking the handprint so it resembled that of a child.

THE NIGHT'S CHILL air started to bother me. My jacket was still draped over one of the kitchen chairs. As I turned to go inside, the flashlight beam passed over the area beneath the back deck.

The deck was supported at each corner by thick posts. Numerous scraps of wood filled the space beneath—probably shaved edges and misfit pieces from long-completed projects. Strips of cloth were stuffed into gaps, worn clothing saved as dust rags for some hypothetical cleaning spree. I stepped closer and kneeled to examine Dad's

Invisible Fences

handiwork. None of the scrap spilled over onto the yard—like a brick-layer, he had expertly packed in enough to fill available space, while still keeping most of the grass clear so he could steer his riding lawn mower over it.

Maybe it wasn't the strokes that killed Dad. He just ran out of places to put his stuff.

That's when I turned to look at the dog houses again. From my position lower to the ground, I could see the openings more clearly. It wasn't the angle of shadow that kept me from looking into each house. All five of them were stuffed to the brim with scraps and junk.

I moved to the back half of the yard, toward the two larger dog houses in the close row. More wood scraps and rags cluttered the first opening. I kicked at it with my shoe and none of the items shifted.

Plastic grocery bags filled the house on the right. The bags were puffy like balloons, tied shut with bow knots. A few of the loops stuck out from the pile. I shifted the flashlight to my left hand, grabbed one of the loops and yanked a bag free. It slid out easily, and the remaining pile of bags kept its shape around the small, deep gap.

When I untied the bag, I found several packages of sugar-free caramels. The candies seemed hard to the touch, and had no doubt gone stale. I pointed the flashlight in the hole I'd created in the pile and moved the light around, catching the glimmer of more loops of blue and white plastic, stenciled fragments of Wal-Mart and Winn Dixie logos. A faint chemical smell drifted from the gap. Probably, as with the refrigerator, things got worse as you went further back. To test my theory, I reached into the hole.

And something bit me.

I pulled back, brushing against another plastic bag, and the entire pile collapsed and tightened over my arm. Sharp edges clawed me through the shirt sleeve, and I felt more stings on my hand, palm, and fingers. Was it a bee's nest? My wrist was caught beneath one of the plastic loops, and the strap wouldn't break—it almost seemed to be pulling my arm in deeper. I panicked and tugged, but each movement brought more painful scratches to my hand and arm. Finally I wrenched my arm free, and several of the bags followed after it and tumbled onto the ground.

Pinpricks and drops of blood covered my hand, and several scratches began to bleed through from under my sleeve. I shone the flashlight on one of the fallen bags. Tiny metallic eyes glimmered back at me and stretched into metallic lines when I moved the flashlight.

Bags full of straight pins?

No. Hypodermics.

For Dad's insulin shots.

The chemical scent I'd noticed earlier now filled the air, a mix of rubbing alcohol and dried blood. Metal tips protruded from various places in the fallen bags. An entire syringe had fallen from the top of one bag, its needle an angry, gleaming stinger.

Dad was supposed to break off the tips and dispose of used needles in a red "hazardous waste" bin. Instead he'd tossed them into plastic grocery bags then jammed them into this toxic pile.

Why? He hadn't built these dog houses until after Mom died. Dad must have been more upset by her death than any of us realized. His inability to throw away useless things struck me then as a strange kind of tribute to Mom. Possibly he had also contracted her germ phobia: he'd moved the needles as far away from the house as he could, while still keeping them on his property.

Germs. God knows how long these needles had festered out here—long enough to rust and grow new bacteria. I might as well have injected poison into my arm.

The pain started to throb. My fear of needles surged up from my childhood, and I dreaded the idea that metal points may have broken off under my skin. I kicked at one of the bags in anger, then hurried back inside to rinse off the wounds.

∽

I WENT STRAIGHT to the kitchen faucet, turned on the water and pushed my hand into the stream. Initially the water ran light pink under my hand, but it soon ran clear. As the water grew slowly warmer, I pulled up my sleeve and moved my forearm back and forth under the stream, turning my wrist slowly with each pass. The temperature grew uncomfortable so I adjusted the faucet, but I wanted to keep the water as hot as I could endure—intending to scald away any possible infection.

After a healthy blush covered my hand and forearm, I turned off the water and examined the wounds. They didn't look as serious as I'd feared—small dots on the hand, a few tiny scratches near my wrist and one longer one atop my arm. To my relief, all the bleeding had stopped. And no sign, thank God, of broken needles beneath my skin.

I was angry at myself for getting in such a panic. And for doing something so stupid as to reach blindly into a darkened heap of trash. Then I was angry at Dad for placing those needles there to begin with—as if he'd deliberately set a trap for me. What was he thinking?

Finally my anger shifted to those hypothetical thrill-seeking trespassers. If they hadn't drawn me out of the house, I never would have hunted and poked through the back yard after dark. Of course, I hadn't found any kids out there, and probably imagined the whole thing to begin with—which brought my anger full circle, back to me.

Then a squeal of tires sounded from the road in front of the house, followed by a scrape of metal and a loud thump.

In that instant, I revised my theory of late-night pranksters. Instead of young children, I thought of teenagers, piled in a car and hooting at my parents' house as they drove by, maybe throwing a bottle or a beer can toward my car at the bottom of the driveway. I grabbed the flashlight (still switched on where I'd set it beside the sink), rushed to the front hall and pushed out the door. I jumped over the porch steps and hit the ground running. Night air brushed at my injured hand, cooling the faint burn as I raced over the lawn toward the road.

Not that I'd be able to fight a whole group of teenagers. The LightDriver had the heft of 2 "D"-cell batteries, but its cheap plastic casing would fall apart if I tried to use it as a club. Still, a rush of adrenalin drove me toward the curb, hunting for any property damage, ready to shake my fist at retreating taillights, yell threats at the vandals' car once the occupants were too far away to hear.

I stopped short of the concrete curb, at the end of the driveway. The road stretched empty in each direction, curving to the right at a distant "Slow" sign that drivers usually ignored. I could see a few neighboring houses, their porch lights dark. In the driveway, my Taurus wagon looked untouched, and there wasn't any damage to the mailbox (a popular target for teenage vandals).

But a rotten, musty smell hovered in the air.

The smell seemed to rise from the eight Hefty bags I'd lined up for tomorrow's trash pickup. The green bags looked shiny and black in the dark, their only color from the yellow plastic ties locked around each closed top. I stepped down from the curb, and saw that one of the bags, third from the end next to the mailbox, was torn open in the side. Garbage and sludge had spilled part-way into the street.

Jesus. Just what I needed.

It was one of the kitchen bags. I saw the white corner of the vegetable bin from the refrigerator, the rancid carrot slop no doubt supplying the strongest of the odors. Zip-lock bags of other rotten food had sluiced onto the sidewalk. I had the morbid thought that these bags looked the size of kidneys or other internal organs, sliced from a person's side with a deep, jagged knife.

And it did look like the larger bag had been cut with a knife. Heavy duty bags won't tear easily, which is the reason they print warnings on the package: "Danger of Suffocation. These garbage bags are not toys. Keep them away from children and pets." A foot-long gash appeared in the side of bag, evenly parallel to the ground. The cut was too precise to have resulted from an accidental shifting of the bag's contents.

Well if it had been teenagers, they surely weren't happy with what they found. There's no incentive to slash open other plastic treasure bags after the first one spills out such foul-smelling garbage. The theory provided a good explanation for the squeal of tires I'd heard from inside. The teenagers drove away in a hurry: a peel out.

Leaving me to clean up the mess. It wouldn't be easy moving this stuff around, especially with a scratched up right hand and fears of new infection. I set the flashlight in the gutter portion of the curb, then lifted a Zip-lock bag by its corner with the fingertips of my left hand.

I was still freaked out after the nest of syringes, so I didn't want to reach too far into the open gap of the Hefty bag. Instead, I lowered each small bag into the torn gash, then poked gently with a finger to force it inside. The bags had an awful, sloshy consistency. It felt like I was poking at someone's stomach.

Once I'd finished, I briefly considered the idea of dragging all the bags back toward the house to prevent further mischief, then decided it was too much effort. Easier to simply get some packing tape from inside and return to patch the hole.

I bent down and retrieved the flashlight.

That's when I noticed the wedge-shaped chip where the street met the concrete gutter.

"Not too close, now, Nathan."

Cracks in the asphalt, and a missing chunk like someone had taken a bite out of the road. A niche to link with the interlocking tip of a child's tennis shoe.

An exact match to a visual aid from my past, the obstacle that tripped an unwary boy to his death in Dad's version of "The Big Street."

That image was burned so clearly into my childhood memory, and I'd swear this was the same shape. It wasn't a mark that would occur naturally, like a pothole that cracks and expands with the change in season. It formed more of a smooth, clean break—as if my father had cut it with some secret tool he'd kept all these years. Did he make this sign out of habit, as a territorial marking for any dangerous crossings near his home? Or through foresight, to have everything in place for future tellings of the story, ready to warn and delight the grandchildren he never had? Maybe he'd hidden this scary image in hopes I'd discover it, a kind of final farewell. He knew I loved his stories when I was little, and he'd never fully accepted that I'd grown up.

I placed my adult foot next to the curved niche, as if to follow that fictional boy in his foolhardy dash across the street. I thought of the sounds I'd heard while inside. The screech of tires on asphalt, followed by a scrape of metal.

Then a thump. Like a body hitting the road.

Was it possible, beneath the high-pitched squeal of tires…Was it possible I'd heard a child scream?

I could smell it now, stronger than the spoiled food from the opened garbage bag: the bitter, smoky reek of burnt rubber.

I aimed the flashlight over the road. No tire marks, that I could notice. But a stain of faded liquid darkened part of the street. The stain appeared at a familiar angle and distance from the niche near my foot. Years ago, my younger self observed the exact same shape in a road many miles away.

The outline of a boy.

My body shook at the thought, maybe a suppressed shiver from the November chill. I imagined an answering vibration from the street, the rumble of an approaching vehicle.

Nothing was there, in either direction, but I hesitated to step closer. The warning of my father's story held me back, just as his raised arm had once blocked my path into the road. I swept the flashlight's beam over the stain. Had my father painted it there, dripped oil to soak into the asphalt, outlining the shape I remembered: splayed legs, head twisted flat against the right shoulder?

A tremor went through me again, and the flashlight rattled in my hand. Its beam faded to a dim glow.

And the dark shape in the road started to move.

An arm first, unbending at the elbow then reaching up. Then the head, an inky smear that bubbled up over the flattened body. The other arm broke from the surface and swelled like a flexed muscle. Both arms pressed flat against the street, pulling the torso up with the faint wet sound of a scab peeled too early from a wound.

The shadow crawled forward on its hands, dragging the legs out of the road behind it.

Crawling toward me.

It paused about a body's length away. I stood there, transfixed and terrified. I could smell it: an awful mix of tar and burnt rubber, oil and blood.

Its head swung from one shoulder to the other with the click of a cracked neck, and it struggled to stand. The shadow's legs shifted, unsteady, and its arms swayed to maintain balance. Ripples flowed over its surface as it moved, a shaken mass of black gelatin.

When the motions settled, I tried to distinguish features in its face. Thick bubbles rose to the surface, hinting at the placement of an eye or nose, or popping with the sound of faintly parted lips.

Its right arm raised, a finger extended. It pointed at me.

Then the entire shadow burst, its image washing over me in a shower of black oil.

HEAVY LIQUID POURED over me. I tried to shake it off my hands, then pushed my fingers under my glasses to wipe syrupy blackness away from my eyes. An ashen sludge pressed against the corners of my mouth, threatening to force its way inside.

Dear God, what's happening?

Then it was completely gone.

No thick, smothering liquid. Only a light sheen of nervous sweat on my forehead and at the back of my neck.

I still held the flashlight in my right hand, its beam dim but resilient. My hand was pink from where I'd held it beneath the hot water; the small scratches and needle pricks looked clean.

Perhaps I'd had some weird reaction to the hypodermics. A hallucination.

The shape in the road...I passed the weak light over the shadowy outline. It was still there, but flat against the ground and less definite in shape. Unthreatening. Except I was still too afraid to step next to it in the road. And my right arm trembled so much that I'd gripped it with my left hand to keep the flashlight steady.

My scratched wrist itched beneath the cuff, and I pushed the sleeve further up my arm. Again I saw that pinched sunburnt look to the skin, held too long under hot water.

The wrist was white where I'd gripped it. The impression was smaller than my hand, though, like a child had grabbed and twisted the sensitive skin.

Enough. It's as if I was trying to work myself into another panic. My breaths came in heavy rasps, and I almost didn't trust my strength to carry me back inside the house. I sat down on the curb, a safe distance from the shape in the road and a few feet from the row of garbage bags. Rotten odors from the opened bag lingered strongest near the mailbox. The wind hung still, but drifts of the smell still carried to where I sat.

I cupped my left hand over my nose and mouth, and my breaths washed warm over my palm in heavy exhalations. The sound echoed deep and frantic, and I concentrated on slowing the breaths, softening the nervous tremors.

As I tried to calm myself, my breathing grew more irregular. A rattle and gurgle rose in my throat, then a strange flapping rasp added a new, desperate rhythm. To shut out the noise, I pinched my eyes tight and held my breath.

The flapping rasp continued over the expected silence.

A heavy weight shifted in the garbage bag closest to me.

THE BAG BULGED at the center. I aimed the flashlight, casting a white spotlight with an irregular yellow center, like a firefly. The light transformed slick plastic into a curved mirror that reflected the curb and street and trees behind me, my face distorted and open-mouthed in surprise.

But it wasn't my face. A head was pressed against the bag from the inside. The fleshy tip of a nose strained against the bag, pushing the plastic outward in a small rounded cone. The flapping rasp scraped out from a taut oval stretched over the open mouth. Plastic whistled with each failed breath.

Someone inside the bag. Suffocating.

My reaction was instinctive. I didn't think, *How did that person get in there?* Or devise a vague yet plausible sequence of events: some conflation of my previously-imagined mischievous children and mean-spirited teenagers, with the older boys stuffing a kid from the first group in the bag and sealing it up, that child (yes, the head was small, like a child's, like—I didn't dare tell myself—the head of the awful threatening shadow that rose from the road just moments before), that child unconscious and unmoving until a terrified, gasping awakening.

My only thought: *I've got to get that kid out of there.* This was no hallucination: I saw a wrinkled forehead, brows raised in panic; saw the agonized expression of the child's open mouth, and could practically count the rows of teeth fighting against the stretched bag.

I leaned over the bag and fumbled with the plastic tie. The bag's opening was twisted into a firm rope, the locking tie pulled to its tightest available notch. I dropped the flashlight to the ground so I could use both hands, trying to curl the flat yellow wedges and thread them back through the tie's small opening. But the tie was designed to be much easier to seal than to remove, and I didn't have enough room to maneuver my fingers.

Desperate rasps urged me to act as the plastic swelled out then sucked in over the child's gasping mouth.

Break the seal. Let some air in.

I reached beneath the tie and grasped a loose fold of the bag. The plastic stretched as I pulled it apart with both hands, but it refused to break.

The bag remained rooted to the ground, heavy with the weight of the trapped child.

My knuckles whitened with tension, and the scratches on my right palm flared up in renewed pain. I tried to push my thumbs through the stretched fold, but the plastic wasn't taut enough beneath my nails.

More rustles and squeaking rasps of plastic over the child's mouth. My own breathing grew more desperate, my throat constricting in helpless sympathy. Time was running out.

Over the mouth. That's where the plastic was stretched to its limit. It might be taut enough.

I dropped to my knees, my hands finding the shape of the head and grasping it on each side to hold it steady. The texture of hair fluttered beneath my fingertips; an open jaw pressed against the heels of my palms. The child's face felt like skin instead of slick plastic.

Leaning close, I whispered towards one of the ears: "Don't be afraid. I'm trying to help."

And I plunged both thumbs into the taut area over the mouth.

The plastic stretched back, my thumbs warm as they passed over a wriggling tongue. The child's jaw tensed beneath my palms and I pushed my hands closer together to keep the joint from snapping shut. "Don't close your mouth," I whispered, afraid of being bitten—and also afraid my hands would press together too hard, crushing the child's head.

My thumbs pressed deeper. I held the head steady to keep it from pulling back.

Deeper.

Plastic stretched, and my thumbs hit a hard surface at the back of the child's throat.

The head shook beneath my hands in quick surges. Gag reflex.

Nowhere else to go, I pushed my thumbs together and pressed against the tongue, forcing my thumbs down the throat.

Deeper.

The head tried to shake some more. I held it steady, but the face felt brittle like an eggshell.

Deeper. The stretch of plastic.

Then a pop, and the shrill whistle of escaping air.

With it, an incredibly foul smell: musty and brackish, the scent of disease and death.

And, carried in the gasping expelled breath, a whisper.

A whisper of my name.

~

MY HANDS PULLED away, and I fell backward onto the lawn.

The bag shifted. The rattle of bones.

Then more of the bags shifted. More of the suck and release of stretched plastic over anxious mouths.

Faces pressed out from each of the bags, as if staring at me through a curtained window.

Too many to save.

Then a series of soft cracks, like the rude snap of chewing gum. Musty odor forced its way through tiny holes. Each bag acted as a bellows of foul air, squeezed to expel syllables over diseased vocal cords.

"Nathan," they called.

I pushed my hands over my ears and clambered back toward the house.

~

"WHAT TIME IS it?" Pam was too groggy to register anger, at least for the moment. Her voice drifted lazily from the speaker. I leaned forward and spoke into the recessed panel in the recliner's armrest.

"Late. I'm sorry."

Next I heard the rustle of bed sheets, a blind hand groping for the clock on the end table. "You're still at the house?"

"Yeah." A dim light shone from the hallway behind me. I'd lowered the living-room shades and closed the curtains. "Something's happened." I wasn't able to disguise the fear in my voice.

"What's wrong now?" A faint hint of impatience, or maybe disbelief—as if Pam already decided nothing more could go wrong. Even so, the familiarity of her voice offered comfort.

"I think Dad got worse after Mom died, worse than we'd realized. He kept even more stuff: newspapers, junk mail, spoiled food—with brand-new storage bins he never bothered to fill with anything. Instead, he stuffed wood scraps and rags up under the back porch. And remember those dog houses I told you about?"

"Sure."

"Five of them on that raised hill at the back of the yard. All of them packed to the brim with garbage. The biggest one was filled with a bunch of those plastic grocery bags, tied shut at the handles. I reached in and pulled one out, and my hand and arm got all scratched. Several bags were filled with hypodermic needles."

"Jeez."

"Like Mom's story about drug fiends in the woods, back in Maryland. Except these were from Dad's insulin shots. He used the needles, bagged them up, then stored them in one of the dog houses."

"More trouble than actually throwing things out the normal way."

"Exactly. He had some odd reasons for what he did, some weird logic."

"I've always thought that."

"No, Pam. Something more. At the funeral home, I didn't mention all the details about Dad's last story. It was about me as a boy, and it was really gruesome. In the story, I cut off my finger—on purpose, okay—then wrapped it up in a box and hid it in the house. Dad was disoriented before and after, but as he told the story he was completely lucid. Like the old days. He'd summoned the strength of mind for a specific purpose, as if he needed to tell me this particular story. But the story didn't make any sense. Unless he was simply trying to creep me out—back then, and even now as I'm cleaning the house. I swear, Pam, it's like I spent the whole day half-expecting to discover severed body parts in a shoebox."

"You always put too much faith in Dad's stories."

"Listen. I came up with this analogy a while back. You know those invisible fence gadgets they sell for dog owners? The animal comes too close to a radio signal near the edge of the property, and it triggers an electric shock in the dog's collar. The stories were warnings to keep us in line, and that's how they worked for me. If I got too close to the Big Street, for instance, it's like something zapped me in the head. Reflex. Classic Pavlovian conditioning."

"Can we save the philosophy, or dog psychology or whatever? It's after four o'clock, and—"

"There's more," I said, my voice rising. I wanted to keep talking with my sister, and I knew I was avoiding the point, starting to ramble. But it would sound too crazy if I simply blurted out what I thought was happening: that for some unknown reason, my parents or their stories were haunting me; that I'd seen some kind of apparition, actually laid my hands on the face of a ghost. The trappings of psychology, an indirect approach through metaphor and analogy, gave plausibility and poetic truth to my account. "It's like Dad left traps here, or like some part of Mom stayed behind in the house she wouldn't leave while she was alive. Emotional triggers, maybe, like how those needles in the back yard reminded me of Mom's warnings about dope fiends. I got stuck by a few of those needles, Pam. The whole night started to get weird on me."

"What, you think you got drugged by something?"

"Maybe it was only the shock of reaching into a bag of needles. You know my phobia, and how I'd freak out about rust, tetanus, or dried blood. Then I thought I heard one of those kids out front."

"Kids?"

"That's what woke me up to start with. I'd fallen asleep in my old bedroom, and I heard a tap and some kid's laugh outside the window. The locals would have known Dad died, and Mom's spooky stay-at-home reputation might have drawn them to investigate the empty house. I was going to chase them down and surprise them."

"They woke you up?"

"Yeah."

"You're awake now, right?"

"Well, yeah." I'd paused briefly, as if I had to stop and think before answering. "Of course."

"Nathan, here's what you do. Get out of that house. Go back to your apartment, and take a break from the cleanup for a day or two."

"I will. I will." In the dimly lit room, I stared at the curtains I'd closed earlier. I hadn't wanted anyone to look in. "It's late, though. I'll wait until morning."

"Get help if you need it. With the cleanup or…with other things. You seemed pretty together at Dad's funeral, and it was nice to hear you'd come to terms with that mess from the past—you know, Aaron and the creek and all."

"I still think about it."

"I'm glad you remembered."

"Doesn't matter that we were only little kids. Things like that stay with you, Pam. It changed everything."

"Of course it did. Watching your best friend drown. Probably feeling responsible, like I did for—"

I gasped.

※

"NATHAN? OH GOD, Nathan, I thought you knew." Pam pleaded, as if afraid I wouldn't respond. "You mentioned him to Aunt Lora the day of Dad's funeral—how sad or sorry you were about Aaron. I really thought you'd remembered." Her words cracked in the speaker; they seemed to vibrate through the chair cushions on either side of my head. "I shouldn't have said anything."

"No, no. It's all right." My voice projected a clinical calm, probably far more ominous than the nervous tremor I'd displayed during my previous ramblings. "Tell me."

~ Invisible Fences ~

"I can't, Nathan. All these years we never discussed it. Not really."

"Because of me. You protected me."

"My little brother."

"That's why I gasped: I started to remember. To feel the truth. I can't explain right now, but I need you to tell me everything. I need you to tell me, Pam."

Because there was another reason why I gasped.

~

IF YOU'RE SURE, Pam said.

She began with the syringe Aaron had transformed into a squirt gun, the bait that lured us deep into the woods. Twisted paths, Aaron leading the way with goofy certainty. The downhill trudge, our discovery of the flooded creek. How they both made fun of my muddy clothes, and Aaron revealed he'd tricked us and hadn't actually found his needle in the woods.

(Yes, I thought to myself. Go on.)

How, in retaliation, I'd dared Aaron to climb the log that spanned the roaring stream.

(I've always admitted that part, and regretted it.)

Aaron slipped and fell in the water, and I laughed at him.

(No, I didn't laugh right away. Did I?)

Aaron was out of reach. We told him to swim, but the current was too strong in front of him. He tread water, hands cupped and arms waving.

(Yes. Like a mime in a windstorm.)

As for ourselves, neither Pam nor I had yet learned how to swim. She came up with the idea of a human chain, holding my arm to extend our reach from the water's edge. Aaron, tired and scared, liked the idea, but I'd refused to step close to the creek.

(The awful smell. But the water was also deeper than I remembered.)

Then Pam told me—if I was *certain* I wanted to hear more—Pam told me how I'd done this thing with a stick. A low-hanging branch I'd bent then ripped from a nearby tree. I held it out to Aaron, pushing it clumsily close to him, possibly interrupting the rhythm of his treading arms, slapping at the water and yelling "Grab it," but the four-foot branch too heavy in my grip, an out-of-control wobble and somehow the tip pressed against his shoulder, snagging the shirt. It almost looked like I intended to push Aaron under the water.

(I was trying to help.)

She told me how Aaron did go under, then flailed up for a second, caught in a current that gripped him from beneath to drag him away. "Swim," I had yelled. "Why don't you swim?" His body rushed down the creek. Aaron's arms flailed, and he dropped beneath the surface.

(No, that was a cardboard box. It caught a spin in the current, then sailed out of sight.)

Pam didn't mention a cardboard box. She told me how I'd yelled after Aaron, begged him to swim, then shifted to cursing—words she'd never heard me use before, angry wild shouts and name-calling and then more tearful pleas for him to swim.

(Oh. *I* had cursed at *him*.)

Long minutes passed beside the creek, each more breathless, more hopeless. Pam had reached out to hug me, but I shrugged away and ran back through the woods.

"ARE YOU ALL right, Nathan? You've been pretty quiet."

"I'm just…processing." Despite deep layers of memories that conflicted with Pam's version of events, I knew she was telling me the truth. But so many pieces still didn't fit. It was like heavy lifting, my mind trying to shift and tug and force each new revelation into place. "When you caught up with me, Pam…you told me, 'He's right behind us'."

Silence for a moment. Then Pam said: "You asked me how Aaron would find his way out of the woods. It was like you'd already forgotten what happened. I guess I just wanted to calm you down, since you'd been so hysterical back at the creek. So, yeah—I told you Aaron was following us."

"I saw him."

"When you looked behind that first time, a wave of relief just washed over your face. I wasn't going to take that away from you. So I said it again and again as we ran toward home: 'He's right behind us. Keep going.' A couple times, your expression when you looked over your shoulder was so convincing. You almost made me believe my own lie."

I closed my eyes, trying to picture what happened next. "We went straight home," I said. "Mom called me into the living room and—"

"No," Pam interrupted. "I had to practically carry you inside. Mom yelled for Dad so loud he could hear her from the garage. We both looked awful, but you were warm with fever and nearly fainted."

"I remember being sick for a few days..."

"More like a week. We protected you from the search and recovery of Aaron's body, the investigation, Mom's long tearful phone calls with Mrs. Lieberman. I had to explain on my own how it was all an accident, how we did the best we could but weren't able to pull Aaron from the creek. It was so awful, Nathan. In the newspapers and everything. Nobody in the neighborhood would speak to me. I wanted to talk with you about it—to ease my mind I guess—but obviously couldn't. Dad went through a pretty tough time, too."

I stared at the curtains again, trying to trace patterns in the dark folds. "Wait," I said. "Wait. I saw Aaron later. At the swing set."

"One day while you were still sick, I walked in to check on you and your bed was empty. I never guessed you'd have the nerve to wander over to the Lieberman's back yard."

"David was there. And Aaron sat in one of the swings."

"The swing set was still broken when I arrived," Pam said. "I heard you yell. David had you on the ground and was pounding your back with his fists. I pulled you away, and David chased us to the end of their yard, warning us never to come back. The guy was always kind of a jerk—but he'd lost his little brother, you know?"

"It's like I can still see Aaron sitting there in the swing, staring at me. Angry and refusing to speak." Another revised memory shifted awkwardly into place. "I told David I'd tried to help Aaron out of the water, but he wouldn't believe me. So I looked right past him, and begged Aaron to speak the truth about what happened. That's when David threw the first punch."

Pam sighed, relieved to be near the end of the story, and also relieved she'd finally told it to me after all those years of silence. "The whole family had to move after that," she said. "Just packed up all that junk and moved, practically in the middle of the night. We had to, before we got chased out by an angry mob or something—like those frenzied, torch-waving townspeople who storm Dr. Frankenstein's castle."

I gave a quick laugh to acknowledge Pam's comparison. "I don't remember the move at all. It's like I suddenly appeared in a new house in Alabama. New house, but a lot like the old one."

"We protected you, Nathan. It seemed like the right thing to do."

"Maybe it was," I said.

Pause. "You think you'll be all right?" Pam asked. "I mean, it's a lot of stuff all at once."

"Yeah, I'll be okay. I really did need to hear everything. Thanks for telling me."

"Sure. Call me tomorrow, okay?"

"I will. Not so late next time, though—right?"

"Right. Good night."

"Good night, Pam. Bye."

My arm trembled as I reached over to click off the phone.

A lot of stuff all at once, indeed. I took a few deep breaths to brace myself.

"Hello, Aaron," I said.

Surrounded by the musty smell of the creek, amid the rustle of curtains and the crackle of dry newsprint, I heard my name again.

~ Invisible Fences ~

I'D GASPED FOR two reasons when Pam revealed that Aaron had drowned. First, despite what I'd remembered for so many years, an instantaneous awareness that Pam spoke the truth. Second, the growing dread I was no longer alone in my parents' house.

It had been difficult to remain calm, to keep my sister talking so she'd tell me everything, everything, without worry that I'd fall apart. Her words reshaped my childhood memories, wrenched my past into new perspectives. As she spoke, an extra presence struggled into the room, breaking through into a world I'd always assumed I understood.

Until that point, my experiences that night had been terrifying, yet dream-like. An air of unreality separated me from the supernatural events: I was a spectator, simply waiting for the movie to end. I knew it would end, because there was no *reason* for it. My father and I had grown more distant, but children commonly aged away from one parent or another in their later years. There was no reason why he would lay traps for me as punishment, why he'd choose to haunt me though his stories simply because I loved him maybe a little less than I had as a boy. As for Mom, memories of her certainly lingered over every scrap of paper she'd written on, every item she'd hoarded around her couch in the living room. If ever a person's spirit could attach itself to a place, Mom's spirit could claim her favorite area in the house she'd always refused to leave. But if she haunted the house, she wouldn't haunt me. The two of us had grown closer towards the end of her life. We'd made peace.

The other possibility I'd considered was Jamie, her spirit summoned by the tumble of plastic bowling pins, her face pressed against the side of a plastic bag like the croup tent she'd pounded at with tiny fists in the hospital where she'd died. Again, though: no reason my baby sister would choose to haunt me.

But Aaron. Aaron had a reason.

As Pam spoke, I realized Aaron had borrowed the energy of the house, the crowded connotations of objects and sounds and smells from my childhood; he harnessed the residue of my grief and regret after the deaths of both my parents, inhabiting the evocative spell of their cautionary narratives.

The slap at the window, the scratch of needles, the rising shadow from the road and the faces pressed gasping against stretched plastic... All of these had been *attempts.*

Aaron wanted me to recognize him, to see his features in the bubbles of tar and blood and oil from the road, to remember his expression in the face I'd held and nearly crushed in my hands, the awful musty smell of the creek rushing from the punctured opening with the spirit's first attempt at speech.

But Aaron needed something more: my full awareness of what had actually happened that long-ago summer.

Not simply that I'd watched him die, but that I'd hatched some stupid plan with a stick that must have pushed him under the water. I'd cursed him for drowning, then ran away like a coward.

My best friend.

Near the end of my conversation with Pam, the shadows in the curtain formed a child's outline. Aaron's face appeared gradually, damp hair matted to his head, and skin the color of pencil lead smeared across a white page. He wore the familiar blue-striped shirt, now sullied with mud and algae. The apparition moved forward with uneasy steps, as if unable to connect with solid ground. Water dripped on the carpet. I wondered if Pam could hear the faint splashes over the phone line.

It stepped closer, one arm raised to point an accusing finger. Instead of a fingernail, a crusted scab pruned darkly over the tip. Skin on Aaron's face rippled with each shift through the air of the room; dark blotches of rot appeared on each cheek.

Aaron stopped when he reached the front of the chair—and I'd kept talking to my sister. When I laughed at her joke about an angry mob at Frankenstein's castle, I was afraid I'd *keep* laughing, a nervous tremor shaking my entire body. She told me the family had protected me, and I agreed it was for the best—even as the ghost of a dead child bent at the waist and brought his face within inches of my own.

Aaron's eyes were muddy and expressionless. His breath was a hot, rancid breeze.

With feigned calm, I agreed I'd call Pam again tomorrow. But to disconnect the phone, I needed to move my trembling arm close to Aaron's leaning form. I was terrified I'd brush against his chest: would I touch him, or would my arm pass through where he stood?

I thought I felt the weight of water droplets against my legs.

I greeted Aaron, and he whispered my name.

His small hand reached toward my face, and I could feel the scratch of a scabbed fingertip against my cheek.

EPILOGUE

NOW, WHEN I think back to that day at the creek, I wonder about my motives. Shouldn't my friendship have helped me overcome my aversion to the water? Could my momentary anger with Aaron have subconsciously influenced my clumsiness with the stick? Was it even remotely possible that I'd deliberately attempted to hurt my best friend? If so, what kind of person did that make me?

AS I'VE MENTIONED, my sister and I used to hate those old haunted house movies without a real ghost, the cheap monster movies that never showed a monster.

In this story, Aaron is the real ghost. I'm the monster.

I SOLD MOM and Dad's house, eventually. Following Pam's advice, I stopped sorting through the junk and simply hired movers to haul everything away.

If the new tenants saw any signs of a ghost, I never heard about it. Nobody ran screaming back to the real estate office to demand a refund. No rumors of a haunted house arose in the neighborhood and followed me back to my apartment building.

Why would they? The ghost came away with me.

DO YOU SEE the point of the story, Nathan? We all cut parts of ourselves away, but we never lose them. Things stay with us—souvenirs with memories attached. We can't always choose what to keep, what to throw away.

SOMETIMES, I'LL FEEL the stab of needles in my hands or feet, like the onset of arthritis—and perhaps that's all it is.

At night, I occasionally hear a squeal, crash, and thump from the direction of the small road in front of my building.

And Aaron. Aaron's with me a lot, offering me "toast" before I'm half awake each morning, inviting me for a walk in the woods.

That's the Aaron I prefer: the one who appears when I'm less inclined to blame myself for a few moments of weakness when I was only seven years old.

In less-forgiving moments the other Aaron reaches from the shadows, screams for me instead of my sister because I was his friend, screams across the years I'd forgotten him, denied the sights and sounds and smells of a living boy dragged beneath those awful murky waters.

The smell of that creek stays with me now. It follows me from room to room.

Invisible Fences

Through it all, another voice haunts me, my childhood voice blended with my present one, angry, resigned, heartbroken, as if life is something a friend would give up willingly or out of spite, as if I can once again erase my worst mistakes even while the truth pulls at me with the force of a rushing current: "Swim. Oh, why, *why* don't you swim?"

CEMETERY DANCE PUBLICATIONS
PAPERBACKS AND EBOOKS!

DEAR DIARY: RUN LIKE HELL
by James A. Moore

Sooner or later even the best prepared hitman is going to run out of bullets. Buddy Fisk has two new jobs, bring back a few stolen books of sorcery, and then stop the unkillable man who wants to see him dead…

"Gripping, horrific, and unique, James Moore continues to be a winner, whatever genre he's writing in. Well worth your time."
—Seanan McGuire, *New York Times* bestselling author of the *InCryptid* and *Toby Daye* series.

SOMETHING STIRS
by Thomas Smith

Ben Chalmers is a successful novelist. His wife, Rachel, is a fledgling artist with a promising career, and their daughter, Stacy, is the joy of their lives. Ben's novels have made enough money for him to provide a dream home for his family. But there is a force at work-a dark, chilling, ruthless force that has become part of the very fabric of their new home…

"Thomas is one of those outstanding Southern writers—seemingly soft, languid, maybe even lazy, when actually what he is, is cotton wrapped about a razor. Half the time you don't even know he's gotten you until it's too late."
—*USA Today* and *NY Times* Bestselling author, Charles L. Grant

THE DISMEMBERED
by Jonathan Janz

In the spring of 1912, American writer Arthur Pearce is reeling from the wounds inflicted by a disastrous marriage. But his plans to travel abroad, write a new novel, and forget about his ex-wife are interrupted by a lovely young woman he encounters on a London-bound train. Her name is Sarah Coyle, and the tale she tells him chills his blood…

"One of the best writers in modern horror to come along in the last decade. Janz is one of my new favorites."
—Brian Keene, *Horror Grandmaster*

Purchase these and other fine works of horror from Cemetery Dance Publications today!
https://www.cemeterydance.com/